THE BRASS KEY

THE SECOND BOOK OF LOWMOOR

RICHARD POOLE

SIMON AND SCHUSTER

For Will again
and Sandra

SIMON AND SCHUSTER
First published in Great Britain in 2006 by Simon and Schuster UK Ltd,
A CBS COMPANY

Simon & Schuster UK Ltd
Africa House, 64-78 Kingsway, London WC2B 6AH.

This book is a work of fiction. Names, characters, places and incidents are either
the product of the author's imagination or are used fictitiously. Any resemblance
to actual people living or dead, events or locales is entirely coincidental.

A CIP catalogue record for this book is available from the British Library.

ISBN-13: 978-0-6898-7549-6
ISBN-10: 0-6898-7549-5

1 3 5 7 9 10 8 6 4 2

Typeset in Garamond by M Rules
Printed and bound in Great Britain by
Cox & Wyman Ltd, Reading, Berks

www.simonsays.co.uk

Also by Richard Poole:

Jewel and Thorn
The Iron Angel

CONTENTS

Prologue: The Shrivelled Claw   1

1   An Unwelcome Revelation   9

2   Greasing the Trapeze   22

3   At the Sign of the Water Rat   34

4   The Silver Whistle   53

5   Sisters   73

First Interface: A Carrier Pigeon   91

6   Elixir of Death   99

7   Out of the Frying-Pan   115

8   The Pale Hermit   133

9   Out of the Sky   146

10   Big Bones, Little Bones   165

Second Interface: The Missing   179

11   In the White Giant's Skull   189

12   Big House, Little House   203

13   Into the Crypt   220

14   The Scarebird   235

15   The Artefact   254

Third Interface: The Stone-Woman   267

16   Jewel Alone   277

17   Scavengers   296

18   Sight and Seeing   309

19   Moira Black   325

20   The Rook Storm   345

21   Pursuit   360

22   The Return of Punch   373

23   The Two Moons   386

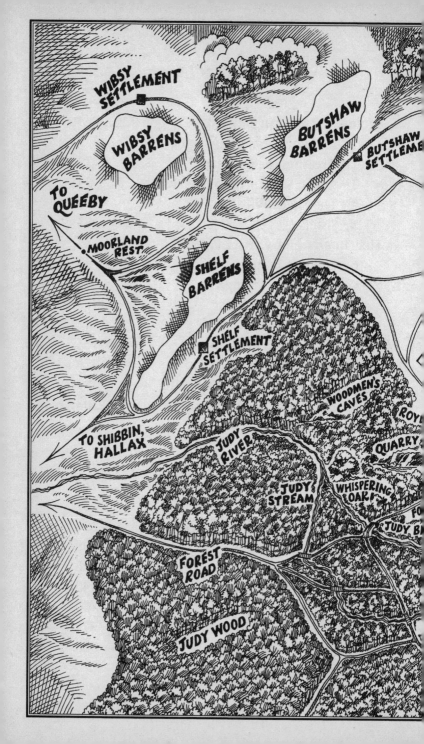

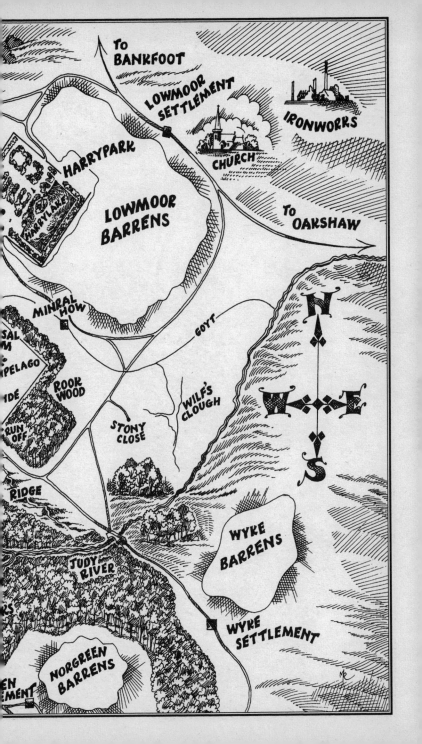

PROLOGUE

THE SHRIVELLED CLAW

The girl walked up to the blue door, seized the owl's iron head and delivered a trio of sharp raps.

She was fourteen and pretty, with long-lashed grey eyes. Her hair, chestnut-brown and lush, hung down her back. She brushed it night and morning, loving the sheen and swing of it and the way it lingered against her cheek.

The Syb was a washed-out creature. Her hair was sparse and straggled, her lips thin and dry, her skin as wrinkled as a crab apple kept for too long in the dark. Only her eyes still seemed young. They were blue as lake-water and alive with irony.

The girl spoke confidently. "My mother says you asked for me."

She hadn't the least idea why. She wasn't a native of Oakshaw. She and her mother had come over from Lowmoor to help her aunt, who was expecting her third child. It had proved an exhausting labour. The Syb had been sent for to ease her pain and had stayed to help the midwife; the child – a boy – was safely delivered. The girl had fetched and carried, and more than once had noticed the Syb's sidelong glances in her direction: as if the Syb was *appraising* her . . .

"So I did," said the Syb in a voice as dry as the rest of her. "Do come in, my dear."

1

The girl went past her into the house.

She didn't like old people. Their bodies were withered and used up. They smelt of sourness and decay. She hated the thought of being touched with scaly, knobbly, sticklike fingers. But this old woman was a Syb, and Sybs, of course, were special people.

A small fire burned in the hearth. May had been cold this year, the earth reluctant to shuck off winter. The room had the same herby smell as the Syb's house in Lowmoor. She'd been inside that house just once, to pick up a jar of preserves.

"Let me look at you," said the Syb.

She stood in the sharp light from the window. The blue eyes sought to pierce her, as if to root out her secrets. But she rebuffed the Syb's gaze. What an ugly old witch she is . . . I will not be intimidated.

The Syb murmured, as if to herself, "She is; I do believe she is . . . I suspected it the very moment I clapped eyes on her . . ."

"Suspected what?" demanded the girl.

"Well might you ask, child."

"Don't call me child. I'm not a child."

"You are, though you also are not."

A riddle, the girl thought. That was Sybs all over. Silly self-important creatures, always playing their little games.

"Why did you ask my mother to send me?"

The old woman rubbed the skin between her nose and lip. It was drawn and puckered there, with the ghost of a moustache. Then she said: "Come. I have something to show you."

Curiosity twitched in the girl. She followed the Syb across the room. On a table, a cloth was draped over some object or other: it might be a pot or an ornament.

Like a conjuror, the Syb whisked the covering away.

"What is it?" asked the girl.

"Ah!" The old woman smiled. "That's the question, isn't it?"

The girl was provoked to irritation by this coy mysteriousness. She felt a sharp urge to give the doddering crone a slap. But, controlling the temptation, she concentrated on the object. Set on a wooden pedestal-stand, it was in shape roughly spherical and in colour a dull yellow, and had the jagged, irregular surface of a raw chunk of quartz. It might have been half an inch across.

"What you mean," the girl said bluntly, "is you don't know. Am I right?"

"What do I know?" said the woman. "I'm only a tired old Syb."

Tiresome old Syb, thought her visitor. And not much of a Syb.

She tried again: "Where did you get it?"

"From a pedlar. But don't ask me where *he* got it from. Most probably, he stole it."

The woman lowered her body into a stiff-backed chair. Then she gestured at the crystal. "Touch it," she said.

The girl looked at her. "*You* touch it," she said.

"I cannot – well, not with my bare hands anyway. It gives me a kind of shock . . . unless I wear gloves or cover my hands with a cloth."

"And you want *me* to touch it? You've got to be mad!"

"I'm no madder than you, girl. Go on now, touch it. If I'm right, you won't get a shock."

"Why not? Why should I be different to you?"

3

"Because you *are* different. You are *very* different."

"Different? I'm young and you're old? Is that what you mean?"

The Syb cackled like a crack-voiced bird. When the fit was spent, she said: "If you refuse to touch the stone, you cannot be what I think you are. But if you do, I think you'll find out just how different you are."

The girl did not like the old woman's bantering tone. Nor the way she'd been laughed at. Nor the sense of a challenge issued. But the Syb had boxed her into a corner. If she didn't touch the crystal now, she knew she'd lose face.

So she stretched out a hand and touched the thing with a fingertip.

Nothing happened. Emboldened, she let her palm fall onto the stone. It was warm against her flesh.

Then, without warning, under her hand light sprang up. She jerked her palm away. At the heart of the crystal a tiny sun had been born. As she watched, it began to pulse.

"It's alive!" she exclaimed.

"So it is," said the old woman. "What you are seeing is its heart. It has that as humans do." She paused, then added dryly: "Most humans, at any rate."

The girl hesitated, but some force (internal? external? it was impossible to tell) brushed aside her diffidence, and her hand crept back to the stone. This time she kept it there. Each pulse-beat seemed to pass up her hand and into her body. She closed her eyes and let her body fill with the sensual rhythm. The stone was charging her with light . . . light that was energy. Then, impossibly, thrillingly, her body leapt from the tawdry room to hang in black space. Stars and suns came wheeling past, an end-less uprush of sparks from some far-off galactic fire. Her body, a solar crystal, flamed at the heart of the firmament. She felt a wild exhilaration.

Then her fingers were scorching. Opening her eyes, she snatched them back. Their bones and sinews glowed with an inner radiance.

But the glow began to fade, the transparency to wane. The crystal's sun-pulse wasted. As she watched, the light died. The stone was as it had been when she'd first set eyes on it.

But *she* was not the same. She felt deprived, dispossessed, emptied out like a snail shell. She looked longingly at the crystal. Already she wanted to reach out, lay a hand on it again. She wanted the sun with its yellow beat, the quickening leap among the stars, the thrill as she lost and found herself. Without it, her life would be a shadow of a life.

The old woman said eagerly: "Something happened, didn't it? Something strange. Tell me now."

The girl looked at her slyly. "If I do, will you give it to me?"

The Syb cackled. "Give you the crystal? Silly girl! Why would I want to do that?"

"It's no good to you. Why, you can't even touch it."

"It's mine. I sit here in this chair and look at it."

"I want it," said the girl. "Sell it to me, *please*."

She had saved a little money. But even as she asked, she knew it couldn't be enough. Very well, she thought, I'll beg, borrow or steal the rest, I'll do whatever I have to do—

"Such a thing is not to be sold."

"Everything has its price . . . so my mother says."

"So everybody says. Look at me. What could I need?"

"*Please*, old woman. *Please, please* sell the crystal to me."

"I will not sell it, child."

Fury erupted in the girl, a fury she'd never felt before. A voice of stone spoke out of her: "If you won't let me have it, I shall take it away from you."

The Syb cackled again, as if the notion was absurd. Then, leaning forward, she grabbed the girl by the wrist. Her grip was surprisingly strong.

The girl reacted without thinking. Lifting her free hand, she tried to push the Syb away. But as her palm made contact with the old woman's chest, a bolt of lightning erupted from her and jolted through the aged body, making it leap like a fish.

The girl shook, a fern-frond in the aftermath of a blast. What on earth had happened? How . . .?

Whatever it was, it was final. The old woman sat lifeless. Her mouth, caught in a cry at once silent and appalled, showed a bony ridge of gum and a few stumpy, blackened teeth.

Still she clutched the girl's wrist. The girl tried to pull away, but the Syb held her fast as if she meant to keep her there. The girl stared at the shrivelled claw. Its flesh was spotted, its skin threaded blue-purple with veins. Nausea rose in her throat. Then, in a frenzy of loathing, she unpicked it finger by finger.

She backed away from the corpse, then spun upon her heel and looked wildly about her.

There was no one else in the room. Only the shadows in the corners seemed to watch her. *They* knew.

"Take me away . . . Take me away . . ."

Had the crystal whispered to her, or had she imagined the

voice? She wrapped it quickly in its cloth, tucked it down inside her jacket and slipped out of the house. As she hurried through the streets, her new self was practising the lies that she would tell.

1

AN UNWELCOME REVELATION

A booted foot prodded Thorn Jack in the base of the spine.

"Where's Blacky? Where's Denny?" Rafter demanded. "What's happened to them? You know, don't you, brat?"

Thorn had been lost in thought. Knees pulled up, arms wrapped around them, he sat on the green covering of the giant tabletop outside the multicoloured marquee in which the Spetch twins lived. His wrists were bound together. Soon, surely, he'd been thinking, I'll be called in to talk to them – get my orders for this mission to recover their stupid key. Another wild duck chase? Damn and blast the pair of them . . .

He looked up. Rafter glowered down at him. A storm cloud must be brewing in the henchman's head, for Thorn could see its darkness in his mean, sunken eyes.

"Just love to cut my throat, wouldn't you, Rafter?" he said.

"Not until I'd carved a few patterns on the rest of you."

Thorn laughed. "Chance would be a fine thing. Harm me, and the Spetches will have your guts for garters. Racky Jagger will carve you up and serve your tripes on a plate."

"I'm not frightened of Racky Jagger. He's just passing through. Here today, gone tomorrow: that's Jagger – always has been. *I* don't trust him and the bosses don't trust him neither."

"Everybody's favourite, that's old Racky."

"Where are Blacky and Denny, you worm? They should have been back from the wood by now. "

"Were you never taught to say 'please'?"

"*Where are they*, you settlement cretin?"

"Why don't you ask Racky Jagger? He doesn't know where Denny is, but he could tell you about Blacky."

"Jagger's no friend of mine. He talks to the bosses, no one else."

"Is that right? Then get this: your pal Blacky's dead. He fell down the stairs at the Punch and Judy Inn and broke his neck."

"He's dead?" There was a pause while Rafter struggled to take this in. "What about Denny?"

"Denny fell into the river when the railing gave way. He and Racky were wrestling on the balcony of the inn. But Denny got out of the river and Jonas Legg hid him. Right now, he's somewhere in Judy Wood being entertained by a friend of mine. He'll be back – if the Woodmen don't catch him."

"The Woodmen? Who's this friend of yours?"

"That's my business."

"That's where you're wrong, Jack. It's very much *my* business."

Grabbing Thorn by the hair, Rafter jerked his head back. Pain sprang in Thorn's scalp but, balling his fists, he brought them up as hard as he could underneath Rafter's chin. Rafter grunted, let go of Thorn's hair and staggered back.

"I'm going to kick you into the middle of next week," he snarled.

"No you're not," said a voice.

Racky Jagger was approaching from the direction of the steps that led down from the tabletop to the floor of the room. The green carpeting had deadened the sound of his footsteps.

"What do *you* want, Jagger?" Rafter demanded angrily.

"*You* to make yourself scarce. Just for a while, Rafter. I want a private word with the lad."

"I can't leave my post," declared Rafter. "Bosses' orders."

"I'm not asking you to leave, just to back off a bit. Let's say, to the table's edge."

"Over my dead body."

Racky said agreeably: "That can be arranged, if you insist. Alternatively—"

A coin had appeared in his stub-fingered hand. Racky spun the coin into the air and caught it again.

"A silver piece," he said. "And yours for doing – well, nothing."

The two men looked at one another. Then Rafter held out his hand and Racky dropped the coin on his palm. Rafter's fingers closed on it. After a last, terse glance at the bald man, he walked away.

When Rafter was out of earshot, Racky sat down in front of Thorn, crossing one ankle over the other and resting his elbows on his knees. It was a posture Thorn was familiar with from their journey through Judy Wood.

"Now we can talk," Racky said.

"I've got nothing to say to you."

"What, after everything we've been through together?"

The old, sardonic Racky. As if, thought Thorn, Whispering Oak was a bad dream and the knife at his sister's neck nothing more than the figment of a fevered imagination.

One corner of Racky's mouth flirted with a smile. He said: "You don't *really* think I'd have harmed Haw, do you?"

11

Thorn considered this, then said: "I think you'll do whatever it takes to get whatever it is you want. If that includes murder . . ."

"I'm shocked you should think so little of me, Thorn. Didn't we fight the stoats together and defeat the crayfish?"

"Yes. But what about what happened at Judy Bridge? Did you fake your fight with Denny? You pretend ignorance of the Spetches, then turn out to be their ally. What am I to make of that?"

"Maybe that I like to play both ends against the middle. Look, you've talked to Rafter. Don't you suppose he would stick a knife in my back if he got the chance?"

"He's not the only person I know who's pretty keen to do that."

"Ask yourself something, Thorn. You know I want something from you. Would it have served my cause if I'd cut your sister's throat? That was just a little charade. I was forced to improvise when those women turned up. I couldn't let them kill the brothers."

"You've got a smooth tongue, Racky. Words cost you nothing, do they? They're like smoke; they come, they go. I don't know when you're acting and when you're doing something for real. I wonder if you do yourself. You're just like Mr Punch."

Racky laughed. "You flatter me, lad. Punch is immortal; I sadly am not. Look: there's no reason on earth for the two of us to be enemies."

"There's every reason," said Thorn. "You betrayed me, and I'll never trust you again."

"All right. Let's say, for the sake of peace and letting bygones

12

be bygones, that I made a mistake in abandoning you in the Echo Hole. Incidentally, congratulations on your clever escape. I'd have said it was impossible. How did you get out?"

Thorn kept his mouth shut.

"Fine, keep your secret. I suspect it had something to do with those brands you had in your pack – I've not seen their like before – and the tunnels under the oak, though to my knowledge no one has ever dared explore them before. But you and I shouldn't be enemies, we ought to be allies. There's nothing we couldn't achieve together – your determination added to my experience . . ." He leant towards Thorn. "Listen. I've got the run of this place. The crazy twins trust me. Their henchmen are fools and easy enough to outwit. I'll make a pact with you. Swear, on your love for your sister, that you'll give me what I want – the strange crystal you stole from Wyke – and I'll get Haw out of this."

"What? You'll help her escape?"

"That's what I'm saying. I'll trust you to hand the crystal over when the three of us arrive safely back in Norgreen."

Thorn contemplated the stubbled, imperturbable face before him. "You're incredible, Racky," he said. "Give me one good reason why I should ever trust you again."

"Very well, if I must." Racky had leant forwards to offer to help Haw escape; now he straightened his back. "You are my son, Thorn Jack. Or should I call you Thorn *Jagger*?"

Thorn stared at Racky Jagger. If a mere pair of eyes could have peeled away skin, sliced through bone and burrowed deep into the soft tissues of a human brain, his would have ferreted out the truth from the man who sat so near to him, his face inscrutable. The silence lengthened. At last Thorn got to his feet. Looking down, he said, in a voice as firm as rock: "You're a liar, Racky Jagger."

"I swear, on the soul of the woman who gave me birth, that what I've told you is the truth."

"You don't believe in souls."

"Then I'll swear on her memory. I'll swear on anything you like."

"I believe you would. But swearing's nothing to you. It's words again, isn't it? You're a liar, Racky Jagger. My father was Davis Jack, a man everyone admired. Not a traitor, a foul bag of filth who grabs a young girl and holds a knife to her throat."

"Harsh words, Thorn. Perhaps words I deserve. But it doesn't alter the fact that you're my son and I'm your father – not a certain Davis Jack of hallowed memory."

"I don't believe you. You're asking me to believe that . . . You and my mother . . .? It's disgusting, impossible."

"Is it? What do *you* know about passion? You've only just stepped across the threshold into manhood. You've only just begun to scratch the surface of life." He paused to let these words sink in, then continued: "Ask yourself this: how is it that of all the sisters of all the brothers in the world, the mad twins should kidnap yours? A girl living beyond the wood, unknown to them, insignificant?"

But Thorn's brain was in such a whirl that it was difficult to think.

"Come on, Thorn," Racky pressed him. "How long before the penny drops?"

"Because *you* told them about her – and about me?"

14

"Got it in one, lad. They wanted someone special to go and get their key back. *You're* that someone special."

Thorn opened his mouth to speak, but Racky pre-empted him.

"No," he said quickly, "don't ask me why you're special. I'm not going to tell you. And I won't tell you, either, why I'm not prepared to tell you. Let's get back to the kidnap. You surely can't imagine that that telltale feather was left *by chance* by your pool? It was carefully planted. It was only a matter of time before you happened on it. I knew of your fondness for the place – I'd followed you and Haw there; you didn't see me, of course. The Council were helpless till that feather turned up. But once it did, they were sure to come and ask for my help: who else in Norgreen has knowledge of the distant world? Then, once I told them the feather came from over beyond the wood, they were never going to commit men to search for your sister. They'd send me and one or two others. If you had any guts at all, you'd insist on coming. And so you did. It couldn't have been better when your uncle got the sweats: that left just the two of us – what I'd wanted all along. Racky Jagger and Thorn Jack – father and son. Alone in Judy Wood . . .

"You see, Thorn, I *really* had to know if you were my son. I mean, the son of my spirit, not just the son of my loins. I had to know if you were capable of rising above a settlement's soft existence and taking on the unpredictable dangers of the big world. Capable, in fact, of becoming a man like me – not a do-nothing like Davis Jack. Well, you didn't disappoint me. The way you conquered each challenge (some of my making, some not – not least the way you managed to get out of the Echo

15

Hole) I don't mind saying that you exceeded all my hopes. Thorn, you are truly my son. I'm proud of you."

Well before Racky had finished talking, Thorn had ceased to look at him. He could no longer bear the sight of Racky's earnest face. He strove to absorb what he'd heard. There was, he had to admit, logic in what Racky had said. And yet . . . and yet . . .

He said accusingly: "It's a strange sort of father who puts his son's life in danger."

"But I only endangered you once – the crayfish hunt. And that was a calculated risk. It was you who put your own life in danger at Brokenbanks. As for Whispering Oak, I fully expected to pull you out of the hole."

"And what about Haw?"

"We'd have gone to collect her first. Or rather, *I* would. All I had to do was tell the Spetches you'd died in the wood. I'm an excellent liar. With no further use for the girl, they'd have released her to me. Or, if necessary, I'd have bought her from them. Then, when the three of us were back in Norgreen, you'd have given me the crystal – as I still hope you will."

"I would, would I?"

"Yes. Unlike me, you're an honourable man."

Thorn looked down at Racky again. Sitting in the same relaxed posture as before, he seemed confident his point of view would prevail. When Thorn spoke again, his sarcasm was withering.

"No, I'm not a bit like you in that, am I, *Father*? To you a sense of honour is a millstone round one's neck. It would really cramp your style. But other people's honour – that's something to be used."

Racky said nothing. For a time his voice had spun its web, but now the full monstrous impossibility of his claim rushed in on Thorn anew. Oh, Racky was plausible, wickedly plausible, but then, he was cunning and – as he'd just confessed – an inveterate liar.

Thorn said: "You don't fool me, Racky Jagger. You've gone too far, you've said too much. Not content with everything else you've done to harm us, you want to take my father away from me, besmirch the memory of my mother. Well, it won't work. I don't believe you. I *won't* believe you."

Racky got to his feet. On the breast of his hide jerkin – the left breast, over his heart – was a pocket with a bone button. He now undid this button, reached into the pocket and took from it something circular and flat. He held it out towards Thorn. It was an old metal locket. Racky now thumbed its catch, and the lid sprang open.

"Tell me what you see," he said.

Curiosity impelled Thorn to move closer to the man. He looked down into the locket. Curled up inside it was a lock of dark hair.

He couldn't take his eyes away. But now it wasn't what was in the locket that he was seeing, but that characteristic movement as his mother tossed her long hair away from her face. Those night-black tresses, wavy and lustrous, that he still could picture though he couldn't remember her face . . .

Racky said: "Sixteen and a half years ago your mother gave me this. She cut it off herself. She must have known she was pregnant, but she never told me. She was always secretive. She was stunningly beautiful, with a wild, fierce spirit. She had

17

many admirers – including Davis Jack. But she only ever gave herself to me – of that I'm sure. If I asked her to marry me once, I must have asked her ten times. She would never say yes. She liked to keep men dangling, enjoy her power over them. A month or two after she gave me the locket, we had an argument. Something snapped in me. I told her unless she agreed to marry me there and then I was off – I'd leave the settlement for a time. She didn't believe me – couldn't bring herself to credit that any man who professed to love her could turn his back on her like that. But still she wouldn't say she'd marry me, so I went. It was my first taste of travelling. I'd intended to be away for no more than two months, but things happened and it was almost a year before I returned. And what did I find? She'd married Davis Jack. She wouldn't even look at me. Everybody, naturally, assumed you were Davis's son. Only I knew better. I've had my eye on you for years, Thorn, watching you grow, and now the time has come for me to reclaim you as my own."

For some moments after he'd finished speaking, nothing happened. Then, with a striking adder's speed, Thorn dashed the locket from Racky's hand. It struck the floor with a clack, bounced and rolled away on its edge.

"Get away from me!" he shouted, a kind of madness in his soul. "Get away from me! Get away!"

"If that's what you want," said Racky Jagger.

Calmly he stooped, picked up the locket and walked away.

"Why couldn't I kill him?" asked Jewel Ranson, picturing Lanner Spetch's grin as she aimed her arrow at his heart. "I was geared up to do it and then, at the last moment, I couldn't – couldn't let go of the arrow. I don't understand . . ."

Rainy Gill considered her friend.

"You mustn't blame yourself," she said. "To kill a man in cold blood – that's not an easy thing."

The two sat in the cell underneath the rattery, backs propped against the wall. Beneath them, the floor was sprung like one big mattress. Above their heads, the hinged halves of the ceiling were open. Leech the ratman was up there somewhere. Every so often he'd come and smirk at them, obviously enjoying this double reversal of fortune. Earlier in the day, Jewel and Rainy had taken him captive and forced him to do their bidding. Now they were his prisoners. Even if they'd wanted to, they couldn't have climbed out. The walls were too high, too smooth. You got in and out by a ladder that was let down from above. Right now it was out of sight.

"But I *hate* Lanner, I *hate* Zak," said Jewel forcefully. "I *want* both Spetches dead."

"I know," said Rainy. "But sometimes what we want and our ability to achieve it are a long way apart."

"I came here to kill them. Now they've got the two of us doing what they want. I've been telling myself I'll kill them next time I get a chance – when we come back with this key. But what if I still can't do it then? I owe my father their deaths."

Rainy was angry too, but she knew that what you can't change you simply have to bear.

"Do you?" she replied. "I don't believe your father would impose such a debt even if he were able to. It's only in your own mind that this thing exists."

19

"Maybe, Rainy, but it *does* exist there, and until the day I pay it I shall never feel free."

"Free?" echoed Rainy. "None of us are ever that. We sometimes think we are, but it's an illusion – believe me."

"Maybe you're right," said Jewel gloomily. "Just when I thought we'd got clear of Crane Rockett, Briar Spurr and that monster Deacon Brace, they return to haunt us. That young man and his sister – why did they have to be here? Things were hard enough before; now they're so complicated I . . ."

Her voice tailed away. So complicated, thought Rainy, that you can't express them.

"Those two want to be here no more than we do," she replied. "We're all four like puppets with the Spetches pulling our strings."

She fell silent. What more was there to say? Jewel was silent too, no doubt brooding on the turn events had taken, and the uncertainties the future had in store.

Rainy's heart went out to the girl. If Jewel could only have been dissuaded from this project of revenge . . . but that had never been an option. Jewel might look slight, appear delicate, but she possessed a tough spirit, a nature stubborn and resolute. She would go on to the end – whatever that was, good or bad – and live with the consequences . . . *if* she survived, that is.

But the project, Rainy saw, had been doomed from the start. The notion that a fairground juggler and a girl of fifteen could outwit the twins, the extraordinary twins with their wealth, their henchmen and on their own ground – and, monstrous though they were, the twins *were* extraordinary, you had to grant them that – well, it was absurd. Hadn't she known in her heart that their quest was bound to fail?

Yes, she supposed she had. Yet knowing it hadn't stopped her from committing herself to the venture. Now why was that? Because she couldn't let Jewel take the brothers on alone? Because she doubted Jewel's ability to kill in cold blood? Because, in the brief time she'd known her, she'd come to care for this girl more than anyone else she knew, with the exception of her father?

A startling idea struck Rainy; that Jewel called forth feelings she'd never expected to feel: the protective, sheltering instincts a mother feels towards a child.

Though in age, she thought, I'm more like a sister than a mother.

Can this really be me – me, the independent spirit, worldly-wise, a little cynical, not easily deceived? Can it be I'm not the woman I always thought I was?

2

GREASING THE TRAPEZE

Thorn sat cross-legged on the floor. The cord was chafing his wrists, but he paid no heed to this. His mind contained two drums, which beat a relentless counterpoint.

The first drum insisted: *Jagger's your father. Jagger's your father. Jagger's your father. Jagger's your father.*

The second drum declared: *It's a lie. It's a lie. It's a lie. It's a lie.*

His head sank onto his knees.

Think, he ordered himself. *Think . . .*

The lock of hair. *Hair . . .*

He thought: my mother had black hair, black as a blackbird's feathers. But other people have black hair too. Who's to say the lock is hers? Racky's a liar, he admits it. How convenient he happens to have this locket in his jerkin. Something real – you can see it, touch it, hang a story around it. Not just one story – many stories, depending on circumstances.

Even if it's hers, there's no proof she gave it to him. He could have stolen it from her. Cut it off while she was sleeping . . . *Sleeping?*

Racky Jagger is *not* my father. Davis Jack is my father.

Then a new thought struck him. If Racky's my father, why did he betray me to the Spetches? What sort of a father betrays his son? What possible reason could he have?

22

So his mind spun its circles, round and round, round and round – as a father, holding his son by the legs, whirls him in circles till he sets him on his feet and the child collapses from giddiness.

Racky Jagger says he'll get Haw out of Roydsal – if I trust him . . . I can't trust him. I won't trust him.

Someone kicked him in the leg. Thorn looked up.

Lippy. Beyond him stood a leering Rafter.

"The bosses want you, kid."

Anything, thought Thorn, to get these drums out of my head.

Lippy unhooked a flap of the tent and gestured Thorn to go through.

An astonishing scene met his eyes.

Four spindly metal gantries dominated the area. To each, a ladder was fixed. The two outer gantries faced one another, and were identical. The two inner gantries stood side by side, and were also identical. From the right-hand one of these, a trapeze swung to and fro. Sitting on its horizontal bar, clad in a torso-hugging scarlet singlet and tights, was flame-haired Lanner Spetch. As Thorn watched, he twined its ropes around his ankles and dropped to hang upside down, his sinewy arms loosely dangling. There he swung, back and forth, back and forth – mesmeric.

Catching sight of the newcomer, he waggled his hands and shouted: "You're upside down, Thorn Jack!"

"Come off it, bro! It's you that's down-side up!"

Identical to his brother, apart from his blond locks, Zak

Spetch stood on a platform positioned two-thirds of the way up the outer left-hand gantry. He wore a yellow singlet and tights, and gripped the bar of a second trapeze. As Thorn watched, he thrust the trapeze away from him. It looped towards the dangling twin as Lanner came swinging back, but though the trapezes came close there was no danger of a collision. Having reached the top of its arc, the vacant trapeze fell back and returned to Zak, who reached out from his gantry and deftly caught it with one hand. He waited for a while, calculating the right moment, then grasped the bar with both hands and launched himself into the air, kicking out with his legs. Lanner reached the top of his arc as Zak was rising towards his and, as Lanner fell back, Zak threw himself – arms outstretched – towards his twin.

Despite himself, Thorn caught his breath. Surely Zak must fall and smash to pulp on the ground . . . But a firm *smack!* sounded as pair of hands slapped pair of hands – and there was the blond, lithely dangling from his brother's strong, saving arms, grinning like an idiot.

The brothers drifted to and fro, then Lanner let go of Zak, who fell to earth and landed lightly in a thick pile of cushions. Lanner swung his body up, grasped the bar of the trapeze, hauled himself onto his seat and untwisted his ankles. Then, having stood up, he urged the trapeze higher by bending his knees and thrusting like a child on a swing. Attaining the necessary height, he reached out and grabbed the stanchion of his own outer gantry, transferred himself to its platform, secured the trapeze; then, disdaining his ladder, slid to the ground down one of its struts. The two brothers now joined hands and tripped across the floor towards Thorn and Lippy, their faces aglow with smiles. Halting inches away, they bowed graciously in tandem, each sweeping the floor with an outstretched arm. A smell of sweat came off the pair. Lippy warmly applauded, but Thorn made no move to follow. Yet if he'd seen the act at a fair, it would have stolen the show.

"Lippy, introduce us!" commanded Zak.

Keeping his face straight, Lippy obliged. "Thorn Jack – the Flying Twins! Please show your appreciation!"

Thorn brought his palms together in a parody of clapping. "Impressive," he observed ironically. Then found himself adding: "Where did you learn to do that?"

"We come," said Zak, "of a line of fairground performers. Our father, Leo, taught us the business. The three of us had an act: Leo and Lanner caught and I flew. Very swish."

"Until," volunteered Lanner, "poor Father broke his neck. Imagine: some dastard greased the bar of his trapeze!"

"Probably someone's husband. Dad was a devil for the ladies."

"Life was never the same again," said Lanner mournfully.

"Never the same," echoed Zak.

"But we keep ourselves in trim to honour the old man's memory."

"The tyrannical old sod."

"Never had a good word for us – no matter how hard we worked."

"It also keeps us fighting fit."

"On our toes."

"On top of things."

"Until the day," Thorn broke in, "someone greases *your* trapeze?"

Lanner and Zak exchanged glances, then burst out laughing. Thorn regarded them coldly.

Lanner's face became serious. "Right, kid," he said, "we've serious things to talk about."

Haw Jack stood at the foot of the rumpled cot in the wooden cell. The cubicle had no windows; barred openings in the roof let in whatever daylight was able to penetrate the windows of Roydsal's vaulty, cobwebbed hall. Here she'd spent every night but one since her arrival.

She was gazing at two rows of scratches in the wood. One was set above the other. The marks were shallow, just off vertical and regularly spaced – the work of a tidy mind. The same mind which now counted them for the umpteenth time. In the upper row, five; in the lower row, seven.

She'd made the marks with a hairpin that had somehow survived the journey here: five for the number of nights that had passed on that journey; seven for the number of nights that she'd spent here at Roydsal.

This little ritual had in its small way helped to get Haw through. Each time she marked off a night, she was asserting her existence against the drag of time's passage and her enforced inactivity.

Turning away from the scratches, she sat down on the cot and rested her hands in her lap. Sitting thus, she radiated calm – serenity even: a quality some Norgreen mothers, when they noticed it in her, wished might rub off on their own impetuous daughters. "Haw's so different from her brother," such a parent might remark, perhaps adding that Thorn was an impulsive youth, inclined to be headstrong. A stranger might well imagine, seeing Haw and Thorn together, that they couldn't be brother and sister, so different were they from one another. Haw, several years younger, was slim and brown-eyed, and had curly auburn hair, freckled skin and a straight nose. Thorn was compact and muscular; his eyes were blue, his nose snub, his complexion clear, and he liked to keep his all-but-black hair short-cropped.

Looking at Haw now, you wouldn't have guessed that her mind was in turmoil as questions tumbled through it, one hard on another's heels. Why did the brothers want this key? Who were Crane Rockett and Briar Spurr, and where did they live? What had Thorn to do with them? Who were the woman and the girl, and where had they sprung from? What was Racky Jagger's game?

She'd reacted with astonishment when, earlier that morning, Racky opened the door of her cell, bound her wrists and took her up to the twins' marquee on the tabletop. She'd asked him what he was doing, but he'd made no reply. They'd arrived just in time to stop the unknown girl and woman shooting the twins. Haw would have preferred to have arrived too late and found the twins already dead.

She'd been taken to the big tent a single time before, six days previously. When she got there, the twins were smoking that awful pipe of theirs and their brains seemed messed up, for all they did was weave nets of nonsense in which she floundered – until, her mind spinning, she told them to their faces they were a pair of silly men, more like children than proper grown-ups.

"I hate you!" she'd cried. "And when Thorn gets here he'll kill you – he's the best archer in Norgreen – and then you'll be sorry!"

Perhaps she'd thought this would frighten them, but they'd only laughed the more, clutching at one another and rolling about on their couch, and soon after that she was sent back to her cell . . .

At which point in her musings, the door was unbolted and a figure walked into the cell.

"Thorn!" she cried.

Moments later, sister and brother were in one another's arms. The intensity of their feelings made speech impossible, and they simply clutched one another, tears moistening their eyes.

But at last they found their voices. Are you all right? . . . *Are you?*

Haw insisted that she was. As for Thorn, he was fine.

Each demanded the other's story. Haw went first, but had little to tell. Three men – whose names in due course she found to be Blacky, Rafter and Denny – had grabbed her at the pool. That first day was the worst, with her not knowing what was happening. Arms and legs tied, an old flour bag over her head, she'd been carried, slung like a sack over this man's shoulder, then that man's, then the other's. On the second day they'd allowed her to walk, without the bag – just so long as she made no trouble.

In the early days of their journey, Blacky – the nastiest of the three – had sometimes threatened her with a beating. But she realised soon enough that his threats were idle words: he and the others were under orders "on no account to damage the goods" – as Denny, the nicest one, put it (if kidnappers could be nice). They took it in turns to scout ahead, and if they spotted other travellers they would all slip into the trees.

There was no chance of escape. When at night they made camp – also well clear of the road – she'd beg them to tell her who they were and the reason behind her kidnap, but all they ever said was: "You'll find out, Missy. Shut your trap!" until she saw it was futile to ask. But from their conversation she gathered that the place they were making for was a mansion beyond the wood, a house built in the Dark Time whose masters – "the bosses", as the three men called them – were twin brothers.

The men seemed in awe of these twins. It also became clear that they hadn't the least idea why their masters had selected her, and no other girl, as the object of their mission. Their favourite topic was the size of the bonus they'd receive when she was safely delivered. They were looking forward to arriving at an inn where they'd get decent beds and food. She'd perked up on hearing this: perhaps she'd have a chance to get away from them there. But the chance never arose. Bound and gagged, she was spirited into the inn under cover of darkness, and locked up in a small room. "Shout all you like, kid," Blacky had told her. "No one will ever hear you." The inn was close to running water: the sound would probably drown out any noise she could make. Next morning they were off again.

When, a couple of days later, they arrived at Roydsal, she was shut up in this cell; until, that is, the night before, when she'd been moved to the rattery. And Thorn knew the rest of it.

Thorn's story took longer to tell. He began at the beginning with his rite of passage at Wyke and stealing of the ruby crystal – but not only did that event now seem to have happened a lifetime ago, its significance was utterly changed by Racky Jagger's behaviour. Then his journey through the wood – with its excitements, its triumphs and the betrayal at Whispering Oak – came tumbling from his mouth like thawing snow from a pitched roof.

But, for the first time in his life, Thorn withheld things from his sister. He made no mention of the strange girl, Emmy Wood, who had helped him escape the Woodmen. Quite why he kept this secret he didn't know, but the notion of talking about Emmy made him uncomfortable. He also failed to mention the conversation he'd had that morning with Racky. Racky's claim to be Thorn's father was no fit matter for Haw's ears: she had enough to worry about. As for Racky's offer to help Haw escape from Roydsal if Thorn promised him the stone, he'd no desire to broach that: Haw might not understand his reasons for turning Racky down . . .

But in all this, Racky Jagger was clearly the dominant figure and Haw, with her quick intelligence, latched on to him straightaway.

"I'm starting to understand," she said slowly. "Racky knows the Spetch twins, so he sets up my kidnap in order to bring you here. *You* are the one the brothers want to get them back their key . . . The kidnappers leave the yellow feather, and you and Racky set off on the trail. But then, after Judy

Bridge, he takes you off to Whispering Oak? *That's* what I don't understand."

That's the trouble with not telling the whole truth, thought Thorn, you can easily get caught out.

"To be honest, I don't understand it myself," he said slowly. "Racky knew at Norgreen that I'd been to Wyke, of course — but how he knew I'd stolen the crystal . . .? I can only think he had a secret source of information. He also knew at Whispering Oak the crystal wasn't in our house, so either he searched it himself before we left or someone else did it later, an accomplice of his. Anyway, it's at the Punch and Judy Inn that things start getting complicated. I suspect Racky and the Spetches had arranged to fake a fight on the balcony. Maybe Blacky was to escape while Denny got himself captured and led us to Roydsal. Instead, Blacky broke his neck and Denny fell into the river. Now Racky changes plans. He takes me upriver and traps me in Whispering Oak—"

"From where you surprise him by escaping. And the next thing we know, he's here, holding a knife at my throat, saving those horrible twins' lives and putting you into their clutches. So now you're stuck with the task of going and getting them back their key . . . I hate them, *hate* them."

"That makes two of us," he said, not unhappy to get off the subject of Racky Jagger. "I feel sick every time I have to look at their smirking faces. Which I was doing just now, because I've come to you straight from them. They agreed to let me see you before I left. I leave today."

"*Today!*" So soon, thought Haw. She'd just got her brother back and now she was losing him again. What if he were killed

31

on this expedition? Pushing the thought aside, she said, "Were the girl and the woman there?"

"No, only me. As it turned out, the twins didn't have a lot to say. Crane Rockett and Briar Spurr live in a house called Minral How. Like this place, Roydsal, it belongs to the Dark Time. It's enclosed by high walls, so it's not easy to get in. And, like the twins, Crane Rockett has henchmen. His right-hand man is this fellow called Deacon Brace. 'Watch out for him,' Lanner warned me. 'He'll swat you like a fly if you go buzzing too close.' I don't think he was joking. 'So how do I get in?' I asked. 'That's up to you – and Jewel and Rainy,' said Zak. 'If I were you, I'd simply try speaking to Rockett first. Offer him this.' And Zak tossed a fat bag of coins across to me. 'Not that Rockett's likely to trade.' 'And if he doesn't?' I asked. '*Then*,' Lanner said, 'you'll have to don your thinking cap.'

"After that they told me how to get to Minral How. This house, Roydsal, is perched on top of a ridge. Below, to the north, the land drops away to a dam built by the giants – Roydsal Dam. To get to Minral How, you can go around the Dam, but it's quicker to go across it. There's a small settlement, Damside, midway along the southern shore. It's mainly fishermen and their wives, but there's an inn there. If the weather's good, a boatman will probably take us across for a price. On the far side of the Dam is a long waterway called the Goyt. It runs all the way to Minral How and passes in under the walls, but it's too dangerous to navigate. Still, there's a track along the bank that you can follow to Minral How.

"That was all they had to say. But I had a question for them. 'This morning,' I began, 'you told me I'd been singled out to undertake this mission—' That was as far as I got. Zak interrupted me. 'And that's all we're prepared to tell you, so don't waste your time asking. There are certain situations where ignorance may turn out to be a positive advantage.' 'Just make sure,' Lanner added, 'that you speak to *both* the Master and the Mistress of Minral How.'"

"How very odd," said Haw. "But then those twins are raving mad."

"Maybe," Thorn agreed. "But they seemed sane enough while they were talking to me just now."

The two went on talking until the door was thrown open. Rafter stood in the frame.

"Come on, Jack, the bosses want you out of here today."

Thorn got to his feet. "I need a moment to say goodbye."

Rafter considered this, grunted, then went out and closed the door.

Brother and sister embraced.

"Go carefully, Thorn," said Haw, and kissed her brother on the cheek.

"I will," he promised. "Trust me: I'll be back for you."

He kissed her in his turn. At last, reluctantly disengaging from her arms, he turned away, walked to the door and was lost to her once more.

3

AT THE SIGN OF
THE WATER RAT

Thorn was waiting when Jewel and Rainy – packs on their backs, bows in their hands – emerged from the rattery, closely followed by Leech, the ratman. The pair came towards Thorn, halted and stood looking at the young man. Thorn returned their steady gaze.

Jewel saw a young man of middling height whose sturdy legs and broad shoulders suggested a physical strength beyond his years. His face was characterful rather than handsome, his eyes blue, his complexion clear, his dark hair short-cropped. He carried an air of maturity; he looked dependable.

Thorn saw a girl who might be a half-inch shy of his own height. She was slim and delicately boned, her narrow face enclosed by straight black hair that dropped to her shoulders. Had she been one of a flock of girls, he might have thought her ordinary; but eye to eye with him, she was not to be dismissed. She radiated determination.

For a time, no one spoke. The atmosphere seemed charged, and Rainy, observing the two of them, sensed strong wills measuring each other up.

"We need to talk," said Jewel at last.

Thorn cast a glance at Leech, who was watching them intently. "First let's put some distance between ourselves and this place."

Jewel nodded her assent.

They went down the side of the building, through the overgrown garden and under the ivy-hung arch to the approach road. Passing the ruined outbuildings and the fallen trees, they came to the ancient gateposts from whose capstones great hook-beaked birds glared down at visitors, welcome and unwelcome alike. And then along the road that followed the crest of the ridge.

"Hang on a moment," said Thorn, when they'd gone a little way.

On his way here he had concealed his pack and weapons in a crack in the dilapidated wall that ran alongside the weed-infested giant-made road. Now he retrieved them. As Jewel and Rainy watched, he strung the bow and ran his fingers along the sprung wood. He was glad to have it back. He felt half-dressed without it.

"Now I'm up to speed," he said.

They set off again.

"It's time we talked," Jewel said.

"Fine by me," said Thorn, and told them what he'd learnt from the twins about Minral How.

"I suggest we go down to Damside," he finished, "see what the weather and lake look like, then make a decision on whether to walk around or take a boat."

"That seems reasonable," said Jewel, and looked enquiringly at Rainy.

"I agree," said the juggler.

"Right," said Jewel. "Now: there are things *we* know and you don't – things you need to hear about the Spetches and the people at Minral How. But first we want to hear your story: Rainy and I need to understand how it is we find ourselves on this expedition to save your sister's life. If we're going to join forces, we must be able to trust one another: which means being frank. I came to Roydsal to kill the Spetches; the last thing I expected was to end up running their errands. Key or no key, kill them's what I'm going to do – next week, next month, next year: whenever."

"Fine," said Thorn, "but you'll have to join the queue. Noboby kidnaps my sister and gets away with it." He paused. "Look, I'm sorry that my business with the brothers messed you up. But freeing my sister comes first. Let's make a pact. You help me get the brass key; then, when Haw's safely out of their hands, we'll go after them together. Three will have a better chance of doing it than two."

"Fair enough. I'll hold you to that," said Jewel.

"You won't need to hold me to it. I keep my promises."

Then, for the second time that day, Thorn launched into his tale. Beginning with the raid on Wyke, he omitted only what he'd omitted in his earlier account to Haw: his adventures with the Woodgirl and his talk with Racky Jagger.

Jewel and Rainy listened intently, and after he'd finished there was a silence.

Then Jewel said slowly, "So, we have not one but *two* mysterious objects, a brass key and a ruby crystal. The key's the important thing to the twins. But, to Racky Jagger, it's the crystal that matters most . . ." She looked thoughtfully at Thorn. "But there's a hole in all this."

"A hole?" queried Thorn.

"A Racky Jagger-shaped hole. Jagger wants the crystal badly. But you going off to Minral How — that's the last thing he wants. Who knows how long it'll be before he sees you again and gets another chance at the crystal — if in fact he ever does."

She took some quick steps and positioned herself in front of Thorn. The young man stopped dead. Rainy, frowning, halted too.

"Is there something you're not telling us?" the girl demanded of Thorn.

"Of course not," he said. "I've told you all you need to know."

"All I *need* to know is not all I *want* to know." She gave him a piercing look. "Has Jagger talked to you today?"

"Of course not," Thorn declared. "When could he have done that?"

"You tell me. Jagger strikes me as a resourceful man."

"One or another of the Spetches' men was watching me all morning."

Jewel laughed. "You're a pretty good liar, but not good enough," she said. "I'm not going a step further until you tell me what Jagger said."

Thorn considered, then said: "All right. I did speak to him today. He said he'd get Haw out of Roydsal if I swore on my love for her I'd give him the crystal when we got back to Norgreen."

"But you rejected his offer. Why?"

"He betrayed me," said Thorn. "I don't believe a word he says."

"I don't suppose you do. But this time, surely, you'd nothing to lose by trusting him. *He* wants the crystal as much as *you* want your sister back." She paused, searching his face. "Is there something you're still not telling me, Thorn Jack?"

"I stole the crystal for Haw. Nobody gets it except her."

"But what good is the crystal to you? You can't even handle it. Surely it's worth giving up if it gets your sister freed and you out of this expedition. Thorn, you're holding something back."

"I've told you everything," he insisted.

"No you haven't. Come on. Why did you turn his offer down? What else did he say to you?"

Jewel stepped close to Thorn and locked her eyes on his. Younger and shorter as she was, and a slighter figure by far, he felt the strength that dwelt in her; she made him feel – ridiculously – as if she were the taller one. He wanted to pull his gaze away, but found the action impossible.

"What else did he say, Thorn?"

"No – nothing," he faltered.

Jewel lifted a hand and laid her fingers against his cheek. Her touch was cold.

Thorn knocked her hand away. Anger welled up in him, and he opened his mouth to throw out an irate torrent of words, but an expression of such profound sympathy had appeared on the girl's face that all at once he felt unmanned.

Jewel said quietly: "Jagger hurt you, didn't he? Not in your body – in your soul."

At that precise moment, Thorn wearied of his burden. Why not tell this girl? For better or for worse, their lives were intricately entwined. Freed at once by this change of feeling, but overcome by a sense of shame, he turned his face away from hers.

"Racky told me he's my father – my true father, not the father . . . that's, I mean – Davis Jack, who . . ."

He faltered to a halt. There was an almost palpable silence.

Rainy had watched enthralled while the dialogue proceeded. Now, at the moment of climax, she was amazed afresh at her friend. Jewel had touched Thorn with only the briefest of touches, but it had provided her with the key to unlock his resistance. Truly she was formidable: single-minded and relentless. And Rainy had little doubt that had the contact lasted longer, Jewel would have read in Thorn's mind what Jagger had told the young man.

Jewel said: "There's a part of you that believes Racky Jagger, isn't there Thorn? Though of course you don't want to."

"Yes," he admitted. "The very idea makes me gag . . . but I can't rid my mind of it, it's eating away at me. I barely remember my father – he died in a hunting accident when I was two. My mother abandoned Haw and me just months after Haw was born. Nobody knows what happened to her."

"Well, I understand now why you refused Jagger's help. You probably can't bear the thought of having him anywhere near you. And as for being bound to him by a promise, beholden to him—"

"I'm *not* beholden to him. He got me into this mess. What sort of father betrays his son for a chunk of coloured rock?"

"I don't know. But your crystal's no ordinary rock, that's for certain. This journey you two made – you said he worked to earn your trust. Did you two become close?"

"We shared adventures, came to seem comrades, I suppose. But I never really got close to him. There was always a distance between us. He told me this morning that in the wood he was testing me. He wanted to know if I really was his son – a free spirit, not some tame settlement man."

"And are you?"

"I don't know. But it looks as though I'm going to find out."

They went on down the road, Thorn preoccupied with his thoughts and Jewel with hers. Roydsal's grimy chimney pots had long disappeared from view.

The morning was grey and still, and the broken walls on either side of the stony, weed-sprung track, spotted with yellow lichen and riddled with knotty growths, seemed forlorn in the frail light, monuments to nothing so much as collapse and despondency.

They came in due course to the junction where the road to Roydsal met the road that southwards wound down to Judy Wood, and northwards to Roydsal Dam and the road to Harrypark.

Thorn pointed towards the wood. "That's the way I came," he said.

Jewel and Rainy stared at the thickly clustering trees. A green-dark mass lumped beneath the grey heavens; it stretched away to merge seamlessly with the lowering sky.

"What a forbidding place," said Rainy. "It's hard to imagine it ever coming to an end."

"But it does," said Thorn, "and beyond lies Norgreen. How I wish I was back there, and all this had never happened."

"But it did," observed Jewel. "Look, you've told us your story – it's time I told you mine."

"I'd like to hear it," said Thorn.

So, as the three travellers descended Roydsal Ridge, Jewel began to talk, telling of Shelf Fair, of her father's brutal murder and her subsequent realisation that the twins had killed him.

Taking up the narrative, Rainy then described how the twins had gambled away the brass key – their most treasured possession – to Briar Spurr at Rotten Pavilion in Harrypark the summer before.

"So now you know *why* you're going *where* you're going," she finished.

"I do and I don't," said Thorn. "We still haven't the slightest idea what this key's for."

"What it's *for* is irrelevant. We have to get it – *that's* what matters."

The story passed to Jewel again, and she described the sequence of events at Rotten Pavilion that led to Tarry Ramsbottom's death and almost ended in her own. Thorn listened with fascination and a growing sense of the formidable opposition that Crane Rockett and Briar Spurr, and their deadly shadow Deacon Brace, could pose.

"You *do* seem to go in for narrow escapes," he commented, when Jewel had told how Parker Catt had pulled her out of Harrylake.

"So it seems," she agreed.

41

"And you have *two* scores to settle — not only with the twins on your father's behalf, but with Deacon Brace on your own."

"Yes. And now, because of you, I shall meet Brace much sooner than I ever expected to. It's strange how things turn out."

"Perhaps," Thorn mused, "fate intended us to meet. Let's hope we enjoy the same luck at Minral How that you enjoyed when you won that wager with Briar Spurr."

"Yes, let's," Jewel agreed, and caught a fleeting look of amusement on Rainy Gill's face. Rainy knew as well as Jewel that luck had played no part in the wager.

Arriving at the road that ran parallel with the Dam, they turned west towards Harrypark and Shelf. A couple of pushcart pedlars toiled past, going in the opposite direction; they exchanged salutations.

The three westbound travellers took the track that branched off to Damside. Narrow and bordered by dense grasses that towered above them, the track passed through a gap in a broken wall and angled down the hill-slope.

Sometimes, on straight stretches of the road down from Roydsal, they'd sighted the Dam way below in the valley bottom. To Jewel's sensitive gaze, it seemed to lurk there, awaiting them like a sentient creature; but, like the wood earlier, the further reaches of its pewter-coloured waters soon lost themselves in the misty afternoon light.

All through the morning the sky had stayed cloud-covered, and now, as afternoon wore on, it grew still darker and a drizzle began to fall. Soon it was raining heavily. On they trudged, sick of the grass that threatened to swallow the track they were following.

It was with relief that at last, without warning, they emerged from the meadow onto the edge of the Dam. Its retaining wall was constructed of stone blocks, and Rainy was reminded of the lake surrounds back home in Harrypark; but these blocks were still more massive than those of Jugdam and Harrylake. Roydsal Dam had been conceived on altogether a different scale. Several times bigger than Harrylake, which itself dwarfed Jugdam, it – like them – was a product of artifice, of the great minds of the Dark Time, when the giants had built huge and mysterious structures.

They advanced to the Dam's edge and looked down: the drop to the surface of the lake was some three feet or more. There was little or no wind, and heavy raindrops plummeted straight into the reservoir. In the indifferent light, the water, sullen, unfriendly and lethargic, slopped against the unyielding stone. As they scanned the grey distances, the Dam seemed vast – endless even, its cluster of islands invisible in the rain-drenched haze.

It was Rainy who expressed the feelings of all three travellers: "I don't like the look of these waters. We could always walk round."

"So we could," said Thorn. "But the weather's against us today. Let's get to the inn. If it's fine enough tomorrow I think we ought to cross by boat."

"Yes," said Jewel. "I'm sure the Dam will look different with a bit of sun on it. Walking round will add at least a day to our journey. What do you think, Rainy?"

"I've got a bad feeling about this Dam. But I'm probably being irrational. And in any case, I'm outvoted."

"That's decided then," said Thorn. "Right, let's get on to

Damside before the light fails altogether and we blunder into the lake."

The rain refused to relent, the stones were slippery underfoot and they'd all had more than enough by the time they got to Damside. The settlement – if the place deserved that description – consisted of a dozen scattered houses (some little more than hovels, though all had garden-plots and sheds), and a two-storey inn with a rough-and-ready rattery that looked as though it would accommodate three animals at most. Below, in the inlet above the high-water mark, and seemingly at odds with the modest size of the settlement, were two large boatyards, each equipped with a slipway and furnished with a stout jetty. To each of these a fishing smack was moored, also a couple of sleeker sailing boats with tall masts. Several dinghies were drawn up on the muddy slope.

Not an inhabitant was in sight. The travellers paused outside the inn to examine its sign, motionless and slick with rain. In the dim light they could just make out the bewhiskered snout of a rat paddling solemnly through greeny, waved-flecked water. But the inn's curtained windows glowed redly from within, and the place had a welcoming look.

They entered and found themselves in a tidy, homely bar. A fire was burning in the hearth, and the room radiated cheer. Three men glanced up from their game of dominoes and fell to studying the arrivals with obvious interest.

Behind the bar-counter, a brawny woman with bare arms was drying a beer-pot. She had coarse features, a thick mass of wavy blonde hair and large, circular purple earrings.

"Hello, me ducks!" she boomed in a deep and somewhat masculine voice. "Welcome to the Water Rat! What can I do for you?"

"Some hot food," said Jewel, "and, if you have them, beds for the night."

"I certainly do," said the woman. She examined them with humorous eyes. "How many rooms is it, then?"

"Three, if you have them," said Jewel.

The woman grinned broadly. "Three's what I have if three's what you want."

"Then please take us to them," said Thorn. "We'd like to dump our packs and get out of these wet clothes."

"Acourse, me ducks," said the woman. "If you'll come along with me . . .

"Call me Mags," she told them, as she led them up the stairs; Mags Topliss was her name.

Their rooms were neat and clean. A gaily-chequered counterpane covered Jewel's bed. Pottery ducks flew on the walls, receding from biggest through lesser to least as they beat with motionless wings towards a destination destined never to come an inch closer. Unslinging her pack, Jewel stripped off her wet clothes, then fell back upon the bed with the idea of testing the springs. It will do, she thought. There was water in a bowl, albeit cold, and a fluffy towel. She washed her hands and face and considered herself in the mirror fastened to the dresser-top.

What had the woman meant by that question about rooms? *Two* rooms would have meant two of them sharing a room. Herself and Rainy? Somehow, she didn't think that was what

45

the woman's manner had implied. No, she was pairing them off: Jewel and Thorn . . . *Rainy* and Thorn.

All of a sudden, Jewel found her mind a confusion of thoughts. A man and a woman sharing a room meant only one thing, but Rainy – Rainy was so much older than either Thorn or herself. Had she ever been in love, had a sexual experience? Rainy of course had told her of Harry's – the master of Rotten Pavilion's – unrequited passion for her, but she and Jewel had never discussed sexual matters in general. Surely Rainy must have some experience. And Thorn? What of him? What did *he* know of love? Young men, she'd heard it said, were often interested in older women. Rainy, perhaps, would make a desirable lover for Thorn.

Jewel, to her surprise, felt a rush of resentment and an odd discomfiture. Was she jealous? Perhaps it was a result of her inexperience. For Jewel, though knowledgeable in many of the world's ways, knew next to nothing at first-hand of young men. She'd never had a boyfriend, never been kissed on the lips. How could she, when her life had been one continual round of travelling and business? Even female companions of her own age or thereabouts had been few and far between. Her father, with his characteristic bluntness and cynicism, had warned her about boys, adamant that they only ever consorted with girls for what they could get out of them.

Oh dear, she now told herself, as she looked at the serious face that looked back at her from the mirror; my world's completely upside down. I know so much about death; I came close to killing a man; it seems that I've been granted powers few human beings have ever possessed. But what do I know about boys? No more than a sparrow knows about the life of a frog.

46

Dressed now in dry clothes, her hair dried and combed, she went downstairs to find Thorn and Rainy already sitting at a table behind pots of light ale, talking quietly together. They fell silent when Jewel appeared. Jealousy assailed her afresh. She stumped off to the bar and rang the bell vigorously to summon the absent landlady.

"I've only two hands, ducks!" the woman declared stiffly, wiping her hands on her apron.

"Another ale, please, Mrs Topliss," said Jewel.

"Please, call me Mags," said the woman, her annoyance short-lived.

The ale drawn, she disappeared again to attend to their dinner.

Jewel joined Rainy and Thorn. They exchanged small talk about their rooms, which turned out to be similar, down to the flying ducks and the design of the counterpane, then lapsed into silence. They might have talked about their mission, but the domino-players at the next table inhibited their conversation. Thorn thought the men a rough-and-ready bunch, but they behaved like locals. It seemed as good a time as any to raise the matter of passage across the Dam.

He framed a question in his head and was on the point of voicing it when one of the men beat him to speech.

"Well now, it's not often we see young folk like yourselves in these parts. What brings you to Damside, I wonder?"

"We're travelling," said Thorn.

The man had blue eyes, a humorous face tanned and parched by decades of wind and sun, and a straggling beard that had long since turned to grey. Despite the warmth of the room, he wore a cap upon his head.

"Did you hear that, lads," he boomed, "it's travelling he says he is. Now there's a thing!"

A second man, whose bulbous nose was as red as a raspberry, produced a series of guffaws that showed off his graveyard teeth. "Travelling!" he chortled. "Travelling!" As if the notion were the funniest ever invented by humankind.

"Better believe it," said the bearded man. "As a way of getting about, it's never yet been shown to fail!"

The third man looked puzzled, as if the joke was beyond him, but the red-nosed man now collapsed entirely. When his laughter turned to coughing, the third man took to patting him gently on the back.

The bearded man fixed Thorn with his blue, miss-nothing eyes. "But travelling implies a *from* and a *to*, a here and a there. So: where might you three be from, and where might you be a-going?"

"That," said Rainy decisively, "is *our* business, I think."

"Woman got a tongue on her," said the third man, still patting. Gangling, with lank hair as pale as winter straw, he was the youngest of the three by a considerable margin.

"Sharp, too," said the bearded man. "Sharp enough to fillet a fish. Better watch yourself, Spindle."

"What's the betting," said Broken Teeth, who now had control of himself, "that *you two*" – he pointed to Jewel and Thorn – "have run away from somewhere. What's the word? *Illooped?* While *you*" – he pointed to Rainy – "are the fairy godmother what waved her wand and made it all happen!"

"*Eloped*, you dunderhead, Stocky," decreed the bearded man. "Well, you could be right. Capable of anything, kids at their

48

age. Get sudden fancies into their heads. Don't know their arses from their elbows."

"Ah, it's love," said Stocky. "Isn't love a fine thing!"

"What would you know about love? All you know about is fish."

"I've had my bit of romance," said Stocky defensively.

"What? The time you kissed Mavis Trout and she slapped your face?"

"A misunderstanding. Mavis was lovely!"

"That's a matter of opinion. And when it's mine against yours, there's no contest, matey. Mavis was a cold fish if ever there was one."

Stocky brought his pot of ale to his mouth with such force that it crashed against the few stumps that still remained to him. Was that, wondered Jewel, how he'd come to devastate them?

Fortified by the draught, the fellow spluttered through his outrage: "What do *you* know of Mavis?"

The bearded man winked at Jewel. "Ah, wouldn't you like to know!" he told Stocky with a leer.

"Oh, you're all talk, Lacky."

Lacky smiled. "Talk costs nothing and passes the time. Don't knock it. Spindle, your round. Rustle us up three more pots."

Spindle downed the rest of his ale and carried their pots to the bar, where he ducked out of sight in order to fill them from a keg resting on trestles near the floor.

Jewel was wondering how to respond to the men's ridiculous suggestion that she and Thorn had eloped when Rainy said, "Perhaps you can help us. We're looking for a boat to take us across the Dam tomorrow."

"*Are* you now."

There was a thump from behind the bar, and Spindle shot into view, rubbing his head vigorously.

"What are you doing, Spindle?" said Lacky. "Trying to knock your head off? I wouldn't if I were you! There's nothing like a head for helping you find your way around!"

Spindle grinned uncertainly, as if *his* head might be the one exception to this rule. Lacky turned back to Rainy.

"Well, I can't say you've come to the wrong feller. Allow me to introduce myself: Lacky Dawes, Captain, boatman extraordinary. Motto: go anywhere, do anything – providing, you understand, the price is right. And passage across the Dam doesn't come cheap, let me tell you."

"I don't suppose it does," said Rainy. "But if we walk round, nobody here will be any the richer."

Lacky chuckled. "Point taken, Missy. Let's *negotiate* then. Now this here" – he indicated the man with graveyard choppers – "is Stocky Ricks, my second-in-command."

"First mate," said Mr Ricks self-importantly.

"And that fine young man over there behind the bar is Spindle, occasional crewman and the best bottle-washer in the whole of Damside."

"That's me!" said Spindle, rising up from behind the bar with a pot of ale in each hand.

"Pleased to meet you all," said Rainy.

Spindle returned with three pots of ale and set them down on the table.

"*Now,*" said Captain Lacky Dawes in a businesslike voice, "a crossing of the Dam is no mean proposition. It takes time, skill and guts." He paused significantly. "Do you take my meaning, Miss?"

"I think we do," said Rainy.

"She do," said Stocky, rubbing his hands. "She do!"

"Why guts?" enquired Jewel.

"Guts!" said Stocky. "Guts!"

"Quiet, Stocky!" ordered Lacky. "Why guts? Well, I wouldn't expect a young lass to understand the word."

"Try me," said Jewel.

"*Try me!*" repeated the first mate with a strangulated howl.

"If you don't shut up, Stocky, I'll ram your pot down your throat," said Captain Dawes menacingly.

The Captain turned back to Jewel.

"The Dam's big. Boats are small. Sailing's no simple matter. There are islands, shoals, currents that boats do well to avoid."

"Not to mention the Great Pike!" blurted the re-seated Spindle.

The Captain favoured the lank-haired man with a withering look. "How many times have I told you, Spindle, that the Pike's an old wives' tale?"

Spindle fixed his eyes on his full pot of ale and said: "Seen it with my own eyes, I have, and more than once. A monster all dark green with a snout like a ram and eyes like fire!"

Jewel glanced at Stocky Ricks. Since his sudden shutting-up his face was blank, unreadable.

The Captain tapped the side of his skull. "I'm afraid my crewman here suffers from an overactive imagination. Take no notice."

"Swallow a boat in one gulp," muttered Spindle to himself.

51

"Listen to me," said Lacky Dawes. "Man and boy, I've sailed this Dam for forty years – no one longer. Never a whiff of such a creature. Oh, there are legends, I grant you, and the waters are dangerous – but a Great Pike? Piffle!" He took a long swig of ale. "So, we'll talk money, shall we?"

"Yes," said Thorn. "But it's on the understanding that we go tomorrow morning. If the weather's too bad to sail, we'll be setting off on foot."

"I'm not such a fool as to risk my boat in a high wind," said the Captain. "A bit of a breeze, that's what we want. Blow us across in no time." He tapped the side of his nose. "And this here organ tells me termorrer will be just the day for it."

"Let's hope so," said Thorn.

They began to bargain. As he'd promised, the Captain's services did not come cheap, but at last they agreed a price, half to be paid in advance. Lacky's eyes gleamed as Thorn counted out the sum.

The coins disappeared into Lacky's pocket. Again he tried to prise the travellers' business out of them, but once again they blocked his probings. At last the men went back to their game.

The travellers talked desultorily for a time, then in came Mags Topliss bearing a tray of steaming plates. Fish pie! Well, what else?

The travellers were hungry, and tucked in with a will. The click and slap of wooden tiles on the neighbouring tabletop accompanied them through the meal.

4

THE SILVER WHISTLE

The following day dawned dry and bright, with barely a cloud in the sky. The three travellers breakfasted well, paid Mags Topliss and left the inn. The swimming rat squeaked as they passed underneath the sign.

There was breeze enough to stir the Dam's waters into ripples, but not nearly enough to threaten to swamp a good-sized boat: ideal weather for their crossing, as Captain Dawes's canny nasal organ had prophesied. They found him, his mate and his crewman aboard one of the sleeker vessels, making preparations to sail. It was a four-foot sailing boat with a wheelhouse/cabin aft of the mast. Espying his passengers, the Captain called them aboard. While Rainy chose a seat to the rear of the wheelhouse on the port side of the boat, Jewel and Thorn went forward. Jewel sat on the port-side bench a little way behind the bows, Thorn somewhat further back on the starboard side.

Lacky, at the wheel, began to bellow out commands. Stocky cast off fore, Spindle aft; then they hoisted the mainsail. The breeze discovered it, and slowly, as if blindly feeling its way, the boat nosed out into the vast expanse of the Dam.

More orders followed, and Jewel and Thorn learnt some new sailing terms as foresail and jib added capacity to the mainsail. Soon the boat was spanking along, tossing up spray whenever

53

the prow cut through the crest of a ripple. To Jewel, it seemed a water bird, skimming an ungrudging surface.

"This is wonderful!" she exclaimed. "What a lovely boat!" – thrown back to the mate, who was stationed just fore of the mast.

"So she should be," Stocky replied. "Had a big hand in building her myself, didn't I? Lacky and I learnt the boat-building trade from Lacky's dad. Old Captain Dawes sailed these waters many a year, but he's dead now, rest his soul."

Time passed and Damside receded, dwindling to a smudge in the distant inlet. Soon there seemed only sky and water and, between them, the boat in the immensity.

Standing up, Jewel peered into the distance. "Are those the islands?" she asked.

"Aye, the archipelago," said Stocky. "You've two good eyes, I'll give you that."

"I heard there are Sybs living there."

"You heard right, lass. Two of them there are. Syb-sisters – which is a rare thing. Getting on now. We take them goods from time to time; do a bit of trading, like. Ferry visitors across. Not that there are many. The sisters aren't the kind as welcomes uninvited guests."

Sitting down again, Jewel stretched out her arms and gripped the varnished wood of the gunwales. Closing her eyes, she sank her consciousness into the timber. The rush of keel against water became inward and intense, her sails billowed with the breeze and her boat-spirit exulted as it sped through the waves.

Thorn too was staring out past the bowsprit, but he couldn't see any islands, even if he stood up. Jewel's eyesight must be better than mine, he thought.

Then he went back to the subject that kept poking up into his thoughts: Racky Jagger. Perhaps it had been a mistake to turn down Racky's offer. What chance had he now, as the distance grew between them, of discovering the truth about the past? Who could he go to for an unprejudiced view of Racky's claim? Morry and Taylor? Had his aunt and uncle known of his mother's relations with Racky, but concealed them from him to save him the hurt? . . . Minny Pickles – the Norgreen Syb? Sybs divined things beyond the grasp of ordinary people.

But then, he thought, only one person knows the truth – and that's my mother, and in all likelihood she's dead. I shall probably never know.

Catching a movement out of the corner of his eye, he started to twist around. Too late: the blow took him on the base of the skull and pain flashed in his head. He tried to lift a hand, but his muscles had turned to jelly and he slumped sideways on the bench. Vaguely he registered a hand as it invaded his pocket; then he passed out.

Lost to herself, Jewel saw or heard none of this. Not till something yanked at her waist-belt did she dreamily open her eyes.

Spindle stood over her, a club poised in his hand. He grinned lopsidedly.

"Your nice, fat moneybag: that's what I want, girl!" And he pulled at her belt again.

Rainy, aft of the cabin, was gazing out over the stern when she heard steps approaching. Swivelling round, she saw the Captain just a couple of paces away, a knife poised in his fist.

For just a moment, as their eyes met, Lacky hesitated. Perhaps he was in no hurry, thinking a woman no match for

55

him. Perhaps he'd paused to savour the thought of what he was going to do. However it was, Rainy's reactions, honed by years of juggling, proved the faster. In a trice, she was on her feet. She brought her right hand up, made a fork of two fingers and jabbed them viciously into his eyes.

The knife clattered to the deck. With a sharp cry, Lacky staggered back and clutched his face. Rainy kicked him in the groin. He yelped, doubled up and crumpled onto the boards. She kicked him in the ribs.

She'd have gone on kicking him, but at that moment a cry sounded from further down the boat. Jewel! Leaving the fallen man Rainy hurried forward, past the wheelhouse, where Lacky had tied the wheel to keep the vessel on a straight course.

Spindle stood over Jewel, a club poised in one hand, the other hand dragging at her belt. With both hands Jewel was gripping his upraised arm, striving to prevent him from stoving in her skull.

Glancing sideways through the narrow gap between the mast and the bellying foresail, she glimpsed Stocky Ricks in the process of hoisting Thorn's limp body over the side.

The choice was a grim one, but she didn't hesitate. Rushing upon Spindle, she grabbed a handful of his hair and yanked at it with all her strength. The gowk shrieked and let go of Jewel.

"Thorn's in trouble!" Rainy shouted. "Go to him! Now!"

"Thorn?" cried Jewel.

"Go!" Jewel ducked away beneath the boom.

Rainy and Spindle were grappling now. As he landed a glancing blow with his elbow to her cheek, she trod hard on his foot. He shrieked again and fell back. Seizing her chance, Rainy punched him as hard as she could on the end of the nose.

56

Blood burst from his nostrils. He staggered backwards, arms flailing, a look of alarm on his face. Then she hit him a second time, and he toppled over the gunwale into the deep, rushing waters.

Next moment, she felt a stabbing pain low down in her back. It sucked the energy out of her and she froze, unable to move. There came a second decisive blow, and she twisted and collapsed onto the deck. Above her loomed the Captain, tears streaming down his face, his knife bloody in his hand.

"Bitch!" he spat out.

Far above his head the sky was a perfect, vibrant blue.

That's how it should be, she thought, and was immediately conscious of the irrelevance of the notion. Or was it relevant after all?

The jib flapped as a mild gust struck its triangle.

"Jewel . . ." she whispered.

Then her vision began to cloud. The blue was deepening into night. At last the sky was utterly black, but her eyes were still open, still fixed on the depthless air.

Stocky Ricks had Thorn's body half-draped over the side. As Jewel sprang across the boat, the mate gave a final heave and Thorn's limp legs went slithering over the rail. Jewel tried to grab his foot, but her fingers closed on air. As she leapt up onto the bench that ran along beneath the rail, Stocky seized the hem of her jacket, but her momentum tore her free and she threw herself overboard.

The shock of the cold water brought Thorn to semi-consciousness. Involuntarily, he opened his mouth and swallowed some water; then his head broke through the surface. He gasped and kicked feebly, but his body felt heavy as lead, and he went under again.

On the yacht, the first mate had rejoined his Captain. Grinning, Stocky waved the bag of coins he'd removed from Thorn's pocket.

But Lacky Dawes swore loudly. "Damn Spindle for a fool! That girl's moneybag was chocker. Now we've lost the main prize."

"But where is he?" asked the mate.

Lacky spat. "Gone overboard." He pointed down at Rainy. "That bitch bested him."

"The silly beggar can't swim!"

Cruelty twisted Lacky's mouth. "Then he'll never find a better time to learn, will he?"

Stocky stared at Lacky.

"Right," said the Captain. "Let's bring her about. Stand by with a lifebelt in case you sight Spindle. But those two – if we spot 'em, we'll run the pair of 'em down."

Surfacing for a second time, Thorn gulped in more air. Again he tried to kick but again he went under.

Then an arm came snaking around him and he was propelled upwards. Once more he broke surface.

"Jewel!" gasped Thorn, as her head appeared above the waves. Water slopped into their faces as they rose and fell with the ripples.

"Can you tread water?" she asked.

"I – I think so." He was coming around now.

"What sort of a swimmer are you?"

"Not bad."

"Could you make it to land?"

"I can try." But the water's cold, he thought, it's a long way, and we can't even see where we're going. "Give me a moment to catch my breath."

They trod water.

Thorn asked: "Did you see what happened to Rainy?"

"No." Jewel was worried about her friend. "The last I saw of her, she and Spindle were fighting. She shouted out you were in trouble."

Trouble's a mild word for what we're both in now, thought Thorn, and coughed as water swilled into his mouth. "OK. Let's get moving."

They began to swim. Then, out of nowhere, the boat's prow was coming at them.

"Dive, Jewel!" Thorn cried.

They kicked their legs up to the surface and dived down desperately. The keel swished by above them, churning the water directly below it, sending them whirling in its wake like bottle-stoppers in a maelstrom.

They fought to the surface in time to see, above the yacht's retreating stern, the Captain glaring at them.

"They're trying to run us down!" cried Thorn.

"Then we haven't a chance," she gasped.

He thought: we're both going to drown. I shall never free Haw. I shall never find out if Racky Jagger's my real father.

But a voice sounded in his ear: *Thorn Jack, what a lot you*

59

have to learn! Startled, he looked about him. So clear was the voice that its owner might have been present, serenely floating just a matter of inches away. Then the voice came again: *Use it on water as a last resort.*

Use what on water . . .?

Of course! He pulled at the chain around his neck, splashing water up into his face, and got Minny Pickles's silvery whistle out from under his shirt.

"What are you doing?" asked Jewel, over the slapping of the wavelets.

"I wish I knew," he answered.

He put the whistle to his lips and blew forcefully into it. A tiny water-jet shot out. He blew again. Again. But the thing made no sound, just as he knew it wouldn't – or none a human could hear.

Nothing happened. He blew again.

Nothing happened. Nothing could happen. It was a toy, a piece of nonsense. An old woman's little joke.

Still, the links had saved him underground, those and the lucifers. *Believe*, he told himself.

A great head broke from the waves. It rose up and up above them, a figment ripped from the ultimate nightmare.

It was a fish – but a fish such as neither of the humans had ever seen or expected to see. Its massive head sloped into a rounded wedge of a snout in which a wide and blubber-lipped mouth was set like a trap. Olive-grey, its skin was mottled with darker blotches; its flat, lidless eye regarded them with superb detachment. Then it opened its jaws and showed off two rows of savage teeth. If it was minded, it could gobble the pair of them down in a single gulp.

It's the Great Pike, thought Thorn. Spindle was right: it *does* exist.

He blew the whistle again, but nothing altered in that eye. It was as empty of expression as a stone. It did not blink.

Beside him, Jewel was too horrified – that, or too fascinated – to utter the least sound.

Then she heard the flap of sailcloth.

"The boat! It's coming back!" she cried.

The pike moved quickly away, its dark body cutting the surface. It had to be four feet long. Then, from a different direction, the sailing boat came at them again. It was twenty . . . ten feet away. They watched, unable to move.

But the pike lifted its tail above the waves, a gigantic fan. Silvery drops cascaded from it. Then, as the boat passed below, it smashed down amidships.

The craft snapped like a rotten branch. Prow and stern reared from the water and the two surviving boatmen were tossed into the Dam. The pike dived, turned about and came up again, its great head jutting from the waves. It paused by the shocked, bobbing men, as if to consider some deep question. Stocky Ricks cried out in terror. Lacky Dawes beat feebly on the water with his hands. But if he thought to scare the fish that way, he thought wrong. The fearsome jaws opened, scooped up the yelling mate and swallowed him as if he was nothing more than a titbit before a feast.

Lacky Dawes was howling now. But the pike was inexorable. It caught him up and closed its jaws with a mighty slobbering smack, then turned and swam across to Jewel and Thorn. It came right up to them – so close they might have put out trembling hands and touched its muzzle. Then its mouth opened again.

Beyond the spiky fence of its teeth, a bearded head appeared, followed by Lacky Dawes's shoulders.

"Help me!" he cried.

You're beyond help, thought Jewel.

Lacky struggled to his feet and stood for a moment, staring balefully out from his fishy cavern. But the pike jerked up its head and, pitching forward, the Captain was impaled on the bone-needles that were its teeth.

Jewel shut her eyes. This was too horrible to see. But Thorn watched as if mesmerised.

Lacky's right arm, outflung, twitched, and the man fetched a deep groan in his last extremity.

Then the pike's upper jaw dropped like a spiked and pulleyed gate, impaling its victim from above, and the Captain vanished for ever from the living world of men.

The pike sank beneath the waves. If it comes up underneath us, we're goners, thought Thorn.

And the fish did swim beneath them, like a long green-dark shadow, its outline wavering under the water. But its head was past now, and still it moved on. Then it surfaced, and the humans felt an unexpected firmness under their feet. Next moment, they clutched at one another in amazement and disbelief as they found themselves sprawling on the fish's slick back. It was all they could do not to slide off into the water – but they managed to stay aboard. *Aboard!* They were riding a lake monster! Jewel was a little way behind the pike's head, with Thorn seated to her rear.

But no sooner had they steadied themselves than the great fish reared up out of the water, almost standing on its tail. The teenagers clutched at the slippery beast in an attempt to find a grip. There went the stern of the doomed boat, sliding beneath the surface in a roil of spume!

The pike sank back amidst a scatter of flotsam. Something floated up, brushing against the creature's flank – Thorn's rucksack, still afloat. He reached down and hooked it out.

"Rainy . . ." said Jewel. "Can you see her anywhere?"

Thorn scanned to one side, Jewel to the other, but there was no sign of the juggler.

"Rainy!" Jewel shouted. Again: "Rainy!" And again.

Thorn took up the cry. But there was no answering call. Just the unending slop of waves against the pike's flanks.

"Can Rainy swim?" asked Thorn.

"She's a very good swimmer. She could swim to shore from here, if anyone could . . ."

But she won't because she can't, she thought with sudden certainty.

"She's dead," said Jewel simply.

"You can't know that," objected Thorn.

"How can you know what I know?" she said with sudden vehemence. "You aren't me and you never can be. She's dead . . . I know she's dead . . ."

All at once she began to cry. Trails of tears joined the trickles that straggled down out of her hair. A huge pain was in her heart and her every sob wrenched at it.

Thorn moved closer and put an arm round her shoulder. He didn't know what to say.

63

With a violent convulsion, Jewel shrugged his arm away.

"This is *your* fault," she accused him. "If it wasn't for you and your sister, Rainy and I wouldn't be here. And the Spetches would be dead."

To Thorn, this seemed grotesquely unfair; yet also true.

"You're shivering," he said. "We need to get to shore."

"But Rainy . . ." whispered Jewel. She sniffed and rubbed her eyes. "She's the best friend I ever had. The *only* friend," she said. "Now I've lost her. It isn't fair."

He reached out and put a hand on her shoulder. This time she didn't shrug it away. The pike was in motion now, cruising smoothly away from the wreckage of the boat.

At last Jewel made a snuffling sound and turned to him.

"It isn't your fault, Thorn. It's the fault of the Spetches. *They* killed my father, *they* kidnapped your sister. Now I've lost Rainy because of them. How I hate them, hate them."

With fierce twistings of her hands she wrung water out of her clothes.

"Tell me," she said in an abrupt switch of subject. "What *is* that thing around your neck?"

"It's a whistle the Syb gave me before I left Norgreen. She told me to use it on water."

"Well, at least you're good for something."

"I wonder where this great brute is taking us," said Thorn, defeated by the erratic to and fro of her mood.

"Not back to Damside, I hope."

Thorn was scanning the horizon. But all he could see was water. Water everywhere . . .

"We're too close to the Dam surface to see very far. We shan't sight land until it's right on top of us. But if you ask me, this fish knows exactly what it's doing."

She stared intently ahead. "I get the feeling that it's making for the islands."

"Why do you say that?"

"Oh, just a feeling."

"Why would it take us *there*?"

"Your guess is as good as mine."

She looked down at the pike's back – a muddy green, slick with water – and stroked its scaly skin with the tips of her fingers. Somewhere in its enormous fishy head there was a brain, a directing intelligence. I wonder, she thought, if I could get inside its mind and find out what it's thinking. Well, it's worth a try.

She looked away from the animal. For a moment her gaze rested on the waters flowing past; then she shut her eyes. She put her hands palm-flat on the tough, slick skin and let her whole body relax.

In a happier time she might have gone – as she had earlier on the boat – for innocent purity of sensation: oneness with the liquid rhythm of the great fish's motion. But that would be frivolous now.

Her consciousness slipped between the plates of its scaly hide and sank down through the packed layers of flesh that formed its body. The pike was overwhelming in its simple massiveness, from its butting snout, all the way down its flanks to the whippy rudder of its tail. And with a deepening awareness of the creature as a thing of flesh, blood, bone and nerves, came a sense of age. Oh, the pike was ancient!

The burrowing worm of her consciousness came at length

to the animal's spine, the sinuous cable of spiky bone around whose firm foundation this mansion of flesh was built. Unopposed, she penetrated the master nerve that carried messages from the pike's brain to every extremity. Up this she flowed to the command-centre itself – to be stunned by the flash and whirl of countless pulses as they pursued one another or played random games of tag, crisscross-leaping like mad sparks of mental fire. She narrowed her search, and now – yes . . . Here was the quiet region where memory was located. She began to trawl it, immersing herself in snatches of an alien existence. It was repetitious and limited. But here was a sharper recollection – of gulping down, recently, with cold satisfaction, one, two human beings. She searched for a glimpse of Rainy, but found none. The fish knew nothing of her.

Encouraged, Jewel withdrew from that region of the brain and began her search afresh. Now she was looking for something immediate, something revealing of the pike's present intention. She returned to that knot of spongy circuitry where activity seemed intense. She fused with it, and whizzed and jumped, exhilarated by frantic motion, till she grew gradually to perceive a sensible pattern in the pulses. An image began to form in her linked brain: out of the fuzzy confines of a circular frame, a plumply-jolly elderly woman with bright eyes, reddened cheeks and untidy screws of hair extended a wrinkled hand towards her. Jewel-pike sensed the pats as light taps on her upthrust snout; but with them came satisfaction. Now a second woman appeared beside the first. She was thinner than her companion both facially and bodily, with pale skin and grey hair tied tightly back in a bun. Although less obviously benevolent, her features claimed a family resemblance with those of the fatter woman in respect of noses and lips. She tossed something into the air. Jewel-pike opened her mouth smartly and caught it. Straightaway a memory-sensation of great sweetness flooded through her and she thought: *again.* At which point the Jewel that was not-pike realised that the memory was also a desire. More than that, it was an anticipation – the fish was determined to make what had happened before happen again. And soon.

"Jewel! Jewel!"

She was snatched back so suddenly to the body on the pike's back that she could do no more than stare at Thorn Jack in confusion.

"You were far away!" he said.

"Was I?" she mumbled. "Must have been day-dreaming . . ."

He said: "You were right. The islands are straight ahead."

The pike was making for a channel that separated two islets. The one on the left was merely a tumble of rocks, and unenticing. The one on the right was considerably bigger; vegetation grew there – mostly bushes, and a few trees, battered by the wind.

Soon they entered the channel. The fish forged through it, cleaving the water-surface with ease. More islets lay beyond, none of any great size. The pike changed direction and, skirting another bare islet, took them into a further channel. Here the water, sheltered from the breeze that stirred the exposed surface of the Dam, was almost unruffled.

Then, straight ahead, Jewel and Thorn saw what had to be

the archipelago's heart. Generously endowed with trees, its full extent as yet unrevealed, the island made a statement of its importance by means of the stout wooden jetty that jutted out into the Dam. It – she! – was the bride at the gathering, the gracious centrepiece; the surrounding pips of land no more than a cluster of dowdy attendants whose presence was necessary in order to do her honour.

Beside the jetty, moored fore and aft, bobbed a sailing boat half the size of Lacky Dawes's craft. The pike came closer to shore. Jewel raised an arm and pointed.

"There! At the end of the jetty . . . See what I see?"

Thorn considered. "Looks like a bell."

"Just what I thought . . ."

At the end of the jetty stood a stout, tall post topped with a horizontal arm that projected over the water. From this – its lower rim a good two feet above the gently licking waves – hung a large brass bell. A rope dangled from its clapper, its end trailing in the water.

Thorn said: "Should we ring it?"

"I'm not sure we'll get the chance."

The pike swam up to the jetty and nudged the rope with its snout. Then, opening its jaws, it took the rope in its mouth and began to swing it to and fro. The bell tolled with sonorous clangs. Six times it struck; then the fish let go of the rope. Satisfied with its efforts, it now seemed content to wait.

Time passed. Thorn scanned the trees and bushes that grew along the banks, and recognised ash, gorse, rowan, alder and a good deal of hawthorn. At the far end of the jetty, a track dived into undergrowth.

From this a woman now emerged and walked out along the jetty, her boots smacking the planks. She halted at the end and looked down at the great fish and its bedraggled passengers.

"Well now, Lucius," she said, "what have you brought us today?"

As if in answer, the pike lifted its snout out of the lake and slapped it down on the water-surface. Then it opened its jaws.

Jewel had expected one or both of the women she'd glimpsed in the pike's mind to appear on the jetty, but this woman was neither of them. She might, Jewel reckoned, be in her mid- or late-twenties. Her hair was cropped short; her face ended in a tiny purse of a mouth and a narrow chin. Her strongest features were her eyebrows: black and emphatic, they angled in to point towards the upper end of her nose – which was small and non-descript.

The woman slipped a hand into her pocket, took out something small, and dropped it into the pike's mouth. Its jaws shut with a snap; then, after a moment, opened again. The ritual was repeated. The woman then turned her attention back to Jewel and Thorn.

"Bit cold for a swim, don't you think?"

"Definitely," agreed Thorn. "But it wasn't our idea."

"Oh? Whose idea was it?"

"A boatman called Lacky Dawes. We hired him to ferry us right across the Dam. But about halfway here, he and his crewmen attacked us. Took us by surprise. They were after our money. We ended up in the water."

"And Lucius brought you here . . . Now why did he do that rather than eating you? He isn't one to pass up a snack."

69

"He's had one. He ate Lacky Dawes and his first mate. Our companion has disappeared, along with a crewman."

Thorn was reluctant to mention the Syb's whistle.

"So Dawes got eaten? How inconvenient – he was useful to us. A rogue, of course, but a useful rogue. Well, I suppose you'd better come ashore. Though what my mistresses will make of you is anybody's guess."

She tapped the end of the jetty with the heel of her right boot. The pike promptly turned its head away and manoeuvred alongside. Thorn picked up his pack, then he and Jewel stepped off the fish onto dry land. Their boots squelched on the jetty's surface, leaving damp prints on the wood.

The pike now backed up to face the woman once more. Again it opened its mouth twice to receive its reward. Two, it seemed, was the appropriate number in the circumstances, for after the second sweetmeat, without more ado, it turned tail and swam away.

Then, without a word, the woman turned her back on them and set off along the jetty.

As they tracked her through the undergrowth, Jewel said: "Does this island have a name?"

"It does. Nettle Island."

"Nettle Island? Why?"

"Obviously, because of the nettles that grow here."

Jewel looked about her. "I can't see any nettles."

"Patience, girl. You will. The island's infested with the things."

"What's your name?" asked Thorn.

"Zinny Muffin," said the woman.

70

Thorn was expecting her to reciprocate by asking their names, but, as she made no move to do so, he said: "I'm Thorn Jack. My friend's Jewel Ranson."

"Fancy that," said Zinny Muffin.

Nobody spoke for quite some time. Jewel's thoughts went back to Rainy. I'll have to go to Harrypark, she thought, tell Rainy's father and all the others. It was a daunting prospect . . .

Zinny was right about the nettles. Once through the trees, they entered an area where, to judge by what little they could see of their surroundings, nothing else much seemed to thrive. The pathway became a narrow avenue between dense growths of the tall plants. Browned stumps, lopped just above ground level, showed where stalks had been felled to make for safe passage through. They went carefully ahead, daintily stepping among the stumps, ducking to evade the occasional stem that drooped across the avenue, its furry, broad-bladed leaves pretending harmlessness. But Thorn remembered the first nettle stings he'd had as a child, how they'd swelled into white lumps, making his arm blaze with pain until the friend he was with tore a piece off a dock leaf and told him to rub it on the stings. A strange remedy, but it worked. What an odd mixture was nature: now threatening, now soothing; now for you, now against . . .

"This is a funny place to live," he said, realising too late that it was a sentiment their guide might not be expected to approve.

But Zinny Muffin threw back her head and burst into a waterfall of startling, birdlike trills. Her version of laughter, Thorn supposed.

Zinny ceased as abruptly as she had begun, then stopped and looked round at Thorn. "Strange?" The word was loaded with contempt. "Oh, it's strange all right, boy. But *everywhere's* strange. The world's full of madness. I'm surprised you haven't noticed. And you a pike-rider!"

Was that a grin on her face? She turned away and marched on.

Thorn and Jewel looked at each other. Jewel shrugged, and offered him a sympathetic smile. *What you can't alter you've got to put up with*, he thought – a favourite saying of Aunt Morry. The rest of the walk passed in silence.

At last the field of nettles gave way to gorse bushes. They were brightly in flower, the massed blossoms like the yellow beaks of closely clustering birds. Zinny skirted the first plant, then took them through an archway of slanting, ropy stalks. Beyond the gorse, the track angled up a grassy, rabbit-cropped slope. This they climbed. Where the ground levelled out, grass gave way to a mossy floor. Over on the far side of this emerald space, sunlit and warm, Jewel and Thorn saw a steep bank, much corded and knotted with the exposed roots of the trees that lifted their trunks above it; and the Syb-sisters' house.

5

SISTERS

The Sybs' house was an oddity. Thorn's first thought was that it had been struck by a landslide, for its side walls and pitched roof (complete with a matching pair of jaunty chimney stacks) plunged straight into the face of the mossy, root-riven bank. But then he thought: no, it was built like this. The hill must be hollowed out behind.

The front of the house was many times longer than it was deep. The lower part, up to the level of the windowsills, was made of stones of various shapes that had been cemented together. Above that point, the walls were wooden. An errant tree-root had been incorporated to form the angle between the frontage and the left-hand side-wall. Five or six inches in girth, it rose almost vertically from the earth to loop back high above the roof and bury itself in the hillside.

The house was well sited. Water came trickling down the moss-thick bank at a distance of no more than a dozen feet from its right-hand wall and collected in a pool. From this the excess escaped over a stone-slabbed lip and drained away as a shallow rill through a kitchen and herb garden.

As a house for a pair of Sybs, it could hardly have been bettered.

Left of centre in the frontage, a wooden porch projected, its blue-painted door wedged open by a stone shot through with white veins. Zinny Muffin stepped through to the inner door (also blue, as were the window-frames and sills), threw it open and walked in. Thorn and Jewel followed and found themselves in a living room that reminded the young man of that of Minny Pickles, the Norgreen Syb. A combination of workroom and parlour, it divided itself into two portions. The working portion was defined by the two large tables and the metal sink where the Sybs prepared their syrups, potions and preserves. This lay to the left. On the right was a hearth in which a fire smouldered, with a kettle on its hob, and two battered armchairs and a rocking chair. A good number of cupboards stood against the walls, and where there were no cupboards there were shelves cluttered with jars, bottles and boxes of all shapes and sizes. From the ceiling hung bunches of drying herbs, and the air was pungent with the intermingled odours.

Busy at one of the tables, with her broad back to the door, was a large-bodied woman clad in a long, purple dress and a black knitted shawl. She either hadn't heard them enter or was choosing to ignore them, for she continued vigorously to pestle away at something or other in a mortar until Zinny Muffin walked round to the far side of the table and attracted her attention.

"Zinny!" said the Syb. "You're back."

Zinny said nothing, but gave a sidelong jerk of the head in the direction of Jewel and Thorn.

The Syb turned towards them, still holding her pestle. Jewel knew her immediately. It was the first figure she'd seen inside the mind of the pike.

74

"Goodness me! You're wet through! What *have* you been doing?" The old woman spoke with a mixture of censure and concern.

Thorn was about to answer when the Syb swept on: "Oh, don't tell me now. Later. First things first." She turned to Zinny Muffin. "Zinny! Don't just stand there, get towels for these two. And a couple of blankets while you're at it! Make some tea! Fetch Lily! She's lying down – one of her headaches. And don't take no for an answer!"

Zinny promptly left the room. The Syb bustled to the fire and, picking up some sticks from a stack to one side of the hearth, heaped them on the glowing embers. She then dipped her hand into a cloth bag that hung to one side of the fireplace and flung what looked like a cloud of dust onto the fire. The flames leapt up, crackling and spitting like the very devil.

The woman gestured to Jewel and Thorn. "Over here, my dears. You must get out of those wet clothes. Then we can dry them."

But when Jewel and Thorn showed little enthusiasm for disrobing there and then, the woman smiled and said: "What a shy pair of rattikins! Not brother and sister then? Not accustomed to trotting around the house in the altogether?"

"I'm afraid not," said Jewel. "Is there—"

"—somewhere you can undress?"

Just then Zinny returned, carrying blankets and towels.

"Zinny, show them each to a bedroom. Now, children – if children's what you are . . ." she winked at them slyly. "When you're dry, wrap yourselves up and bring those wet clothes back here."

75

"This way," said Zinny curtly and set off back towards the door through which she'd just come. Jewel and Thorn trooped obediently off in her wake.

As the trio disappeared, the woman smiled, rubbed her hands together and muttered to herself: "Now we'll have some fun, sister."

Zinny led the way through a storeroom and turned into a long corridor with a window at each end. Here all the rooms were set on the right, presumably to take advantage of the daylight that would come into the house through the frontage. Halfway down the corridor was a junction where a new passageway led off to the left. Glancing along it, Jewel and Thorn saw that it disappeared into gloom – penetrating, by the look of it, deep into the hillside. But Zinny carried straight on, to halt at the next door.

"One of you in here," she said. "The other in the next room." When the young people hesitated, looking uncertainly at one another, she said: "Make your minds up! I haven't got all day! I've work to do!"

"You take this room, Thorn," said Jewel.

"Right," he replied. He took the towels from Zinny and gave one to Jewel, then did the same with the blankets. Zinny immediately shot off down the corridor.

Thorn grinned, "See you soon!" and went into his room.

Jewel walked on to the next door.

The room was lightly furnished but pleasant. Curtains and bedspread matched one another in pastel shades of yellow and green. There were a chair and a small dresser. On the floor lay a couple of rugs.

Jewel dropped the blanket and towel, and sank down on the bed. She felt empty, bereft. She'd lost her pack and everything in it, but that was nothing to losing Rainy.

Rainy . . . oh, Rainy . . .

With difficulty she damped down the threatened return of tears. Must do something, she told herself.

With an effort she dragged off her boots (by now half-stuck to her feet) and began to strip off. As she towelled her body dry, it occurred to her to wonder why the Sybs needed so many bedrooms. An answer wasn't far to seek: hadn't Lacky Dawes mentioned that from time to time he ferried guests across? People, probably, who felt the urge to consult a Syb. Or, better still, consult *two* . . . A pair of Syb-sisters would surely be extrapowerful, since their minds must be assumed to be closely attuned to one another.

Which caused Jewel to think of her own developing abilities, and of her natural inclination to keep their existence secret. As yet she knew nothing of the temperamental makeup of these Sybs. They might be entirely benevolent, but you couldn't depend on that. Best, she thought, to behave as if I'm an ordinary girl – a stupid girl, even. It mightn't, of course, be possible to fool a pair of Sybs. Still, I won't know unless I try . . .

She was dry now except for her hair, but had no comb to comb it with. So, wrapping herself in the blanket (which was huge and had been dyed in irregular patches of yellow and blue) and gathering up her clothes and boots, she went back to the living room.

Thorn, also wrapped in a blanket, sat near the fire in an

armchair. The plump Syb had squeezed her body into the rocking chair. The second woman Jewel had glimpsed through the mind of the pike occupied the second armchair: the sister Syb. Lily, the first sister had called her earlier.

"Jewel Ranson?" said the plump woman. "Fetch yourself over here. Zinny – take those clothes. You know what to do with them."

"Do I?" said Zinny rebelliously. But she came up to Jewel and held her arms out for the garments.

"What *is* she to do with them?" Jewel asked.

"What you normally do with dirty clothes: wash them, you silly girl! You wouldn't want to spend the rest of your life in a blanket, would you?"

"Perhaps she would!" said the other Syb, and tittered at her fancy. The skin of her face was as pale as her sister's was rubicund, but her eyes glinted with mischief.

Jewel passed her clothes to Zinny (who disappeared with them from the room), then advanced towards the fire.

"Sit there, girl!" ordered the plump Syb, pointing to the hearth. "Dry your hair. Lily, pour her some tea."

"Yes, sister," said Lily.

Everybody, it seemed, was in thrall to the red-faced Syb.

The pot sat on a table by the pale sister's elbow. Lily poured a steaming mug and set it on the hearth by Jewel.

"There, drink that, girl. It'll do you a power of good."

"What is it?" asked Jewel.

"Water and fruit and a few simples. Guards against chills, you know. It's my very own recipe."

"It's very good," put in Thorn, who held a mug in his fist.

78

"Very clever with herbs, our Lily," said the first sister proudly. "Cure anything, she will, just so long as it isn't dead!"

Lily smiled modestly.

"She'd have a go at the dead too, if I let her!" added the Syb, with an odd glint in her eye.

"Oh, Rosy!" exclaimed her sister. "You say the wickedest things!"

"Poppycock, Lily, I'm good as gold, as well you know. *If*," she added obscurely, "gold is good – and it may not be."

Jewel was now sitting cross-legged with her back to the fire. Ignoring the ambivalence of this last remark, she said: "It seems Thorn has told you our names. May I know yours?"

"You may. My name is Rosy Puckfloss," said the plump Syb. "My sister there is Lily, and we are mistresses of this island."

"Pleased to meet you. You're very kind."

"What did you expect – that we'd turn you away from the door?"

"I'm very glad you didn't. This is a lovely house. Have you lived here many years?"

"More years than a rat has claws, but not so many as it has teeth. We've lived in a number of places."

"How did you come to Nettle Island?"

"By boat. How else would we come?"

"I meant – how did you *learn* about the island?"

"Oh, the wind is blessed with voices, and human beings do not lack tongues. You're fond of questions, Jewel Ranson."

Jewel assumed what she hoped was her friendliest smile. "Well, questions *are* the quickest way of finding things out."

"And you like to find things out. Well so do we, don't we, sister?"

"That we do, sister," said Lily. "So let us ask a few. Zinny has told us of Captain Dawes and how the Great Pike brought you here instead of eating you. Now why would he do that?"

"And *don't* try to fob us off like you fobbed off Zinny," warned Rosy.

There was a pause; Thorn looked at Jewel and Jewel looked at Thorn. Then Thorn said: "I have a whistle. I blew it and the pike came and rescued us."

"A whistle!" exclaimed Rosy. "There's a thing! May I see it?"

Reluctantly, Thorn reached into his shirt and brought out the whistle. Slipping over his head the green ribbon from which it hung, he passed it to the Syb.

Rosy examined the object, then handed it to her sister.

"Where did you get this?" she asked.

"From a Syb. I was to use it on water, she said."

"Were you, now . . . And what was the name of this Syb?"

"Minny Pickles."

"Minny Pickles?" Rosy and Lily looked at one another, then burst into laughter. Thorn and Jewel watched with astonishment as the tears rolled from their eyes.

"Minny Pickles!" said Rosy at last. "So that's what the old mole calls herself these days!"

"Where does she live, this Minny Pickles?" asked Lily.

"In Norgreen – where I come from."

"Norgreen . . . that's over the wood. You're a long way from home."

Thorn looked from one sister to the other. "Do you know Minny?"

"Oh yes, we know Minny," said Rosy, her red face shining. "We know her as well as we know ourselves."

Thorn was puzzled. He glanced enquiringly at Jewel, but she met his look with a shrug. Well, she'd never set eyes on Minny: what could she know of the Syb?

He stared into the fire, and was reminded of the day he'd been summoned to the Syb's house, which lay outside the settlement. They'd sat and talked, sipping her excellent elderberry wine, and she'd warned him against trusting Racky, and given him the gifts that had twice now saved his life. As he focussed on the bristling, yellow fangs of the flames, he recollected the reverie into which, just before he left the house, Minny had fallen, and into his mind came some curious words she'd uttered, not to him but to herself: *Is it the same for them, I wonder? They too must be getting old . . .*

He thought: *they*. Could *they* be the Syb-sisters? If Rosy and Lily know Minny, then Minny must know them . . .

Something chimed in his head – and there, dangling in his mind like a chain, was a sequence of words: Puckfloss . . . Pickfloss . . . Pickloss . . . Pickles . . .

"Minny's your sister!" he cried.

Rosy said: "Congratulations. You got there in the end, Thorn Jack." The Syb's tribute was heavily undercut by sarcasm.

Lily said: "Minny's our elder sister – born a Puckfloss, like us. But it seems the name's not good enough for her now. Shame on her."

Why would she change it? wondered Thorn. He was on the point of opening his mouth to frame more questions when he noticed that Jewel was staring him in the face. She gave a slight shake of her head, meaning: hold your tongue, Thorn.

So he said nothing. Looking from one to other of the sisters, he saw that each appeared preoccupied with her thoughts. Rosy's eyes glistened as they caught the flickering flames, but there was something glassily cold in her inward-dwelling gaze. Like the eyes of a toad, he thought . . . Dark waters lay between Norgreen's Syb and her younger sisters, and it was best not to disturb them.

Jewel had borrowed a comb from Lily. She slowly drew it through her hair, lifting a tress and letting it fall. She seemed absorbed in the task. Her hair too was dark, yet as it dropped from the teeth of the comb the smooth tress snatched at the firelight and seemed to ripple-shine like water. It's beautiful, he thought . . .

Lily was the first of the sisters to rouse herself. "Where are you two going?" she asked.

Thorn considered. "Across the Dam."

"Yes. But why?"

"This is my rite-of-passage," he said.

"Is that so?" This was Rosy. She was clearly unconvinced. "Well, you've got halfway. How will you manage the other half?" She giggled. "If, of course, swimming isn't your chosen means of progress!"

Jewel said: "We saw your boat. We could pay for passage across."

"Well, it's true we have a boat." Rosy looked mockingly at Thorn. "But we never help a liar – it's a principle with us."

Am I so see-through? thought Thorn.

"Well it's just that . . ." He stopped. "We've undertaken this mission—"

82

"A mission? How exciting!"

Thorn hesitated again.

Jewel said: "You may as well tell them, Thorn."

"All right. We're travelling to Minral How to recover something for the Spetch brothers. They kidnapped my sister, Haw. They'll free her when I bring them what it is that they want."

The sisters looked at one another. "Now *that* is so fantastic," said Rosy, "it might just be true. And what *is* this object?"

"A key – made by the giants."

"And what does the key open?"

"We don't know. They wouldn't tell us."

"That's the Spetches all over," remarked Lily to her sister.

Rosy turned to Jewel. "What's *your* part in all this?"

"I'm helping Thorn," said the girl. "We're friends." She met the Syb's piercing gaze with her most innocent expression. She was speaking the truth, of course, albeit speaking it sparingly. Murder and revenge were not things to speak of here.

Before Rosy could follow up, Thorn stepped in. "So – you've met the Spetches?" he asked Lily.

The pale Syb glanced at her sister, then said: "They came here once – for a consultation. A pair of snakes, if ever I saw one."

"But amusing snakes," said Rosy. "I like people who make me laugh."

She looked challengingly at Jewel.

Even murderers? Jewel wanted to say. But she did not.

Lily said: "And they loved our nettle ale. Zak simply couldn't get enough of the PF Special. You must try it before you go."

Rosy said: "Oh let's not talk of them going yet. They've only just arrived. Besides, their clothes are soaked through."

"They must stay the night," said Lily.

Must we? thought Thorn. Yes, I suppose we must.

"But tomorrow?" he said. "Will you take us across the Dam?"

"Oh, it's Zinny who sails the boat. Which isn't very often," said Rosy. "Best wait till tomorrow morning – see what the weather says."

"It's nice for us to have a bit of company," said Lily. "Especially young folk. We don't see many young folk here. Zinny's young*ish*, of course, but not young like *you* are."

"Full of the sap of youth," said Rosy dreamily. "As we are not." She leant forward, so that her rocking chair creaked. "Imagine, Thorn Jack: if you could decant that sap, distil it, manufacture an elixir that would turn age into youth . . ."

Her eyes glittered in the firelight.

"That's impossible," said Thorn.

"Is it? It would once have been deemed impossible to cast from silver a whistle that would summon a great fish. And then it was done. Impossible things are improbable things that haven't happened yet."

Thorn spent part of the day sorting out his clothes and the rest of the gear in his pack. Everything was dank and soaking, and had to be thoroughly cleaned. That went, too, for his quiver, still attached to his pack. His arrows were undamaged, though they had to be dried out. But he had lost his bow, as had Jewel; so in the afternoon they set out to find saplings suitable for making into new weapons.

From the front of the house, paths led off in several directions. Rather than simply retrace their steps to the jetty, they chose a path which took them along the mossy bank – the sea of nettles below to the left – before dropping down to pick its careful way underneath and through a mass of thickly-growing bushes. Here Thorn located a growth of strong but springy stalks. He cut two with his knife. Then he and Jewel followed the path till it petered out on a stony headland.

They sat down on a log. A scatter of rocky islands lay off to the west of them. The sky was grey and the breeze had stiffened. It blew directly down the channel, teasing the waves into peaks and streaking them white. To Thorn they resembled fully-extended birds' wings.

"What do you make of the Sybs?" asked Jewel.

"They seem friendly enough," said Thorn. "We can't complain about our welcome."

"No, but that house . . . something bothers me about it. Or maybe it's the atmosphere there. It's hard to say."

"Zinny doesn't seem very happy."

"That's hardly surprising. I don't think *I'd* be happy to be at Rosy's beck and call. She's quite a tyrant. Still, it's more than that."

"What, then?"

"I wish I knew. I wonder why Minny Pickles changed her name from Puckfloss . . ."

"Me too. No one in Norgreen has the slightest idea she's got sisters. She never talks about her past, where she came from, that sort of thing. But I keep thinking about the whistle . . . It's almost as if she *knew* we'd cross the Dam, get into trouble and need the Great Pike to come and rescue us."

"If she saw you in the water – saw with her inner eye, I mean – that would explain why she gave you the whistle."

"If she saw me in the water, she must have seen me in the Echo Hole at Whispering Oak, too. I wonder, could she also have seen me here, on Nettle Island?"

As Thorn was speaking, Jewel felt a vibration in the log on which they were sitting. Passing into her body, it flashed up her spine into her brain. It was as if she'd received a direct signal from the young man, albeit an involuntary one. He was thinking of another gift the Syb had given him, a phial containing liquid he hadn't yet had cause to use.

"Oh well," said Thorn, "there's little point in beating our brains. We'll be gone from here tomorrow."

As the breeze gusted suddenly into her face, ruffling her hair, Jewel wished that she could share the young man's confidence.

Thorn took another draught of PF Special and studied the pale-yellow liquid with eyes that had recently become more than a little bleary.

"Ale from wettles – *nettles*," he corrected himself. "Who'd have thought it possible? Why doesn't it sting your tongue?"

"The secret's in the process," said Lily mysteriously. "We extract the juice, then it's watered down, and fermented, and combined with other ingredients."

"But you *must* plandle the hants," Thorn persisted, waving a hand in the air. "How come you don't get stung?"

"We're very careful. We wear special, thick gloves the nasty nettle-hairs can't pierce."

Thorn and Jewel were sitting by the fire with Lily and Rosy.

Zinny Muffin was there too, a little further from the hearth, sitting on an uncomfortable-looking three-legged chair with a high, hooped back.

"Well, I take my rat off to you. I mean *hat*. It's marvellous stuff." Thorn took another swig. "Best ale I ever tasted."

"How many ales *have* you tasted?" put in Jewel. She was both concerned for Thorn and annoyed with him. Men! They were never satisfied with one glass of ale; they had to have four or five. Her father had been the same. And Thorn was only sixteen.

"Lots and lots and pots and pots," said Thorn, his voice slurred and dreamy.

"I don't believe you," said Jewel.

"I never lie," replied Thorn, "except when I'm drunk. And I'm never drunk." And, forgetting that he'd heard this brain-teaser from a friend whose father was a famous toper, he giggled at the profundity of his wit.

"Nettle ale," said Rosy fulsomely, waving her pot in the air so that the liquid slopped over the brim. "What could bear truer witness to the genius of humankind?" She had drunk as much as Thorn, and she too was showing the effects. "A genius embodied in my dear sister Lily, who could transform a rabbit's turd into a pearl if she so wished."

"Don't be disgusting," admonished Lily, who had drunk much less than her sister. "And I couldn't, as a matter of fact. No one could."

"I know someone who could," said Rosy belligerently.

"Who?"

"Querne Rasp."

87

Jewel gave a start, then glanced at the Sybs to see if they'd noticed that she'd recognised the name. Neither, it seemed, had. Rosy was slumped in her rocking chair, gazing as if hypnotised at her pot of ale, while Lily's attention was wholly focussed on her sister – at this moment clearly something of an irritant to her. But when Jewel looked at Zinny Muffin, she saw the woman eyeing her with what looked like suspicion. Jewel met Zinny's glance boldly, and it was the woman who looked away.

"Querne Rasp?" exclaimed Thorn. "Who's he when he's at home?"

"*She*, Thorn Jack," said Rosy. "Querne's a woman and a Magian. No *man* could have done it. Though in fact she was only a girl when she cast the three whistles. A lass of seventeen."

"*Three* thistles – *whistles*?" said Thorn laboriously.

"Yes, three. All the best things come in threes. Minny got one, Lily got one, and the third she kept for herself."

"What's a Magian?" asked Thorn.

"A woman with exceptional powers."

"What, like a Syb?"

"More like ten Sybs rolled into one. No, Magians can do things a Syb can only dream of. Wonderful things. Terrible things. They're a law unto themselves."

"Love to meet one," said Thorn, who was fighting a losing battle to keep both his eyes open. As soon as he got one open, the other would snap shut.

"Would you? Well, watch out if you do. Cross a Magian, and believe me she'll have your tongue on toast."

"Take no notice of my sister," Lily told the goggle-eyed

Thorn. "It's not at all likely you'll ever meet a Magian. Few people ever do."

"Has Querne Rasp been here, then?" asked Jewel, who had listened to the conversation with secret amusement mixed with relief. The Sybs had no idea she was no ordinary person.

"Here? No. And she wouldn't be welcome either. If she knew—"

"Rosy!" snapped Lily.

"What?" Rosy looked woozily at her sister. Her slumped position in her chair had made her plump cheeks into jowls – as if the fat behind her face had made a recent (and unwise) decision to sink towards her chin.

"You know what!"

"I know what, of course I do. And I know what's what as well. I know who and where and when and why and all the double-yous. The double-mes, the double-wes, the honey-bees and jumping-fleas. I know—"

"Sister, you're rambling."

"Syb can ramble if she wants to."

"I think you should ramble off to bed."

"Another little drinkie first."

"You've had enough little drinkies."

"ANOTHER LITTLE DRINKIE FIRST!" Rosy had bellowed out the words, and now she lurched out of her chair. Her impetus took her several steps forward before she managed to pull up. The rocking chair rocked emptily. "Tiddely-pom, tiddely-pom," Rosy muttered to herself, swaying precariously. Then she staggered forwards again until she fetched up against the table on which a jug of ale sat. She grabbed the jug and refilled her pot, spilling some liquid in the process.

Lily turned to Jewel. "It's times like this I wish I'd never learnt to brew ale."

"Well you did, Lily, and I love you for it," said Rosy. She took a deep draught of ale and smacked her lips loudly. "Kissy-kissy," she said to the pot, eyes shut, lips a-pout.

"Sin in haste, repent at leisure," observed her sister phlegmatically.

FIRST INTERFACE

A CARRIER PIGEON

Racky Jagger was lost to the world.

He was reading a book.

The ancient volume lay flat on the floor and Racky stood on top of it. Wrapped about each foot and tied with twine around each ankle was a square of clean cloth. This to minimise the damage he was doing to the book. To be honest, he felt guilty about this method of reading. Trampling on the people whose lives he was absorbed in was an insult both to them and their long-dead creator. Still, what could he do? Even if, in recent years, he hadn't grown a touch close-sighted, he'd have had to read this way. Any human would. And he might well be the only reader the book would ever get. The Spetch twins found his love of reading bizarre, regarding the pursuit as the height of frivolity.

As he scanned each line of print, his head moved from left to right, then swung back to start the next. Every so often he took a couple of paces backwards to bring fresh sentences into view. At length he stepped down off the book, read the last few lines and, bending, lifted the corner of the page. The paper was thick and stiff, its outer margins spotted yellow. When he'd brought it up vertical, he stepped back onto the volume and walked to mid-page in order to press the leaf flat. Then, stepping across the depression where the sheets were folded into the book's spine, he repositioned himself and continued to read.

> . . . fancy you felt for Linton? Because misery and degradation, and death, and nothing that God or Satan could inflict would have parted us, *you*, of your own will, did it. I have not broken your heart – *you* have broken it; and in breaking it, you have broken mine. So much the worse for me, that I am strong. Do I want to live? What kind of living will it be when you – oh God, would *you* like to live with your soul in the grave?

He felt such an uprush of emotion that he could not go on reading. He stepped down off the book and sat on the edge of the page. But though his back was now turned on Heathcliff's bitter sentences, the words burned in his brain: ". . . would *you* like to live with your soul in the grave?" He'd read *Wuthering Heights* three times before, and each time he'd read this passage it had cut him to the quick. For in the forsaken Heathcliff and in Heathcliff's betrayer, Catherine Earnshaw, he, Racky Jagger, saw a brutally clear reflection of himself and Berry Jack – Berry Waters, as she'd been before she married *her* Edgar Linton (pretty, clean-cut, long-limbed, archer-hero Davis Jack, the smarmy darling of Norgreen) a mere fortnight after Racky had set out.

For the hundredth – *five*-hundredth – time he roundly cursed himself for his youthful foolishness. *Why* on that far-off day had he lost patience with Berry – lost, worse, his temper? *Why* had he walked out of Norgreen? The irony was that he knew the answers to these questions. Nothing he could do, could say had brought her to the point of saying: yes, I'll marry you. Putting some distance between them had seemed a good idea at the time. Then, in his youthful romanticism, he'd entertained the conviction that visiting far-off places would invest him with a glamour Berry would find irresistible on his return. Few Norgreeners had travelled further than the nearer settlements, some not even that far; and wouldn't he, Racky, come back with great stories to tell, tales in whose sunshine he could bask like a lizard? He'd intended to be away no more than a month or two, and had told Berry so. But he'd got into deep water in Hallax settlement, and it was the best part of a year before he returned to Norgreen . . . To find her married to Davis Jack, and mother of a son his every instinct told him was his. Thorn then was five months old, which meant he'd been conceived before Racky had left Norgreen. Davis could only be the father if, before Racky left, he too had enjoyed Berry's favours. Which Racky found impossible to believe, *impossible* . . .

One day, when Davis was off hunting, he'd gone to the house and confronted her. Bitter words had passed between them. He accused her of betrayal, she him of abandonment. He'd been away so long that she'd concluded he was dead. And Davis was so in love with her; and Davis pressed her so hard; and Davis could have had any girl he wanted; and she, Berry, was pregnant.

"With my son!" he'd yelled at her.

"He's not your son!" she'd shouted back.

She was lying, he was sure. He seized her in his arms. She didn't attempt to pull away. She was more beautiful after the child than she'd been in the time before.

"Who could love you more than I? You know I'd kill for you, I'd do anything you asked. What would *he* do for you?"

93

"Don't say such terrible things," she pleaded.

"Is he a better lover than me? Do you melt in his arms?"

"Don't, Racky – please . . ."

"Leave him!" he urged her. "Come away with me now!"

"I can't, Racky, I can't."

Then Davis Jack came through the door, and stared wild-eyed at them.

"What the hell are you doing, Jagger?"

"I'm talking to the woman you stole from me!" Racky cried.

Davis threw himself at Racky, but Racky's travels had hardened him, and he was a tough and cruel opponent. He knocked Davis to the floor and got his hands around his neck. He would surely have strangled the man, but quick-thinking Berry must have grabbed a pot or pan. She hit him smartly over the head. When he regained consciousness he was lying out in the street with a painfully throbbing skull and a lump the size of his thumb . . .

". . . would *you* like to live with your soul in the grave?" Yes, that was what his life had been like after finding Berry married and his son lost to him. And then, soon after Haw's birth, Berry had disappeared, dashing his hopes that she would turn to him. Who did she think she was punishing? Him? Herself? Both of them?

A scratching sound impinged upon his self-recrimination. How long, he wondered, had it been there?

Rising to his feet, he went across to the little wooden door and undid the latch. When he opened it, a pigeon came walking into the room, head jerking forward and back in the machine-rhythm of its kind.

"Hopper! Good boy," he said, patting the bird's neck. "Have you something for me today?"

The pigeon cocked an eye at the squat, unshaven man. Of course the bird had. He wouldn't be here otherwise.

Kneeling, Racky untied the twine that secured the white scroll and pulled it away from the bird's leg. Then, lifting the lid of a nearby box, he took from it several fistfuls of seeds, which he put down on the floor for the pigeon to peck up.

He took the scroll to his chair, sat down and opened it out.

> *Bring your payment from the twins.*
> *Call on the way at Nettle Island.*
> *I have reason to believe you'll find a second treasure there.*

The note was unsigned but authentic, no doubt of it. The handwriting said *Querne*, as did the obliquity of the message – just in case the note should fall into the wrong hands. Besides, how many others did he know who could write? The same number who could read. Number them on the fingers of one hand, no more than that.

Damn the woman. Now he wouldn't have time to finish his favourite book. Rebelliously, he thought for a moment of delaying, but only for a moment. He knew that he would do – as he always did – her bidding; that her power over him, her magnetism, was undiminished. No, he had to get himself into the saddle – soon; this morning, even.

After, of course, he'd seen the twins.

*

95

But Lanner and Zak were out riding. To fill the time before their return, Racky packed his saddlebags, took them down to the rattery and asked Leech to prepare Bumper, the ageing saddle-rat he'd left here on his last visit to Roydsal. Then, chafing at the wait, he strode up and down in front of their fatuous marquee.

Ah, here they were at last!

"Racky!" exclaimed Lanner. "So you're about to leave us?"

"Yes."

"Oh dear! We *do* so enjoy your company."

"Indeed we do," echoed Zak. "It's so stimulating. We shall be lost when you're gone. May we enquire as to the reason for this all-too-sudden decision?"

Racky was immune to their polished insincerities.

"You may enquire, but you won't get an answer," he said.

"Racky, you're such a spoilsport!"

"Zak, I don't give a damn what sort of a sport you think I am. I want my payment. Then I'm off."

Zak turned to Lanner. "He wants his payment, bro."

"I heard him, bro. He didn't say *please*."

"Some people have no manners."

The brothers turned their amiable murderers' eyes on him.

Unperturbed, Racky said: "Manners are for people who have a use for such things. I, as you're both well aware, have none."

"That's telling us straight, bro," said Zak.

"Yes, bro," said Lanner, "that's calling a spade a spade . . ."

". . . a doorknob a doorknob . . ."

". . . a walking-stick—"

"Just give me what you owe me and stop beating about the bush!"

"Oh, Racky," implored Lanner. "Would you deprive two wretched souls of one of life's chiefest pleasures? We *love* to beat about the bush."

"Don't I know it. But you beat that particular bush to death some time ago." Racky paused, then said significantly: "I hope I don't have to tell Querne that you dragged your feet."

"Racky, what a shocking thing to say!" complained Zak.

"Querne is one of our *very* oldest friends," asserted Lanner.

This was true. But, for the life of him, Racky couldn't see what Querne professed to see in the vicious pair. She found them highly amusing, but their relentless whimsicality got right up Racky's nose.

Zak said to Lanner: "Will *you* fetch it, bro, or shall *I*?"

"I will," said Lanner.

Racky watched the redhead pass inside the marquee. It occurred to him that the brothers were keeping him out of the room in which they stored their precious things. The perception amused him: he'd never been much interested in gold and silver and gems, and found the mere thought of pursuing wealth stultifying. He'd seen what it did to some of the people who possessed it – turned them into mouths demanding more and more to devour.

Lanner returned with an object well swaddled in cloth.

"Here it is. Our debt to you is now fully discharged. And once again, our thanks for putting Thorn Jack into our power."

Lanner smirked as he said this, and Racky felt like smashing his fist into the handsome face. But, controlling the urge, he said: "Show it to me."

Setting the bundle down on the floor, Lanner unwrapped the cloth to reveal a crystal the colour of bluebell petals. Thorn Jack would have recognised it as the mate – in size and texture, if not in colour – of the ruby stone he'd lately filched from Wyke Treasury. Lanner did not touch the stone.

"Where did you find it?" asked Racky.

"We didn't find it," said Zak. "It had already been found."

"So who did you get it from?"

"A man. Well, he *was* a man when we met him. He isn't anything now."

"I don't suppose he is," said Racky. "All right. Wrap it up."

Lanner passed the bundle over. "Nice to do business with you, Racky."

Racky nodded, turned on his heel and walked away.

"Till next time, then!" Zak Spetch called after him.

Racky stopped and looked back.

"That depends," he replied, "on whether there *is* a next time."

6

ELIXIR OF DEATH

Thorn lifted his head from the pillow, uttered a groan and let it fall back. It felt twice its normal size. Inside it, a demon with a hammer was banging a gong monotonously. His mouth felt dry, his tongue swollen, his body sweaty and limp – a squirming extension of his head, and good for nothing.

Why did I drink so much last night? It wasn't as if he hadn't got drunk before and suffered for it. A few months earlier, a friend who'd successfully come through his rite-of-passage had wangled a barrel of beer out of his father, who was a brewer, and entertained his pals. Next morning Thorn had entertained a headache much like this one, and had vowed: never again! So much for vows, he thought. So much for learning one's lesson.

Getting up was unthinkable: the hammering demon would go berserk. Thorn would have to lie here without so much as twitching an ear until his unwanted visitor tired of him and took himself off to another ale-soaked idiot's head.

At which point, the demon beat out an intricate rataplan.

"Ouch!" responded Thorn. Then realised that he'd actually *heard* the added thumps. They were sounds; they had their point of origin outside his skull. Someone was knocking on the door.

"Who is it?" he called out, and reeled from self-inflicted pain. The door opened.

"Me."

Heroically (as he thought) Thorn lifted his head from the pillow and saw Jewel framed in the doorway.

"May I come in?" she enquired.

"You can if you like. But I'm not (*groan*) good for very much at the moment."

He let his head fall back on the pillow.

Jewel came over to the bed and looked down at him. "Not feeling so good today?"

"No."

"Too much to drink last night?"

"Yes." Has she come to torment me? he wondered.

"Bad head? Feeling sick?"

"Terrible head." Why couldn't she just go away? Hadn't he earned his misery?

"Thought you might have, so I've brought you a hangover cure. Rosy swears by it. She had hers long ago and is already up and about."

"Up what?" Jewel seemed to be speaking from the other side of the world.

"Come on, Thorn. Shift. Stop feeling sorry for yourself."

"What? You'd deprive me of my only consolation?"

He raised himself on an elbow. His head was about to split. The halves would fall off his shoulders and go rolling about the floor.

Jewel smiled brightly and thrust a cup towards his chest. He blinked, but made no move to take it from her. She grimaced.

"You *do* remember how to drink, don't you?" she said. "You managed it last night – managed it all too well."

He blinked at her again, and she divided into two. Both Jewels looked sarcastic.

"Right, this is how it's done. You raise the mug to your mouth, pour the liquid into it – doing your best not to spill – and swallow."

"All right, all right, Jewel, I'm not a baby," he grumbled.

"If you aren't, you're doing a very convincing imitation of one."

He frowned, took the cup from her and knocked half of its contents back.

"Ugh! This is awful!"

"Good. Drink up. I'll talk to you later when your brain's more receptive. If, that is, you haven't inflicted permanent damage on it."

She walked towards the door, then stopped and turned.

"Incidentally, it's too windy to take the boat out at the moment. So, fortunately, we're not wasting time."

She smiled with exaggerated sweetness and went out.

Thorn's head flopped back on the pillow and he moaned as the brute shock of the impact echoed through him.

Jewel walked down the corridor. Glancing along the passageway that tunnelled into the hillside, she noticed that a couple of lights were gleaming in the darkness. Oil-lamps, it appeared, had been lit along the walls.

What's down there? she wondered, and felt the powerful drag of an impulse to investigate.

She hesitated, however. I oughtn't to go poking about. The Sybs wouldn't approve.

But the drag was too strong. And something was wrong in this house – she felt it in her bones.

She looked both ways up the corridor. No one was in sight, so she set off down the passageway.

It was stone-floored, but its walls were composed of wooden planks. More planks had been laid laterally to form a ceiling to hold back the soil. The passageway was dry but musty. Jewel trod lightly; she mustn't slip or make a sound. One or both of the Sybs were probably down here. She didn't relish the notion of facing a Rosy in a rage: the Syb would be a termagant, she was quite sure of that.

She passed the first wall-lamp and went on to the first door, where she stopped and listened for a time. No sound reached her from within. She grasped the knob but didn't turn it. There was keyhole beside the knob and she knew that the door was locked. She let her mind relax and open itself to influence. Soon she sensed fermenting liquid cased in stout, ageing wood, and smelt a smell she'd smelt before – recently. This was a storeroom for barrels of nettle ale, and harmless – if you didn't move in permanently, that is . . .

She went on up the passageway, passing the second lamp, and stopped by the second door. Voices murmured within – but what it was that they were saying . . .? No, she couldn't make it out. The passageway was dark ahead. She was about to retreat when something made her change her mind – a sudden impulse, a mental twitch, a thing obscure in origin but not to be ignored. Stepping right up to the door, she laid her forehead against the wood and for a second time let her body go slack, her arms hang loosely at her sides. She concentrated on the sounds . . . and yes, syllables were acquiring definition. Soon she could make out words, then a coherent conversation – as if the door were equipped with ears and she were part of the door.

". . . Lily, come on now, you know what you've always said: *the answer lies in the blood.*"

"The blood, yes . . . But if I'm wrong . . . What if I'm wrong?"

"You're not wrong. You're never wrong!"

"Why can't I be? Others are."

"Others are not you. You've no match anywhere. Even Querne admired your skill."

"But I've never attempted anything as difficult as this. What if I fail? They'll die for nothing."

"Why should you fail? Imagine, Lily: at last, an elixir of life! To be able to live for ever!"

"It sounds more like an elixir of death, if you ask me."

"Poppycock, sister! Think of the wisdom we'd accumulate, living life after life – think of the good we could do the world! We'd be the greatest benefactors humankind has ever known! What, weighed in the scales against that, are a couple of lives? They're nothing – less than nothing!"

"They're hardly nothing to Jewel and Thorn."

"They're children. What sense have they of the value of life? They're headstrong and careless, just like all young people. They think themselves immortal. Without the whistle they'd have drowned yesterday, and that would be that. But you and I, sister, we contain a world of knowledge. It would be a sin not to put it to use."

"A sin? But—"

"Listen: now's the time, the perfect time. When will we get a better chance? Nobody knows these two are here – only Zinny, and she won't tell."

"But it's *murder*, Rosy, *murder*!"

"Look at it this way, sister. It's either their deaths or ours. Which would you rather have it be? How many years are left to us?"

"But it's wicked – wicked to kill . . ."

Lily's words tailed away. Jewel sensed a weakening in the pale Syb's resistance. So too, it seemed, did Rosy.

"Wicked! That's just a word – a word for fools and old women! And you, sister, are both!" Her scorn was scorching. But, just as suddenly, her tone changed and once again became seductive, sinuous. "It will be so simple, easy, sister. A sleeping potion in their tea. A silent knife across their throats. They'll die without ever feeling pain! Think of all that blood – youthful, hot – to put to work!"

"But how will I ever live with myself?"

"How will you live with me if you don't?" Rosy spat out the words. "If you don't do this, Lily, I'll make your life a living hell. You'll think the twitterings of your conscience child's play in comparison. Now: will you do it or won't you?"

"If you put it like that, sister—"

"Oh I do, sister, I do."

"Then I suppose I must."

"Of course you must. It's the only thing. Now, what we'll do is this. We'll persuade them to stay tonight, saying we'll take them ashore tomorrow. Then we'll drug them. Agreed? Is that simple enough for you?"

"Simple enough, sister."

"Good. But we've lingered here too long. Let's get back to the parlour and be nice to our young guests."

"How will I look them in the face?"

"The same way you did last night. Smile, and think of the future stretching out ahead of us. Now, let's be about it."

Footsteps moved towards the door. Jewel shrank back from the wood. She wanted to flee, but her feet seemed rooted to the ground.

The doorknob began to turn. She'd never get back to the corridor. At last her muscles unlocked themselves. She moved swiftly into the darkness further down the passageway, running one hand along the wall as she went.

Gloom swallowed her up. Halting, she leant back and sought to still breaths that seemed in the darkness appallingly loud. She heard the door unclose, then a patter of footsteps as the Syb-sisters emerged. There was a metallic *click-clack* as a key was pushed into the lock, engaged the wards, was withdrawn. She held her breath. Then the footsteps pattered again, receding down the passageway, and soon she could hear them no more.

She stayed like that for quite some time, her thoughts spinning and spiralling, while she sought to still the headlong rush of her blood.

She pictured the Sybs, a pair of old women who might have been somebody's grandmothers, nurturing, kindly and wise; yet their minds were bent on murder, on slitting throats and drinking blood.

My blood, *Thorn's* blood. She shivered in the blackness.

Was that why they'd isolated themselves on the island? To pursue dark experiments, prey on chance visitors?

But she knew and she'd outwit them. She was a Magian, wasn't she, and they were merely a pair of Sybs. If I can't outwit them, she thought, I don't deserve the powers I have.

Gradually her blood stilled, and she breathed evenly.

It was then she realised that there, where the small of her back was in contact with the wall, was a curious nub of heat. Not the heat of her body transferred to the vertical surface; no, intenser than that – a local, fist-sized glow as if a heat-source was making itself felt from the other side.

But it's *not* a wall, she thought, it's a door – another door. For her hand had encountered the doorknob.

Whatever was causing the heat was calling to her – *to her*, Jewel Ranson, and to no one else. It seemed to say: *I am here. I am waiting for you. I am here, here . . .*

She turned about and touched the door with her fingertips. In just one spot, the wood was hot, though not unbearably so. Outside that area it was cool.

She knew without trying the knob that the door was locked.

I wonder, she thought . . .

She slid her hand across the surface of the door till she found the keyhole. As she'd expected, the key was missing. Inserting her little finger into the socket, she closed her eyes, concentrated and conjured up first one delicate mental tendril, then another and another. These she sent snaking down her arm into her hand, then down her finger and out through the end into the lock mechanism. They engaged with the wards, and with a *click!* twisted them.

Jewel opened her eyes and smiled. That had been almost too easy.

The room was hers to investigate. She opened the door and peered in. It was pitch dark inside.

I need a light . . .

A thought struck her. She moved back down the passageway. A gleam of light defined itself, then the floor, walls and ceiling came into view. In their haste to return to the parlour, the Sybs had forgotten to extinguish the pair of lamps that burned on the wall.

She removed the nearest from its holder. It was a simple metal container in which a wick floated on oil. She carried it carefully back to the room, slipped inside and gently closed the door behind her.

If she'd expected something momentous to seize her attention, it did not. Her flickering light revealed nothing out of the ordinary. She saw a couple of broken chairs, an old bedstead, a rickety table. A heap of rotting rugs, several dust-begrimed flagons. The place was a junk-room. Then something did attract her eye: on top of the table stood a jar – big, black and made of glass. In itself the jar was not in the least interesting, for it was an ugly thing; no – it was interesting because it was the same height from the floor as the heat spot that had drawn her into the room.

She went over to the table and looked down at the jar. It was a bulbous object capped with a circular, round-knobbed lid. It resembled a big teapot without a spout or a handle.

For a moment her courage faltered. What if she lifted the lid and something frightful leapt out – a poisonous spider, for instance?

But the top of the jar was thick with dust. It hadn't been touched in a long time. Could something living survive in there? It seemed extremely unlikely. And what spider could radiate heat? No, whatever the jar held, it couldn't be an animal.

Tentatively, she touched the glass with a single fingertip. Here was a strange thing: the glass was cold. Yet the patch on the door had been hot . . . It didn't make sense. Perhaps the jar was empty, and had nothing to do with the door . . .

But there the jar sat, smack in the middle of the room, imposing its presence on everything, drawing everything to its centre – chairs, bedstead, flagons, rugs, and the trespasser herself.

Jewel raised her free hand and let it hover above the jar. Nameless fears nibbled at her. Then, commanding herself not to be such a coward, she grasped the knob and lifted the lid.

Nothing emerged from the jar.

She put the lid down on the table, held the lamp near the jar's opening, leant above it and looked down.

All that she could make out in the jar was a whitish rag. A common or garden rag, a piece torn from a garment or a sheet. If there was something inside the jar, it had to be underneath the rag. Yet to find out, she'd have to put her hand inside the jar . . .

She slipped a hand into the jar and lightly fingered the rag, then poked it with a finger. Something was certainly wrapped inside it, something hard but not hot. She pushed her fingers underneath it and managed to lift it up. But with her hand inside the jar, it was too big to come out through the hole.

Jewel withdrew her hand. She set the lamp on the tabletop. Then, grasping the jar with both hands, she lifted it and tipped it upside down. The rag and what was inside it promptly dropped through the hole and landed on the table with a gentle *thud*.

Dust puffed out in all directions.

Jewel sneezed. A small explosion.

Nerves a-tingle, she listened. But there was no sound of footsteps outside in the passageway. Surely no one could have heard . . .

She set the jar back down on the table, took hold of a loose corner of rag and pulled at it. The object did not move, so she gave it a strong tug. As the wrapping unpeeled, the object went rolling across the table towards the edge.

Jewel stuck out a hand. As the thing met her palm, there was a sharp green flash, and she jerked back. The object had came to a stop on the very lip of the table. It lay there, teasing her. Why, it's a stone, she thought.

But an odd-looking stone. Neither smooth like a pebble nor uniform like rock, it was jagged and irregular, and dark green in colour. It's a crystal, she decided. But what sort of crystal emits a flash when you touch it?

She knew the answer, of course. A crystal like the one Thorn had stolen from Wyke. A crystal like the one Racky Jagger was keen to have.

Tentatively, she prodded it with a finger. A faint, pale-green glow stirred deep within the crystal, then went out as she broke contact. Loosely, she cupped a palm about it: the glow returned and strengthened.

Now here was something interesting. Thorn hadn't been able to handle the crystal he'd found, but she could handle this one . . .

Suddenly, caring nothing what the consequences might be, she grasped the crystal with both hands and lifted it up to her face.

The light intensified, enlarged, became an emerald radiance that spilled out between her fingers. It bathed her face with light and striped the dingy walls of the room, putting the lamp's efforts to shame. The crystal grew warm and began to throb, and each separate pulse passed up her arms and through her body, causing her whole being to quiver. Her brain registered the pulses as a series of mental jolts. Yet far from being hurtful, these spasms thrilled her; she felt her consciousness expanding, enlarging her sense of self, till she felt wise and benign beyond the reach of her years. The crystal was hot now, but strangely the heat did not burn. *I, I, I!* exulted the girl's consciousness.

Now her brain speeded up: images flashed across the screen of her inner eye with dizzying rapidity, so fast they overwhelmed her and she couldn't take them in. Then, when she thought that she could bear no more, that her head would split asunder, the rush stilled.

She was drifting above water in a clear blue sky. The water was bluey-green, with wave-crests that lifted and broke white. A lake perhaps, or a dam? No, this expanse of water was too big to be a lake or a dam. A strange word came to her: *ocean . . .*

Now, far beneath, appeared a boat of a kind Jewel had never seen before. It possessed not a single sail. It had a broad, flat deck that was almost featureless – except towards the stern, where a metal structure rose up. This was dominated by a great chimney that trailed a long pennant of smoke.

The boat fell away below, and Jewel was carried at speed across the watery waste. Now, in the distance, appeared a blossom of greyish smoke. It came, she saw, from a mountain – a curious flat-topped cone rising sharply above an island. As she neared this, she saw that the cloud was a cloud of ash, and along with this the mountain was busily spewing out gobbets of fire. Looping into the swirling air, they rained down on the blackened earth around the fevered cone, burning and steaming in their fury.

As she passed over the lip of the cone, she saw with horror what lay inside: a seething, roiling, spitting mass of molten orange rock. Like an arrow, she plunged towards it.

It will annihilate me, she thought, and struggled against the downward force. To no avail – she was sucked into the maelstrom.

But was not destroyed there. A flame sprang up at the core of her being. It was exquisitely thrilling and she surrendered herself to it.

Anyone entering at that moment would have beheld the girl glowing like an emerald coal, transfiguring with her radiance the room's tawdriness.

"Ah, you're up!" said Rosy, grinning. "Feeling better now, are we?"

"Much better," said Thorn, "thanks to that concoction of

yours." He grinned. "The PF Special really packs a punch. Amazing."

"It does, doesn't it? But then you're only a young lad, and not accustomed to strong liquor. When you get to my age—"

"I doubt I ever would, if I went on drinking *that* stuff." He glanced around the room. "Jewel not here, then?"

"I don't know where she is. She had breakfast ages ago. Are you hungry, Thorn Jack?"

"Well, I could manage something, I think."

"How about bread and strawberry jam? Lily makes the jam."

"Then it's bound to be excellent. Yes, that sounds just right."

"Zinny, do the honours. And make some tea while you're about it."

Zinny was busy at one of the tables – mixing dough by the look of it. "I've only one pair of hands," she complained truculently.

"Then use them!" snapped Rosy.

Zinny slammed down the dough and marched off to the pantry.

Lily, working at another table, watched as she went inside.

"One of these days," she said, "that girl will revolt."

"Revolt my foot!" exclaimed Rosy. "She's just asserting her independence – not that it exists except inside her imagination."

"Do you think she doesn't know that? No, mark my words: one day she'll revolt and then there'll be trouble . . ."

"Fol-de-diddle!" cried Rosy, and her fat jowls shook.

I'll be glad to get off this island, Thorn said to himself. God save me from fratching women.

*

Jewel came back to herself. She was standing by the table. On the table lay the crystal. The light had gone out of it. Inert or quiescent, it seemed to brood on its own darkness.

She turned her attention to her body, but if she expected it to be changed that expectation was disappointed, for it looked just as it had been before she picked up the stone. She poked her stomach with a forefinger: it felt just like a stomach should. Yet the enhanced sense of being, the deep rapture the crystal had brought her, she remembered vividly. The temptation to repeat the experience straightaway was strong.

But she did not give in to it. Caution, said reason, you know too little about this stone. It mastered you, controlled you – you were not in control of it. It may be dangerous, destructive, you need to know more about it. Next time you explore it—

Next time? she thought. It isn't mine to take away . . .

But didn't it call to me? Through the jar's black glass, through the thickness of the door, through the air between the door and the jar, didn't it call with its heat? It's been waiting here for me. All I have to do is take it . . .

But Jewel had never stolen in her life, and she hesitated.

It belongs to the Sybs, she thought. Still, what use have they for it? If they had one it wouldn't be here, stuffed in a jar in a back room. And *why* is it here? Obviously because it scares them. They don't dare touch it. They know it's beyond them. But it's not beyond me. It knew me, revealed itself to me. It ought to be mine.

It was then that she remembered the elixir of death, that the Puckfloss sisters were plotting to kill her and Thorn, and the world became simple again.

113

She wrapped the crystal up in its cloth and started to hunt around the room. In a corner, she found what she needed – an old rucksack. She beat the dust out of it and put the crystal inside.

Then she sneaked back to her room and slipped her plunder beneath the bed.

7

OUT OF THE FRYING-PAN

When Jewel came into the living room, the two Sybs were working at one of the tables. They called out friendly good mornings, then went back to what they were doing. Only Zinny, it seemed to Jewel, stared at her suspiciously – Zinny just being Zinny? Jewel ignored the servant and went over to Thorn.

"Feeling better now?" she asked.

He smiled. "Much better. Er, sorry about last night. Would you like some blackcurrant tea?"

"Yes, that would be lovely."

She sat down at the table. As Thorn was pouring her a mug, Rosy came up beside her.

"It's still windy at the moment – much too windy to risk the boat. It doesn't look as though we'll be able to take you ashore until tomorrow."

"Are you cer—" began Thorn, but Jewel cut across him.

"That's fine," she said briskly. "Tomorrow it is, then." She turned to Thorn. "But I'm going to take you out for a walk, Master Jack – blow your cobwebs away."

"Must you?" he said. "I'm still feeling a bit weary."

"All the more reason to go for a walk."

"Sometimes you remind me of my Aunt Morry," he said. "*She's* a fresh-air fiend."

115

"Last night you reminded me of my father," she retorted. "*He* didn't know when he'd had enough either."

"Well, I've learnt my lesson," he said. "I shan't ever get drunk again."

"That's funny. My father used to come out with those very same words. Neither he nor I believed them."

"Well, I'm *not* your father," Thorn replied crossly.

Jewel grinned, and sipped her tea.

"Thorn, there are several important things I've got to tell you."

They were sitting on the log, looking out towards the channel. The wind blustered into their faces, pinching the water to whitecaps.

"I'm all ears," said Thorn.

"These are *serious* things," she said, not much liking his light tone.

"Then I'm all *serious* ears."

She looked doubtfully at him, but he seemed attentive enough.

"Right. First, I didn't tell you everything about myself."

"You didn't?"

"No." Jewel paused, and snapped off a stalk of grass. He watched as she began to twist it around her fingers.

"Look," she went on. "Do you remember the sisters talking last night about Magians?"

"Er, vaguely," he said. "Sort of super-Sybs, aren't they? They mentioned one – a weird name, I don't recall it."

"Querne Rasp. Actually I'd heard her name before – from

Elphin Loach, the seer in Harrypark. I told you about Elphin, how she helped to save my life."

"Yes."

Jewel was feeling embarrassed, but she made herself go on. "Well, Elphin thinks I might be a Magian . . ."

"What, you!" exclaimed Thorn. But the smile on his face died when he saw how sternly the girl was regarding him. "I'm sorry," he said, "I didn't mean . . ."

She smiled faintly. "I wasn't sure for some time that I believed it myself. I wasn't going to speak of it just yet, but now I must. I've been experimenting, you see, and I'm convinced that it's true."

"What sort of experiments?"

She untwisted the stalk of grass and tossed it into the air. The wind whisked it away.

"It's difficult to describe them. But I can sort of go out of myself into other things. All sorts of things – water, wood – even into the pike when we were riding it yesterday."

"The Great Pike? You're kidding!"

"No. When I was inside its mind I saw Rosy and Lily. It was thinking of them. It brought us here because they give it sweet-meats, and it expected a reward."

Thorn was silent. He was looking at her oddly, as if he was torn between belief and disbelief.

Well, I don't blame him, she thought.

"But then, earlier this morning, just after I left you, I saw some lamps burning along that passageway that runs into the hillside, and I went down there. Rosy and Lily were talking in a room. I couldn't make out what they were saying at first, but

117

I used my powers, and then I could hear them quite clearly." Once again she paused. "Thorn, they're planning to kill us."

"Rosy and Lily! I don't believe it! They're just harmless old women with a taste for nettle ale."

"Don't you believe it. Why do you think they hid themselves away on this island? They're obsessed with developing an elixir of life. Lily thinks the key to it lies in human blood – young people's blood. That's why they're going to kill us."

"Hey – Rosy did say something yesterday . . . I remember now – she was talking about decanting the sap of youth, and she mentioned an elixir."

"Well, she was serious. She's the leading light in this. I don't believe Lily wants to kill anybody, but Rosy's a fanatic. Murder's nothing to her, just a means to an end."

"Did they say how they were going to go about killing us?"

"They'll drug us tonight. Then . . ." She made a slicing movement across her throat with one hand.

Thorn mused for a few moments.

"Look at the weather," he said. "If the wind would only drop, we could sneak off and steal the boat. But it's out of the question."

Jewel regarded him steadily. "Minny Pickles gave you a third gift. A phial containing a potion—"

"How do you know about that?"

"I told you: I'm a Magian. The last time we were sitting on this log, you thought of it."

"So I did." He looked at her suspiciously. "Are you in the habit of reading my mind?"

"I've *never* read your mind, Thorn. I wouldn't dream of it. It was just a random impulse I picked up through the wood.

Things sometimes happen that way with me – like a Syb getting a sending."

Her evident earnestness persuaded him.

"So, yes, the phial . . . Ah, I see what you're thinking. You've guessed what it is, and I rather think you're right. What's good for the mouse is good for the rat!"

She grinned. "Exactly! . . . There's something else I need to tell you."

"Something else?"

"Yes. You told me about the crystal that you stole from Wyke for Haw . . . It was dark red, you said, and it glowed when you touched it and sent a kind of shock through you."

"That's right."

"Well, I found a dark-green crystal in a room down the passageway. It called to me . . ."

"I hope you didn't touch it."

"Oh but I did. I held it—"

"You held it? Impossible!"

"What's impossible for you may not be impossible for me."

Was Thorn looking at her with jealousy in his eyes, or was she imagining things?

"Have you any idea what it is?" he asked.

"I can't be sure, but I think it's a source of power. When I held it, it lit up and made my mind expand. I saw these hurtling images – too many to make sense of. And I floated above the earth." She paused. "I stole it – I hid it under my bed in an old bag."

"Good for you, Jewel!" he said. "But I wouldn't tell Racky Jagger. He might have your brother kidnapped!"

"*You're* my brother now," she said, and laid her hand on his.

They sat on without speaking, and the sough of the wind filled their silence.

"Why do you stay here?" asked Jewel.

Zinny Muffin twisted her head to look up at the girl. The two were collecting water from the pool in wooden buckets. The wind blustered about them, but not as strongly as earlier.

"Where else would I go?" she said.

"Anywhere you liked. A settlement: Shelf, Lowmoor."

"I'd be a square peg in a round hole."

"Why? You're a good worker. You're quite pretty when you forget to put on a scowl. You could easily marry."

"Marry?" Zinny snorted. "Don't notice much, do you? Not all of us are loveable like you, Jewel Ranson."

"You could be, if you wished."

"Rubbish. People are what they are. They never change. They're like stones."

"Stones crack, or wear away. Pebbles were big stones once."

"But their natures don't alter. Once a stone, always a stone. And that's what *I* am – a stone." She laughed unpleasantly.

Jewel thought: There's pain in her laughter. I wonder what has made her the way that she is?

"I don't believe that," she said.

"Believe what you like, it's true. Look at you: you're nice now, but in six months, a year, who knows what you might be like. You might be a tyrant – like Rosy. Or worse."

She picked up her buckets and walked away towards the house. Jewel remained for a time by the pool, watching the water as it trickled down the mossy face of the bank. The green of the vegetation reminded her of the crystal when it came alive in her hands.

Could I change? she wondered. If I did, what would I be?

The wind blew dark strands of her hair across her face.

The afternoon was ageing. Soon it would die into evening. But, as the nights were shortening, it wouldn't be dark for quite some time. The wind had dropped considerably.

The Sybs had subsided into their chairs, clearly weary. Zinny Muffin was stoking the fire.

"How about I make us all some tea?" Jewel suggested.

"Tea?" Rosy opened drowsy eyes and looked at her.

"Or would you prefer ale?" Jewel added helpfully.

"Too early for that," Rosy replied quickly. "Tea, for now. We'll save the PF Special for later."

So, thought Jewel, *that's* where she's going to put the drug . . .

"Tea it is, then." She got up and filled the kettle, then set it on the hob. "Fruit tea for you, Zinny?"

"Why not?" said the woman. "If you can manage to make it."

"I'll do my best," said Jewel, ignoring her superciliousness.

When the kettle boiled, she took it over to the table and filled the teapot. Now the leaves had to mash.

She had stationed herself with her back to the other occupants of the room. The phial with its mysterious markings – **Z Z Z** – was in her left hand. She had probed it with her mind and knew what it contained: a potent sleeping potion. Anyone who drank a few drops would sleep till morning. It had been tightly corked, but she'd easily pulled it out. The mugs were ranged in

121

front of her. On top of one lay a strainer to catch floating leaves. She lifted the lid of the teapot and stirred the brew with a spoon. Let it settle, then pour. Add a few drops of the Syb's potion to three of the mugs, stir and serve.

As she began to pour the tea there was a loud *crack!* from the fire and a glowing splinter leapt out. It landed on the rug beyond the hearth and began to sizzle. Thorn shot out of his chair. As the Sybs watched, he seized the fire-tongs from their rack, gripped the ember in their pincers and dropped it back among the flames.

"The reactions of the young fair make me dizzy," said Lily.

"And envious, sister?" said Rosy.

"That too," Lily agreed.

Rosy chuckled. "Never mind, dearie. There's always death to look forward to!"

Jewel handed out mugs of tea to the two Sybs. The phial was safely back in her pocket.

"I don't know how you can make jokes about death," she observed.

"Just wait till you get to be our age," said Lily. "You'll find you can joke about anything."

"*Any*thing and *every*thing," Rosy embellished. "*If* you get to be our age." She cackled again.

"It sounds as if you know something we don't," said Jewel.

"Perhaps I do." Rosy giggled, and took a sup of tea.

"Like to tell us what it is?" said Jewel.

"If I did, you'd know what I know," said Rosy.

"What's wrong with that? What's the point of knowledge if you don't seek to share it?"

"What's the point of knowledge if you throw it to the four winds?"

"Don't you think that's a selfish attitude?"

"Selfish?" For a moment it looked as if Rosy would explode. Then she seemed to rein herself in. "What's the point in arguing? You'll be gone tomorrow, lass."

"True," said Jewel, "and you'll be here – you and the nettles."

"Us and the nettles," said Rosy. "The PF Special and the blood puddings." And she giggled so hard that she had to pull out a handkerchief and wipe her streaming eyes.

Lily looked disapprovingly at her sister. "Pull yourself together!" she said.

"Blood puddings!" Rosy repeated under her breath, and blew her nose.

Not long after, head thrown back, mouth ajar, she was snoring. There was a thump. Lily's mug had slipped out of her hand. She too was fast asleep.

"Lily?" murmured Zinny. But when she tried to rise from her chair she fell back, defeated.

"What did you put in the tea?" she croaked. "Have you poisoned us?"

"Poison," said Jewel, "is no more than you deserve. But it's only a sleeping potion. You'll be fine in the morning."

Zinny struggled to stay awake, but at last her eyes closed. She too was asleep.

"Time to get our packs," said Thorn.

When they came back into the living room with their packs and bows, the three women were lying as they'd left them.

Thorn looked down at Rosy.

"We ought to slit her throat," he said. "*We* might have escaped her, others may not be so lucky."

"Part of me agrees with what you say," conceded Jewel. "But there's always a chance that she'll change, isn't there?"

"Is there?" said Thorn. He didn't think so.

"Time to go," said Jewel.

They'd reached the door when, behind them, a voice said clearly: "What's this? Leaving, and not a word of farewell?"

They turned on their heels. Eyes wide open, Zinny was lounging in her chair, on her face a half-smile.

"You didn't drink the tea," said Thorn.

"Not likely. I'm not the fool you take me to be. Unlike these two." She gestured towards the two recumbent Sybs.

"If you knew, why didn't you warn them?"

"Why should I save them from their own stupidity? Besides, you've earned your freedom. How you knew what they had in store for you, I don't know. I only know that, in your place, I'd never have guessed."

Jewel said: "Come with us, Zinny. Now's your chance to break away."

"I don't think so. Nettle Island suits me. And when they die, I'll be mistress." Looking at Thorn, she added: "Pity you didn't cut their throats. One of these days, I might just have to do it myself."

Jewel said: "I was about to wish you luck, but now I don't think I shall."

"It's you who'll need the luck, out on the water in this weather."

With these ominous words in their ears, Jewel and Thorn left the house.

*

As they walked through the nettle field, a rift opened low in the sky and the westering sun drove a broad, yellow beam down through the breezy air.

The trim little sailing boat was rocking by the jetty. They clambered aboard and stowed their gear under the stern thwart.

"Do you think we can sail this thing?" Jewel asked doubtfully.

"What's the alternative? Take the tiller, Jewel. I'll cast off."

Thorn unloosed the mooring ropes, then jumped back on board. Just then a wave lifted the boat and bumped it against the jetty. Thorn fell over in the scuppers.

"Great start!" said Jewel wryly.

Thorn grinned and got back on his feet. He unfurled and hoisted the mainsail and they were quickly under way.

Their first task was to navigate their way through the islands. But not the way they'd come, since their intended destination was the northern shore of the lake – the opposite shore to Damside. Thorn had watched how Stocky Ricks had handled the jib boom, and how Lacky Dawes had tacked, using the direction of the wind. The water wasn't so choppy in the channels between the islets, and once they'd got into the way the little craft handled, they made decent progress. While the sun remained visible, it shouldn't be impossible to steer the correct course. If the weather continued to improve, Thorn calculated, they ought to be able to make land before nightfall.

At last they emerged from the archipelago and moved out into the Dam. The swell rose higher here, and the sailing boat bucked as it met occasional crests. But it was a sleek craft, and when they found the right tack it went bowling along, at times almost jumping out of the water.

Nothing to it! thought Thorn.

Then, in a sudden shift of wind, the boat leapt and heeled, swinging the jib towards Thorn. He ducked, and the boom whipped over his head. As he crouched, looking up towards the sun, it disappeared, swallowed by bruised billows of clouds.

"We're going the wrong way," he called back to Jewel.

"Can we change tack?" she replied.

But the breeze had strengthened, and though they tried hard to get themselves back on course, they were unequal to the task. The boat sped along still faster, the sail bellying out, the ropes creaking and straining.

"We'll have to run before the wind," shouted Thorn. "That's all we can do."

Now, with the sun gone, evening arrived early. As the clouds thickened still more, the first drops of rain pricked the water's restless skin. Soon it was pouring. Like a pair of half-drowned rats, they held their stations in the boat – Thorn grasping the side-rail and nervously eyeing the bulging sail, Jewel grimly gripping the tiller – while the boat bounced across the water, tossing up sheets of spray.

"Can you see the shoreline yet?" Jewel shouted down the boat.

"Not yet. I can't see far ahead. We'll either hit a rock or run aground. Cross your fingers."

Not very practical advice, when it required all her strength to keep them on a straight course.

The boat flew on. Whoever had built it had done a good job, for the sail didn't rip, the mast crack or the rigging snap. But they were shipping water now from the incessant rain and

126

spray, and Thorn set to bailing with an old wooden bucket. As fast as he threw it overboard, however, more water arrived, and he was fighting a losing battle. Unless they made shore soon the boat would sink and they'd be drowned.

He broke off from bailing and went aft to speak to Jewel. Then, taking their packs and weapons, he struggled up to the bows and stashed the gear beneath a thwart. Returning aft, he changed places with Jewel. She began to bail. He'd given no reason for the switch, but she surmised why he'd done it. If the boat beached, or hit a rock within reach of the shore, she'd be nearer to the prow and would stand a better chance of getting safely to land. Also, as the bow rode higher in the water than the stern, if the boat began to sink, it would sink stern-first.

Ladling furiously, she thought: surely it can't end like this? But it could, she knew, it could. Only too easily . . .

On the stern thwart, Thorn was up to his ankles in water. It was slopping over the side, the boat was about to be swamped—

Then Jewel cried out his name. A high, giant-made wall had appeared ahead of them, no more than thirty feet away. Directly in front of it, a ridge of jagged rocks thrust out of the water like black teeth.

Then – "Steer to the right!" she cried.

Further over there were no rocks, and the height of the wall dropped back to a mere few inches above water level.

Thorn hauled on the tiller and the rudder moved a little, shifting the boat's heading somewhat. He redoubled his efforts, wincing with the strain, and the boat responded, coming round still more. It was now heading towards the low section of wall.

Away to starboard, more high wall materialised from the gloom. The low section appeared to be positioned in a corner of the Dam. Against the vertical face of this parapet the swell rose and fell, and water was driven over it and through the gap.

The boat dipped into a trough; then, when it seemed that its prow must collide with the face of the parapet, was lifted up on a sinew of swell. Riding up at a steep angle, the keel screeched alarmingly as it scraped against stone, and for a moment it seemed as if they'd slip back into the Dam. The boat hung there perilously, then the prow dropped and the keel slammed down on a level surface. Great plumes of water fountained up on both sides, and Jewel and Thorn were sent sprawling in the scuppers.

Picking themselves up, they looked hopefully over the side. But they didn't like what they saw. The parapet on which the boat rested could be little more than five feet wide. Beyond the prow and the far lip of this shelf lay a gulf of darkness.

"It's the run-off for the Dam!" Thorn shouted. "We must get out!"

"I'll get the packs," Jewel cried.

But as she started along the boat there came a rush of water from aft, and the craft went sliding forward as if launched on a slippery slope.

"Oh my God!" Jewel exclaimed.

The vessel had come to rest with its prow projecting over a massive vertical drop. Twelve feet below lay a square, stone-floored basin where the overflow was conducted down a channel that disappeared among shadowy bushes and trees.

Jewel seized Thorn's backpack and slung it along the boat. Then, grabbing her precious rucksack and both their bows, she clambered back. Thorn had remained on board as ballast, and now he helped her over the side. But, as he stepped up on a thwart, another wave struck astern. The boat went sliding forward again. Thorn jumped over the side, landing in a wash that would have swept his feet from under him and carried him away had Jewel not thrown her arms about him and anchored him to the spot.

The boat had completed its final voyage. With infinite grace and an air of resigned martyrdom, it dived off the parapet and disappeared from sight. Amid the tumult of wind and water, the impact of its fatal arrival below counted for nothing.

Spray blew in off the waves and rain continued to fall. Jewel and Thorn stared at the butt-end of the Dam's retaining wall. A metal ladder, its uprights rooted in the stone blocks of the parapet, climbed the height of the wall, but it had been designed by giants for giants, and its rungs were three times as far apart as Thorn was tall.

There was an inrush of water, but, clutching the metal upright, they managed to stay on their feet. A really big influx and they'd be swept over the lip . . .

"Can you shin up?" asked Jewel. It was beyond her, she was sure.

"Perhaps," replied Thorn – but the wall must be six feet high, and the metal pole was too thick to grip. This was a far cry from climbing the knotted rope to Emmy's tree house . . .

Handing his pack to Jewel, he wrapped his arms and legs around the pole and tried to haul himself up it. The rain drummed on his head. He got a few inches, but then his weight and the slick surface of the metal defeated him, and he slid back again.

"It's no good," he concluded. "But if we can't climb up, maybe we can climb down . . ."

With his back to the wall, he moved along the ledge to the brink of the drop and peered down. One slip, or an irresistible rush of water and he'd be gone, to be broken by unforgiving stone and swirled away downstream. Starting above his head, the wall that he was hugging ran down at a steep angle, at once the shoulder of the basin and a wall that held up the grassy hillslope beyond it.

To climb down the sheer rock would be impossible. On the other hand . . .

He returned to Jewel.

"I think I can see a way. But it's not going to be easy."

From a pocket of his pack he extracted a length of rope. One end he tied to one of the legs of the ladder. Then he made a couple of loops around his waist and edged forwards to the drop. Water came pouring around his legs and threw itself into space. When it had gone, he cast the free end of the rope after it.

Yes. It was long enough.

He unhooked his pack. Then, standing on the slippery brink, he held the pack in his free hand, swung it in a broad arc and flung it through the air. With a thump, it landed safely in the grass on the hillside. Allowing himself a brief smile, he hauled the rope in and went back for Jewel's pack. He repeated the process, then did the same with their bows. Everything landed safely beyond the shoulder of the basin.

Now came the tricky part. He returned to Jewel and explained his plan.

She nodded. "Anything's better than staying here. Let's give it a go."

Thorn knotted the loose end of the rope around the girl. Now the two of them were connected by the cord to the iron ladder. As they edged to the brink of the drop, a fresh cascade of water buffeted their legs. But the rope held them fast.

Jewel sat down on the edge of the drop, then eased herself over. The rope went taut as Thorn took her full weight. Then he was lowering her, paying the rope slowly out, gritting his teeth with the strain. She was fairly light, but her clothing was soaked; he could have done without that.

Another spurt of water came, and Jewel disappeared in the deluge. But when it had gone, she was there, dangling some way beneath the parapet, her back to the basin.

"OK. That's the distance," called Thorn. "Now do your stuff."

Jewel kicked away from the wall, twisted her body and scrabbled for a handhold. The side-wall of the basin was built of roughly-dressed blocks of stone, but years of pouring water had eroded the filling between them here, and Jewel was able not only to get her fingers on a knuckle of rock, but the toes of her boots into a horizontal fissure where two blocks met. This took her weight off Thorn, who paid out the rest of the rope as she edged along to the shoulder, got a leg over the edge and pulled herself to safely.

She sprawled on the down-slope, panting, then shouted out: "Done it!"

Standing, she stepped out of the looped rope and let it go. Then she crawled back to the edge to observe Thorn's progress.

Thorn hauled the rope in. He was more heavily-built than Jewel, and had to untie and retie the rope around his chest. But, unlike the girl, he had no one to let him down, no one to stop the rope chafing against the parapet's lip.

He dropped the looped rope over the edge; then, keeping the line taut, let himself over after it. His boots slithered on the slippery rock as, grimacing with the strain of his own weight, hand under hand, he let himself down the face of the basin. Water came pouring onto his head, but he hung there grimly till it had passed, then carried on.

He was almost level with the fissure Jewel had used, when a second jet descended. Like a curtain it enveloped him, beating upon his head.

It was then that the rope parted. Chaperoned by the last of the gush and still gripping the snapped-off end, Thorn plummeted towards the stony surface below.

8

THE PALE HERMIT

Jewel watched as the heavy fall of water engulfed Thorn. But when it had gone, he too was gone, dissolved away in the cascade.

She stared at the blank, wet wall, willing him to reappear. But such magic was beyond her, and she looked down into the basin. Where the water had crashed upon the stones, it churned and tumbled; then, rediscovering an element of order, foamed away down the channel made for it.

She searched anxiously for a glimpse of his body – his head, a foot, a waving hand, some sign that he might have survived the drop – but there was nothing. Soon the last of the water had passed down the slope into the shadows of the woodland, leaving her crouched on the edge of the drop in the drizzling rain.

She climbed numbly to her feet. Then, abandoning their gear, began to descend the hill-slope as quickly as she could, hampered by the thickness of the grass but unwilling to trust herself to the slippery stones of the basin's edge. Wet grass whipped against her face and wrapped itself around her body, seeking to pull her down, and more than once she tumbled over, but got up again and continued. She beat clawing brambles away and got scratched for her pains. Yet she had little hope; even if Thorn had survived the fall without serious bodily hurt, he'd most likely be drowned.

And he put me before himself, just as Rainy did, she thought . . . First Rainy, now Thorn . . . Am I cursed or something?

At the foot of the slope, the escaped water formed the shallow beginnings of a stream. Rain-sogged grass grew thickly along its edge. A fresh outrush arrived bounding, eager to get ahead. As she followed the stream further into the wood, the water deepened. Fresh gouts of water, foam-flecked, went merrily roiling past. She felt weary and soul-sick. She could see no sign of Thorn. Then, in a spot where the steam opened out into a pool, she saw, sticking pathetically up out of the water, the prow of the sailing boat. And there, a little further down, wedged between some rocks, was the snapped-off mast. The sail was still attached and now spread itself downstream, forlornly rippling like an abandoned banner.

Wiping away the useless tears now threatening to overwhelm her, and pushing aside her exhaustion, she went on.

Thorn felt, rather than heard, the rope part above his head. As he hurtled downwards, he sucked in a deep breath. Then he landed, and water crashed and roared in his ears.

The overflow that had come to earth before him cushioned his fall. But though it saved his life, saved him from breaking a single bone, it wasn't done with him yet. He was plunged into the maelstrom and madly whirled about. He fought to get to the surface, but was seized and dragged away by a masterful undertow.

Blinded and deafened by churning water, he kicked against

the current, but it refused to let go of him. His backside bumped the bottom. Still he was rushed on. He managed to turn so he was travelling feet first; now, if he were to collide with anything, his feet would take the impact. He let his body go loose. He held his breath manfully. At last the speed of his movement slowed. Again he kicked out, but his right foot caught on something (part of the wrecked sailing boat) and his body was dragged around; then the current had him again.

On he went, flailing and kicking, desperate now to reach the surface. His wrist struck something (a rock?), sending a sharp pain up to his elbow. Then his head broke through into air and he took a grateful gulp before he was pulled under again. But his momentum was slowing now; again he bobbed to the surface and this time stayed there. He drifted downstream, sucking air into his lungs, looking for somewhere to climb out: but the banks were high and dense with growth. Tree-trunks rose up into the shadows. This was definitely a wood.

The water was moving placidly now: the anger had all gone out of it. He floated slowly into a pool. Glancing about him, he saw that the left-hand bank sloped down to the water; at last, he thought, and struck out for it.

But as he neared land, an immensely tall, wildly-bearded man emerged from the shadows to stand poised above Thorn, a wickedly-barbed spear pointed at the young man's face.

Thorn threw up an arm in instinctive self-defence, but the man threw down his weapon, dropped into a squat and extended a long arm.

Thorn put out a hand and was hauled out of the water as if he weighed next to nothing.

The man wore moleskin trews, a moleskin jacket and a matching cap. He grinned broadly. "I took you for a water vole. Thank the seven stars that I thought before I threw. I don't always."

Thorn stood dripping and shivering. His wrist was bleeding where it had grazed the rock.

"You're a sight for sore eyes," said the man, with sympathy and humour. "Twilight swimming's one thing. I've been known to do it myself. But swimming with your boots on is something else altogether."

"I don't remember getting a chance to remove them," said Thorn.

The man looked thoughtfully at him. "I smell a story here. Look, my hut isn't far. You can dry yourself there and tell it to me, and eat and sleep. One night mind – no more. Hospitality only stretches so far with me."

"You're very kind. But somewhere in this wood is my friend. I must find her first."

"A friend, eh? Better and better. But you're in no condition to go looking for anyone."

Then, like a hare, the man cocked his ears to listen.

"You won't need to go looking. Here she comes!" he announced.

Jewel's head came into view, bobbing along through the grass. She was filthy, soaked to the skin, bramble-scratched and exhausted. Yet when she saw Thorn she let out a cry, stumbled towards him and threw herself into his arms.

"I thought you were dead," she said, as they clung to one another.

"If he is," said the tall man, "then you are dead too." He considered for a moment. "I suppose you both could be apparitions in one of my sillier dreams." He patted Thorn on the shoulder. "No, too wet," he declared, "altogether too wet. You're both definitely alive."

Jewel stepped back from Thorn. "Who are you?" she asked.

"She's a suspicious one, your friend," said the tall man to Thorn.

"With good reason," he replied. "People keep trying to kill us."

"Sadly," said the man, "that's the sort of world it is. Which is why I live in this wood and keep myself to myself. But you asked me my name. Up at Damside, they call me the Pale Hermit – or worse things. But my name's Lorcan Brace."

"Brace?" repeated Jewel, and looked sharply at the man.

"That's my name. Why? Have you heard it before?"

"Yes and no." Jewel was reluctant to say more.

"Let me guess. You've heard tell of – or, worse still, you've met – my son Deacon. My *beloved*, my *only*," the Hermit added with heavy irony.

"Your *son*!"

"Even monsters have fathers," said Lorcan Brace.

"Yes, we have met," said Jewel. "It wasn't a pleasant experience."

"There's one thing you've got to grant Deacon – consistency. That – and his height – are his inheritance from me; the rest of himself he invented." Lorcan paused. "Young woman, you look almost as wet as your friend here. I offered him food and a roof for the night. The offer's good for you too. Will you accept?"

Thorn looked at Jewel. "I'm happy to accept," he said, "but I'll go with your decision." He pointed to where Lorcan's spear lay in the grass. "If he'd wanted to kill me, he could have done it already."

She gave a nod. "We accept," she told Brace.

"Good. Follow me," said the Hermit.

"Hang on," said Jewel. "What about our packs and bows?" She mustn't lose the precious crystal.

"Tell me where they are, and while you dry yourselves I'll fetch them."

"That's good of you," said Jewel. Could she trust him? She thought so.

The Pale Hermit smiled. "One malevolent Brace in the world is quite enough."

And so saying, set off through the wood.

"By the way, my name's Jewel," said Jewel. "This is Thorn."

"Jewel and Thorn: beauty and pain. Well, they often go together. They say opposites attract. Is that the case with you two?"

"I've never thought about it."

Lorcan laughed. "Haven't you? I believe you: hundreds wouldn't."

Beauty and pain, thought Thorn, as they tramped a well-trodden trail. That was a novel idea. Almost novel enough to distract him from the squelching in his boots.

"This is getting to be something of a habit," commented Thorn. He was towelling his hair.

Jewel said: "It's good you can joke about it. I bet you didn't feel much like joking when your rope snapped."

Thorn grinned and took a swig of hot tea. "Not much," he agreed. Then said, with mock exaggeration: "My whole life flashed before me."

She raised her eyebrows.

"To tell you the truth, it didn't," he said. "I don't believe I thought of anything except dying. That's an idea big enough to keep anyone busy."

They were sitting, wrapped in blankets, in front of the fire in Lorcan's hut. Their wet clothes hung on a creel that dangled down from a rafter. The room was spartan, but neat and clean – the living space of an ascetic. Its only approach to orna-ment, propped against the wall beside the hearth and the height of the room, was a bark-stripped, fantastical knot of roots: nature seeming to strangle itself, yet growing nonethe-less, both ugly and beautiful. Mud and wattle, with a stone-built chimney and capped with a roof of thatched reeds, the hut stood beneath an old beech tree and merged so fluidly into the landscape that they hadn't noticed it until they were almost at the door.

That door now opened, and a draught fluttered the flames as Lorcan entered with their gear. He dumped it on the floor and stripped his moleskin jerkin off.

"Feeling better now?" he asked.

"Almost human," said Thorn. "We were lucky to meet you."

"Yes," said Jewel. "But why were you out and about on such a vile night?"

The Hermit grinned. "Still doubtful about me, Jewel? Well, it's easily explained. When the weather gets rough like this and a spate of water comes down from the Dam, fish get carried along with it. Hence the spear. You wouldn't have seen it, but there's a net across the stream below the pool I found you in. It keeps the fish from swimming further. My very own food source. Though you'll get rabbit stew tonight, as you can tell from the smell." He waved a hand towards the pot simmering on a metal trivet. "You're hungry, I suppose?"

"I should say so," said Thorn.

The Hermit gave spoons to his guests, took a couple of hand-carved wooden bowls from a cabinet, ladled stew into them and handed them steaming to Jewel and Thorn; then sat down in a chair by the fire.

It was easy to see now why he was called the Pale Hermit. Instead of flickering yellowy-red in the light thrown up by the fire, his face seemed white: cloud-white or chalk-white, as if behind his cheeks no blood flowed to colour them.

He's wrong, thought Jewel, to believe he only passed two qualities on to his son; he gave Deacon his pallor, too.

"Aren't you eating?" she asked him.

"I ate before I went out. But I'll have some tea."

He poured himself a mug and watched as the pair tucked in.

"This is very good," said Jewel.

"Food tastes better when you've earned it," said their host pointedly.

"We haven't earned it," she said.

"You will. Thorn has promised me your story. So eat up – you've talking to do."

Not, however, before they'd had a second generous helping. Then, sated and more inclined to go to sleep than hold forth, Thorn roused himself and gave the Hermit a selective account of their adventures from their arrival at Damside to his appearance in the pool.

"Hmm," said Lorcan Brace. "Your story does nothing for my faith in human nature. Or rather, my lack of it." He laughed coldly. "Lacky Dawes . . . Nasty echo, that." He paused, then went on: "There have been rumours before now of people vanishing in this region. Some years ago I had Lowmoor's Headman visit me – him and a bunch of armed men. Very grim and determined. They were a search party – one of their people had gone missing. I couldn't help them – I'd never heard of the man, never seen him. They didn't like the look of me, but they left me alone. Settlers, you see: they can't get their heads around a loner like me. Of course, I didn't tell them I was Deacon Brace's father. If I had, they might have killed me just for that."

This was Jewel's opportunity. "Speaking of your son . . ."

"Ah! I wondered how long it would take you to get to him."

Jewel blushed. "Not very long, I suppose," she admitted. "But he murdered someone I knew – a harmless fellow, a gambler. When I confronted him with the truth, he beat me and threw me in Harrylake. I almost drowned."

Lorcan frowned. "I thought something was nibbling at you – though not anything quite so bad. Well, perhaps I owe you some account of Deacon. I say 'account' – I can't explain him; I'm not sure I understand him. You see, I don't know whether people are born evil or whether evil creeps into them as a result of what life throws at them, how it twists them. Not that there was anything special about Deacon's early life. He was unfortunate – but you can say that of lots of children."

He stopped briefly and seemed to reflect, then resumed his narrative.

"I was a baker once – a trade I learnt from my father. Me and my wife – her name was Sal – lived in a settlement called Bankfoot. That's a long way from here to the north. Just an ordinary settlement, nothing unusual about it. Sal was a lovely woman, a good wife, a good mother. Deacon was our only child. We wanted others, but it didn't happen. I suppose Deacon was spoilt. I used to tell Sal she was spoiling him, but she'd say: 'He's my only son, Lorcan. Who else am I going to spoil if I can't spoil him?'

"Sal was a painter. She painted pictures of the countryside, and sold them or traded them, and we lived comfortably. Now I don't know if you know, because it seems harmless enough, but painting's a dangerous business. Why? Because painters have to make their own paints – you can't just buy them. Paint comes from two sources – plants or soft rocks. You squeeze plants to extract the dye, crush rocks to produce a dust. You then add water or oil, depending on what kind of paint it is you want.

"Painters are secretive about where their colours come from. The rarer the colour, the more secretive they are. And the rarer, the more remarkable the colour, the more risks they'll take to obtain it. By 'risks' I mean that some of these substances are poisonous. They're all right when the picture's painted and dry, but they're dangerous to process. You can breathe in dust, you can get liquid on your skin. Sal knew the dangers, of course – she wasn't an idiot; but she was obsessed, as many creative people are. Now I don't know whether what killed her was some new substance she was experimenting with, or whether it was all her years of exposure to the stuff. But she died. She took a long time to die, and it was terrible. It started as a rash, then it spread and she fell sick. She hadn't the strength to rise from the bed. She wasted away before our eyes.

"*Our* eyes. Deacon, of course, had to watch all this. He'd always loved his mother more than he loved me. In fact, I don't know whether he ever had anything much in the way of feeling for me. If I'd died and Sal had been spared, maybe things would have turned out different. But they went the way they went.

"Deacon was ten at the time. He was devastated. At first he was withdrawn, numb with grief, as they say; except that grief isn't numb – it's like a continuous pain in your heart, sucking the life out of you. Then he started to go wrong. He misbehaved in settlement school, wouldn't do as he was told, became cheeky and violent. He was beaten several times – though never by me, I couldn't have done it – but it didn't have the slightest effect on him, unless it was to reinforce his increasing waywardness. His mother's death was a burning glass and he was the sun – determined to destroy and not caring what he destroyed.

"He blamed me, of course. He needed someone to blame and I was the obvious person. 'You shouldn't have let my mother paint. You knew the dangers, Dad. It's your fault, your fault!' As if I could have stopped her! She wasn't the kind of woman who's going to do what men tell her. She did what *she* wanted to do, and that was one reason I loved her. I tried to tell Deacon this, more than once, but he wouldn't listen. He'd start shouting, kicking and punching, and swearing like an adult.

143

"Well, to cut the story short, matters came to a head when he attacked another child. Over something and nothing, it was. The kid was two years older than Deacon but he didn't have a chance. He lost an eye, and Bankfoot Council asked the two of us to leave.

"So I became a travelling baker. We'd stay a while in a settlement, then Deacon would do something and we'd have to leave again. We eked out a sort of life, which went on till he was eighteen. Unbeknown to me, he had a relationship with a girl, and when her father found them together, he killed the man. Stuck a knife under his ribs. Then vanished from the place.

"I didn't see him again for some years after that. I suppose I could have settled down, remarried – but I couldn't do it. I'd stay for a time in a settlement, then I'd up and leave. Travelling eased the ache in my heart – if anything did. Then I came to Lowmoor and heard at last where Deacon was – this house built by giants called Minral How. Working for a man called Crane Rockett – a rich fellow. So I went to see Deacon. I hammered on the gate till he came out. He'd always been thin, but now he seemed cadaverous, as if his hurt had fed on his flesh in the absence of anything better. His skull, arms, legs, were just skin stretched over bone. He said: 'What do you want, father?' 'I came to see you,' I said. He laughed. 'Well, now you've seen me, you can go.' And he turned on his heel and went.

"That was four years back. I haven't seen him since. But sometimes rumours reach me of his doings – dark deeds. My son. What else should I call him? . . . I found this wood and built this hut. I expect to die here."

He paused. Jewel and Thorn sat silent. Neither knew what to say. Then Lorcan Brace said: "There's just one thing more. It's the question I ask myself. I ask it over and over and I can't answer it. Do you want to know what it is?"

Jewel wasn't sure she did, but felt obliged to answer, "Yes."

"If Deacon hates me so much, why didn't he kill *me*?"

9

OUT OF THE SKY

That night, Jewel and Thorn bedded down in their sleeping bags in front of the fire, while Lorcan retired to his pallet.

Next morning, over breakfast, he asked: "Where are you making for?"

Thorn hesitated, shot an enquiring glance at Jewel, then answered: "Minral How, as it happens."

Lorcan said: "Now there's a surprise."

"You don't look surprised to me."

"Nothing much surprises me. Expect the unexpected and you'll never be surprised. But Minral How's a bad place. Why are you going there?"

"It's a long story, but it's something I" – he looked at Jewel – "*we* have to do."

"Then it must be important."

"It's a matter of life and death."

"Does it involve Deacon?"

"No."

"But you'll see him, I expect . . ." Lorcan studied the crumbs on the plate in front of him. "Perhaps you could give him a message for me." He looked up at Jewel and saw the doubt in her face. "No, of course you couldn't," he said. "Forget I said that."

After breakfast, he took them to the place where he'd found them.

"Follow the stream," he told them. "There's a track of sorts on this side. I often walk that way. The stream runs to the edge of the wood. There's a high rampart there, part hill, part earthwork. It's too steep to climb, and it's topped by a wall – or what's left of a wall. I sometimes wonder if that's the only change we make to the world – shifting stones from place to place." He produced a dry chuckle. "Well, turn left and follow the rampart to the north-east corner of the wood. There's another wall there, but it's not much of an obstacle. Go over that and up the slope. You'll see open, rolling country and a road that goes north to Lowmoor. Minral How's north-west. You could cut across country, but it's hard going, trackless. Alternatively, you can follow the Lowmoor road, turn west at the junction and come to the house that way. You'll see it from the road – a huge structure of blackened stone surrounded by a high outer wall. It's better defended than many settlements I've seen. But there's a gate, and it'll be manned by a gatekeeper. Not Deacon though: he's above such routine tasks . . . Well, goodbye and good luck to you."

Jewel and Thorn said goodbye and shook the Hermit's pale hand, then set off along the stream. When they looked back, he was gone.

The stream meandered through the wood, tinkling or chuckling, twisting and turning as the land rose or fell, as the water found its way, and they went along with it, happy to cede the matter of direction to nature. Occasionally, tributary streams united with it, and a couple of these they had to cross. But in

147

both cases makeshift bridges in the shape of fallen branches lay across them (or had they been hauled into place by Lorcan?) and there was no need to get wet again. The Hermit had told them the wood's name: it was Rook Wood. But the rooks lived in the treetops of its north-eastern corner, and they could hear no cawing yet.

At mid-morning, between the trees, they spotted the rampart that bounded the wood to the east. Soon they stood below it. Perhaps twenty feet high, it rose almost vertically, was turfed and topped by a dry-stone wall. Time had turned this into the semblance of a gigantic broken jaw. Some stones had tumbled into the wood, and lichen, moss and even plants grew on many of them, changing rock back into grassland, lumpy and blocklike.

The stream dived into a culvert – a dark tunnel arched with stones. Perhaps, on the far side of the earthwork, the water emerged, but here their relationship with this ambiguous daughter of the Dam came to an end. Turning left, they began to follow the rampart north.

The going was painfully slow. There was no trail here, the ground was boggy and rough, blocked by snapped-off branches and the occasional fallen tree, and frequently they were forced to turn back and find an alternative way through. Noon came. They rested, quenched their thirsts and ate some food Lorcan had given them. Then resumed their trek.

Some time later, rook-chatter came at last to their ears, discordant and querulous. High in the beeches, on their black clots of nest or claw-clenching on a twig, the sleek birds were at it hammer and tongs.

"It's a wonder they don't murder one another," said Jewel.

"They're just talking," said Thorn. "They're pretty harmless, rooks."

The afternoon was well advanced when they reached the corner of the wood. The previous day's clouds had cleared, the sky was blue and it was warm. Rooks came wheeling out of the trees and flapped away cawing, black shapes with air-blown voices pursuing obscure bird-missions.

The northern extremity of the wood was marked with a dry-stone wall, but like that on top of the rampart it had fallen into decay. Much colonised by ivy, it wasn't difficult to climb.

Standing on a mossed and ivied stone, they saw that beyond the wall lush grassland stretched away, rising up to the height of the rampart. It was there, where the broken wall of the earthwork came to an end, that the Lowmoor road must run. They'd already decided to take the roundabout route. Better safe than sorry; by now they knew only too well what sorry meant.

It was a struggle to get up the hill. The grass was long and still wet from the previous day's heavy rain, and the grass stalks clung to them, unwilling to let them pass. Soon they were wet again.

At the top of the slope they found a stony track. A narrow strip running along a giant-made road, it was clearly much used, for cart tracks ran along it. Ahead was Lowmoor; behind were Damside, Roydsal Hill and, beyond it, Judy Wood. The going would be better here. Still –

"I don't think we'll make Minral How before dark," observed Thorn.

"No," said Jewel.

"Still, there's plenty left of the day. We can camp on the roadside. We'll get there tomorrow."

Jewel said nothing. She seemed reluctant to talk – had seemed reluctant all day.

Deacon Brace – that's who she's got on her mind, thought Thorn. It seemed to him that his courageous friend was frightened of very little. But Deacon Brace . . . Had the renegade son of the Pale Hermit the power to scare her?

It seemed so. Still, despite everything Thorn had heard about the man, Brace as yet seemed abstract to him, a parody of a human being, a walking skeleton dressed in clothes.

The road ran on between grassy expanses. Fields, probably, in the Dark Time when the giants had walked the earth. He imagined them striding through the grass – no, over it. Heck, it wouldn't even have reached their knees. And their stride: not two inches but two feet . . . more! If they happened to pass now they'd go by without seeing him – or they'd accidentally tread on him, creeping along down here. What, he wondered, would they think if they saw a human? What would they call such a creature? A midget? But they'd have midgets of their own race; humans wouldn't even rank as midgets to them, with their heads butting the clouds . . .

Thinking of clouds caused him to glance up into the sky. There were one or two up there, drifting just perceptibly. Then he noticed something else away to the east – some kind of bird. He kept his eye on it . . . It was coming in their direction. But it was oddly unbirdlike . . . It didn't flap its wings . . . It simply glided along.

Jewel was plodding steadily a few steps ahead of him; she hadn't seen the thing in the air.

He took some quick strides, caught her arm.

"Jewel! Stop! Look! Do you see – there in the sky? Is that a bird or isn't it?"

The girl followed his pointing finger.

"Well, it's got to be a bird . . . But . . . there's something strange about it . . ."

"Just what I was thinking . . ."

"Still, what could it be but a bird?"

Thorn knew what he wanted to say, but to say it seemed absurd. Then he said it: "A flying machine?"

She turned to him. "Impossible!"

"That's what I was thinking." He grinned.

She frowned, then looked back up at the sky.

Still it came nearer.

"That's no bird," she declared.

And, a little later, as if now she too couldn't believe what she was saying: "Is that a man up there?"

They gazed, entranced. The thing had wide, swept-back wings in the shape of a broadened arrowhead. Below this, in a triangular frame, his body lying face-down in some sort of sling, hung a helmeted man. A spider dangling from an airborne web . . .

One moment, the impossible thing was sailing serenely on. The next, it wasn't. A distant crack came to the watchers' ears, followed by a curse. The mechanism lurched to one side, then went into a sideways dive.

"It's going to crash!" cried Thorn.

As the craft passed overhead, they saw that one of its wings was bent. Inside his frame, the flier lay prone. As man and machine came skimming towards the field, the flier let his legs swing down below his body. Then he was down: long grass silently swallowed the black wing.

"Come on!" exclaimed Thorn.

He plunged into the field. After him went Jewel. But the grass was high and wet: they couldn't see ahead of themselves and had only a vague idea of where the machine had come to earth.

Nevertheless they struggled ahead.

"Somewhere around here, do you think?" gasped Thorn.

"I think so," managed Jewel, who was also breathing hard.

They went left, circled round, but couldn't locate the machine.

"*Hello there!*" cried Thorn. "*Can you hear me? Call if you can!*"

There was no reply.

"Perhaps he's unconscious," said Thorn.

"If he isn't dead."

They went on searching and calling, treading the grass down, making ever more tracks. Increasingly frustrated and increasingly tired, crossing and re-crossing their own trails, they found nothing.

"He can't have disappeared," said Thorn. "He must be here somewhere."

"Perhaps he got further than we thought," Jewel suggested. "Wait! Why didn't I think of that before!"

As Thorn watched, she lay chest-down on the flattened grass, her left ear to the ground, her hands palm-flat on either side of her head. Eyes closed, she lay for a while as if asleep, while a breeze stirred the tips of the surrounding sea of stalks and the sun continued to shine.

What on earth was she doing? Then he recalled what she'd told him about the powers growing in her. How by blanking out her thoughts she could enter into things . . . Well, if by this method she could find man and machine, he'd gladly bow to her.

Time passed. Her eyes opened and she smiled up at him.

"I know where he is," she said, getting to her feet. "He's hurt and unconscious. I can feel his pain through the earth. This way."

She pushed into the wall of stalks. Thorn followed without speaking.

Not long after, they found him – strapped in his harness, motionless: a young man in his mid-twenties under a mess of ripped wing-fabric and twisted metal struts. One leg was awkwardly doubled beneath him, and there was blood on his cheek where he'd banged himself landing. On the framework of the machine not far from his right hand hung a bell.

She knelt and put her hand on the doubled-back leg.

"It's broken," she said.

Thorn considered the situation. "If we can cut his harness free, perhaps we can carry him back to the road."

"Right. Let's try that."

Thorn took out his knife and severed the ropes that connected straps to frame. Then, carefully, they manoeuvred man and harness out of the wreckage.

"I'm glad he's slim," commented Jewel. "If he'd been heavily-built . . ."

Leaving their packs and bows behind them, they hefted the injured man and carried him back towards the road. They had to rest several times on the way, and by the time they emerged

153

from the field they were breathing heavily again and feeling very tired.

"One thing's for sure," said Thorn. "We can't go any further tonight. We'll have to make camp here."

Jewel agreed. "I'll fetch the packs. You stay with him."

He didn't argue. He might not himself be able to find the flying machine. But Jewel could. He'd no doubt about that.

He squatted beside the unconscious man. He had a pleasant face, fair hair that flopped over his forehead, and a neat moustache. But as of now, his face was almost as pale as the Pale Hermit's. Blood had trickled down his chin, but the cut was superficial.

Who are you? Thorn wondered. Where have you come from? And where on earth did you get the inspiration for this mad jaunt?

The man groaned, then murmured something. Thorn couldn't make it out. The man groaned again. A little later, his eyelids fluttered and he murmured a second time. But again the words – if words they were – were unintelligible.

Now his eyes opened. They were greeny-blue and slowly came to focus upon Thorn. "I . . . You . . ."

"You're among friends," said Thorn. "But you've broken your leg. I don't know what other injuries you might have."

The man considered this, then began to test his limbs.

"Just my leg I think. It looks like I've got off lightly." Then, to Thorn's surprise, he produced a broad grin. "It's my own fault," he said. "Red told me those wing-struts ought to have been stronger. I should have listened to him."

"Red?"

154

"My brother. Next time I'll build better . . ."

The young man's eyes took on a distant look. Already he was calculating stresses and dimensions.

He's off his head, thought Thorn. You wouldn't get *me* up there.

"Look," he said. "Your leg's got to be splinted. It's going to hurt. As soon as Jewel gets back with our packs, I'll scout around for something to use."

"Jewel. Is that a man or a woman?"

"A girl."

Just then Jewel appeared. She dumped their packs and bows on the ground.

"I need to splint his leg," said Thorn.

"Do you know how to do it?" she asked.

"I've seen it done a couple of times – on hunts, when people got injured. We need some wood."

"There was a dead bush a little way back down the road."

"Right. I'll go back – see what I can find. Keep this fellow company." He set off.

"You're Jewel," said the injured man, who'd been eyeing her. "You're very young."

"You're not so old yourself."

"I'm older than I look. A *lot* older than you."

"Is this an ageing contest?"

The man laughed. "My name's Roper," he said. "Roper Tuckett."

"I'm Jewel Ranson. My friend's called Thorn Jack. But how can you be so happy when you've just broken your leg? Think what could have happened – it might have been your neck!"

"No chance of that – I'm indestructible! Besides, I've too much work to do to waste my time dying."

"What work? Building flying machines?"

"That – among other things."

"But what if we hadn't seen you crash – hadn't brought you out of the field? You couldn't have crawled out of there."

"Red and Lucy would have tracked me down. They knew which way I was coming. Did you see my bell? All I had to do was ring it. They'd have homed in on that. They'll be along soon with a cart."

"What if you'd stayed unconscious – or been too injured to ring the bell?"

"Then they'd have fetched Snicker."

"Snicker?"

"My saddle-rat. He'd have sniffed me out. He's done it before. He couldn't love me more if I was a rat like him. Or a doe, to be precise, since he's a buck."

"Who are Red and Lucy? Let me guess: your brother and sister."

"Right. Excellent guess! They love me almost as much as Snicker does."

Jewel thought of asking him how you could compare the love of a rat to that of a human, but she decided against it.

"Ow!" exclaimed Roper, and screwed up his eyes.

"Your leg's hurting," said Jewel.

"Just a bit," he admitted.

"Try to rest. Thorn should be back before too long."

She laid her hands gently on Roper's leg, and concentrated.

"Hey – how do you do that?" he exclaimed after a while. "The pain's almost gone."

Just then Thorn arrived, and Jewel was saved the trouble of manufacturing a reply. He carried a number of straight sticks.

"These should do the trick," he said, "till we can get proper splints."

"Fine," she said. "By the way, your patient's name's Roper. So rope him up good!"

While he worked, she maintained her focus, damping the pain, containing it. She could do this, she found, without going out of herself – and despite her tiredness.

I'm developing, she thought, getting more skilful, powerful. Then a new thought sprang up in her mind: perhaps I could heal the break?

At once she rounded on herself: no; that's arrogance, vanity. I'm beginning to think I'm God. I might make things worse, do some permanent damage.

"Roper says his brother and sister will turn up soon," she said. "With a rat-cart."

"Let's hope so," said Thorn, "for his sake. We've no way of moving him. If no one comes, one of us will have to go for help."

"I'm sorry to be a nuisance," said Roper, "but progress involves risk and inconvenience."

"Your risk, our inconvenience," said Jewel.

"If you put it that way, yes. But progress for one is progress for all."

"Meaning that, one day, we'll all be flying around in contraptions like yours?"

"Meaning exactly that. Except that they'll be more advanced models, of course."

"Unless you break your neck first."

"I've told you – I'm not going to die for some time yet."

"Who told you that – a Syb?"

"A Syb?" Roper laughed. "Sybs are overrated. I grant that their knowledge of herbs – where they have it, and not all of them do – can be genuine knowledge, but the rest of what they pretend to be about – foretelling the future and all that – is a lot of guff. Sheer superstition and deliberate obfuscation."

"Is it? Why obfuscation?" Jewel tasted this new word with her tongue.

"Why? I should have thought it was obvious. To impress simple minds and gain power and prestige."

Jewel was tempted to argue the point further, but decided against it. This wasn't the time.

Thorn stood up. "Best I can do," he declared.

"It feels good to me," said Roper. "Many thanks."

Jewel transferred her palm to Roper's forehead. "I think you should try to sleep now," she told him.

"Got a potion handy?" he joked.

"No . . ."

"Then I shan't be able to."

But before long, his eyes closed and he was asleep.

"How do you do it?" asked Thorn.

She smiled. "Nothing to it! Fancy forty winks yourself?"

He grinned. "Thanks for the offer, but I reckon I'll stay awake. You might turn me into a snail!"

"You'd make a very nice snail. But I'm not a magician."

"I'm not so sure about that. Which, I suppose, makes me one of those simple people our friend here despises."

So was I, once, she thought; but not any more. Once upon a time, and a time not long before, she'd been certain of her own identity, her own nature. She was Elliott Ranson's daughter, a travelling tradeswoman. She was strong-minded, a touch rebellious but, when it came down to it, filial and well-behaved. Now she was certain of nothing. She'd become someone else. The idea disturbed her.

They settled down to wait. A travelling pedlar went by, harnessed to a small cart. He gave them a suspicious look, a perfunctory nod, and passed on. The afternoon lengthened, and the sun began its drop towards the western horizon. Roper slept peacefully. Jewel thought again about the break in his leg, how she might re-marry the bones. An attempt would become necessary if his siblings didn't appear.

Then a cart pulled by two brown rats came into view. A man and a woman – both, she thought, a little older than Roper – sat side by side up front, the man driving.

Jewel and Thorn got to their feet. The cart halted next to them. The driver looked down at the man sleeping on the ground.

"Is that my brother down there?" he asked.

"Are you Red Tuckett?" asked Thorn.

"That's me," said the man.

"Then the answer's yes. As you can see for yourself."

The man sighed. "What's the damage this time?"

"A broken leg."

The young man turned to the woman next to him. "I told him he'd come to grief, but he never listens to me."

"Nothing special about that." The woman turned to Thorn

159

and Jewel. "Roper, I'm afraid, never listens to anyone. Half the time, he doesn't even listen to himself."

They got down from the cart and Thorn and Jewel stood back to let them get close to their brother.

They certainly looked like siblings. They had the same reddish-brown hair, brown eyes and clear-cut looks. They little resembled Roper, and it occurred to Jewel that the injured man might well have a different mother.

"We saw him come down in the field over there." Thorn waved an arm. "We managed to get him this far, and put his leg in a splint."

"We're much indebted to you," said the woman. "I'm Lucy Tuckett, by the way."

"I'm Thorn Jack. My companion here is Jewel Ranson."

The four of them shook hands.

Then: "Which way are you travelling?" Lucy asked.

"Northwards," said Jewel.

"Then you must come and spend the night with us. It's the least we can do to express our thanks."

"Well, as a matter of fact—" began Jewel, keen not to be delayed.

"We insist," said Lucy firmly. "You look as though you both could do with a bath, a good meal and a soft bed."

Jewel and Thorn exchanged glances.

"I won't deny that," said Jewel. "Well, if you're not too far out of our way . . ."

"That's settled then."

"What's settled?" Roper was looking up at them.

"So you've woken up, have you?" said Lucy. She spoke with

a sort of amused exasperation – the expression, Jewel imagined, of many years' exposure to her brother's vagaries.

"Yes. So now you can lift me onto the cart," Roper declared. "Then fetch the Airbird. I'm not going back without it. These two know exactly where it is, and if you don't get it today you might never find it."

"You see what he's like?" said Lucy to Jewel, whom she seemed to have earmarked as a sympathetic female.

"I see," replied Jewel.

"Women," said Roper disgustedly. "They always stick together."

"Do you wonder?" said Lucy.

"I'll give you a hand," said Thorn to Red, and together they lifted Roper and laid him in the cart – which was capacious and contained at the top end a pallet, as if kitted out for just such an emergency as this.

Then, while Roper waited with Lucy, Jewel and Thorn went with Red to get the Airbird. The two men carried the contraption out of the field. It proved surprisingly light, and they were able to carry it – in spite of the resistance put up by the thick grass – to the road. Red now brought out some tools and expertly disconnected parts of the framework. When this was done they were able to load the Airbird onto the cart. Just enough room was left for Jewel and Thorn, and when they'd climbed up and disposed themselves near to Roper, off they went.

Red drove steadily north, but they still hadn't reached the junction of which the Pale Hermit had spoken when Red abruptly turned east. In the Dark Time a broad avenue might have run here between field and hedgerow, but now it was choked and only faint wheel-tracks marked where the rat-cart's passage kept open a way through the high and riotous growth. When the track began to rise, Lucy, Thorn and Jewel got down and walked behind the cart. Roper complained loudly as it rattled along, telling his brother to drive with a little more consideration for his passenger's state of health. As if he has a choice! thought Jewel. But Red was evidently used to Roper's moans, for he took not the slightest bit of notice and pressed on.

The light – already beginning to fail – dimmed further as they passed under the shadow of a stand of ancient elderberry trees. Emerging, the track ran alongside a block of stone perhaps four feet long, a foot and a half high and the same across. As the cart turned around the end of the block, Jewel and Thorn saw other blocks lying like a broken barrier in front of them. The cart passed down between two of these and came out into a large clearing. All around, more great chunks of stone were haphazardly strewn. They came in a variety of shapes and sizes, but all possessed six sides and squared-off corners. Some lay athwart others or leant up against them.

With its back to one of the blocks lay the Tucketts' house: Stony Close. It had a single storey and as a piece of architecture was unremarkable, but to its central structure a couple of wings had been added, and it looked capable of accommodating a pretty big family. Off to one side lay a cluster of subsidiary buildings, one of which was obviously a rattery. The clearing also featured an extensive kitchen garden.

Red halted in front of the house. As he did so, the door opened and a man and a woman came out.

"Roper!" exclaimed the woman. "What have done to yourself?" She hurried across to the cart and flung her arms around him.

"I'm perfectly all right, Mother!" Roper was struggling to disengage himself.

"You're not all right!" she cried.

"He's got a broken leg," volunteered Lucy, as she got down from the cart.

"A broken leg!" Mrs Tuckett exclaimed.

"Mother! You're smothering me!"

"If you ask me, he *wants* smothering," said the man, who seemed amused by the pantomime.

"He's *your* son and it's *you* he takes after," the woman accused him. "If anybody deserves to be smothered, it's you!"

"He takes more risks than I ever did," said the man, who was plainly her husband.

"He's *exactly* like you. Two broken bones a year, till you handed the dangerous tasks over to him."

"There'd be no progress otherwise," he said mildly.

"Progress!" said the woman. "You're obsessed, both of you!"

"He'll mend," said her husband phlegmatically. "If you let us get him inside. But who are these two?"

Jewel and Thorn had got down from the cart and were listening to the exchange.

"The ones who found him," said Lucy, "and strapped up his

163

leg. I've invited them to stay." And she proceeded to introduce Roper's rescuers to her father, Matt Tuckett, and her stepmother Petal. Petal was embarrassingly fulsome in her thanks; Matt contented himself with a hearty, "Pleased to meet you," and a vigorous handshake. Then Matt and Red carried Roper indoors, and the others followed.

10

BIG BONES, LITTLE BONES

There were more Tucketts to come. By the time Jewel and Thorn, freshly bathed, emerged from their comfortable rooms in the east wing to join the family at the dinner table, four more had declared themselves. There was Wilf Tuckett (Matt's father), Lasker Tuckett (Matt's brother), May Tuckett (Lasker's wife), and July Tuckett (May and Lasker's teenage daughter). Jewel wondered what would happen if July ever gave birth to a daughter in December. Thorn hoped no more Tucketts would emerge from the woodwork: he was struggling to remember their names.

Eight Tucketts sat down with Jewel and Thorn to eat; Roper sat separately by a low table at one end, his splinted leg suspended in a sling that Red had rigged in accordance with Roper's specifications – this would save the leg, its owner explained, from resting on its own bones.

The meal wasn't far advanced when Matt Tuckett addressed his guests. "So, where are you two off to, if you don't mind me asking?"

Jewel and Thorn had anticipated the question. They'd considered lying, but had rejected it on the grounds that it might only get them into difficulties. Thorn said: "We're go-betweens. The Spetch brothers up at Roydsal have sent us to negotiate the return of an object of value from the people at Minral How."

Red whistled. "You move in exalted company."

"Dangerous company too." This was Matt. "I hope you know what you're doing."

"We know what we're doing," said Thorn. We don't, of course, he thought. We know *why* we're doing it, yes. But *what* we're doing? No.

"If you don't mind me saying so," continued Matt, "you're an unusual pair of negotiators – some might say strange."

"Strange? Why?" asked Jewel, somewhat nettled by the remark.

"Well, you're both very young – only the age of July here."

"And young people are incompetent?" she fired back.

"*Inexperienced* is the word that comes to mind."

"But Mr Tuckett," broke in Thorn, "how can you know what experience the two of us have had?"

"I can't. But experience is useless unless you reflect upon it. Age brings perspective, caution, subtlety: qualities not readily located in the young."

"Take no notice of my son," said old Wilf Tuckett, speaking for the first time. "I'd swap the qualities he speaks of for energy, passion and courage any day of the week." He turned to his son. "You were quite a firebrand when you were young, Matt. But now you're middle-aged and soft, and your children are taking over."

"Firebrand I may have been. But I made mistakes then that I wouldn't make now."

"Mistakes are part of life. It's by making mistakes we learn. If

166

the young aren't going to make them, they might as well be born old."

"Well, I don't mind saying I've made a few," said Thorn.

"If we're going to start confessing, I'll go first," said Roper. "I'm only twenty-two, yet I've made more mistakes than I care to remember."

"What a refreshing admission," said Lucy. "You behave as if you're always right – as if you were born perfect."

"People can't be perfect. Even for things, perfection's hard. Only ideas can be perfect."

"Oh, why's that?" asked Thorn.

"Because ideas exist in the mind – bright, shining, tantalising. The trouble starts when you try to turn them into realities. There's always a gap between the idea and the thing."

"Like with your flying machine?"

"The Airbird? Yes."

"But if you know you'll never do justice to your idea, what keeps you going?"

"The belief that, bit by bit, I'll get closer and closer to it if I just keep plugging away."

"If it doesn't kill you first," said his mother resentfully. "Roper, I don't understand you at all. What idea's worth more than a life?"

"Our ideas are all we've got," replied Roper passionately. "It's only ideas that lift us above animals such as rats."

"What's wrong with rats?" asked Lasker Tuckett, who was the family's ratman. "I've spent all my life with them. They're affectionate, they're loyal, and if you treat them right they'll always do their best for you. Which is something I can't say of every human I've met."

"You've lived so long with rats you've started to think like them," said Roper.

"So at least," retorted Lasker, "you allow that they think?"

"In a rudimentary way. But they're not capable of ideas. They're not capable of *reason*."

"Oh, reason. Everything comes down to reason with you. Reason, reason!"

"Yes, reason. I persist in believing that the world is rational, that nature obeys laws. If we can work out those laws, we can dominate our world."

"Only one thing dominates our world, and that's God."

"God? God's only a fancy name for human ignorance. We can't account for the world's existence, so we invent God to explain it. But God's just lazy thinking. Where is he? I've never seen him. I only believe in things I can see, hear, taste, touch."

"Godless, that's what you are," declared Lasker with satisfaction. "You'll come to a bad end one of these days."

"You mean God will punish me for not believing in him? That's a story for keeping little kids in line, not fit for adults. You really ought to keep away from Ranters, Lasker. They're apt to rot your brain."

"It's ideas that rot your brain. Roper, why can't you be happy with the world as it is, instead of always meddling with it?"

"Meddling's my nature, Lasker. If God made me, he made me meddlesome."

"But you don't believe that."

"No. I get my meddlesomeness from my father: that's what I think."

168

Thorn decided to break in. "I talked to a Ranter once about the giants and the Dark Time. He believed that the giants achieved perfection, and that God took them up into Heaven as a reward."

"Heaven?" exclaimed Roper. "What's that? Pie in the sky!"

"I've heard that theory," said Lasker, ignoring his nephew's jibe. "But it's wrong, not to say heretical. The giants are down in Hell, getting tortured by devils—"

"Devils!" chortled Roper, and slapped his injured leg – only to wince with the pain.

"—*Tortured by devils*," repeated Lasker. "And why, young man?" he asked, directly addressing Thorn. "Because of their arrogance, their vanity, their worship of *reason*!" He paused to savour his success in proving Roper's God to be nonsense. But Roper was quivering too much to return to the battleground. Lasker went on: "Consider the Barrens, places blasted, purged of unclean life. They're a warning, the living evidence of God's righteous wrath, and we should pay heed to them. If we make the same mistakes as those who went before us, we shall be punished like them! Annihilated! Snatched away to Hell and tortured for ever!"

"What about," said Red, who'd been silent for quite some time, "the skeleton we've found? *That* wasn't annihilated."

"Skeleton?" said Thorn, pricking up his ears.

"Let me explain," said Red. "Quite recently, we – in fact it was July – discovered the skeleton of a giant in a place not far from here: a valley we call Wilf's Clough after guess who. Tell him, July."

"We went for a picnic," she said, "and I saw this whitish

169

thing. It was sticking up out of the ground. I told Roper about it. I thought it was a rock, but he wasn't so sure."

"We dug around it," said Red. "It was a huge finger bone. And there, under the soil, was the rest of the hand. So we dug further, and found an arm. The whole limb was over two feet long! As you can imagine, all this digging took one hell of a long time. Still, we kept at it. Nobody, as far as we know, has ever before found a giant skeleton. We followed the shoulder bone along till we came to the skull—"

"Which we've just excavated." Roper had stepped in. "Fascinating. Worms or maggots had long since gobbled down its brain—"

"Roper!" exclaimed Petal. "Must you really say such disgusting things when we're eating?"

"Why not, mother? That's how nature works. Anyway, because the jaw had come loose I was able to get inside the skull and clean the soil out of it. You can sit down in there. Imagine! A dead giant's head! A bone room!"

"I helped with the digging," said Lucy, "but I won't go in there. Just looking into the empty eye-sockets makes me shiver."

"It's just bones," said Roper. "The same as we've got in our own bodies, except bigger."

"A lot bigger," said Lasker. "It's unnatural. I can sense the evil emanations lurking around it."

"But we still haven't mentioned the most interesting thing," said Red. "There was a hole in the front of the skull about half an inch round. And in the cavity itself was a chunk of metal a little smaller than the hole. The worms hadn't eaten that! It seems reasonable to suppose the metal object made the hole."

"Yes," said Roper. "Could the giants have had a weapon that could fire a piece of metal right through bone? Why not? Other artefacts we and other people have found suggest a degree of sophistication in designing and making things that's far in advance of anything our culture's capable of."

"If Roper's right," said Lasker, "and one giant killed another one with a powerful weapon, that only goes to prove they weren't perfect, like some Ranters want us to believe. No, they did wicked things. Which explains why they're in Hell."

"Lasker, why do you never listen to anything I say?" said Roper wearily. "To believe that some of the giants were violent is one thing. To say the whole race is now in Hell is irrational. There's no necessary connection between those propositions."

"On the contrary," said Lasker, "the Barrens must be explained."

"I don't disagree with that. But, as far as Barrens are concerned, we've no facts to go on. In the absence of facts, we can't construct any theories."

"Could Jewel and I see this metal object?" enquired Thorn.

"Of course," said Red. "I'll pop out and get it."

He got up and went out of the room. He came back with a stubby chunk of metal and dropped it with a metallic thump on the wooden tabletop.

"It's lead," he observed.

Thorn stroked the object with his fingertips, then stood aside for Jewel.

The girl debated briefly. Caution said: do nothing! Do not reveal your powers! But curiosity, the desire to know, drew her towards the thing. It lay there, blunt and black, issuing a mute

171

challenge. And there were other motivations. Matt Tuckett had impugned her youth. As for Roper, he annoyed her with his assumption that abstract reasoning was the only way to the truth. Jewel might be fifteen, but she knew better than that.

Surrendering to temptation, she laid her hands on the ugly lump and let her eyelids drop.

Instantly, she became the focal centre of the room. Furniture, crockery, cutlery, people all arranged themselves around her. No one was eating now. Everyone gazed at this dark-haired, slight figure as she communed with lead and, through it, the Dark Time.

"What's she doing, Mam?" whispered July, clutching at May's arm, awed by this girl not much older than herself.

"Shh!" hissed May, and put her arm around her daughter as if to protect her from something. "Wait and see!" she whispered back.

Even Roper, the great sceptic, couldn't take his eyes away. This girl was so focussed, so absolute in her concentration, that to disturb her was unthinkable.

At last she opened her eyes. Matt was sitting opposite. Just for a moment, it struck him, she seemed absent from her own eyes; then she was back behind them again.

"It's a *bullet*," she said. "It was fired from a weapon that fitted the hand, called a *gun*. You pulled a metal hook known as a *trigger* with your finger, set off a controlled explosion that shot the bullet down a short metal tube called a *barrel*. It was so deadly it frightens me to think of it. That's all I can tell you."

"How do you know this?" asked Red.

"I just know. It's an ability I have. I've only just discovered it. Don't ask me how it works, or where it came from."

"You mean – you're a Syb?" asked Petal.

"No. A seer I met told me I might be a Magian. I now believe that's what I am – for what the name's worth."

"A Magian," said Matt. "But you're just a young girl . . ."

"Yes," said Jewel, and smiled at him. "And completely inexperienced in the wicked ways of the world."

Matt grinned. "I apologise if I offended you."

"Apology accepted. But we ought to return to eating, before this stew gets cold. I'd like some more, if that's possible."

"I've heard of Magians," began Lasker, when they were all settled again.

"You would have," said Roper who, now that Jewel's act was over, had decided she was some sort of fairground performer, and was kicking himself (mentally, that is) for allowing her charisma (which was real enough) to trick him into falling for a hoary confidence trick.

"They're very rare," Lasker went on, ignoring his nephew, "and they can do amazing things."

"There's nothing at all amazing about what Jewel's just said. Red told her our theory, and all she did was embroider it with some words we'd never heard before. A clever trick, a nice performance; she has presence, I grant her that. She'd do well in a fairground show – which, very probably, is where she perfected her skills. I'll happily admit to being impressed by her act. But it was an act, no more than that."

"It was real enough," said Lasker. "This girl is the genuine article. Listen, I've seen a Magian in action once before, and I know. It was in Lowmoor about six years ago. There'd been a murder, but the Headman couldn't decide which of five suspects was the killer. So he called in this Magian – Querne Rasp, such a queer name I'm not likely to forget it. So there she was, in front of Lowmoor Council and about half the settlement, with these five suspects – four men and a woman. What she did was place her fingertips on the forehead of each of them in turn, and close her eyes and concentrate – like Jewel with that bullet. It was all done in silence, but everyone said afterwards that they sensed the power in her. When she'd gone round them, she pointed to one of the men and said: 'This is the man who did it. He's ready to confess.' Then she simply walked away. And what do you know? The man fell on his knees and confessed there and then. They hanged him the following week."

"That's an excellent story, Uncle," said Roper easily. "But as a proof of occult powers, it hardly gets off the ground. What in fact it demonstrates is the power of suggestion. The killer firmly believed this woman would find out the truth. That's why he lost his nerve and gave himself away. She fingered him, he confessed."

Lasker groaned. "Now who's guilty of not listening? You may be brilliantly clever, Roper, with flying machines and suchlike, but your head's as thick as this." He rapped his knuckles on the table.

Thorn had listened to the argument with mounting irritation. Jewel had found Roper in the long grass of the field and now he was daring to criticise her. He said: "Jewel is a Magian, Roper. If you'd seen her do what I have, you wouldn't doubt the fact."

"Well, you're bound to support her, Thorn. You're her friend, after all. But please don't get me wrong," he said to Jewel. "There's nothing personal in what I say. I'm very grateful for what both of you have done for me."

"Nothing personal!" said Thorn. "That's not how it seems to me."

"It's all right, Thorn," said Jewel, laying her hand on his arm. "I understand what Roper means. He sees the world in a certain way, and whatever doesn't fit with his view he rejects."

"You've got it," said Roper. "Facts! That's what I trust!"

"What would it take to prove to you I am what I say I am?"

"Prove it? Conclusively? I don't see how you could."

"Don't you? What if I was to do something you think impossible – like mending the break in your leg?"

"Mend my leg? What with? Potions and poultices? The leg will heal in its own time and just as quickly without them."

"No. Here and now. Using nothing but my mind."

Roper stared at her. As her eyes held his, burning with a dark light so intense as to be daunting, he found his certainty wavering. Was there a chance he could be wrong?

"Very well. Do it."

"And you'll admit you were wrong about me if I succeed?"

"I'll have to, won't I? Eat humble pie, as they say."

Thorn leant towards her and started to whisper in her ear, but she looked at him and he stopped. Then she got up from her seat and walked to the end of the table. Kneeling down beside Roper, she placed her hands on his suspended limb and once more closed her eyes.

People had stopped eating again. The air seemed charged

with silence, as if it was something you could reach out and touch, like wood or stone. Once again, Jewel gathered the room and its contents about her, giving them form and consequence.

She knew how to do this now. She sent probing filaments down through her fingers into the limb. Some pierced this bone, some that. They gathered at the broken edges. The fracture was a tender space waiting to be filled.

The broken bone wasn't a dead thing like a giant's skeleton. It was alive, it could grow. She sensed its inner desire to be whole. Left to themselves, over time, these edges would grow together again. So, in order to mend them, she must speed that process up. She probed the bone, and slowly, she understood its being. To the eye, a bone appeared to be a single, settled thing; but eyes couldn't see everything, eyes could be deceived. Bones were made up of tiny parts, *cells*, that could multiply themselves and join together mysteriously. She poured the virtue of her power into the cells of the broken edges, prompting them to quicken, multiply, bridge the aching space.

The work was intricate, and Jewel was already tired from the day, but she must not fail in this, she must not botch the task.

Time passed. No one spoke. Roper looked down at the kneeling girl. He felt no pain in his leg, was aware of what was happening as a kind of busy tingling, as if countless bees – infinitely tiny and completely fanatical – were working on the construction of an unseen honeycomb. Astonishment grew in him. The leg was mending, he was sure of it. Pallid and drawn, Jewel's face showed the strain of the undertaking, and he felt ashamed of doubting her, wanted to reach out and touch her. He didn't – to disturb her concentration might imperil the operation.

And yet, at the same time, nothing that was happening challenged his picture of the world. There's no magic in this process, he said to himself. It's a fact, like other facts, to be absorbed, made sense of. But he *had* learnt something new: that some minds, rare minds, might possess abilities quite beyond the ordinary.

Call the girl a Magian then – a name as good as any other. For he was firmly of the opinion that new things must have a name – like his own Airbird.

And if the girl could do this, what else could she achieve? His mind reeled.

At last, Jewel withdrew into herself and opened her eyes. She was looking at Roper's leg – but from the outside only now. She knew that the break was good. He would need no convalescence. He could stand, walk, run, fly – break it again, if he wanted.

She felt a sense of triumph: she had proved Roper wrong. But what had she done? Not to *him*, but to *herself*? Everything was changed now. She wasn't the same person she'd been a little while before. The world's weight had suddenly descended onto her shoulders, and she sagged under the burden of the unknown as never before.

This was no good. She must get up.

But she couldn't – not yet.

"Are you all right?" asked Roper.

"Just tired," she said. "It's taken a lot out of me. But your leg's mended now."

"Yes, I know. Thank you, Jewel. You *are* a Magian, after all!" He leant forward and gave her a quick kiss on the cheek.

Then: "Red!" he shouted. "Get me out of these damned splints!"

Red came and looked down at his brother. "You're all right now?" he asked unbelievingly.

"Never better. Get a move on!"

Perplexed, Red began to untie the cords that held the splints.

Only now, laboriously, did Jewel get to her feet. Then the whole family was crowding noisily round. She was hugged and showered with thanks as never before in her life. She conjured up a wan smile.

But all she could think was: what have I done? What have I done?

SECOND INTERFACE

THE MISSING

Racky Jagger was sitting in the bar of the Water Rat. On the table in front of him was an almost-empty pot of ale.

Without warning, he raised his fist and banged it down on the table.

"Damn!" he cried.

The pot jumped into the air. Mags Topliss behind the bar and half a dozen customers shot looks of surprise at him.

Racky ignored them. At this moment, he hated himself.

All the way down from Roydsal, straddling Bumper's strong back, he'd thought about Thorn and the way he'd treated the lad: contemptibly, despicably. What kind of a father betrayed his son to the likes of the Spetch brothers? How could he have brought himself to do it?

Querne wanted the crystals, of course, and what she wanted she must have. She had one from way back, a yellowy-amber one, though exactly how she'd come by it she wasn't prepared to say. Until recently she'd assumed it was the only one in existence; but then the Spetch twins had mentioned this bluish stone they'd lately acquired. Querne was an old friend of theirs, so rather than simply ask them for it – or take it by force, which she could easily have done – she'd got Racky to propose a trade. Was there anything special they wanted? Well, said the brothers, there *was* something – a key. But it was at Minral How, and there was no way Crane Rockett would voluntarily give it up.

Now Querne knew all about Thorn because Racky had told her about him in a moment of weakness, knew also why he was perfect for the job of getting the key. It wouldn't have been too difficult for her to get the key herself: even a ghoul like Deacon Brace was no match for a Magian. But no: Querne had instead proposed the kidnap that would draw Thorn to Roydsal and put him into the brothers' power. All that was required to make the plan run smoothly was for Racky to betray his son.

Which was, of course, the real reason why Querne had thought it up. She loved to humiliate people, to savour the pain she could inflict. He'd seen her do it to others; now Racky's turn had come. For, long before this, she'd made him her slave. Not only that. In Racky's feelings towards Thorn, Querne had sensed an ambivalence that Racky himself had only lately come to understand. Irrational though the reaction was, Racky had long resented Thorn for being son to another man. That Racky believed Thorn to be *his* son counted for little: *Thorn* had always believed himself the son of Davis Jack. By this long-running traitorous act of allegiance, Thorn had denied Racky the substance of fatherhood.

So the plan was set in motion. Racky, to his shame, had played out his pivotal role and it had worked perfectly – the kidnap, the yellow feather, the invitation to Racky to guide the Lowmoor search party. The only drawback was the inclusion in the party of Thorn's uncle; Racky would have to get rid of him.

But then, unexpectedly, things had got complicated. On the morning he was summoned to the Council meeting to look at the feather, a carrier pigeon had arrived with a message from Querne. She'd discovered, a bare week before, the existence of a *third* crystal – a ruby one – in Wyke's Treasury. She'd gone in disguise to Wyke to find the settlement in a state of ferment: the crystal had vanished – snatched in a daring raid the night before her arrival by person or persons unknown. So, Querne now asked: had Racky by chance heard anything? He must secure that crystal too for her, if that were possible.

Racky knew, of course, who that unknown person was. But since Thorn hadn't placed the crystal in Lowmoor's Treasury, the lad must still have it. Racky took himself off to the Floods' house and, finding no one in, made a rapid search of it. To no effect: the lad had taken care to hide the stone.

What could Racky do now? Taylor Flood's sudden illness cut the party down to two: that was good. But Racky could see that Thorn didn't trust him an inch; useless to ask the lad point-blank about the crystal, he'd be bound to clam up. Besides, Racky had his own agenda to pursue: he wanted to test Thorn out, to find out what he was made of while trying to win his trust. This would take time.

Then had come Judy Bridge: Blacky's death, Denny's fall – neither event according to plan. That was when Racky had fixed on a new strategy. He'd trap Thorn at Whispering Oak; Thorn would have no option but to give in to his demands; Racky would go on to Roydsal alone, sweet-talk the twins into giving him *their* crystal – the blue one – liberate Haw

181

and go back with brother and sister to Lowmoor for Thorn's stone.

Hah! Men and their fancy plans . . . destiny had a way of playing merry hell with them.

A single positive element shone out in all this mess. Far from being the milksop that Davis Jack would have sired, Thorn had turned out everything that Racky had wished for; he was the son of Racky's soul. Hadn't he met every challenge in Judy Wood without flinching? Hell! He'd even managed to escape from the Echo Hole, something that the older man had thought impossible. Almost, Racky resented Thorn's success in proving himself. Sometimes, snatching a look at his son as they tramped or made camp, Racky had had to catch his breath. In Thorn's compact, sturdy body, in the firm set of his brow, in his quickness of hand and eye – yes, even in his ignorance of the world, his innocence – Racky had seen, as in a mirror, an image of his younger self. The self that had loved Thorn's mother.

This one positive had its bitter side, however. Racky – man in the middle, puppet-master, fiddle-diddler – was richly reaping where he'd sown: the guilt and anguish of treachery. Just as Querne had planned he should.

I'm my own worst enemy, Racky now told himself. I haven't betrayed my son once, I've betrayed him twice over. I ought to be made to swallow nails.

And Querne – Querne was the she-devil in his dreams. Racky had moments when he hated her as fiercely as he'd once loved Berry Jack, yet he could no more live without her than he could live without breathing. At least, he told himself, when I've acquired the Sybs' crystal, Querne will have three out of the four – and how grateful she'll be then! And he began to imagine the form her gratitude would take . . .

This was no good. He was sitting here, drinking and brooding, when he ought to be making arrangements for his crossing to Nettle Island.

He got up, knocked back the little that remained in his pot, and went over to the bar. "Same again, Mags," he said.

"Something bothering you, Racky?"

"You could say that," he said.

She smiled, but said nothing. She knew better than to ask what it was.

He said: "I need passage to Nettle Island. Is Lacky Dawes about? I thought I'd see him here."

"No. Truth is, he's disappeared. And not just Lacky – his crew and his boat as well. Vanished off the face of the earth – or rather, the Dam."

"Is that so?"

"It's so. The last time I saw him was a couple of nights ago. He was here with Stocky and Spindle. He agreed to ferry three young people across the Dam. They set out next morning, but the boat never came back."

Suddenly there was an urgency about Racky's questions. "Did people go out looking for them?"

"They did. Gimpy Briggs and Rab Barraclough both took their boats out. But they didn't find a thing."

"Could Lacky have tied up at the island?"

"Rab sailed by the jetty, but Lacky's boat wasn't there."

Racky rubbed his stubbled jaw. He suddenly felt hugely weary. "It sounds as though they went down."

"It very much looks that way. But Lacky knows these waters like the back of his hand. And there was nothing in the weather – it was a perfect day. It doesn't make sense."

Racky didn't answer. He took a deep draught of ale. He seemed to Mags to have aged; all of a sudden to have shrunk.

Time passed. He said at last: "Which of the other boatmen do you recommend, Mags?"

"To be honest, there isn't much to choose between them. Gimpy, perhaps."

"I'll need a room tonight."

"It's yours for the asking, Racky."

Racky took himself off to talk money with Gimpy Briggs.

"Racky Jagger!" cried Rosy Puckfloss. "You're a sight for sore eyes! Sit down, sit down."

Racky sat. The sisters flopped into their chairs. Zinny Muffin hovered in the background, watchfully. Racky thought: there's something about that woman . . . Something in her eyes . . . I wouldn't trust her an inch.

"Racky Jagger on Nettle Island! How many years has it been?"

"Too many, Rosy, to remember."

"I remember," said Lily. "Five. But you didn't intend to call. A squall blew up while you were crossing the Dam. Lacky put in and you stayed the night while the wind blew itself out."

"Your memory's good, Lily."

"Lily's trouble," said Rosy, "is she doesn't drink enough of the Special. There's no better medicine for forgetting in the world."

"Then I'd better take a few bottles with me when I go. But speaking of Lacky, I'm told he and his boat have disappeared. He was ferrying a party across the Dam, but never got back to Damside."

"Nor did he, Racky. And what's more, he never will."

"Listen, Rosy. The Spetch brothers and I have a certain interest in those travellers. I'd like to know what happened."

"Greed happened, Racky. Lacky and his men set on their passengers to rob them. Two went overboard. Lacky was trying to run them down when the Great Pike appeared. It capsized the boat, swallowed Lacky and his mate, and brought the two survivors here."

"Who were the two survivors?"

"A young man called Thorn Jack and a girl – Jewel Ranson."

"And the older woman, Rainy?"

"Dead. Went down with the boat."

"And the pike saved them," mused Racky. "I thought that fish would be dead by now."

"That fish will be alive when the rest of us are dust."

"So . . . what happened to Thorn and Jewel?"

Rosy's eyes narrowed. Racky had seen that look before. She said: "We fed them, entertained them, gave them beds for the night. Next day they stole our boat. How's that for ingratitude?"

How's that for half a story, thought Racky. But he said, "So they're safe, at any rate?"

"There was a storm after they left."

"I saw something," broke in Lily.

"Saw what?" demanded Racky.

"I saw the boat drop from a great height in a kind of water-fall. It smashed to pieces on stone."

"And Thorn and Jewel?" he said sharply.

"I didn't see them," she said.

"Serve them right if they drowned," said Rosy, in a voice that dripped poison.

"I don't think so," said Lily. "Something tells me they survived. Is that why you came, Racky? To find about those two?"

"Partly," he replied, reassured by what she'd said.

"There's something more, then?"

"To speak plain, I'm here as Querne's representative."

"Querne Rasp?" exclaimed Rosy.

"What other Quernes do you know?"

Neither Syb answered. One Querne, they thought, was more than enough. Racky went on, "It's come to Querne's notice that there's an object on this island – a crystal. I assume you have it in your keeping. Querne is eager to acquire it. I'll pay you well for it."

"Our crystal . . ." said Rosy. "Now how did she know of that?"

"Querne has ways of finding things out." He didn't add: ways beyond the reach of a Syb – but both women caught the unspoken implication.

The Sybs looked at one another. Then Rosy said: "Of course we'll sell it to you."

For a time they talked money. The Sybs did not prove difficult. Agreement was soon reached.

Rosy got to her feet. "Come, Racky. We'll fetch it together."

Racky understood the meaning of the invitation: there was to be no subterfuge. The Sybs were afraid of Querne. They'd deal openly with him.

He followed the old women; Zinny Muffin walked behind him. The Sybs kindled a couple of lamps, then turned down a passageway that drove into the bank against which their house was built. Rosy unlocked a door with a key on a ring she took from a pocket.

The room was a glory hole, but hardly an interesting one. Racky's eye moved quickly over its clutter of cast-off furniture and rugs and dusty flagons. On a battered old table stood a large black jar.

"It's in the jar," said Rosy. "Take it."

"This is a strange place to keep a precious thing," observed Racky.

"Precious it may be, but we can do nothing with it. Its secrets are beyond our reach."

This was candour indeed. Racky walked over to the table. He was on the point of lifting the lid when he stopped and stared at it.

"Have you handled this recently?"

"We haven't been in here for months."

"Someone else has. Give me a lamp."

Holding the lamp above the jar, he lifted the lid and looked inside.

"It's empty," he said.

"But – but it can't be!" cried Rosy.

She hurried to the table and craned her head over the jar.

"But – it's gone . . . !"

"Are you trying to make a fool out of me?" asked Racky coldly.

But even as he said this, he knew the Sybs were not. Their surprise, their consternation, were genuine enough.

Rosy turned to Zinny Muffin. "What do you know of this?"

"Nothing. I didn't even know about this crystal. And anyway, the room was locked."

"I believe her," said Lily.

"Then who stole it?" said Racky.

"That girl, Jewel," said Lily slowly. "There was something about her."

"Something about her? What do you mean?"

"Now and again I got the feeling she was hiding something from me."

"Hiding what?"

"Herself – her true nature, funnily enough."

Racky Jagger didn't find it funny. Damn and double damn, he thought. Two crystals have now got away from me. Thorn has one, Jewel the other. Querne won't like this one little bit.

11

IN THE WHITE
GIANT'S SKULL

"This is Retty," said Lasker, scratching the rat beneath the jaw. "She's getting on now, very docile, easy to handle. You'll be fine with her."

"If you say so," said Jewel.

Thorn was already in the saddle (on a stout buck called Ticker), so were Lucy, Roper and Red. Thorn, unlike Jewel, had been on ratback before: every Norgreen child was taught to ride at an early age. He looked on with some amusement as, with extravagant care, she eased herself into the saddle and felt for the stirrups with her feet, then sat there rigidly, clutching the rein as if this thin cord was all that stood between herself and catastrophe.

"I'll ride behind you," said Lucy, "but I'm sure you'll be all right."

The little party set off. Roper led them; then came Thorn; after him Jewel, Lucy and Red in that order. As they passed down a defile between two close-set blocks of stone, Thorn said to Roper: "These stones: what *are* they?"

"*Were* they, rather. We've two possible explanations, but either or both could be wrong. They might be the remains of

189

an industrial structure or installation. Alternately, they might be remnants of an old religious site – a place where rituals of some sort were performed in the Dark Time. Maybe once they were arranged in a significant pattern. Anyway, they form a convenient barrier between our house and kitchen garden and nature in her less agreeable moods. Wilf chanced on the place one day – oh, forty years ago – and fell in love with it straight-away. My grandfather has always harboured unconventional tastes. He was fed up with settlement life, wanted to plough his own furrow. He named the house Stony Close. My father was a child then. Our branch of the Tuckett tribe has lived here ever since."

For once, Jewel was listening with no more than half an ear. Instead, she was intent on getting used to Retty's gait. The rat was going along at no more than walking pace, but *walking* was an idea far more appropriate to creatures possessed of two long legs than an animal which sported decidedly short ones. *Slouching* seemed a better word for what the rat was doing. As Retty pitter-pattered along, belly almost scraping the earth, haunches rhythmically pumping, she swayed from side to side, and Jewel was rocked this way and that.

Thorn had warned her about this. "Go with the rhythm," he'd advised, "don't attempt to resist it. That's a sure recipe for saddle-sickness, which isn't pleasant. If you *do* start to feel sick, say at once you want to stop. Don't wait till it happens. If there's one thing that riles a rat, it's getting sicked on. Rats remember and they'll never let you on their backs again."

She wished he hadn't told her that. For now, of course, instead of enjoying her first ride, as she might conceivably have done, she was obsessively monitoring her stomach for signs of sickness. Did thinking about being sick make it likelier to happen? She suspected that it did. Still, Retty did seem docile, as Lasker had promised.

Retty: so named on account of her red-brown pelt. Adventurously Jewel took a hand off the rein and stroked the animal's thick fur. Straightaway Retty threw her head back, unbalancing her rider. Jewel slipped sideways in the saddle, but with her free hand she managed to grab the pommel and steady herself. There'd be no more experiments like *that* for a little while . . .

Instead she tried to concentrate on the passing scenery. They'd left the hilltop and the scattered blocks of stone behind now, and were travelling down a bare, stone-strewn gully.

The trip had been Roper's idea. "Now that we've described it," he'd said, "you *must* come and see our skeleton before you leave." Then added, like a barker drumming up trade outside a booth: "It's a once-in-a-lifetime opportunity, folks! How about it? We could go tomorrow morning."

She and Thorn were both strongly tempted, but they'd felt the need to get on the road, and they said so. Roper was plainly disappointed; he wanted to show his gratitude, and they weren't going to let him.

Then he'd said: "What if we ride down? Wilf's Clough isn't far. Afterwards the three of us can ride to Minral How. Even with a delayed start you'll get there faster than if you went on foot. How does that sound?"

"But I've never ridden a rat!" Jewel had exclaimed, realising too late that she'd conceded ground to him.

191

"Nothing to it. Lasker will fit you up with an even-tempered beast. You'll never have cause to look back, I guarantee it. Well?"

They'd hummed and hawed a little more, but the proposal made sense and they *did* want to see the skeleton, so in the end they'd agreed.

And here they were.

Thorn was speaking again: "Can I ask you something, Roper? I wanted to last night, but you and Lasker started arguing and then Jewel cured your leg."

"Ask me what?"

"About the Airbird. How did you come up with such a machine – out of nowhere, I mean? It wouldn't even have crossed my mind that human beings might learn to fly."

Roper laughed. "It wouldn't have crossed mine either if I hadn't found a giant version of the Airbird three years ago."

"A giant version!"

"Yes. It was a wreck, of course, badly damaged. Its wing-fabric had long since rotted away, but the frame was made of some light alloy that had survived surprisingly well. It was in an out-of-the-way place, and had probably been abandoned where it came down. But what was bad luck for some giant turned out to be good luck for me. I've always been interested in making things – in inventions. I have a forge here, and I also deal with the foundry at Lowmoor settlement, so raw materials aren't a problem. I've also had a thing about flying since I was a child. I used to have these dreams in which I'd take off through the roof of the house and go drifting across the landscape like a bird.

"So, when I found this giant-sized Airbird I saw immediately what it was. I took measurements and began to construct my own machine on the same pattern – human-sized, of course. I built a prototype, Airbird 1, and tested it, then went on from there. Red and Dad help out, but everything takes time. I've flown many times, and so have Dad and Lucy and Red – though not as often as me. The machine that crashed yesterday, Airbird 11, was a new model – lighter, faster, more manoeuvrable than anything I've built before. Or so I'd hoped, but obviously things didn't work out that way. Still, I'll get there. I always do."

They were now dropping down into Wilf's Clough itself. Wind-blown hawthorn and alder and stunted oaks dotted the land, and they heard the breeze sighing as they rode beneath a bush.

Along the valley bottom, water had gouged out a route, and the streambed was pebbled with grey stones.

"Tucketts have always come here for picnics," Roper explained, "so it's surprising none of us spotted the bone before my sharp-eyed cousin. But the ground moves hereabouts from time to time, so maybe some tremor pushed it up to the surface."

The excavation lay on the lee side of a gnarled alder bush. They dismounted and hitched their animals to a weatherworn root.

The exposed bones of the giant – hand, arm, shoulder, skull, the upper part of the spinal column – lay as the diggers had uncovered them. The skeleton seemed frozen in the bizarre act of rising up out of the earth, as if half-resurrected, perhaps with every intention of confronting its killer. Except its killer too was dead, long dead.

They were standing above the hand bones, which were laid out flat and in apple-pie order. The surrounding flesh and sinews might have been newly whisked away.

"He was buried on his back," said Roper, "with this arm at an angle to his side. We want, of course, to go on digging, uncover the whole of him – if a whole body's there. It will take a long time. Anyway, according to my calculations, based on the proportions of our bodies and assuming his will be the same, he would have been about six feet tall – so more probably male than female."

He paused, then went on: "The hand, from fingertip to wrist, is over seven inches long: which makes its length that of the tallest amongst us. Imagine: this man could have stood you on his palm and held you up to his face! You could have stared him in the eye – if you were strong-willed enough. He could have crushed you in his fist."

"Except he's dead, and we're alive," observed Thorn.

Roper laughed.

He set off towards the head. Jewel and Thorn followed. Lucy and Red came after them. Stretching the length of the trench, the bones glimmered against the black soil.

They passed the elbow, the shoulder blade. Now they stood looking down at the skull in its deep, grim grave. The lower jaw had fallen away from the upper, giving the skull a vandalised look. The eye-sockets, their soft orbs long since rotted or eaten away, stared up but saw nothing.

"There, in the teeth," said Thorn. "What's that?"

"Some sort of metallic stuff," said Roper. "Evidently, they had a way of treating teeth that were going rotten, so that their owners could keep them."

194

But what drew Jewel's gaze was the hole at the front of the skull where the bullet had passed through it, leaving radiating cracks. Why had the man been killed? Why?

"I'm going down there," she said.

Thorn turned to her in surprise. Rather you than me! he thought.

The ladder was on the far side. The others looked on with interest as Jewel climbed down to the floor of the trench.

The soil was muddy, but planks had been laid in a rough circle round the skull to form a makeshift walkway – as if the skull were some rare fairground attraction that you had to pay to see. (As it would be, if a canny man got hold of it, she thought.)

She walked round the bulge of the skull, trailing one hand along the up-curving bone like a playful child. Then, without hesitation, she got down on the planks and crawled through the toothed jaw into the skull's vacant dome.

She couldn't stand up here, but she could lie down. So she lay on her back with her knees bent upwards, staring through the right-hand eye-socket at the portion of sky floating up there beyond it. Viewed from outside, the skull bone had gleamed white; but now she was inside it, it had darkened to deep grey, and the blue almost-circle seemed a bright but impossibly distant hatchway of hope.

Then she closed her eyes, and the black that replaced the blue in her field of non-vision shone faintly with the retained after-glow of the heavens.

"That's one strange girl," said Roper, as they gazed down on the skull.

"Wherever did you find her?" said Lucy to Thorn.

"Jewel? I didn't. It was she who found me."

Lucy smiled. "I don't know what your relationship is, but I'll tell you this. You'll never find one like her as long as you live."

Thorn considered this, then said: "We're chance companions, no more. Circumstances have brought us together. It's as simple as that."

Lucy laughed. "Nothing's simple between men and women," she said.

"There you have me at a disadvantage," he said.

"If you say so."

Jewel came crawling out of the skull. She climbed the ladder and rejoined the waiting group.

"What did you see?" asked Red, speaking for the four of them.

"I was behind the dead man's eyes. A man was pointing a gun at me. His face was a mixture of hatred and pain. Then he fired, and the bullet went into my brain. You see, I'd planned to meet his wife and take her away from him. But she'd confessed to her husband, and instead of her, *he* came. Then he brought me here and buried my dead body in the ground."

In silence they remounted their rats and rode away.

They were halfway to Stony Close before Thorn spoke.

"Roper, remember last night's talk about the Dark Time?"

"I remember."

"Well, something's always puzzled me, and seeing that skeleton has brought it into my mind again. Why don't our people have any true memories of the giants? There are myths and stories about them, sure, but they're always, well, fantastic, not tales of believable beings something like us except bigger."

Roper thought for a while, then said: "That's a very good question, and it's one I've asked myself. Trouble is, neither I nor anyone else can answer it with certainty. And certainly not Ranters and those who take their ideas from them. As a people, our memories only reach back so far: three generations, four at the most, then you run into a blank wall. A sort of curtain comes down and closes us off from our own past."

"Yes," agreed Thorn. "The Ranters say we have no past. Go back a handful of generations, and that's when we were created. But you don't believe that, do you?"

"No. I can't accept that the way we live – in settlements, with husbandry, trade and tamed rats and all the rest of it – could have developed in such a short time. I suppose the simplest theory is that there *is* no mystery: we don't have the means to hold on to our history. If more of us could read and write, it might be very different. But hardly anybody can. Even *I've* never learnt."

"Hmm . . ."

Roper chuckled. "Not very exciting, is it? Humans prefer exciting ideas to dull ideas, but for that very reason duller ideas may be preferable."

"What if our ancestors *did* share the world with the giants, but then something happened that caused them to forget?"

"Well, there are Ranters who preach that God blanked out our forbears' memories. Take God out of it, as I would, and you're left with the notion that some kind of mass shock occurred. But we've no evidence of that. *Evidence*, that's the problem, Thorn. Didn't I say last night that in the absence of evidence all you can do is speculate?"

Yes, you did, thought Thorn.

There seemed nothing more to be said.

Later that morning, three riders set out from the house a second time. Roper had promised Jewel and Thorn that he'd accompany them, but it was Red who rode with them.

"You're better with machines," he'd told his brother to his face. "If it comes to physical stuff, I'll be more useful than you."

Accepting the logic of this, Roper deferred to his half-brother. But as a token of his appreciation for what they'd done for him, Roper offered Ticker and Retty to Thorn and Jewel as outright gifts. The young people were touched, but said no: they'd no idea what the immediate future would bring, and so thought it better not to encumber themselves.

"All right," Roper had said, obviously disappointed.

But other gifts were forthcoming. Roper presented Thorn with a bow of metal – twice as powerful, he claimed, as one fashioned from mere wood. Thorn ran his fingers along its gleaming shaft: it was beautiful and deadly. Lucy took Jewel into her room and found her clothes and other items to replace the ones she'd lost in Roydsal Dam.

"Mother's always complaining I never throw anything away. Now I'm very glad I didn't!"

For Lucy was taller than Jewel, and what she was wearing now wouldn't have fitted the girl.

The three set out, peppered with goodbyes and good lucks, waving till they turned out of sight around a stone. At the last moment, in answer to some obscure prompting, Jewel had slipped the green crystal into her saddlebag.

"This is the way to travel!" said Thorn.

Jewel wasn't so sure. Though it was nice not to have a rucksack dragging on your shoulders, scoring red tracks in your skin, (their gear was packed in saddlebags), her bottom was uncomfortable already from the earlier ride. The smarting was mild as yet, but she knew it would get worse. She supposed she'd get used to it – but how long would that take? Or, put another way, how long before they reached the outer walls of Minral How?

"Mid-afternoon," suggested Red.

They rode west, reversing the route of the cart the day before; then turned north onto the Lowmoor road.

Around midday they came to a junction and turned off the Lowmoor road. The new road went to Butshaw and places beyond – and Harrypark, thought Jewel, thinking of Luke Gill.

She was glad to get down from the saddle and stretch her legs in the sun. Her joints had stiffened and her backside felt sore. But after a snack of cold cuts, pickle and bread she was ready to move again.

She began to think of Deacon Brace. That gaunt face, those bloodless lips . . . She'd shortly be face to face with the man who'd almost killed her in Harrypark and who would relish the opportunity to try a second time.

The sun was still high in the sky when Red reined in.

"There," he said, pointing straight ahead. "That's Minral How."

The house was a black clot set squat on the horizon. But as

they rode on, it grew till Thorn could distinguish its separate parts. It was like a settlement all to itself.

The stone wall that bounded the mansion looked in pretty good order. Few stones had fallen from it, and it reared black and forbidding. The house lay at its centre, a stony spider crouching at the heart of a man-made web.

"They say Crane Rockett has many enemies," said Red, "and that's why the house is so well-protected. At night, I'm told, guard-rats are released to roam the grounds. They kill anyone whose scent they're not trained to recognise. I've also heard there are pits and traps of various kinds – though that doesn't seem to make sense, for if there were, wouldn't the rats fall into them? Who knows what's truth and what's rumour?"

"How does Crane Rockett make his money?" asked Jewel.

"He owns the Lowmoor iron foundry."

"Is that right?" said Thorn. "I thought industries like that were always owned by the local guildsmen who work them?"

"Not in this case. It was Creel Rockett – Crane's father – who started the foundry up. He hired people to work for him and paid them a weekly wage."

"But wouldn't that mean that those who do the work don't reap the full rewards of the labour they put in?"

"You've got it, Thorn."

"What a bizarre idea."

"Bizarre it may be, but it's exactly what happens. And it's made the Rockett family rich – disgustingly rich. Rockett could buy and sell the Spetch brothers until they were dizzy."

"I can't imagine anybody wanting to buy *them*."

The outer walls of Minral How were set a little way from the road. As the three riders made their way down the connecting track, the walls grew taller above them. They were six feet high and built of stone. But at the end of the track was a section of wall no more than two feet high. In the days of the giants, this must have been a gateway. Human builders had bricked it up, and entry was now effected through an iron-barred gate. The gate was more than wide enough to admit the largest cart. Its uprights were tipped with spikes.

They came to the gate and dismounted. Jewel could have sworn her limbs creaked as she got down. She started to rub her bottom and winced. Oh dear, she thought, I've blisters there the size of saucepan lids.

The gate's identical halves were chained and padlocked in the centre. Inside the gateway on the left, a little way back from the track, stood a wooden guardhouse.

A man now emerged from the door. He wore a brown jerkin and trews. He came up to the gate and frowned at them through the bars.

"Who are you?"

"My name is Thorn Jack. My friends are Jewel Ranson and Red Tuckett."

"Red Tuckett? I've heard of him. But not you and her."

"That's as may be. I wish to speak with your master and mistress."

"You do, do you? Lots would like to speak to them, but they'll never get through this gate. And what do you want to speak about?"

"That, I'd rather tell them. But it's a matter of importance."

The gate-guard laughed. "That's what they all say. Right, I'll pass the message on, but I can't promise nothing."

He turned away and walked off towards the house, whose façade was largely obscured by shrubs and trees. Soon, he was gone from sight.

Some time later, distantly, they heard a bell toll thrice.

When the guard came back into view, another man was at his side: a gaunt man, a tall man, his legs so long he might have been walking on stilts. Jewel's lips shaped his name, but not a sound escaped from them.

12

BIG HOUSE, LITTLE HOUSE

Deacon Brace peered through the black bars of the gate at the supplicants. His cheek still bore the traces of Gilda Buckle's angry nails. Passing quickly over the two males, his gaze locked on Jewel.

"You!" He smiled frostily. "If my memory serves me correctly, our last chat ended in you taking a little swim."

"If *my* memory serves me correctly, the swim was your idea."

"You needed cooling down. *Have* you cooled down?"

"Let me in and you'll find out."

Deacon Brace laughed. It was the laughter of a skeleton, hollow and mirthless.

"It's nice to find you've kept your sense of humour. Or rather, it isn't."

"Look," said Jewel. "It's my friend who has business at this house, not me."

"Yes," said Thorn. "I'd like to speak to your master and mistress."

"What about?"

"I'd rather tell that to them."

"Tell me; *I'll* tell them."

"I can't do that. But I *can* say that the matter concerns Zak and Lanner Spetch."

"That pair of long-haired freaks? Then you're wasting my time. Mr Rockett and Miss Spurr have no interest in the Spetches."

"All I ask is that you pass my message on — that and my name: Thorn Jack. Let your master and mistress decide whether to see me or not."

"I will not. *I* decide who comes in and who stays out. You three stay out."

"But this is a matter of life and death!"

"Don't insult my intelligence."

"You *must* let me in, you *must*!"

"*Must? Must?* You've had a wasted journey. Tell that to those two clowns in their mausoleum on the hill."

The long-boned man twisted about and stalked away.

"Deacon Brace!" Thorn shouted. "Deacon Brace! Please come back!"

But Brace did not come back. Soon he disappeared from sight.

"Damn!" Thorn kicked out at the base of the gate in his frustration. It responded to his provocation with the faintest of rattles.

The gate-guard grinned. "Careful, lad, you'll hurt yourself!"

Then he went back into his hut.

Jewel, Thorn and Red walked back up the track, leading their rats. Red asked: "What are you going to do now?"

"I'm not leaving without talking to these people," said Thorn.

"You can't do that if you can't get in."

"We'll get in." This was Jewel.

Red would have laughed, if he hadn't seen this girl mend his brother's broken leg. But he had, so he didn't. He simply asked: "Have you a plan?"

"I have an idea. Whether it will work . . ."

"The padlock?" asked Thorn, recalling how she'd gained entry into the Sybs' locked room. "If you start to fiddle with that the guard will see you and raise the alarm."

"That's why I shan't touch it."

"What then?"

She smiled, and explained her idea. There followed a brief discussion. Then, keeping out of sight of the guardhouse window, she padded up to the left-hand extremity of the gate. Behind her went Thorn, his new bow strung and nocked.

The end upright was thick, but the inner ones were less so. Grasping the base of the bar next to the end, she relaxed and began to concentrate. After a time, the iron grew hot, and she was forced to let go.

"It's burning my hand!" she whispered, ruefully rubbing her inflamed skin.

"Then it's no good," he whispered back.

"No – wait. I've another idea."

She went back to Retty and took the green crystal, swaddled in its wrapping, from her pack. Now I know why I brought it with me, she thought. Creeping back to the gate, she took the wrapping off the stone. This time, instead of grasping the bar, she held the crystal against it. She concentrated . . . The heart of the crystal began to glow . . .

The results surprised the girl herself. Not only did the crystal focus her power, it seemed to augment it. In no time at all the bar glowed red, then white-hot like a lightning-spear. Then, turning molten, it began to weep iron tears that dripped onto the earth and gathered in a puddle. Soon the bar had gone. Jewel had felt the heat on her face and hands, but remained unscathed. She moved on to the next bar. Soon that, too, lay liquified.

Jewel moved back from the gate, slipped away to Retty and repacked the precious crystal.

Now Red joined Thorn. Stepping carefully over the still-hot puddle of metal, they squeezed through the gap in the gate and sidled up to the guardhouse.

Red crashed through the door, startling the guard, who was sitting in a chair drawn up to the window. But before he could grab his pike from where it leant against the wall, Thorn was in through the door and menacing him with his bow.

"Sorry," said Thorn, "but we're going to have to tie you up."

The guard began to curse as Red roped him to his chair.

"Carry on like that," said Red, "and I'll gag you. Tightly."

The guard obligingly shut up.

Taking down the keys that hung on hooks on the guardhouse wall, Jewel unlocked the gates, fetched the rats and tethered them to a rail outside the hut.

"Red," she said, "I want you to stay here. Keep an eye on the guard and look after the rats."

"But Jewel," he complained, "I shall miss the main action!"

"Perhaps. But I've already lost one friend. I don't want to lose another. Please stay here. If neither of us comes back, turn around and go home."

He started to argue, but she cut him short: there was no time to waste.

Leaving their bows and quivers behind, Thorn and Jewel set off. Shows of weapons, they reasoned, hardly suggested friendly intentions, and Thorn was intent on trying to win his case with words, not arrows.

Red felt useless as he watched them out of sight.

Minral How had extensive grounds. Back in the Dark Time, all this would have been gardens, thought Jewel. Now it was wilderness. Weeds flourished, grasses sprang up, choking other plants. Several trees had blown down, and lay rotting amidst the chaos. Shrubs had rioted, pushing beyond their allotted limits, interweaving and tangling their branches; ivy and other creepers battened on less mobile growth; flowers had been made to fight to hold a patch of ground and only the strong had survived, seeding and reseeding themselves over the long years. To keep open a way through was as much as the inhabitants of the house could achieve.

The track wound erratically through the undergrowth. Then it forked. They chose the left-hand trail. Passing between a beech tree and an ancient sycamore, they emerged on the top step of what in the Dark Time had been a flight of stone steps. It was still passable: at the left-hand end, dirt and stones had been tipped between the steps and tamped down, forming a steep ramp.

Minral How stood before them. Mentally, Jewel compared Crane Rockett's house with that of the Spetch brothers. Roydsal was plainly the more ancient. It was also of a piece.

Minral How fell obviously into three separate parts, and looked somewhat incongruous. Its central and original block was two storeys high with a roof of thick slates. On either side of a central door were matching windows with stone lintels and mullions. Above each window was set another, with a third above the door. To either side of this original block a wing had been added. The east wing had two storeys, but was set back some way behind the line of the original building. A pebbly crust had been added to it, but large patches had dropped off to reveal the red brick it had covered, so that the frontage was scabbed and blistered as if with a lurid disease. The roof had caved in, leaving a gaping black hole. In sharp contrast, the west wing had only one storey, so that its roof reached little more than halfway up the side of the central block. Its façade held the line with its neighbour. Built of the same stone as the original house, it didn't look quite so out of place as the east wing.

Each wing had its own door, making a total of three in all. The giant flight of steps pointed towards the central door, but, as Jewel and Thorn reached ground level and went forward, it became clear that the track they were on wasn't going to take them there. For now, veering right, it darted towards the west wing.

And – success! – reached it.

Here, side by side, stood a rattery and a carriage-house, their tiny red bricks providing a sharp and ugly contrast with the mansion's blackened stone. Westwards, a second track burst out of the undergrowth. So, had they taken the other fork, it too would have brought them here. Or so, at least, Jewel assumed.

A stout wooden door filled the doorway of the wing. But no giant would now go through it. Down in its right-hand corner a rectangular hole had been sawn or chopped out to accommodate a second door of human dimensions. It was a strategy familiar to Thorn and Jewel from Roydsal.

The bell they'd heard ringing dangled beside this door. Thorn stepped up, undid the tied-up clapper and rang it three times.

After a time, the door swung open.

"What is it now—" a voice began. Then stopped, as its owner (a short, mild-looking, middle-aged fellow now going bald) took in the pair standing outside. "Who are—" he began again.

But Thorn pushed past him and Jewel followed hard on his heels.

"Hey!" said the man feebly.

"I'm here to see Crane Rockett and Briar Spurr," Thorn announced.

"Get out!" spluttered the man.

"Be reasonable: I've only just come in," returned Thorn. "My name is Thorn Jack. My friend's name is Jewel Ranson. I'd be grateful if you'd tell your master and mistress that we're here."

Jewel was looking around the room. An unremarkable space, it was paved with square tiles that were the colour of dried blood. A hearth occupied the middle of the wall to their right, but it had nothing of the dusty grandeur of the marble hearths that featured in Roydsal's better rooms. The single item of giant furniture was a table on the left – a plain, unbeautiful object, but sturdy enough. Time had not yet brought it to its knees.

What the room had most of were doors: four of them – five, if you added the one through which they'd entered the house.

Recovering something of his poise, the servant said pompously: "The master and mistress see no one without an appointment."

"Then make us one – for *now*. What I have to say won't wait."

The man considered his options.

"Very well. Wait here, please."

He closed and bolted the outer door, then set off across the room, making for the single door in the wall opposite. This had been treated in the same way as the outer door, and through it he disappeared.

"Two to one that fellow comes back with Brace," said Thorn to Jewel.

"I'll give you evens," she said.

When the door opened again, Deacon Brace was the first through it. He strode towards Thorn and Jewel, the servant almost running in his effort to keep up.

Halting within touching distance of Thorn, Brace stared at him. "I see you're like her." He inclined his head towards Jewel.

"Am I?" said Thorn. "How?"

"You don't listen."

"I listened before, but I didn't happen to like what you said. I have to see your master and mistress. It's important."

"Oh? To whom?"

"To me."

"Then it isn't important at all. How did you get through the gate?"

"Simple. We walked through it."

Brace grinned. "Very funny. You should have been a comedy act at a fair, Mr Whoever-You-Are."

"My name is Thorn Jack, as I told you before. You'd do pretty well at a fair yourself, Mr Brace."

"Would I? In what capacity?"

"Surely you don't need me to tell you that."

Brace grinned, showing his broken teeth. "That's right, Jack, I don't. In fact I don't need you to tell me *anything*."

"*You* tell *me* something, then – that I can see your master and mistress."

"Persistent, aren't you lad? Well, this must be your lucky day. The master and mistress *will* see you." Brace glanced at Jewel. "*You* they remember from Harrypark. As I do."

"What a jolly little reunion we shall have," said Jewel.

Brace did not react to her sarcasm. "Come with me," he said.

He turned and walked away towards the door through which he'd come. Thorn and Jewel followed him. He seemed to lope across the floor, and by the time he reached the door they were some distance behind.

This inner room was several times the size of the first. It was dominated by a huge, west-facing window whose four panes of glass had, by some freak, survived the long years intact. At each end of the window, heavy curtains hung down. Their original colour was olive-green, but the sun had bleached them pale yellow and moths had gorged themselves on their folds. The sun lanced into the room, irradiating the cobwebs that hung from the low ceiling and doing its utmost to drain even the dead-end whiteness from the back of the giant couch that faced the hearth away to their left.

211

Brace turned towards the window, and they followed him beneath the shadowy underside of a huge table towards a rectangular wooden structure of human size that lay just beyond the table's far overhang. The floor was covered with wooden tiles laid in running arrowy lines, but some had worked loose so that their edges jutted up. Around these Brace carefully steered.

Soon they reached the wooden structure. It was a house within a house. Unlike a human house, however, it had never been rained or snowed on, never battered by rough winds. Rounding its end, Thorn and Jewel sighted the master and mistress of Minral How.

Propped on scarlet and purple cushions, Briar Spurr lay stretched on a snow-white couch. She wore a long pink gown. A purple scarf encircled her neck. She'd kicked off her pink shoes and her bare feet displayed nails painted a lurid crimson. And her eyes – her eyes were large black circles of nothingness.

For a moment Jewel couldn't understand what she was seeing. Then her brain performed an adjustment and the world made sense. Briar was wearing eyeglasses, albeit of an odd kind. Jewel knew something about eyeglasses. Once at a fair, in a distant place, an eye-man had erected his stall next to her father's. Intrigued by the items he was selling, she'd spoken to him during a lull in customers. He'd explained how, in order to correct faulty vision, he ground the lenses to different thicknesses. From time to time, after that, she'd noticed people wearing these objects – even young people. Never before, however, had she seen anyone wearing lenses made of black glass.

This, then, was what it meant to be rich: this and many other things. Briar Spurr had the power to fulfil her every whim . . . Yet possessing such power didn't seem to have made her happy. On the occasions Jewel had seen her, she'd always looked infinitely bored, as if the world held nothing worthy of her interest.

On a table in front of Briar stood a tall glass half-filled with some yellowy-green liquid. Crane Rockett held a similar glass in his right hand. He was sitting in an armchair with his feet up on a bolster. Seeing his visitors approach, he set his glass down on a second table and got to his feet.

Halting precisely six inches short of his master, Brace stuck out a hand to stop his charges from going closer.

He said: "This is Thorn Jack, Mr Rockett. Jewel Ranson you've met before."

"Indeed I have," said Crane. "Harrypark, wasn't it? A bet of some sort. And, following that, unless my memory is playing tricks on me, a sequence of most unfortunate circumstances."

"You could say that, Mr Rockett," Jewel replied evenly. "They were definitely unfortunate for Tarry Ramsbottom, who ended up murdered."

"Yes indeed. Harry went round asking everybody questions. But alas, neither Briar, nor I, nor Brace could help him."

"That's right. But that isn't why we've come here today."

"Just as well," said Crane. "It was a waste of our time then; it would be a waste of it now." He turned to Thorn. "My man Scraggs says you're here on a matter of importance."

He's superb, thought Jewel. We break into his grounds after

213

being refused entry, and he's too polite, or too arrogant, even to mention the matter . . .

Crane said to Brace: "Fetch a couple of chairs, Deacon. Then our guests can sit down."

Our guests! thought Jewel. It was all she could do not to burst out laughing.

"Yes, sir," said Brace, his bony features expressionless.

Soon Thorn and Jewel were seated directly opposite Crane. Briar's couch was a little off to one side. She'd barely moved since their arrival. Her eyes, behind their barriers, gave nothing away.

Behind Crane and Briar stretched the frontage of their house. Its rear and side had been windowless, but its façade made up for that with windows at regular intervals. Graceful living . . .

"Can I offer you a drink?" asked Crane.

"No thank you," said Thorn.

"As you wish. Now please state your business."

Deacon Brace, Jewel saw, had taken a seat at a short distance. But, far from expressing any sense of repose, his body looked taut, ready to leap into action should the situation require.

Thorn had worried about the question of what to say and how to say it as he'd rode to Minral How. Here goes, he thought.

"We're here as representatives of the Spetch brothers," he said. "You know them, I believe."

"I know *of* them," said Crane. "They're a pair of insolent rascals. And that's as much as I want to know."

"But you had dealings with them once – at Harrypark, in the gaming room."

"I wouldn't exactly call them *dealings*: they insisted on a foolish bet and lost. No more than that."

"As I understand it," said Thorn, "it was no ordinary bet. Precious things were wagered. Both sides had much to lose."

"The brothers lost; I won."

Rockett's in an uncompromising mood, thought Thorn. Well, plough on.

"That's why I'm here," he said. "The item the Spetches forfeited was a key of giant manufacture. It was important to them. They'd very much like to have it back. I'm authorised to offer you a handsome sum for it."

"*A handsome sum?*" Crane began to laugh. It was a hearty, jovial laugh that involved the whole of his body; his head wagged, his belly wobbled, his arms twitched, his legs shook. When he stopped laughing, he said: "Surely your friends must know no sum of money, however handsome, could compensate me for the loss of the pleasure I get from having their key – and depriving them of whatever it is it gives them access to?"

"I was hoping you wouldn't say that."

"Oh? And what *were* you hoping?"

"That by this time the key wouldn't be so important to you; that you'd sell it back to them."

"Then your hope was misplaced. I intend to keep the key."

And in the rich man's eyes, Thorn read the finality of that statement.

Crane got up from his chair. "That concludes our business, I think. Deacon, show these people out. And this time, *keep* them out."

"Yes, Mr Rockett," he said.

215

Deacon Brace rose to his feet.

"Wait a moment," said Briar Spurr.

Crane and Brace turned to her.

"You seem to forget, Crane," she said, "that you gave the key to me. It's mine to dispose of – should I decide to do so."

"I gave you the key, yes," said Crane. "But you must understand, my love, that restoring the key to the Spetches is something I couldn't tolerate."

"Oh, and why couldn't you tolerate it, Crane?"

"Surely you don't need me to tell you."

"Oh but I do, Crane, I do."

Jewel looked on, fascinated. Was Briar mocking Crane? He was clearly irritated, but strove to control his annoyance.

"As you know well enough, Briar, I do not forgive slights. I will not allow anyone to make a fool of me. If the Spetches get their key back, it'll be seen as a weakness in me. I'll become a laughing stock."

"What do you care what people think? People are fools, they always were."

"I will not be seen as a fool."

"How do you know people don't already think of you as a fool?"

"How can they?" Crane thundered. "I'm rich – richer than anyone."

Briar spoke coolly: "Even rich men can be fools – greater fools than poor men."

"I will not be seen as a fool."

"So you say. But there's more to these young people than meets the eye."

"I see nothing."

"That's because you're not looking." Briar turned to Thorn: "Why did the Spetches select you two for this little exploit?"

"I don't know why they chose me," Thorn replied. "Jewel happened to be at Roydsal when I was there. She came with me when I left."

"Just like that?"

"Just like that."

"So what's in it for you?"

"My sister's freedom. The Spetches kidnapped her. They'll free her if I succeed in getting the key back for them. If I fail, they'll kill her."

"High stakes . . ." murmured Briar, as if communing with herself. Then she said; "Where are you from, Thorn Jack?"

"I'm from Norgreen," he said.

"And you're how old?"

"Sixteen."

"What's your sister's name?"

"Haw."

"How did you track your sister down?"

"The kidnappers dropped a yellow feather. A man called Racky Jagger thought he'd seen its like before over on this side of the wood. He agreed to be my guide. At the inn at Judy Bridge we were directed to Roydsal. Jagger and I got separated, so I went on alone. I tried to rescue Haw, but the Spetches captured me."

"You live a colourful life, Thorn Jack."

"Not by choice. I simply want my sister back."

"Do you love her, then?"

"More than anything else in the world."

Briar turned to her lover. "Should I give him the key, Crane? Is a young girl's life worth an old brass key?"

"What's this Haw Jack to me? I'm not responsible for her. Anyway, the Spetches are bound to be bluffing. Bluff and bluster – that's their style. They haven't got it in them to kill someone in cold blood."

"They're more than capable," said Jewel. "They murdered my father."

Crane regarded her for a time. Then he said to Thorn: "What happens to your sister is no affair of mine. The key will stay here. There's nothing more to be said."

"There *is* more to be said." Briar set her feet on the floor and began to put on her shoes. Then she stood up.

On the left side of her face, her long black hair had dropped forward to obscure one lens of her glasses. She tossed her head, swinging the hair back and away. In Thorn's memory, something stirred.

"Come with me," said Briar to Thorn.

"What are you doing, Briar?" demanded Crane in a stiff voice.

Ignoring him, Briar led Thorn towards the house.

"Deacon . . ." Crane waved a hand in the direction of his man.

Deacon started towards Thorn.

"Stay out of this, Deacon. It's no concern of yours," said Briar.

Briar walked past the tall man. Brace made no move to stop Thorn. Briar and Thorn went into the house . . .

218

Deacon Brace looked questioningly into his master's face. For the first time since Jewel had met the man, he seemed uncertain.

Crane Rockett said: "Jack is not to leave Minral How with that key. Do you understand, Deacon?"

Brace hesitated, then murmured: "I understand, Mr Rockett." He seemed about to say more, but after glancing at Jewel he walked over to Crane and began to whisper in his ear.

Crane listened to his man. When Brace stopped whispering, he said: "Yes, that would be for the best."

The pair gazed at Jewel.

She saw only one thing in their eyes, and it frightened her.

13

INTO THE CRYPT

The house within a house was a flood of rich colours. Crane and Briar obviously bought the best of everything – furniture, cushions, rugs, lamp-holders, knick-knacks. Briar led Thorn through a living room and a dining room, then into what he imagined was the final room at this end of the house. It was a storeroom of sorts, cluttered with odds and ends – an old desk, a sagging armchair, a cracked oval mirror, out-of-favour ornaments, and several stacks of discarded curtains, blankets, sheets and other assorted fabrics. On a scarred table stood a couple of oil-lamps.

Briar pulled a rug to one side, revealing a square trapdoor set flush in the wooden floor. "Open that!" she commanded Thorn.

Mid-way along one edge, inset into a depression, was a stout metal ring. Thorn grasped it and lifted. The door was heavy, but up it came, revealing a square hole and a flight of wooden steps going down into darkness.

The door was hinged on one side. As Thorn folded it back on the floor, he heard, behind his back, the sound of a struck flint. He turned. The sound came again and a light flared as the spark found the tinder. Briar was lighting one of the lamps. From it she lit the second, which she handed to Thorn.

"Where are we going?" he asked.

"Into the crypt," she replied.

"Why?"

She took off her dark glasses and looked him full in the face.

"To get you what you want."

"You're beautiful," he whispered.

"So men tell me," she said. "But I'll grow ugly soon enough. If I live, that is. Sometimes I think I've lived too long."

Her directness was alarming.

"How can that be?" he asked.

"You're asking questions of a person who has no answers to give. Now, follow me. And don't drop that lamp."

She went down the steps into the crypt and disappeared beneath the floor. Thorn went after her, and found himself in an underground room just high enough to stand up in. Deacon Brace would have had to stoop. Already Briar and her light were some distance away. Thorn crossed the floor after her, his lamp casting a halo like a drifting will-o'-the-wisp. Spider-webs hung like delicate nets from the ceiling – some with inhabitants, some without – and floating strands clung to Thorn as he advanced.

Briar was in the far corner. But Thorn could see nothing there – just the crypt's bare walls. Then he heard a sliding noise. Briar had moved a panel aside to reveal a further recess. She stooped and went through. Thorn followed. This second room was tiny – little more than a box.

"This is where Crane keeps his money and other valuables," said Briar. "He's a highly suspicious man. He thinks people are out to rob him. Perhaps they are. I wouldn't care if they did. It would wipe the self-satisfied smugness off his face." She spoke with surprising venom.

"Why do you stay with him if you don't love him?" asked Thorn.

"Love?" she replied. "Don't speak to me of love."

"Care for him, then."

"As well him as any other. Or better him than many others. He doesn't ask much of me. He's an emotional child."

Thorn didn't know what she meant.

On the floor stood a matching pair of chests. Briar unlatched the hasp of one and lifted the lid. It creaked as it moved, and she let it drop back. The chest was filled with smaller containers: boxes, caskets and cases in a variety of sizes.

"Give me your lamp," she said to him.

He did as he was bid.

"See that long, flat casket? Take it out and open it."

He removed the casket, set it on the floor and opened it. Inside, lapped in some soft crimson material, lay the brass key. It wasn't much more than an inch long. At one end was a flattened ring; at the other, a complex head cut to fit unknown wards.

"Take it and go," she said. "And watch your back. Crane won't be willing just to let you walk away."

"What about you?" he asked.

"I'll be fine. He'll be angry for a while, I expect, but he'll get over it."

She returned his lamp to him, put the casket back in the chest and secured the hasp. Then they left the recess, slid the panel back into place, crossed the floor of the crypt and climbed the steps.

Thorn was first up. He blew out his lamp and set it down on the table. The journey had disarranged Briar's hair. She tossed her head, throwing it back, and Thorn felt a sudden wrench of pain about the heart – half-suspicion, half-recognition.

It's now or never, he thought.

He said, as she set her lamp down on the tabletop: "Are you my mother?"

Just for a moment (or did he imagine it?) startlement flitted across her face. Then her face was again a mask.

She said: "My name is Briar Spurr."

He said: "Names can be changed."

She said: "I'm nobody's mother."

He said: "I'm somebody's son."

She said: "Of course. But not mine."

She spoke with such finality. Was he wrong then, after all?

"The way you toss your hair . . . My mother used to do that. It's the only thing I remember. I've forgotten what she looked like."

"Forgetting's the best thing to do when something goes missing."

"But I can't forget, can I? She abandoned my sister and me. I've always wondered why."

"I can't help you, Thorn Jack."

"I think you can. You're the right age. Why can't you be honest with me?"

"Honesty never did anyone any good, believe me."

"Why are you so cynical?"

"Why is the sun yellow?"

I don't understand you, he thought. But I haven't finished yet.

"Why did you give me the key?"

"Because you say it will save your sister."

"What's my sister to you?"

"Just a name. A pretty name."

"Names are revealing, don't you think? I'm Thorn. My sister's Haw. My mother's given name was Berry. You call yourself Briar. Do you see a pattern there? Thorn, Haw, Briar – don't they go together well!"

"If you say so, Thorn Jack."

"Do you know why the Spetches plucked me from nowhere for this mission? Because I've a special qualification. But when I asked them what it was, they refused to tell me. But if they know you're my mother, Haw's mother, it all makes sense. They believed you'd give me the key in order to save your daughter's life."

And who but Racky could have told them Briar Spurr was Berry Jack? Racky must have spotted Briar somewhere on his travels . . .

Briar's face was sculpted stone. "I'm nobody's mother," she said again.

"Then I'm nobody's son," said Thorn.

He turned and walked out of the room.

Briar took three paces after him, then stopped. There she remained, her eyes fixed on the door through which he'd left. After a time, a tear appeared in the inner corner of one eye, welled up over the lid and escaped down her cheek. She made no effort to wipe it away.

When Thorn came out of the wooden house, Jewel and Crane were alone.

Crane took in what Thorn was carrying, then said: "I advise you not to take that key, Thorn Jack."

"I must," said Thorn.

"You are stealing my property. I cannot allow that."

"It was Briar Spurr's property and she gave it to me." He turned to Jewel. "Let's go."

Crane watched them out of sight, then went into the house. He found Briar in the exact posture Thorn had left her in. If he noted the tear-track on her cheek, he gave no sign of this. He walked up to her and demanded: "Why did you give him the key, Briar?"

She made no reply.

Crane repeated angrily: "Why did you give him the key?"

Still she said nothing.

He seized her by the arms. "Answer me, Briar! Answer me!" He shook her passionately. "Why did you give Jack the key?"

Still she looked through him. He might not have been there, for all the notice she took of him.

The last vestiges of Crane's self-control drained away.

"I told you not to do it!" he shouted. "Why did you disobey me?"

Only now did she seem to see him.

"You don't own me, Crane. I'm not Deacon Brace, I'm not some soulless machine that will do your every bidding. I do only what pleases me."

"Well it doesn't please me."

He slapped her hard across the face.

"You bastard!" she cried and dug her nails into his face.

225

He let out a cry and grabbed her arm, but she seized a fistful of his hair and clung grimly on to it. Blood ran down his cheek. He tried to pull away from her but found himself dragging her after him. Together they staggered backwards and went crashing into the table. It toppled over, and the still-lit oil-lamp Briar had placed upon it smashed, spilling fuel onto one of the piles of fabric on the floor.

Flames ran with the freed oil, and the fabric was instantly ablaze. The second oil-lamp caught fire. But the couple wrestled on the floor as if the only thought in their heads was to murder one another.

"Let go of me, you mad bitch!"

"I'll see you in Hell first!"

They tumbled over one another and Crane went into the burning cloth. Eager for stuff to devour, the flames fastened on his jacket.

Crane screamed and let go of Briar, who rolled away and got to her feet. Then stood looking down at him and the pyre at his back. Flames danced in her eyes, fire answering to fire.

Crane flailed his burning arms. He rolled, trying to douse the flames, but a sheet wrapped itself around him, swaddling him in fiery tongues. His hair flared and frazzled.

Briar smiled as her lover screamed. The house could burn for all she cared – Minral How could burn to the ground. The little house, the big house – and after them, the entire world.

As they crossed the tiled floor, Jewel told Thorn about Crane and Brace: that the two had whispered together, and that then Brace had left.

226

"I think he's preparing an ambush. Maybe gathering extra men."

"Briar warned me," said Thorn. "But I shall fight to keep the key."

"We'll both fight," she said.

She spoke resolutely. Even so, she couldn't see them defeating Deacon Brace.

They went back through the house the way they'd come. They reached the front door unchallenged and Jewel unbolted it. Glancing around, Thorn spotted Scraggs watching them from a side-door.

They went out into the garden.

"Which way?" Jewel asked.

"Let's go the way we came. At least we know the terrain."

They were approaching the built-up steps when the expected challenge came. Out from a spray of weeds stepped Deacon Brace and two men. The men carried heavy clubs, but Brace appeared unarmed.

Having left their bows in the guardhouse, Jewel and Thorn had only their knives.

Brace motioned to his men, and they came slowly forward while he stayed where he was, a slight smile on his face.

Brace thinks this is going to be easy, thought Jewel. And it will be. I know no more about fighting than I do about flying.

Thorn was about to put the brass key on the ground, when a thought struck him. He'd been carrying it by the shank, but if he held it by the ring – yes, it felt solid in his hands – he could swing it like a club.

He said, "Stay there, Jewel," and took several steps forward.

A movement at the top of the flight of steps caught Jewel's eye. It was Red. Instantly taking in the scenario below, he nocked his bow, aimed and let fly. His aim was good. One of the two advancing men fell to the ground, an arrow-shaft protruding from his shoulder.

Deacon Brace spun round and saw Red at the top of the steps. His advantage gone, Red threw down his bow and quiver and came rushing down the slope.

The unhurt man closed on Thorn and swung his club in a high arc. It would have crushed the young man's skull but he ducked beneath it. Then, straightening, he swung the key at his attacker and heard the fabric of his jerkin rip as the wards tore through the cloth. But the man was unhurt. He swung his club diagonally and it swished past Thorn's face. He felt the draught of its passage. The two circled one another warily, weapons poised.

Red was down the slope now. He swung a fist at Brace's head, but the tall man swayed backwards. Red aimed lower, a body blow, and felt his fist impact solidly on Brace's ribs. It would have shaken many opponents, but Brace merely grinned. Then he stepped in towards Red and clubbed him over one ear with a big, knuckly hand.

The force of the blow shivered through Red's body to his knees. As he wavered, Brace punched him on the chin and he slumped to the ground.

A feral gleam lit Brace's eyes. He dropped to his knees and wrapped his undertaker's hands round Red's neck.

Thorn and his assailant only had eyes for one another.

"Come on," Thorn taunted him. "I'm just a lad. What are you waiting for?"

But the man was not to be goaded into making a foolish move. The two stalked one another, searching out an opening. The man whirled his club again, but its arc fell short: Thorn had simply stepped away. Then, abruptly, the man charged. Thorn swung the key and drove it into the man's side. But the man's head struck his chest, and he was flung onto his back. Now his attacker stood above him. Raising his club, he brought it down. Thorn rolled sideways, and the head of the club thumped into the ground. He got up onto his knees, but the man now swung at his head. Thorn ducked and whipped the key at the man's legs. It struck him on the side of the knee. The leg buckled and he fell to the ground.

Thorn was quickly onto his feet. He swung the key for the last time and it chunked into the man's head. His body went limp and blood ran from his nose and ear.

When Jewel saw that Brace had Red by the throat, she ran forward. She grabbed Brace's right arm and tried to haul him off, but he simply let go with his right hand and threw her off contemptuously.

What happened next took even Jewel by surprise. Gathering herself again, she threw herself at Brace and clasped his head between her hands. This feeble action shouldn't have troubled him in the least, but at that moment all Jewel's locked-up emotions – her hatred of Brace and the Spetch brothers, her misery and despair at the loss of her father and Rainy Gill – seemed to combine in one massive and uncontrollable outburst of passion. Energy surged through her fingers and leapt through the man's head, jolting it out of her hands. She fell back, stunned by the discharge; but the effect on the gaunt predator was devastating. His hands went slack and his body lolled, then he slumped sideways and rolled over onto his back.

A moment later, Thorn arrived. Brace was lying on the ground, eyes open, looking upwards. His eyeballs moved in their sockets, as if searching for something. His lips moved, but made no sound.

Thorn laid the key on the ground and unsheathed his knife. He bent to thrust it into the man's neck, but Jewel lifted a barring arm and said: "No, Thorn. Wait."

Thorn watched as the girl set her fingers to Brace's brow. The roaming eyes focussed on her.

"Mother?" he said vaguely. "Mother, is that you?"

"What happened?" asked Thorn.

"I don't know," Jewel answered, "but I do know he's harmless. He'll never hurt anyone again."

"Harmless? How can he be harmless?"

"His mind's gone. He'll be like a child."

She got to her feet and went to Red. As she knelt at his side, his eyelids fluttered, then opened.

"Red?" she said.

His eyes settled on her. "Jewel?" he said hoarsely, then began to cough.

"My neck!" he said. "What happened?"

"Deacon Brace gave it a squeeze. Are you all right?"

Red considered. "I think I'll live."

Thorn stuck out a hand and hauled Red to his feet.

Red pointed to Brace. "Who did that to him?" he asked.

"Jewel," answered Thorn. "The Jewel who mended Roper's leg."

Red grinned. "Remind me never to get into a fight with her . . . So that's the famous key?"

Thorn was retrieving it from the ground.

"It is. It's what we came for. Now we've got it, let's go."

The man with the arrow in his shoulder lay still and watched them pass. But when, at the top of the ramp, they looked back, he had gone.

Deacon Brace had climbed to his feet. Motionless, he stood staring at a clump of yellow roses.

"He's like a man seeing the world for the first time," said Red.

"Perhaps he is," said Jewel. "Or perhaps he saw it long ago, then forgot what it looked like."

They reached the guardhouse without further incident. The gate-guard had tipped his chair over, but his hands were still firmly tied. They cut his bonds and sent him off towards the house.

Then, remounting their rats, they rode out through the gate.

They'd travelled some way along the highroad when a sudden pricking of the scalp made Jewel twist and look back. She reined Retty in.

"Look!" she exclaimed. "Minral How – it's on fire!"

Above the distant black walls, flames were licking at the sky. The three riders sat and watched. What had happened back there?

Thorn pictured the woman who called herself Briar Spurr. Had she set the house on fire?

She's capable of it, he thought. Had she escaped the conflagration? Had she resigned herself to the flames? Surely no one would do that.

No one in her right mind. But what mind was Briar in?

Some enigmatic words she'd said to him came into his head: *sometimes I think I've lived too long.*

He felt loss mixed with frustration. Their paths had crossed all too briefly. Briar had given him the brass key, but nothing beyond that. She'd put up a barrier between her present self and the past. The second big question he wanted to ask – the name of the man who'd fathered him – had never got as far as his lips. Coldly, she'd faced him down.

She was his mother, no question of it. Everything pointed to that fact. But she didn't love him. She had never loved him. That was why she'd said nothing, denied she'd ever been a mother.

He felt a surge of certainty that she'd expired in the fire. Dead. The only person who knew his father's identity, reduced to ash, her flesh blown across the sky.

Stony Close was too far off to be reachable before nightfall. They pitched their tents a little way off the road, in the lee of some bushes. They lit a fire, brewed up some tea and ate food they'd brought. Despite their victory at the house, all three of them felt subdued. They could so easily have lost, and one or all of them killed.

"We'd better mount a guard," said Red, "in case they decide to come after us."

"That seems unlikely," said Thorn. "But it's a sensible precaution."

"I'll take the first watch," said Jewel.

The others tried to change her mind, but she refused to budge. She saw no reason why she shouldn't do her share of the work, she said.

Actually, she was feeling tired – to be honest, very tired; perhaps from the energy she'd expended when she'd seized Deacon Brace. But *I'm damned if I'll admit that to the men*, she told herself.

It was a mild night, the sky was clear, and stars teemed in the black vault. They were so bright you had the feeling that all you had to do was reach up and grab a handful. Then, when you opened your fist, they'd sparkle like diamonds on your palm. She'd tried this as a small child until her mother explained that the stars were far away.

"*How* far?" she'd asked, with characteristic persistence. "Do the birds go there?"

"No. Stars are far beyond their reach."

Then stars had to be very far. For look how high the birds soared in the blue sky of day. But then the stars couldn't be seen. They'd hidden themselves away, like a host of bright secrets . . .

Jewel built up the fire a little and looked at her hands in the firelight. When Deacon Brace fell back on the ground, she was convinced she'd killed him. Had she wanted to? He'd killed Tarry Ramsbottom and tried to kill her too. He deserved to die. Thorn would have killed him if she hadn't put up her hand and stopped him. Why had she done that? Brace was helpless now, an infant trapped in a man's body. He'd be easy meat for one of the many enemies he'd made.

What a twisted world, she thought. And here I am at the heart of it.

Me – along with my living enemies.

14

THE SCAREBIRD

The three riders reached Stony Close around noon the next day. They were welcomed with relief and taken inside.

Jewel's back and thighs were aching. Would she ever get used to riding? She was happy to slump on a couch and pamper her back with a scatter of cushions. The womenfolk bustled about, and piles of food and drink appeared.

"You stay there, love," Petal told her. "I can see you're all in . . . Lucy! Look after this lovely girl."

And Lucy did, pressing food on Jewel until she begged her to stop. Soon after that she fell asleep while, between them, to eight agog Tucketts, Thorn and Red gave a blow-by-blow account of their exploits. When Red told them how Jewel had stopped Brace from strangling him, they treated the silently-slumbering girl to long looks of awe.

"I ought to have gone with you," said Roper, annoyed with himself – and seemingly everyone else as well.

"Now, you know what you're like with a bow and arrow, Roper," said his brother. "You'd have hit Thorn or Jewel."

"Rubbish, Red. I'm not that bad."

Red smiled. He knew better than to persist. His brother would never give ground to him, right or wrong, in an argument.

"How's the leg?" he asked.

"Champion," said Roper. "Good as new. Or even better. I've been in the workshop all morning. Which reminds me," he said to Thorn. "I haven't shown you round, have I?"

"No," replied Thorn. "But really we ought to get back on the road this afternoon."

"Nonsense!" declared Petal. "Jewel's worn out. Just look at her. You must stay the night with us. Let her rest. Go on tomorrow."

Thorn considered his companion. Though her face was relaxed in sleep, she looked pale.

Yes, he thought, we'll go tomorrow. We'll need all our strength at Roydsal.

Probably all our cunning, too.

So, later that afternoon, leaving Jewel still resting (awake now, but taking it easy, sitting chatting with Lucy and May), he went off with Roper.

They went first to the smithy. Here Roper had built a furnace. He used charcoal, he explained, in order to soften and work iron. But his installation was simple when compared with that at Lowmoor. The Lowmoor ironworks led the world, and it was there that he got more complicated jobs done.

"These processes," he explained, "are only in their infancy. It remains to be seen how far we can progress. Knowledge is the key to everything, don't you think? People like Lasker don't want to know. Machines frighten them. They want us to stay just as we are. But humans as a race must move forward or die. The giants possessed tools far in advance of anything here."

"Yes," agreed Thorn. "But doesn't our very smallness put limits on what we can achieve?"

"We mustn't use size as an excuse," declared Roper. "Limitations exist only to be overcome!"

"Even so, do you know, ever since I was a small child I've had the feeling I didn't belong on this earth. It's a matter of scale. The world seems perfect for the giants, but not for us. We're out of place. It's as if some malignant god plucked us out of our proper world, and dumped us here to struggle."

"Other people have told me that. I'll tell you what I tell them: that we only think like this because of what remains of the giant world – what we call the Dark Time, though it was anything but dark. If there were no remains, we'd have nothing to measure ourselves against. But even then I doubt we'd be content with our lot. It's in our nature to be dissatisfied, to aspire, to create. That's why I'm proud to call myself an Experimentalist."

The word was new to Thorn, but it required no explanation. Not here, in Roper's smithy. Not in his workshop either, where he built his flying machines.

Airbird 11 was no more. All that remained was its wing-fabric. He'd melted down its metal parts. He talked with enthusiasm of the new Airbird he planned to build.

"Strength and lightness!" he enthused. "Strength and lightness – that's what I'm after! A perfect blend of opposites – or apparent opposites. My task is to reconcile them, and reconcile them I shall!"

Thorn had little doubt that he would. But where would it end?

Then he smiled to himself. It wouldn't end, he saw; it couldn't. Endlessness was built into Experimentalism. There would always be more to do, new challenges, new horizons. Roper was a hero, but a hero different to those Thorn was used to thinking of – outstanding Headmen, renowned hunters. Roper was a hero of knowledge. He had the spirit of a fanatic. No wonder Lasker argued with him; Lasker, who was content to work with nature as she was.

Except that that wasn't true either, for wasn't Lasker a ratman? Rats in their natural state were feral; in the wild, they were killers. But men had got hold of them and tamed them, made them answer to their needs. Now Roper with his Airbird . . . What was he doing but taming the sky?

"Come on," said the man himself, "and I'll really show you something."

Thorn followed him outside. They went round the back of the workshop and down an alley between two of the great squared-off blocks of stone. Then, turning a corner, Thorn saw that a long, wooden shed stood against the side of the block. Away to the right, the hillside dropped away.

Roper unlatched the door of the shed and motioned Thorn inside.

"Behold! My Airbirds!" He grinned infectiously.

The floor was partly taken up by six flying machines. Their forked wings were lifted above ground level on wooden stands. A light, metal framework hung beneath each wing. In some of these, strap-suspended, were harnesses for their fliers.

"These are the machines that have survived," Roper said. "Others got cannibalised for parts when their usefulness was

238

over." He halted, and patted the wing-blade of the nearest machine. "This is Airbird 1," he said. "I've a soft spot for her. I was tempted to take her apart but sentiment said: *no: leave the poor girl alone!*"

"You – sentimental?" Thorn exclaimed. "I don't believe it!"

"Don't you think an Experimentalist can be fond of his creations? I'm just as attached to Airbird 1 as Lasker was to the late Phyllis, his all-time favourite rat. Are they really so different? Rats might have four legs, but Airbirds have wings. And both have noses and tails!"

Thorn laughed along with his friend.

Roper moved to the next machine, noting changes and improvements. He dwelt lovingly on each particular. The third machine was larger than the others; a pair of harnesses dangled in its framework, one directly behind the other. This, Roper explained, was a training machine; on it, Red and Lucy had learnt to fly.

Time went by. At length they came to the sixth machine.

"This is Airbird 10," Roper announced. "I call her Scarebird. Perhaps you can see why."

Thorn studied the machine. Its wing was larger again than that of Airbird 3. Inside its frame were three harnesses.

"Scarebird was rather a shot in the dark. But she flies."

"With three fliers?"

"Correct," Roper said. "The main flier goes in front; the two behind are subordinate. Sensibly handled, she's very safe. But I haven't yet achieved my main ambition with regard to her – to get Lasker and May into the air. I think May would do it, but Lasker's a real stick-in-the-mud. Of course, beginners require

239

some instruction and some ground-based rehearsal before attempting their first flight."

He stroked the machine's wingtip. "Believe me," he said, "Scarebird flies beautifully. I wasn't confident she would when we first took her up, on account of the extra weight. But she more than makes up for her weight with the size of her wing. Given the right conditions, she just goes up and up. You think you'd bump against the sky! Except the sky's just emptiness – currents of heat, currents of air and lots of emptiness, with the big blue above you that goes all the way to the stars."

"The way you say that," said Thorn, "it sounds like you fancy going there."

"Don't I just!" said Roper. "Maybe one day, someone will. Though not to the stars – to the moon. Do you know" – he tapped Thorn's arm – "I sometimes think the giants might have gone there already."

"To the moon?" Thorn was incredulous. "Even the giants couldn't do that."

"How do we know what they could do? I think most of their civilisation's simply been wiped out. What's left are bits and pieces – nuts and bolts, so to speak. We see walls, reservoirs, a few houses, occasional monuments, and a lot of smaller objects – what hunters call Artefacts – some we can name, many we can't. The giants were Experimentalists, and of a high order too." He grinned. "And for that, according to Lasker, for daring to usurp God's own creative powers, they were bundled into Hell!"

Thorn returned the grin. "You don't believe that, do you?" he said. "So what *did* happen to them?"

"That's the question, isn't it? As far as I'm concerned, there are three possibilities. One, they left and went somewhere else. Two, they were destroyed by an outside force. Three, they destroyed themselves. But as I said when we were talking about the giants the other day, you can't construct a theory if you haven't any facts. Maybe one day startling evidence will suddenly turn up, and at last we'll be able to do more than speculate; but, speaking for myself, I'm not terribly hopeful. Anyway, I've one thing more to show you before we head back. I've been warned not to be late. Petal knows how I lose track of time when I start rabbiting on about my work – as she calls it. She thinks the two of you need feeding up – and my mother's never wrong."

They went out of the Airbird shed to the top of the hill-slope.

Roper said: "Wilf chose better than he knew when he decided to come here. Where else could I have found such an excellent launch pad? And such a convenient one? You run the machine down the hill and when your speed's right – hey! You're airborne! Nothing to it!"

To Thorn, there looked plenty to it.

Roper gestured towards the valley. "Down there, to the east, is Wilf's Clough – where you saw the skeleton."

He turned and pointed south. Off in the far distance, the land rose to a height that made Stony Close seem like a hillock (which it was).

"Roydsal Ridge, as you know. Up there, but further west's where the Spetches live." He turned and pointed west. "Rook Wood lies that way. It sits in a dip, so you can't see the trees from here. Roydsal Dam's on its far side. But that's the way you

241

came, and that's the way you've got to go. When 'go' means walking . . . Unless . . ." He turned on Thorn the mischievous expression of a small boy.

"Unless what? Unless we ride?"

Roper laughed. "I get the impression that, for the time being, Jewel's had as much as she can take of ratback. No, I was thinking of a far less tiring, much faster and infinitely more thrilling mode of travel."

"You can't mean—"

"Flying? Oh yes I can. What else?"

They were relaxing by the fire in the aftermath of the meal. Jewel was thinking: if I stayed here, I'd soon be as fat as an old rat. Then she thought: no I wouldn't. None of the Tucketts are fat. They're always busy. Even Wilf does his share. If I lived here I'd have to work, just as I shall work wherever I happen to end up – if I end up anywhere. But what sort of work?

The answer soon came: the sort of work right for a Magian. But what was that? Identifying criminals, as Querne Rasp had done at Lowmoor? Or what she'd done the other day, when she mended Roper's leg?

At which point she thought of the other things she could do: unlocking doors without a key, melting solid bars of iron, burning out the circuits of another person's brain . . .

Magians could choose to do as many dark things as light – maybe more. What else, as time went on, would she discover she could do? What temptations would her strange powers place in her path? And would she succumb to them?

She came out of her reverie to find Thorn talking about the

Airbird shed – the building where Roper kept his flying machines. He ended by saying how much he'd been impressed by what he'd seen.

Lasker snorted. "Roper's clever, I'll give him that. But it's the cleverness of the devil. We humans weren't meant to go flitting about in the sky. If we were, God would have made us birds and given us wings."

"He did better than that," said Roper. "He gave us the intelligence to make wings for ourselves."

"So," said Lasker quickly, "you admit to him as your maker?"

"I admit nothing of the sort. I speak as you speak for the sake of convenience."

"Convenience! Pah!"

"You two!" said Lucy. "You're a pair. Each of you feeds off the other. Roper, if Lasker didn't exist, you'd be forced to invent him. And, Uncle, the same goes for you."

"Well, we amuse you at least," said Lasker with a smile.

"Up to a point. But you go on so! It gets tedious."

"Let's change the subject then," said Roper. "Listen: while Thorn and I were talking in the Airbird shed, I had a really bright idea."

Lasker groaned. "Oh no! Not another one of them!"

"Lasker, for heaven's sake give it a rest!" May told her husband. "Or you can brew your own beer!"

This dreadful threat did the trick. Lasker promptly buttoned his lip.

"Yes," continued Roper, as if there'd been no interruption. "Why don't I *fly* Thorn and Jewel up to Roydsal?"

"What – in the Scarebird?" said Red.

"What else?" said his brother.

"Is that a good idea? Neither of them has flown before."

"So what? I'll explain how it works, and we can practise moves on the ground before we get up into the air. They're both sensible people – they aren't going to do anything stupid. Consider the advantages. One: they want to get there quickly. The Scarebird guarantees it. Two: flying will save them the physical effort of trekking up Roydsal Hill. They'll arrive fresh, and, what's more, raring to go after the excitement of the flight!"

"They might be scared stiff," said Petal. "I would be, if I flew."

"They're not like you, mother. They've been in lots of tough corners. They'll take the Scarebird in their stride."

"Not if they're airsick," said Red.

"They won't be. Petal can give them some of the stuff Matt takes before he flies. It settles the stomach. He's never been sick."

"What about taking off again?"

"Roydsal's on a hilltop. We land on a slope – and Bob's your uncle! We can simply run the Scarebird off again."

"Well, Roper," Red admitted, "you seem to have the angles covered. The Scarebird's a sound machine, tried and tested, dependable. But what do Jewel and Thorn think?"

"Well, Jewel?" said Thorn. "I'll go with whatever you decide."

"That means you're ready to do it," she said. "And you've looked at this machine . . ." She considered briefly. "Not having to walk back up that great hill has its attractions. And as for flying, if Lucy can do it, why can't I? Yes, let's fly!"

"Good decision!" said Roper. "You won't regret it, of that I'm sure."

That night, back in her room, in the light of her oil-lamp, Jewel sat on the edge of her bed. Beside her lay her pack. Throwing back the flap, she plunged her hands inside and brought out her crystal in a clean, cloth wrapping and set it down on the bed.

Unwrapped, it seemed a chunk of night. Here and there a jag or a facet caught the light from her lamp and gave back a cold gleam. Had it been torn from some rocky matrix, or had it been manufactured?

It had mastered her in the dingy back room on Nettle Island, but put to use at Minral How had done the job she'd asked of it. Well, this time she'd make a deliberate and measured investigation, see what sense she could make of it. I will not be carried away. Placing her hands on its surface, she was for a moment reminded of Deacon Brace's skull. But that had been smooth; the crystal was chunky and pitted.

A glow appeared at its heart, a core of emerald light. As the light grew in intensity, Jewel dispatched a tendril of consciousness into the stone. The crystal mounted no resistance; almost it seemed as if it welcomed the tendril in.

The stone was surprisingly porous. It was made up of tiny veins, much too tiny to see, and along these she travelled as along tracks through a dense forest. The veins were organised in a knot, a complex network of connections, but the knot itself was tiny, and she now perceived that it was only one of many other knots.

And now, as the crystal woke, the veins in the knot began to fizz, and she found herself in the midst of a frantic rush of light-streams that pulsed and sparkled as they moved. She was reminded of her foray into the brain of the Great Pike. So was that what the crystal was – a brain fashioned out of rock?

Selecting at random one of the broken ribbons of light, she moved her point of consciousness to intercept it. As the light-pulses struck her, an image formed in her mind – first blurry, but clearing as she tuned in to it. She was standing above a bed looking down at the person in it. That person was her mother. Her eyes were wide open and smiling up at her. *I'm feeling much better today*, she said. Jewel's father stood by the bed. He grasped her mother's hand in his. *Thank God,* he said. There were tears in his eyes.

Jewel moved out of the impulse-stream. Selecting another, she intercepted it as before. The image steadied and came into focus. An arrow nocked to her bow, she stood above Lanner Spetch, who lay sprawled on his couch. Beside her, Rainy Gill had drawn a bead on his brother Zak. *Please – don't kill me,* Lanner whispered, and threw up a protective hand. But Jewel's bow twanged and the arrow struck Lanner in the heart. Rainy fired in turn, and the shaft hit Zak in the throat, pinning him to the couch.

For a second time she moved and picked out a light-stream. When the image became clear, she found herself in Harrypark, standing beside the Round Pond. Close by, Retty the saddle-rat was lapping from the water. There was a movement in the long grass on the far side of the pool. Something dark and angular had for a moment come into view. There it was again . . . Should she investigate? She had pressing business here, and there might be danger in the grass. Nevertheless Jewel's curiosity was piqued. Confident Retty wouldn't run off if left for a while, she set off around the pond . . .

Jewel withdrew from the impulse-stream and broke the connection with the crystal. She was back in Stony Close. On the coverlet beside her, the crystal's green light was dying.

I proved I could use it, she thought, and now I've proved I can explore it and not lose control. But what was the meaning of what I saw?

She'd tuned into three different scenes . . . Two had presented her with situations from her past life. Yet in neither case had things happened as she'd just seen them happen. In life her mother had died, and the twins had evaded her revenge. What was the crystal doing? Picking scenes of her memories and transforming them into their opposites? Were they dreams, perhaps, wish-fulfilment versions of reality? The strange thing was, they'd seemed so vivid, so plausible – as if they were firm memories of what had been.

But the third scene at the Round Pond? Where had that come from? It hadn't happened, it didn't relate to reality.

Unless – the thought jolted her – it hasn't happened *yet*.

Next morning, flying helmets snug beneath their chins, Jewel, Roper and Thorn carried the Scarebird into position at the top of the hill-slope.

Jewel's nerves quivered. She'd felt strange on waking, as if only half-attached to the world she was in. As if she'd left some small part of herself behind in the crystal – or as if the crystal's spirit had somehow entered into her. She'd had to fight down the urge to take it out of its bag. For today, she was convinced, she would face a great test . . . But what would be demanded of her she was unable to foresee.

Thorn's nerves too were a-quiver – but with the excitement of anticipation. Flying was about to leave the realm of ideas and become a fact.

Like the others, he carried a small amount of food in his pockets. His bow and quiver, like Jewel's, were strapped to the Scarebird's wing-frame. Only he was wearing a pack.

On the previous evening Roper had held forth on many things: heat and air currents, launch and landing techniques, the right weather conditions for flying. Then, with the help of a model, he'd explained how a flier (or three) went about his (or their) business. In order, he told them, to alter direction or change speed, a flier moves to one side or forwards or backwards on the strap that attaches him to the wing. Naturally, the Scarebird demanded a degree of co-ordination from its three fliers. Earlier, on the flat, they'd practised the necessary sequences, which including running together. Only when Roper declared himself fully satisfied had they moved to the hill-slope.

Now he asked if they had any final questions.

"Just one," said Thorn with a wry grin. "How often do you crash?"

If Jewel could have slapped him at that moment, she'd have done it; but he was out of reach, so she made do with an admonition.

"Don't worry," said Roper. "The Scarebird has never crashed. She flies like a dream."

"Like a dream?" said Jewel. "I'm not sure how to take that."

Roper laughed. "Just follow my orders and my lead. Right?"

Together, they lifted the flying machine up off the ground. Jewel's contribution was token, for Roper and Thorn were both strong, and between them supported the bulk of the Scarebird's weight.

"Ready?" asked Roper.

"Ready!" said Jewel and Thorn.

"Good luck!" called Red and Lucy, who stood a little way to their rear.

Roper counted down: "Three . . . Two . . . One . . . Go!"

They ran forward, Roper chanting to keep the three of them in time. The slope wasn't steep, and if they got out of step, they could always abort the launch. But Roper had drilled them well – and, all at once, Jewel felt her feet part company with the ground. The Scarebird floated away from the hill.

Following Roper, Jewel shifted her body until it was horizontal. Now, gripping a crossbar of the framework, she hung prone, looking straight down at the ground. Behind her, Thorn assumed an identical posture. Air slid over and under them, barely impeded in its passage through the sling – as Roper called the craft's underframe.

The earth was fast dropping away as the hill's incline steepened. Riding the air effortlessly, the Scarebird drifted slowly in the direction of Wilf's Clough.

Thorn smiled a secret smile. This was better by far than sailing! He felt not a trace of fear, only immense exhilaration. To be flying like a bird! To do something so many dreamt of, but almost no one achieved! The magnitude of Roper's genius struck him afresh.

Then Roper called out instructions and they went into a lazy curve. Far below, Thorn could see the trench with its partial skeleton. But the giant was tiny now, a wren's bones sprinkled in a minute earth-grave.

The air on his face was suddenly warmer: he felt the Scarebird lift.

It was what Roper called a riser: a column of air moving up from a tract of sun-heated terrain. Keeping the Scarebird in the riser would lift it higher and higher – and he knew they needed height to get them up Roydsal Hill. But the sky was blue, the sun shone, and the wind over Stony Close had been within acceptable limits.

Up they soared. It was as if some invisible god, bending back his massive head, had, right under them, blown a stream of air from his mouth. Up they were carried like a feather or a winged seed, until Thorn felt near to fainting from the utter joy of it.

"How do you like that?" Roper shouted.

"It's tremendous!" Thorn replied, and Jewel threw out "Wonderful!" She looked back at him and grinned, and Thorn grinned as broadly back.

"There's nothing like it!" cried Roper. "Up here, men are gods. If I could get Lasker to fly, he'd soon drop that religious nonsense."

Thorn very much doubted it, but made no reply. Talking up here was far too effortful, and, besides, he wanted to concentrate on the experience of flying.

Still the Scarebird rose upwards. Below, the giant of Wilf's

Clough was no longer discernible. But the thin thread of a stream was strung like silver along the cleft.

Soon they were moving westwards across a landscape of irregular grassy areas bounded by strips of darker green. A mass of trees came into view and quite quickly drew closer. Above the corner of this, black birds glided and flapped: Rook Wood. Beyond lay Roydsal Dam.

Roper, it was clear, was aiming to skirt, not cross, the wood, but their machine had aroused the interest of its inhabitants. Two of the rooks were coming towards them, gaining height as they flew. Roper let them get close, then pressed a bulb mounted on the frame near his hand. A raucous hooting noise sounded, and the rooks turned tail and shot back towards the trees.

"Works every time!" Roper shouted. "Now you can see why I call her the Scarebird!"

They flew parallel with the trees; then, turning more westerly, crossed the corner of the wood. Ahead lay the long, broad up-slope of Roydsal Hill. The ridge itself was high above them, but this was the windward side of the hill – the correct flank on which to find a means of gaining height.

As they drifted across the hill-slope, Roydsal Dam came into view with – far off in the centre, barely detectable in a combination of sun-glare and heat-haze – Nettle Island nestling in its archipelago. The water seemed benign, its surface bluey-green and barely broken by wavelets. Sailing today would be easy, thought Thorn, even lethargic. So long, of course, as the Great Pike swam on undisturbed . . .

For a time, nothing happened; then, abruptly, they were

rising. This time they'd hit a lifter: this, as Roper explained it, was a corridor of air moving up a hill-slope.

As suddenly as they'd hit the lifter, they lost it again. Roper called out to them and put the Scarebird into a turn. The point was to find the lifter again – and again if necessary – and use it to get them up above the ridge so they could land. They found the lifter; and again the craft rose on its invisible pillow of air.

Their height was good. Once more they turned in a leisurely arc until they were over the crest of the ridge. Judy Wood now came into view: a dense expanse of trees stretching west, south and east with no visible boundary except its near, northern edge. They flew west along the ridge and sighted at last their destination: the great mansion of Roydsal, a structure of dark walls against the patchwork greens of the long ridge-crest.

Roper scanned the earth below for a suitable place to land. Which also, of course, must be a place to take off from: ideally a gently-sloping grassless incline.

They'd hoped to put down on the near side of the house. But they were getting closer and closer and Roper still had given no sign.

He called back: "Damned if I can see a spot to land. I'll have to overfly the house. Keep your fingers crossed, people. We don't want to be seen."

As they floated over the slate roof and its blackened chimney stacks, Thorn glimpsed below them, in the narrow space that separated the house from the rattery, a tiny figure. But it did not stop or seem to look up – and then they were out of sight, the rattery falling away behind them.

"There!" Roper was shouting again. "See that bluff below?"

252

In just one spot the ridge sharpened to an abutment, a steep-faced headland that overlooked the wood to the south. Here, exposed to winds of all kinds, the narrowing ridge-crest was bare, and on its northern flank the hill sloped gently away.

"We'll turn and come in from the east, against the wind. All right?"

They bent northwards, then began a gradual counter-turn. The Scarebird was drawing a circle on the featureless face of the air. Roydsal, which had dropped behind them, reappeared ahead. They dropped lower, slowing as they met the wind head-on. The ridge-crest was below them.

"Get ready for landing!" Roper shouted.

Then Jewel, along with the other two, was tilting into the vertical, her feet swinging down beneath her. They slowed still more, dropping almost idly towards the earth. The ground met her feet, and she trotted a few paces as the Scarebird's momentum died.

"Perfect landing!" cried Roper.

Now for the twins, thought Jewel. And, this time, I will not fail.

15

THE ARTEFACT

Thorn banged on the door again. After a while, the cover behind the spy-hole was drawn back. Someone was looking out at him . . .

Rafter's voice, for Rafter it was, said: "You on your own, Jack?"

"That's right," answered Thorn.

"Where are the others – the woman, the girl?"

"They didn't make it. But I've got what your bosses wanted. You'd better let me in."

"All right – but first, back off. I want to see you dump your weapons against the rattery wall."

"Don't you trust me?" asked Thorn.

"Just do it, kid."

Thorn walked across to the rattery, leant his bow against the wall (he'd left his new one behind, expecting to be disarmed), unstrapped his quiver and set it down, then turned to come back.

Somewhat muffled by the door, he heard Rafter shout: "Your knife as well, Jack."

Thorn sighed, unsheathed his knife and dropped it reluctantly on the ground. Then he walked back to the door. The bolts were retracted.

"Inside," said Rafter. "Take five paces and stand still."

Thorn did as he was bid. Behind him, the bolts crashed back into their slots.

"Walk slowly ahead," Rafter ordered.

Thorn walked down the stone passage towards the first room. But, as he passed beyond the corner of the wall, a savage blow struck his ear. He fell sideways to the floor. As he lay there, head a-buzz, blood oozing from his ear, a kick came into his thigh. He struggled to roll into a ball. A second boot arrived, slamming painfully into his back.

"That's enough," came Rafter's voice. "Do you want to have to carry the little bastard up the stairs?"

A voice replied: "Don't tempt me. It might be worth it."

But no more kicks came. Thorn looked up groggily. Above him loomed an angry man, a man familiar to him. Round the knuckles of his right hand was bound a kind of clasp. It glinted metallically. It was this that had torn his flesh.

"Denny Sweat . . ." said Thorn. "So Burner didn't leave you for the Woodmen after all?"

Denny sneered. "*He* was the one who got left for the Woodmen. By now he's yesterday's stew."

"*You* got the better of *Burner*?" Thorn grinned in spite of his pain. "Then fish can fly," he said.

Denny prodded him with his toe. "Get up, you runt! They'll want to see you right away."

"I bet they will," said Thorn, as he clambered to his feet.

Denny was pulling the metal clasp off his fingers.

Thorn touched a finger to his ear; it came away bloody.

"What is that thing?" he asked.

255

"Don't you know?" Denny grinned. "A knuckle-duster, kid."

"They don't have them where I come from."

He watched as Denny drew his knife and tested its edge against his finger. "Real backwoods boy, aren't you?"

"No. Just civilised."

Denny and Rafter both laughed.

"Enjoy your sense of humour," said Rafter. "Its days are numbered."

"If you say so," said Thorn.

Rafter thrust his face into Thorn's. "I've got lots of things to say to you," he said threateningly, "but you'll have to wait to hear them." He stepped back and said to Denny: "OK. Take him up."

Denny gestured with his knife. "Get going, kid," he said. "You know the way. And give me trouble, by all means. Yes please, give me trouble."

They set off across the room.

The brothers were lounging on the couch in a reprise of the postures Thorn remembered from the first time he'd been taken to the marquee. On that occasion, his hands had been bound. Now they were free. But they might as well have been bound for all the use he could make of them. Where, he wondered, was Haw? Would Racky Jagger be guarding her?

As Thorn crossed the floor, Zak drew on the water pipe, held the smoke for a moment in his lungs, then blew a smoke-ring. It came drifting towards Thorn like a signal, promising nothing.

Thorn stopped short of the table on which the water pipe stood. He unshouldered his pack and set it down on the floor.

Lanner waved a hand at Denny. "A chair for our youthful emissary."

Denny grunted, but fetched up a chair. Thorn's ear still burnt, and his back and thigh were sore. He'd have preferred to stand, but decided to sit. Then he waited for one of the twins to speak.

Lanner said: "Your friends – where are they?"

"They didn't make it," said Thorn.

"I can see that," said Lanner. "Have you been careless? Have you lost them?" He spoke languidly.

He doesn't care either way, thought Thorn.

"We were attacked while crossing the Dam by the boatmen we'd hired. Rainy was killed. I ended up in the water. I don't know what happened to Jewel. But I swam ashore and went on to Minral How."

"All by yourself? Intrepid boy!"

"Have you got the key?" said Zak. His pupils were shrunken, like black pearls.

"Yes." Thorn undid the straps of his pack and took out a key-shaped object bound in cloth and tied with twine.

"Give it here," ordered Lanner.

Thorn passed the package across the table. Taking a knife from his waistbelt sheath, Lanner cut the twine and unrolled the cloth. The brothers stared at the object now revealed, then Lanner rubbed it with a finger.

"It's made of wood!" he said.

"What?" exclaimed Zak.

The key was indeed wooden – a crude, quickly-carved copy that Red had obligingly made for him.

"What are you playing at, Jack?" said Lanner.

"I have the real key, but it's hidden outside the house. I'll do an exchange with you – key for Haw."

"No," said Zak. "We get the key. Then you get your sister."

"No," said Thorn. "An exchange – outside the house, on neutral territory."

There was a clatter: Zak had thrown the tube of the water pipe onto the table. He got up from the couch and walked round the table to Thorn. Grabbing a handful of Thorn's hair, he jerked his head back, brought his face close to Thorn's and said fiercely: "You *will* go and get the key. If you don't come straight back, I'll have your sister brought up here and I'll chop two of her fingers off."

Thorn considered this.

"All right," he said reluctantly. "You win. I'll give it to you."

Zak let go of Thorn's hair and stood glaring down at him.

"What made you think that you could bargain with us?" asked Lanner. He seemed amused by the incident.

Thorn's scalp was on fire. Concealing the pain he felt, he said: "You can hardly blame me for trying. The key's in my pack."

Lanner laughed. "So, fancy yourself as a bit of a joker, do you, Jack?"

"The only jokers here," said Zak to Thorn, "are me and my bro."

Thorn said nothing.

"Get the key, Denny," said Lanner.

Denny pulled out a second package and handed it to Zak. Zak slit the twine with Lanner's knife and unrolled the wrapping. Inside lay the brass key.

"You little lovely!" said Zak. "Come to Da-da!"

He lifted the key to his mouth and planted a soft kiss on the shaft.

"So you got it, Jack," said Lanner. "For once, you've surprised me. I didn't think you could do it. Tell me, how did you get it?"

"Briar Spurr gave it to me."

"Did she tell you why?"

"She said she felt sorry for Haw."

"Not much of a reason, is it? Is that *all* she said?"

"Yes. But you told me I had a special qualification for this job, and I think I know what it was. Briar's my mother, isn't she?"

"How would I know?" said Lanner. "But I'm surprised Crane Rockett let you take the key away. Crane's sense of possession is – how shall I put it? – highly developed."

"He wasn't keen on the idea, but Briar persuaded him."

"What a persuasive woman she is. I bet she twists him around her finger." A paused followed. Then he said: "And you got clean away? Didn't Crane send his death's-head, Deacon Brace, after you?"

"No. But later, when I looked back, I saw that the house was in flames. Something must have happened after I left – but I don't know what."

"Hmm . . . interesting. With a bit of luck, Crane and Brace will be howling in Hell by now. Pity about Briar, though. I could have done something for her – or *with* her," he added.

Thorn very much doubted it.

Zak had paid little or no attention to this exchange. Now he stood up.

"Can't wait any longer," he said. "Got to make sure this still works."

"Fine, bro," said his brother. He too got up from the couch. "Shall we give our guest a treat? He's earned it, I think."

"If you like," said Zak.

"Bring him along," said Lanner to Denny.

Thorn and Denny followed Zak and Lanner across the room to a stretch of peach-coloured drape. Pulling aside a flap, he walked through. The others followed. They went down a passageway, turned right, and down another. On they walked, threading the maze, until Thorn had completely lost his sense of direction.

At last, Zak stopped, detached a second drape and led them through the opening.

This room was smaller than the two Thorn had visited previously. It was dominated by a large, box-like shape made of some polished wood. Eight inches long, six deep and four inches in height, its corners stood on wooden blocks, which raised its underside an inch clear of the floor. It was obviously an artefact produced in the Dark Time.

The lid of the box was closed, but a frame had been rigged above it. Midway along the upper surface of the box and close to the front, a ring was set into the wood. From this a taut rope rose up to a wheel mounted upright on an axle attached to the frame, passed over its flanged rim and came down behind the box. At the back, Thorn surmised, there'd be a windlass of some kind to enable the lid to be raised and lowered.

Facing the wooden box were two armchairs. One was

upholstered in red material, the other in pale yellow. Between them was a table, but there was nothing on top of it.

"You two – stand behind those chairs," said Lanner.

Denny chivvied Thorn into place.

The brothers now disappeared around the back of the box. To the creaky accompaniment of the cranked-up windlass, the lid was slowly raised. It was hinged at the back, and opened like a jaw to reveal a lining of black fabric.

When the lid was fully drawn back and (Thorn assumed) the windlass secured, the Spetches returned to the front of the box. Halfway along it was a dark, irregular hole. Its shape betrayed its function: this was the socket for the key.

Zak pushed the brass key into the socket. Then he and Lanner took up mirror positions on each side of the hollow ring that formed the key's head; grasping it, they began to twist, one pulling, one pushing, in a well-practised routine. The key turned with a screeching sound, as of metal tightening. They turned it no more than a half-revolution at a time – and it didn't look easy work.

Lanner retreated to the red chair and dropped gratefully into it. Zak walked to the right-hand corner of the box, where there was a short flight of steps. He dragged the steps across to the head of the key, climbed to the top step and reached down towards the box. Thorn heard a sharp click.

As Zak came down the steps, a faint whirring started up. Thorn's eyes were fixed on the box, whose contents, of course, its height prevented him from seeing. A stiff figure rose into view in the centre, as if pulled up by hidden wires from a supine position. When the figure was erect, the whirring ceased.

The figure was female and perhaps two inches tall. She wore a close-fitting silvery bodice that left her arms and shoulders bare. A many-layered, frilly skirt of a kind entirely new to Thorn stuck out horizontally from her thighs, leaving her legs uncovered. She was made from some hard stuff – metal or pottery or wood – painted over, and both her black hair – drawn tight from the crown and bobbed at the back – and her emotionless features had a glazed sheen to them. Her skirt, however, was made of some gauzy material. Her arms were raised above her head to form an oval, the fingers touching.

Now sounds came from the box. At the same time, the female figure slowly began to revolve.

How to describe the sounds? Thorn had heard the trilling of larks, but what came from the box was far more complicated than anything any bird could have produced, far more poignant and wonderful. The sounds seemed to rise and fall in glittering diamond chains, now to float like the Scarebird and now to tumble like a waterfall, tinkling and ringing like unseen, airy bells – or heavenly bells, for if Heaven existed that was where these sounds belonged.

On they went, until Thorn felt a profound sense of longing and melancholy. He thought of the father he'd never known and the mother lost to him. He felt a dragging pain in his throat, as if his neck had been squeezed or wrenched, and tears came into his eyes. What's happening to me? he wondered. What is it gives these sounds such power? There was nothing like them in his world.

Then, as abruptly as they had started, the sounds stopped and the figure stilled. The whirring recommenced, and the figure, still rigid, slowly toppled over backwards to disappear from view.

There was a long, tense silence. It was as if no one dared to speak, such was the magic cast by the box. The brothers sat as if tranced in their chairs, their red and yellow heads unmoving. Denny was standing behind Thorn, but no sound came from the man, and Thorn guessed he too was spellbound.

Time passed. At last it was Zak who ended the silence.

"How did we live without it, bro?"

"In the way we lived before it. As we shall live if it ever breaks."

"Don't say that, Lanner. Don't even think it."

"But I *have* thought it. The mind—"

"Sod the mind! You think too much."

"No more nor less than you do, bro, and – I'd guess – little differently."

Lanner twisted round and looked over the back of his chair.

"Come round here, Jack," he said.

Thorn walked around the chairs and took up a stance facing the brothers.

"What did you think of that?" said Lanner.

"The box?" said Thorn hoarsely. "It was wonderful."

Lanner turned to Zak. "He says it's wonderful, bro."

"Then he's stealing our thoughts," said Zak. "Because that's what we think."

Lanner said to Thorn. "You'll have to put our thoughts back. We can't have idiots stealing them."

"What do you want me to say?" said Thorn. "That those were the ugliest noises I've ever come across in my life?"

Lanner laughed. "Well, you know the old saying: A lie in time, skiddle-de-dee, keeps yours for you and mine for me."

"No, I don't know it," said Thorn, who thought that Lanner had made it up. "But I'd very much like to know what it was that we heard."

"It's called *music*. Our friend Querne Rasp told us that. The contraption behind you goes by the name of a *music box*."

"I've never heard music before," mused Thorn. "All we have is bells and drums."

"True," said Zak. "Perhaps there's something wrong with us. Perhaps the Ranters are right who say we're all bound for Hell."

Lanner said: "*We're* certainly bound for Hell, bro."

"Maybe," said Zak, "but not today."

The brothers giggled.

"Well now," said Lanner to Zak, "we've a reputation to maintain. What shall we do with this fellow?"

"I've done what you wanted," said Thorn. "You promised to set my sister free."

Lanner assumed a puzzled frown. "I don't remember that," he said. "Do you remember that, bro?"

"Remember what, bro?" said Zak.

"Saying we'd set his sister free."

"Free of what?"

"Good question," said Lanner. He turned to Thorn. "Free of what?"

Here we go again, thought Thorn.

"I'm not playing this game," he said. "Will you set her free or not? Just give me a simple answer."

"He wants a simple answer," said Lanner.

"I hear him, bro," said Zak. "Does he think we're simpletons?"

Lanner said to Thorn, "My brother wants to know if you think we're simpletons."

"I heard what he said. I'm not deaf. Will you set her free or not?"

"What does she look like, this sister?" asked Zak.

Thorn said nothing.

"What's the matter? Rat got your tongue?"

"No," said Thorn. "But it's got yours."

Zak stared silently at Thorn. Then he turned to his brother. "I'm starting not to like this kid."

"What's to like?" asked Lanner. "I've seen prettier moles."

"True, and they make excellent fur coats, which he never will." Zak paused. "So, he wants his sister back?"

"So he says. The question is," Lanner said gravely, "why do bees sting your knees?"

"Moreover," said Zak solemnly, "why do moles live in holes?"

There was a brief silence; then the brothers began to chuckle.

Lanner giggled: "Why do frogs live in bogs?"

The brothers fell about laughing and clutching at one another.

Zak gasped: "Why do sparrows fly like arrows?"

Lanner shrieked: "Why do flies like rabbit pies?"

As Thorn stood watching them, their strangeness struck him afresh. They were more than weird, more than bizarre. Were they mad then? Mad, their behaviour often seemed; yet it was calculated too, it had a kind of logic to it. One moment they acted on whim, the next they acted on reason. They lied, kidnapped, murdered – probably tortured their victims too. Yet only a little while before, they – like him – had been struck dumb by something soulful and infinitely beautiful. How could that be? How could such depraved beings respond so deeply to music?

At last the brothers subsided, pulled coloured handkerchiefs from their pockets and dabbed their tear-wet eyes.

Lanner said: "He'll be the death of us, this lad."

"Unless," said his brother with a snuffle, "we get in first."

He looked speculatively at Thorn, as if measuring him for a noose.

"My sister," said Thorn. "You're not going to free her, are you?"

"Who can know, who can say?" said the flame-haired twin. There was a twinkle in his eye. "So many things are hidden in the dark womb of time."

"I think," said Thorn, "that I can take that as a no."

THIRD INTERFACE

THE STONE-WOMAN

Racky Jagger rode Bumper through the stone-arched gateway of the ancient churchyard and on down the paved pathway. Crazy paving, the giants had called it. It wasn't all that was crazy here.

On either side, grass rioted and eroded tombstones reared – some defiantly upright, some slumping at drunken angles, the names cut into their faces clogged by mustard-bright lichen. He passed a sooty mausoleum. Before it stood a time-corroded angel, winged and demure, head bowed, hands upward-pointing in an attitude of prayer. Beyond her a stand of yews, trunks twisted as if by nightmares, writhed blackly and silently.

He came at length to a wooden building built against the church wall. Outside it, in a paved space, were a number of carts and carriages to which rats were harnessed. Also, tied to hitching-rails, were a number of saddle-rats. Emitting occasional snuffles, they scuffed their paws restlessly or stood dreamily, patiently waiting. Obviously a service was in progress inside the church.

Racky brought Bumper to a halt. As he dismounted, a young man got up from the chair he was sitting on.

"Hello, Racky. You're back then."

"As you see, Fleck . . . Not at the service, today?"

"Not today, Racky. My turn to keep an eye on things."

Fleck Dewhurst was a stout, nervous young man with struggling hair, a potato nose and capacious ears. Like his father, he was a ratman. Fleck lived and worked in Lowmoor, but also sometimes here. The long wooden building was the church rattery.

Racky unstrapped his saddlebags and hooked them over his shoulder.

"Higgins on good form, is he?" he asked the ratman dryly.

"He's a great man," said Fleck.

"Is he? You deserve better."

Fleck said nothing.

Racky went on: "You remember Bumper. Will you stable him for me?"

"Of course, Racky."

"You're a good man, Fleck."

"You're going down, I suppose."

Fleck alone amongst the disciples knew of Querne's hideaway and had set eyes on the Magian. He was sworn to secrecy.

"That's right," Racky confirmed.

"Rather you than me. I can't bear to be underground. I get the feeling I'm trapped."

"We're all trapped," said Racky. "It's just a question of how. Well, see you later, Fleck. Keep the sun warm for me."

But Fleck caught his arm.

"She's beautiful," he said, "but you deserve better, Racky."

Racky took in the young man's serious face, then burst into laughter.

"One to you, Fleck." Then he sobered. "But when it comes to deserving, she's exactly what I deserve."

268

Leaving Fleck with Bumper, Racky followed the path that hugged the base of the church wall until he came to the side entry. The original oak door stoutly repulsed all but the winds, which slipped in through the cracks between its edges and the frame. A door of human dimensions had been hung in one corner and, lifting the latch, Racky entered.

He was in a vestibule. The inner door was wedged open, as it always had been, and he went through and along the south transept of the church. Light sprayed down from a pair of stained-glass windows and, as he passed through the rays, lozenges of colour flowed over him like irradiated water. That, he could enjoy – but not the voice he now heard, haranguing the dusty vaults and alcoves.

Arriving at the nave, he turned down the south aisle – away from that relentless voice. For, at the meeting point of transept and nave, pivot and crux of the edifice, Higgins Makepeace, Grand Ranter of the Church of the Iron Angel, was in full spate: flogging his flock with the harsh-tongued gospel of his God.

Oh, how they loved it! Loved the rapture, loved the pain. How they bent to the thongs of language with which Higgins whipped their souls. For how else could they be uplifted, fly heavenward with the church, become one with the glorious sun?

Racky hurried away from the voice, closing his ears to its swell of sound.

To his right reared ranks of pews, their rigid backs and cramped seats designed to keep giants awake while they worshipped their God. Now they were riddled with woodworm, and bored-out sawdust peppered the floor between the rows. Underfoot were slabs of stone, some engraved with names and inscriptions.

The voice had lost definition, reduced to mutterings in fog. By the time he came to the base of one of the yellow-grey pillars that held the roof-beams in place, the voice could no longer be heard. The pillar was overwhelmingly massive. The giants must have used machines to swing its great stones into place. He refrained from looking up. A single soul of wood and stone, the building seemed impetuously to strain at its foundations, seeking to leap into the sky. Racky couldn't account for the effect it had on him. It was as if this lump of architecture was calling to something buried beneath reason's cool floor – something dark, primitive. He felt he had to resist it.

Racky turned between two rows of pews. His boots kicked up a mixture of sawdust and dust. Down the centre of the church ran a broad aisle, but as he crossed this space he didn't so much as glance in the direction of the east window. He had no desire to sight the Iron Angel himself.

Pews again . . . a second pillar identical to the first . . . and now he was in the north aisle. Here in the wall a door was set, but again a smaller door had been chivvied in one corner. Taking a key from his jerkin, Racky unlocked it, went through and re-locked it behind him.

This was the anteroom to the crypt. In one corner a gaunt stone stairway led down into darkness, but it was useless to humans and Racky instead directed his steps towards a much smaller vent on the opposite side of the room.

This access point was circular. Around it ran a wooden guardrail. On a table beside the hole were several lamps and a metal tin containing flint and tinder. When Racky had lit one of these, he lifted a section of the rail and began to descend a spiral staircase.

A watcher from above would have seen the light linger for a time after its carrier had vanished, burning its way through slow circles. Then that too was swallowed up.

Racky paused for a few moments at the door to Querne's sanctum. Once, on an impulse, he'd looked up her forename in a damp-stained, mouse-gnawed dictionary he'd found at Roydsal. A *quern* was a stone-mill for the grinding of grain. Which made Querne a stone-woman, a heart-grinder, a soul-crusher. Guess whose heart? Guess whose soul? Yet he didn't give a tittle for *her* heart, *her* soul – if she possessed such things, which he seriously doubted. Her compulsion lay elsewhere . . .

He rapped five times with the brass knocker: first two strokes, then one stroke, then two strokes again. Only he and Spine Wrench, Querne's nauseating servant, were aware of this sequence. Then he turned the ring and pushed. The door smoothly unclosed.

"So, the wanderer returns!"

Querne was sitting in her chair.

"Hello, Querne," he said.

Was the room still more extravagant than the last time he'd been here? Since no particular object satisfied Querne for long, it was more than likely. She'd no sooner procure one thing than she'd express a desire for another – the next thing, the new thing that would amuse or titillate. Despite her awesome power, there was something unformed in her, something for which, he suspected, her power itself was responsible. Her original yellow crystal, acquired many years before from a reluctant Syb (as the Magian smoothly put it), nestled like a pampered idol in a cloth on top of a table set within reach of her chair.

And now he'd brought her a second stone.

The room – or cavern (for such it was) – teemed with vivid colour and light. Rugs and tapestries hung from the walls and scattered the harsh rock of the floors. There were cabinets and tables that the Magian herself had fashioned; elaborate ornaments of glass that caught and refracted the light; and, secluded at the toe-end of this L-shaped room, Querne's bed with its taloned feet and viper-headed bedposts: each snake scale-skinned, fork-tongued and ruby-eyed. The light came not from natural lamps but gem-lights she'd somehow embedded in the rock. These she could brighten or could dim as it pleased her – a minor flexing of her power. What she might not do if she was minded . . .? He feared to know what she might do . . .

Unhooking his saddlebags, he swung them onto a table.

"Have you the crystals?" Querne demanded, avarice flaring in her eyes. Then, seeing him hesitate: "Don't tell me you haven't got them." The syllables rang like icicles.

"I have the blue crystal – the one the twins acquired. If you got my last message, you will know the ruby crystal is no longer at Wyke. More of that in a moment. As for the green crystal, the one the Syb-sisters had, that was gone when I got to the island."

He saw fury tighten her face, narrow her eyes, stretch her jaw.

"GONE?" she repeated in a voice like thunder.

"Yes, gone. But I know who has it, so all is not lost."

The hurricane subsided no less quickly than it arose.

"The blue crystal – give it to me."

He took the swaddled stone from his pack and carried it to her. She set it down on her lap and proceeded to unwrap it.

Her need burned in her eyes. As she examined the blue stone, he studied her down-turned face. Its angle served to emphasise its natural shape: which was that of an upside-down tear or droplet pearl. The angle emphasised, too, her slightly in-slanting eyes – grey-irised, under artfully-blackened eyebrows and long lashes. Her nose and mouth were delicate, her hair chestnut-brown. She looked younger than she was: an illusion, no doubt. But then, so much around and about this woman was illusory. Racky was struck by a fantasy: he was dreaming, he'd wake up to find Querne and the realm she'd created suddenly sucked out of time – like the world of Heathcliff and Catherine when the reader, trance broken, walks away from the book . . .

Lightly resting her hands on the stone, Querne closed her eyes. Within moments, an intense blue light flared up in the thing. Escaping between her fingers and the uncovered parts of its surface, it flung itself into the room, drenching every object and surface, colouring hangings and furnishings and even the local, glittering lights. Racky bore the intensity, his eyes still on Querne's face. It seemed to tauten, to age, revealing its sinews

273

and muscles, the shape of the bone beneath the skin; then the Magian's lips parted and she emitted a long sigh. Racky had heard that sigh before. His features hardened; he looked away. The woman was obscene. His barely-suppressed hatred for her flowered in him afresh. He turned and walked towards the door.

He was reaching for the handle when her voice sounded behind him.

"Where are you going, Racky? Come back to me. *Now!*"

He turned to find her earlier self smoothly restored. On her face was a mocking smile. She no longer clasped the crystal; already its blue light was dying.

"Come – sit down," she said. "You look tired. I'll make some tea. Then you must tell me everything."

Damping down the flames of his hate, he drew up a chair.

She was not like other women. To make tea, she didn't put a kettle on a hob. She simply touched the pot with a finger: the water would boil before you'd taken your mental count as far as fifty . . .

Forty-five. Soon after that she was pouring the tea.

"Now, you beautiful man," she said, "I wish to hear every-thing."

"So," she said, when she'd heard him to the end, "it appears we have not one Thorn in our flesh, but two of them: your son and this unknown girl." She smiled sweetly at him. "Each of them has a crystal: the ruby stone and the green. If they knew how to use them, they'd be formidable enemies. But they are children, no more. A little strategy, and the crystals will be mine. And then . . ."

"Then what?" he asked.

"Then I shall be greater than before."

"And what will you do with this greatness?"

"You will see."

"You sound just like the twins."

Querne emitted a peal of laughter. "Now *that* could be taken as compliment or criticism. I tell you what you need to know."

Of course you do, Racky thought. That, my beautiful monster, is all you've ever done.

"So: have you a plan?" he asked.

"If your son recovers the Spetches' key, he'll go back for his sister. Then they'll go to Norgreen and the ruby crystal will reappear. The girl Jewel seeks revenge: for that, she too must return to Roydsal. So long as she has the green crystal, she will carry it with her. It will be your task to cover that end of things: to take possession of both crystals if they should chance to come your way. How you do it is up to you."

She paused.

"But there's another possibility. You say this Jewel has lost a dear friend, Rainy Gill. I know something of this juggler, where she comes from, where she lived. Jewel will – she *must*, it is written in her nature – go back to Harrypark to bear the news to Rainy's father and those close to her. I, therefore, shall go to Harrypark. If Jewel turns up there, I shall take her crystal from her."

"You make it sound easy," said Racky. "But things have already gone wrong once."

"It *will* be easy. Trust me."

He thought: I'd rather trust an adder.

Querne had long red fingernails. With a slow stroke she scored three white tracks across his cheek. He shuddered and shut his eyes.

"You've earned a reward, Racky," she said.

16

JEWEL ALONE

Midday stretched into afternoon. Jewel and Roper lurked at the corner of the house, keeping watch on the doorway and the rattery opposite. Since Thorn had gone inside, little of consequence had happened. Briefly Rafter had appeared, picked up Thorn's weapons and taken them in. Leech, the wizened ratman, had come out, crossed to the rattery, stayed there for a time, then returned to the house. That was all.

"He's not coming out, is he?" said Roper.

"I don't believe so," said Jewel. "It's as we thought: the twins have gone back on their word. We have to assume that Thorn's a captive as well as Haw – though on past experience they won't be held in the same place."

"So," said Roper, "according to what we know, there are five of them and two of us. Not good odds."

"I'm going in alone," said Jewel.

"You can't be serious," said Roper.

"I am," she said, "and you know why. I told you about Rainy. I can't bear the thought of any more dead friends."

"But Jewel—" Roper began.

She seized his head in both her hands. His eyes widened as she stared at him. Belatedly, he raised his palms and tried to push her away. But his effort was feeble; his arms fell back to his sides. His legs turned to water, his eyelids drooped and he sank down to the ground.

She dragged his body out of sight of the door and supported his head on a stone. He would sleep for some time.

"I'm sorry, Roper," she said, "but this is for your own good." And after a moment: "Wish me luck."

She strapped her quiver of arrows to her back. Then, armed with her bow, she walked down to the door and listened. No sound came from within. She leant her bow against the wall. She placed her hands on the spot where she judged the upper bolt to be positioned, took hold of it with her mind and slid it back, muffling the iron so that whoever was on duty in the guardroom would not be alerted; then did the same with the lower bolt.

She pushed the door open. She went in and re-bolted it. She allowed herself a smile as the second bolt went home: this was easier than using physical force would have been.

Quietly, she walked down to the end of the passageway. She risked a glance into the room, but could not see anyone. She crawled across to the guardhouse wall.

The rust-red tiles that covered the floor were cracked and uneven. Gaps appeared between the tiles and the bottom edge of the guardhouse wall. Laying down her bow, she slipped her fingers under the wall. The guardhouse had its own floor . . . This gave her an idea. Gripping the angle, she set herself to concentrate . . .

Inside the room a man was sitting, staring out through the window. Silently his wooden chair began to sprout tendrils – out of the seat, out of the back. Its occupant sat on, oblivious.

The woody cords grew out and down – long, serpentine, dangling.

Suddenly from below and round from behind the cords came whipping, to wrap themselves tightly about the man's thighs and torso. One of his arms had been resting in his lap – it was roped to his leg; the other had been raised to scratch an itch on his scalp and it escaped pinioning. Letting fly an oath, he tried with his free hand to drag a cord away from his chest. He couldn't move it even a fraction. And now another cord leapt up and fastened down the fighting arm. He was trussed like a rabbit on a spit, ready for roasting.

Jewel came into the room and looked at the man. It was Lippy.

"You!" he cried. "But what—"

"Quiet!" she ordered him, and laid a finger on his lips. The red-pink skin trembled, then began to bubble. Fresh alarm showed in Lippy's eyes. He opened his mouth to scream, but even as he did so his lips erupted with fleshy polyps. Within moments they had united, sealing his mouth with new skin. Lippy struggled like a madman, but was unable to speak a word.

Jewel looked at the frightened man. You're not so lippy now, she thought.

She said coldly: "After a day the skin will shrivel; you'll be able to speak again. Be patient and you'll survive. Panic, you'll end up dead. Not that I care either way."

Now she placed her hands on his head, closed her eyes and concentrated. When her eyes opened again, she looked quietly satisfied.

Outside the guardhouse she nocked an arrow to her bow and, carrying it as Rainy had taught her – at waist-height and pointing downwards, went swiftly across the room. Her first move had gone as planned, but she'd been lucky in that she'd had to deal with only one man. Two could have caused her problems. From here on, she knew, she would have to improvise.

Uneventfully, she crossed several rooms in turn until she came to the entrance to the old, high-ceilinged hall.

She reached out to grasp the latch of the door-within-a-door, then took her hand away. There was a diagonal crack in the wood. It was a hairline crack, but it had given her an idea.

Laying down her bow and arrow, she placed a hand on each side of the crack. Then she set to work. Slowly, silently, the crack began to widen as she compressed the woody fibres.

When she judged it wide enough, she set an eye to the crack. Away across the hall floor was the wooden cell where Haw was imprisoned. In front of it a man stood. He was armed with a pike. Jewel couldn't make out his features, but then he turned to his right and began to walk around the cell. It was Rafter, she was sure. As Rafter went down the left side of the cell, a second man appeared from around the back to the cell's right. He too carried a pike. When he reached the front of the cell he stopped. Jewel didn't recognise him, but she knew who he was. Denny Sweat had returned from the wood. That meant there were six men in the house.

She leant for a time against the door, then picked up her bow and arrow and took a second shaft from her quiver. She nocked both arrows, tightened the bowstring and put her eye to the crack.

In the hall now, Rafter appeared from round the back of Haw's cell while the second man turned down the side.

Holding the bow with one hand at the point where the arrows crossed the sprung wood, Jewel opened the door and slipped into the hall.

Rafter spotted her straightaway. As Jewel levelled the bow and aimed, he shouted out a warning.

Down through the arm stringing the bow, into her hand, thumb and forefinger and into the sleek, twin shafts ran some of the virtue of Jewel's power. Then the arrows were in the air.

Rafter thought the girl insane. How, at such a distance, could even the greatest of archers hope to hit a mobile target? And *this* archer was a mere slip of a girl, who'd fired not one arrow, but two. They weren't even coming towards him! A smirk came into his face. Pictures of what he'd do to her when he'd caught her tickled his mind.

Denny Sweat had swivelled round. He too had seen the archer.

But something odd was happening. The two arrows had parted company, seemed to be swerving in the air . . . Rafter's smirk evaporated and was replaced by a frown. Now, one of the arrows was making straight for him.

On the other side of the cell, seeing an arrow coming towards him, Denny moved to one side. The arrow bent in flight. Denny took to his heels and ran – but the arrow struck him high in the thigh and he collapsed, clutching his leg.

Rafter threw himself flat on his face and heard the *zing!* as the flying shaft ripped the air where he'd stood.

He was safe. He rolled over.

And couldn't believe what he was seeing. The shaft that had missed him was looping up and over. It seemed, impossibly, to have lost none of its speed. He followed its arc, struggling to understand this breach in nature. Then it was dropping straight towards him.

He ought to have twisted sideways, but his body refused to move. He let out a shrill scream. It was the last sound he made.

The arrow speared his neck and buried its metal tip in the floor. Rafter jerked, his eyes popping; a gurgling noise came from his throat. He coughed, and blood-bubbles formed and burst on his lips. He grasped the arrow and tried to pull it out of his throat, but couldn't shift it. He felt as weak as an infant. He struggled to suck air into his lungs, but his windpipe was shattered.

I'm going to die, he thought.

High above his head hung a glittering cluster of diamonds. Its beauty struck him as absurd. He half-lifted a limp hand; then it flopped back to the floor.

Jewel, a third arrow nocked, had set off across the room. She came and looked down at Rafter. In the protuberant balls of his eyes, his pupils shone like black pearls. Blood smeared his slack mouth. From his neck more blood was dribbling to form an irregular lustrous pool. She felt nothing for this man – neither pity nor horror – and, turning away, she walked around the rear of the cell.

Denny had propped himself on an elbow. His back was to Jewel. White-knuckled he clutched his pike, holding it out in front of him at an angle to the floor.

Jewel said: "Throw that weapon down. If you don't, I'll kill you."

Denny twisted, wincing with pain, and glanced over his shoulder. Behind him, his unlikely opponent had levelled her bow at his head. The pike clattered to the floor.

She circled carefully round him and kicked the pike to a safe distance. Denny leant back on his elbow, a bloody hand gripping his thigh where the arrow stuck out of it.

"Rafter?" he said. His mouth had gone dry.

"He's dead. As you will be – if," she promised, "you give me the least trouble. Do you understand what I'm saying?"

He nodded. That fact he understood, but nothing else to do with this girl.

"What are you?" he asked.

She gave him an icy smile. "Too much for you, little man."

She picked up the pike and started to walk away from him. But she stopped and looked back, as if prompted by an afterthought.

"This is your second reprieve," she said. "Make sure it's your last."

Denny tried to swallow, but something seemed to be gripping his throat.

Jewel unbolted the door of the cell and threw it open.

Haw was standing beside her cot, her eyes fixed upon the door.

"Jewel?" she said, scarcely believing what she was seeing.

"You're safe now," Jewel said.

But Haw stood as if in a trance, and it was Jewel who went forward and put her arms round the other girl. She was two years older than Haw, but felt infinitely older.

Haw drew back from her. "Where's Thorn?" she asked.

"The brothers have him."

283

"He isn't with you?"

"There's no time for questions. You must do as I say." She drew the girl out of the cell and pointed to Denny's pike. "Take that and, if need be, defend yourself," she said.

Then she went back to Denny. "Into the cell," she ordered him.

Denny turned, and began to pull himself backwards along the ground. Pain furrowed his face.

In the meantime, Haw had spotted Rafter's body on the floor.

"Did you shoot them both?" she asked.

"Yes," Jewel replied.

"Is Rafter dead?"

"Yes."

Haw looked at Jewel in awe. "I'm glad you killed him," she said. "Rafter was a bad man."

As soon as Denny Sweat had dragged himself into the cell, Jewel bolted the door on him.

"Right. Let's go," she said.

As they hurried through the building, she told Haw about the Scarebird and Roper Tuckett outside.

"Go to Roper and stay with him. If Thorn and I haven't joined you by the time Roper wakes, you must both go back to the Scarebird and wait there for us."

"But I want to stay with you," objected Haw, "and help Thorn."

"You're a brave girl, Haw, but I have to face the twins myself." And I can do it better, she thought, if I don't have *you* to worry about.

She took Haw to the outer door, let her out and shot the bolts. On the way back, she looked in on Lippy. He was red-faced but alive.

"Remember – patience!" she said, and left him to his punishment.

But, as she was going past the corner of the guardhouse, a man flung himself on her. She went sprawling with the man on top of her. The breath was forced out of her lungs and a knife jabbed into her ribs.

Her body exploded with energy. Her assailant was flung off into the air. He landed a clear foot away and went sliding along the floor. His knife skittered away from his grasp.

She got to her feet and felt her side. She was bleeding but the cut wasn't deep. She thought: my body defended itself before real damage could be done.

Her attacker was Leech, the ratman. He lay on his back, whimpering. His face was badly scorched, his knife-hand five charred stumps. Wisps of smoke curled up from him.

He must have found Lippy, then lain in wait for her.

She considered him dispassionately, the last of the Spetches' men. Had she happened to be an ordinary person, she'd be dead. But she wasn't an ordinary person. Leech had never had a chance. Kneeling by his side, she touched his forehead and knocked him out. He would sleep for at least a day.

Only the twins remained. Racky Jagger, she knew from Lippy, had left the house some days before.

She was climbing the long staircase to the tabletop marquee when a painting on the facing wall of the room caught her eye.

The picture was wild and riveting. In the foreground, a woman who had snakes instead of hair was menacing a youth. She was red-eyed and furious. He was handsome, wore a helmet and clutched a gleaming sword and a mirror. Strangely, he wasn't looking at her. Instead his gaze was fixed on the mirror, in whose circular pane of glass appeared a reflection of her head. In the background, to left and right, were a number of stone figures, as if arrested in action.

Jewel had no idea who these characters were, but the story the picture told was clear. The woman with the snaky head was a monster who turned you to stone; the stony figures were her victims. If the youth looked her in the face, he too would turn to stone and join her frozen gallery. Hence the mirror to get him close enough to deal her a killing blow.

I ought to be on the side of the youth, thought Jewel. But she had no feeling for him. It was the raging, serpent-headed woman with whom she identified.

She went on up the staircase, then across the green carpet to the marquee and its maze of corridors, concealed entrances and secret rooms.

For the first time, she was struck by the strange symmetry of the impending confrontation. The brothers had murdered her father in a labyrinth of glass. Now she herself must seek revenge in a maze of coloured cloths . . . The twins had surprised her father in a room of distorting mirrors. She would repay the compliment.

She undid the entrance flaps, then, gripping each flap with a hand, closed her eyes and relaxed. In her mind, she travelled the corridors, locating entrances and rooms. Time passed; still she stood there like a statue of a girl. When at last she opened her eyes, a tracery of the place shone clear in her mind. But of Thorn and the twins, strangely, she could find no sign.

She went first to the room where the twins sat and smoked. It was empty. The water pipe stood on the table; no smoke curled from its top. She visited several rooms in turn. One was the twins' bedroom, where among rich, gauzy pastel drapes a formidable bed stood, easily big enough for four.

In another room she found nothing but two armchairs and a huge box. Above the box was a pulley-wheel to enable the lid to be raised and lowered. The box had a keyhole, and intrigued her, but she had no time to waste.

The last room to which she came she'd heard about from Thorn: the room equipped with trapezes where the brothers exercised, transforming themselves into the Flying Twins.

It was here that she found them.

Here, too, that she found Thorn.

Hands and legs tightly bound, he hung high above the ground at the heart of the assembly, midway between the gantries from which the trapezes hung. A rope was knotted about his ankles and looped over a second rope. This stretched across the tops of the inner gantries and down to the platforms on the two outer gantries. There, its ends were tied to rings.

The brothers stood on their platforms, facing each other across the rig. Their trapezes were tied to the poles. Each held a sharp knife. They seemed relaxed and carefree; they hadn't a care in the world.

And, indeed, why should they have? Hadn't they got their key back, at little cost to themselves?

Jewel drew back from the slit through which she was peeping, and considered. It was clear to her now why it had proved beyond her powers to pinpoint Thorn's whereabouts or the position of the twins. It was because they were in the air, only tenuously linked to the ground she stood upon.

This was a dangerous situation. One false move on her part and the twins would cut the ropes . . . If either were to succeed, Thorn would plunge to his death.

She dismissed out of hand the notion of firing arrows at them. The arrows might only wound them, or they could (as Rafter had done) dodge the first pass, giving them time to sever the ropes.

She sat cross-legged on the floor, and struggled to think. Courageously and deliberately, Thorn had walked into Roydsal, conscious that the twins would probably break their agreement. *I have to try*, he'd told her. And yes, he'd had to try. But the twins had run true to form. Thorn's fate lay in her hands. She knew he trusted her, believed in her. He knew she could open locked doors, he'd seen what she'd done to Deacon Brace. And yet, what if his confidence in her was misplaced? What if he'd overestimated the potency of her powers?

There *has* to be a way I can save him, there *has* to be . . .

Her thoughts twisted and turned through blind alleys with locked doors.

Then an audacious idea pushed up a green shoot in her mind. The tendril grew and uncurled. Could it really work?

Well, what else was there? Damn the twins, she'd *make* it work . . .

She commenced her preparations . . .

Some time later, she undid the flap and stepped into the room.

The twins were still on their platforms. They were chatting and joking. Above them Thorn dangled, gagged and trussed, gently revolving. As she watched, Lanner whipped the knife at the rope, just missing it. The twins laughed. How soon before they tired of tormenting him?

Jewel walked towards them. Blond Zak spotted her first.

"Bro! We've a guest!" he exclaimed.

Lanner turned and looked down.

"Well, if it isn't little Jewel! We were told you were dead."

"Talk about bad pennies!" said Zak.

Jewel halted beside the nearest of the stout metal poles that supported the platform on Lanner's side of the rig. Leaning against the pole, she looked up at the flame-haired twin.

He said: "Your timing couldn't be better. Your friend is just about to attempt a death-defying drop."

"Yes indeed," echoed Zak. "A feat never yet achieved in the whole of fairground history!"

"For reasons," said Lanner, "far too obvious to repeat."

"For," said Zak coyly, "if you drop things, they fall—"

"And go *splat!* when they hit the ground—"

"Human skulls especially."

"Just like *yours* would, if *you* fell?" Jewel observed impassively.

Zak flashed a grin at her. "Not us. We're *in*human."

"You said it," Jewel said.

Lanner frowned down at her. A thought had just occurred to him.

"How did you get in?" he asked.

"Wouldn't you like to know?"

Lanner frowned. "Where are our men?"

"Here and there," she replied.

"She says 'here and there'," Lanner informed his brother.

"I heard her," replied Zak. He told Jewel: "I don't know what the hell you think you're playing at, girl. A word in someone's ear and his sister will be dead." He jerked a thumb at Thorn.

"Then give it," said Jewel.

"Leech!" Zak shouted. "Leech! Get yourself in here!"

But Leech made no appearance.

Lanner said: "He must have gone to check the rats. But he'll be back soon enough."

"He *won't* be back," said Jewel.

"Won't be back?" said Zak.

"Not today," said Jewel.

"Then it looks as if the two of us will have to sort you out."

"All *two* of you?" said Jewel. "Will two of you be enough?"

"More than enough for *you*, girl."

"If you say so. Start whenever the fancy takes you."

For the first time, the brothers' self-possession seemed to waver. They looked at one another as if they couldn't believe their ears.

Jewel lounged by the pole, caressing the metal with a hand.

"Which of you killed my father?" she asked. "I'd like to know. Of course you're equally guilty. But who wielded the knife?"

Zak pointed to Lanner. "He did," he said.

Lanner pointed to Zak. "He did," he said.

The twins grinned identical grins.

Jewel said wearily: "You never let up, do you?"

"Letting up's never been our style," said Lanner.

"Until now," Jewel murmured.

"Not now either," said Lanner.

Twirling about, he whipped his knife at the rope, just missing it. Then grinned down at Jewel like a malevolent gargoyle.

"Look at you," said Jewel. "A pair of cowards threatening a bound and helpless man. Which of you is man enough to come down here to me?"

The smile faded from Lanner's face. He glanced across at his brother.

"I've had enough of her," he announced.

"Well, bro," said Zak, "you were never the patient type."

Wrapping his arms and legs around the nearest gantry upright, Lanner began to slide down.

He got no more than halfway when he came to a stop, his feet at least six inches above Jewel's head.

Below him, both of the girl's hands were gripping the pole.

"Bro!" he cried, "I can't move!"

He looked wildly around, as if seeking an explanation for what was happening to him.

"I'm stuck to the pole! Help me, bro!"

Zak shouted: "Hold on, Lanner!"

Unfortunately, holding on was just Lanner's problem.

That girl, thought Zak – she's doing something to the pole.

"Stop!" he shouted and pointed at Thorn. "Stop! Or I'll cut him down!"

291

But Jewel might have been deaf. As Lanner cried out with fear, Zak frenziedly sawed at the rope. He'd cut through just half of its strands when it parted with a crack. As the cut end leapt away, Thorn dropped headfirst towards the floor.

But, instead of smashing up, his body sank into its surface, cushioned as if by thick sponge.

Zak goggled with disbelief. What was happening to the world? An icy spasm tripped his heart.

Lanner, glued fast to the pole, had fallen silent. He was staring at his hands. His fingers and fists had turned silver. A metallic skin was creeping up his forearms from his wrist.

And they were cold – oh, so cold!

So were his legs between feet and knees. He glanced down: the same malignant tide was crawling up his thighs.

He opened his mouth to scream, but was able to produce no more than a half-strangled wail. The infection was in his chest, which was also touching the pole. His vocal cords were half-frozen. His torso was rigid. And now he felt the murderous coldness creeping up his neck.

"Kill her, bro," he whispered. "Kill her for me . . ."

The metallic skin reached his chin and locked his mouth shut. It climbed his cheeks into his forehead. His every hair turned silver-grey as the flame-coloured tresses shivered outwards from the root.

His trapped eyes roamed their sockets. He was a man of flesh and blood inside a hard shell of silver.

Then his blood turned to mercury, his heart to a steel casket, and his eyes ceased to move.

Jewel let go of the pole and hurried across to Thorn. The

floor did not sink beneath her; it had already regained its firmness. Reaching down, she untied his gag.

"You took your time, Jewel," he said.

She said tersely: "Your sister's safe." Then she hacked at his ropes.

He smiled. "I knew you could— look out!"

Jewel threw herself sideways.

Gripping a rope, Zak swished through the air where she'd been standing. Had she not moved, he'd have kicked her in the head with his outflung feet.

Some way beyond her, he dropped to the ground. The rope swung back like a pendulum. He pulled a knife out of his belt.

"I'll cut your heart out for what you've done to my brother."

Jewel was lying on her stomach. She'd used her hands to break her fall and her palms were flat on the floor, almost directly beneath her shoulders. Under the threadbare covering stretched a smooth bed of slate.

Zak took a step towards her; then a second; then a third. He was no more than inches away when he found he could go no further: the soles of his bare feet seemed stuck to the ground. For long moments he struggled to pull them away, but he couldn't shift them.

His ankles began to stiffen. Looking down, he saw that the skin there was turning blue-grey. Unable to drag his eyes away, he watched his calves slowly change colour: a weird kind of paralysis was crawling towards his knees. He tried throwing his body forwards to break the floor's grip on him, but succeeded in doing no more than bending forward from the waist: his heels flatly refused to part company with the ground.

He glared at Jewel. "What are you doing to me, bitch?"

Jewel lay as she'd fallen, looking back at him past her elbow. "I think you know that," she said.

To Zak, it felt as though his legs had become encased in solid rock. And still the paralysis crept upwards – it was almost at his groin.

But his arms were still free, and he still held his knife. Drawing back his right arm, he flung the knife at the girl.

Jewel had no time to move. The knife struck her beneath the armpit and buried itself to the hilt.

Along with the shock of pain, a sudden weakness flooded her. But, clenching her jaw, she kept her hands flat on the floor. She had to finish what she'd begun, lest the process reverse itself.

Zak could do nothing. The rocky shell had reached his hips. He touched it with a fingertip; its surface was smooth and cool. With the idea of ripping it off, he tried to insert his fingers beneath it, but found there was no space between skin and stone: where one began and the other ended it was impossible to tell. If he tore the stuff away, he'd be stripping his own skin.

I'm a dead man, he thought.

How was it his life had come to this – defeat at the hands of a mere girl? His life which was *their* life – his twin's and his own; for the two of them had lived like a single being since their birth?

But he knew what the answer was. They'd made a fatal mistake. This Jewel was no mere girl. How was it he and Lanner hadn't realised what she was? But, then, how could they have known? In the mirror maze the girl had been nothing, powerless. If they'd cut her throat then, none of this would have happened. Or if Querne had been here . . . If . . . If . . .

It was at his neck now. Had Lanner broken, at the end? Well, he, Zak, wouldn't break. A vicious smile appeared on his face.

"You wanted the truth . . . here it is."

Jewel, clinging to consciousness, heard his voice as one hears the sough of a distant, bitter wind.

"It was me who killed your father – that puffed-up, pompous underwear salesman. And do you know something, girl? I *enjoyed* killing him. I'd kill him again if I could."

It was then the creeping stone caught and immortalised his smile: a gargoyle, grinning into the face of vacancy.

Only when his yellow hair had faded to blue-grey, and was as lifeless as the bed of slate that Jewel lay upon, did she allow herself the luxury of at last passing out.

17

SCAVENGERS

Jewel awoke to find herself in bed in the mirror-room. Above her head, and stretching away down the gallery, the ceiling-lamps hung glittering, reflected and distorted in the restless rectangular panes. She sat up, and around her several Jewels did the same – except that they were no more than parodies of her, absurdly compressed or distended. But all were pale and puzzled: not least by the fact that, pulling up the loose shift that she wore, she found no wounds. That was strange . . .

"Not strange at all!" declared a version of herself who seemed to be all mouth and eyes. "What's the good of being a Magian if you can't heal yourself?"

No good at all, thought Jewel. She pulled the bedclothes aside and swung her feet down to the floor. A pair of slippers was by the bed; she put them on.

"And where do you think you're going?" said a stern, familiar voice.

Behind her, on the far side of the bed, stood her father.

"Get back in bed," he commanded. "You need to rest, recover your strength."

"I feel fine," she retorted.

He shook his head sadly. "That's my daughter – wilful to the last!" He paused, then went on: "I've got a bone to pick with you. You never said you were a Magian. Now if I'd known . . ."

"If you'd known, what?"

"Then I'd have held an auction and sold you to the highest bidder!"

"*What?*"

"Only teasing!" Elliott Ranson grinned. "Where's your sense of humour, girl?"

"It's in tatters right now."

"So much the worse. In adversity – that's when you need it most."

"But it doesn't get you far when someone sticks a knife in you. And, in case you didn't notice, I was doing my level best to avenge you at the time."

"And a very good job you made of it. Turning one of those louts to iron and the other one to stone, now that was resourceful! If only you could bring your old dad back to life! It's no joke being buried, with only worms for company."

"Worms?"

"Actually, it's not as bad as all that. Some of my best friends are worms. We have long conversations about the meaning of life. Or do I mean death . . .? Funny thing is, life and death seem much the same to worms . . . Well, Jewel, must pop off. Man to see about some frocks. Be good, daughter mine. Or evil. Whichever!"

And he slipped out of the room.

"Father!" she cried. "Father!" And ran after him. But the floor gave way beneath her, and she fell into nothingness.

*

297

"Jewel?" a voice said. "Jewel?"

Jewel opened her eyes.

She was lying on her back under a cover of rabbit fur. She was bumpily in motion. She could hear the rumble of wheels. Beside her knelt Haw, gazing at her with concern. Beyond Haw's head, all was blue.

"Are you all right?" asked the girl.

"I . . ." But Jewel foundered, still half-tangled in her dream.

Haw smiled. "You were talking in your sleep. Well – mumbling to be honest. You've got a touch of fever. It's the wound, I expect. Those dreadful twins had smeared poison on the knife."

She put her fingers to Jewel's forehead.

"Well, that's good – you're not as hot as you were."

Poison, thought Jewel . . . "What was I talking about?"

"I don't know. It didn't make much sense. You said 'father' several times."

"Did I?"

She started to lift her head and shoulders, then let them fall back. Her side was sore.

"Where am I?" she asked.

"In a rat-cart, on the way to Stony Close. Thorn's driving."

"A rat-cart?"

Haw grinned. "We borrowed it from the Spetches."

Jewel managed half a smile. "Stole it, you mean?"

"Well, the twins aren't going to argue. Neither are Denny, Lippy and Leech – they've enough to worry about. Still, they're alive." She laid a hand on Jewel's shoulder. "You were terrific up there. I can't imagine how you did it."

298

"I can't imagine myself. Something seemed to take me over. It was like some inner force was making decisions, directing me. If I'd once stopped to think what I was doing . . ." She grimaced.

"I'm glad you didn't," said Haw. "For Thorn's sake and mine. And I'm glad you killed those three. They didn't deserve to live." She stopped, as if to consider, then said passionately: "I wish I was like you, and could do amazing things. But I'm just ordinary."

Jewel drew her right arm from under the fur and took hold of Haw's hand. The girl seemed so young, while she herself felt ancient. Am I really only fifteen? she thought. I feel more like fifty.

"You're not ordinary," she said. "And to tell you the truth, I'm a bit scared by what's happening – happening to me, I mean. It's happening so fast, and I don't know where it will end."

"You'll be all right," said Haw. "You're good, not like those twins. You'll always do the right thing."

Will I? wondered Jewel. I wish I could be as sure about myself as you are. Then a fresh thought struck her. "Where's Roper?" she asked.

"He had to fly the Scarebird back. Thorn helped with the launch. But he's back again now. And not just Roper. Look, up there!"

She pointed north. Squinting against the glare, Jewel made out a pair of specks, black stars against the heavens. Infinitely slowly, they floated, keeping watch.

Weariness washed like a wave through her body. She closed her eyes. Haw was saying something.

She fell asleep again.

*

She woke to an absence of motion and a ceiling above her head. She was in bed at Stony Close – the room she'd slept in before.

What time of day is it? she wondered. Morning? Afternoon? It certainly wasn't night. Although the curtains were drawn, there was daylight beyond them. How long had she slept? A whole night through?

Under the bedding, she moved a hand and touched the place in her side where Zak's knife had found its mark. Poisoned, she remembered. A square pad covered it – a poultice, probably. Around her body went a bandage to hold the dressing in place. Gently, she prodded herself and was surprised to feel no pain. There was no dressing over her ribs where Leech's knife had cut into her. Experimentally, she lifted her head and shoulders up from the bed. No pain greeted the movement. She sat up, threw off the covers, and shifted the pillows to prop her back.

Her bed was one of two in the room. The other had been slept in – by Haw, of course. So: one night at least had passed.

She examined the skin above her ribs where the ratman's knife had cut her. It was unmarked. Now for the more serious hurt. She pulled loose the neat bow someone had tied in the bandage. When it was gone, the poultice stayed in place, stuck down to her skin. She peeled it off, then used the bandage to wipe away what of its gummy stuff the pad had left behind.

A small, pinkish area was revealed on her skin. But in its centre, instead of a knife-wound, sore lips sewn together, was a thin red scar: fading testimony to Zak Spetch's last despairing action. Her body had repaired itself while she'd slept.

She got out of the bed, gave herself a good wash using the water in her bowl, and dressed in the fresh clothes that lay folded on a chair. Then she pulled back the curtains.

Warm sunlight flooded in.

Hello world! she thought. And then: I feel ravenous.

Later that morning (for morning it was – she'd slept through the first leg of the journey, then through a night spent under canvas, awakened briefly the next day, then slept through a night in Stony Close), Jewel, Haw and Thorn lay sprawled on thick grass in sunlight. They'd walked some distance from the house; here they could talk undisturbed. Not that they had anything to hide from the Tucketts; rather that they wanted a quiet spot, clear of distractions. Haw, long imprisoned, couldn't get enough of the open air.

For a time they talked about what had happened, exchanging their separate stories. Then, glutted with the past, they turned their thoughts to the future.

"What are you going to do now, Jewel?" Thorn had asked the question, and he was fearful of the answer. Or rather, fearful of one possible answer: that Jewel meant to bend her steps in a direction different to his. It's not that I love her, he told himself; then struggled to say exactly what it was he felt for her. I'm just used to her. We've shared such tremendous adventures. Life will be pale apart from her.

Life at Norgreen, he thought. How am I going to go back to that? The old settlement existence, with its regular, seasonal rhythms, would seem dull after recent weeks. Even hunting held little attraction. What was shooting the odd rabbit to a man who'd fought for his life – against stoats, crayfish, men? Perhaps there was something Racky-Jaggerish in him – a love of travel, alien places, the thrill of the unforeseen, danger.

But I've got to return to Norgreen. What else can I do?

He looked apprehensively at Jewel. She too seemed to be thinking.

Haw exclaimed: "Oh *please* come to Norgreen. You can be my best friend!"

"I'd love to be your best friend. But I'm sorry," Jewel replied, "I can't come with you." Then, seeing Haw's huge disappointment, she added: "I've something important to do."

"What's that?" asked Haw.

"I've got to go to Harrypark. I owe Rainy's father an account of how she died. Other people who cared for her, too. And I must do this in person."

Haw snapped off a stalk of grass and glared at it.

"But you can come *after* you've done that, can't you?"

"Yes, I can. And I'd like to. But you'll be gone from here by then. And travelling the wood alone is dangerous, as you know."

"But you're a Magian!" protested Haw.

Jewel smiled. "Even for me it's dangerous. I'm not immortal, Haw."

"Well then." Haw turned to Thorn. "Why don't we stay here and wait for Jewel to come back? Then we can all go home together."

Thorn said: "But the Tucketts may not want us hanging around, getting under their feet."

"We won't be under their feet," said Haw. "I can work in the kitchen garden. You can hunt and help Roper. You could even learn to fly – I know you'd like to."

"I suppose I could," said Thorn. He moistened his lips. Haw had touched a nerve. "Well, Jewel, what do you think?"

"If the Tucketts are agreeable, I don't see why not. But I could be away a week."

"A week?" said Haw. "That's nothing. A week here will pass quicker than an hour in that rotten cell."

Jewel and Thorn exchanged smiles.

"You've got a persuasive sister," said Jewel.

"Don't I know it!" agreed Thorn. "Right. Let me put the idea to the Tucketts. If it's OK with them, we'll stay here and wait for you. If it isn't, well, we'll have to think again, won't we?"

"Wonderful!" cried Haw.

She walked back arm in arm with Jewel, Thorn tagging along behind.

"I can't wait to show you our favourite place," she said.

"I can't wait to see it. Just so long as you promise not to get kidnapped again!"

"Nobody would dare to kidnap me with you around."

"Hey, what about me?" said Thorn.

Haw flew to her brother, threw her arms around his neck and, standing on tiptoe, kissed him on the nose. "Don't be jealous," she told him. "Jewel's my best friend now, but you're still my brother."

"Brother? What does that mean?"

"It means that I'm the only one can kiss you on the nose."

Thorn grinned at Jewel. "If it's nothing worse than that, I suppose I can just about live with it."

"It sounds as though you haven't any alternative," said Jewel.

Next morning, mounted on Retty, Jewel rode off from Stony Close. Lasker had pressed her to take the rat – it would speed her journey. Roper had offered to fly her there, but she'd politely declined. She told him what she'd told Thorn and Haw earlier – that she needed to go alone. Adding, to soften the rejection, that there was nowhere near the Gill house to set an Airbird down with any hope of getting the flying machine back into the air.

But she was happy to take Retty. The rat would be companion enough on the journey – undemanding, amenable. And as for riding itself – well, surely with time her bottom would get saddle-fit (if not saddle-shaped, she thought).

The crystal, well wrapped, was in one of her saddlebags. Since her last experiment, she hadn't felt strong enough to touch it. The crystal seemed to work two ways. You could make use of it, if you stayed single-minded and kept control; but let it take hold of you and it would carry you away.

She didn't anticipate using it in Harrypark; still, you never knew. And she thought she might show it to the seer, Elphin Loach. Since more than one crystal existed, it was possible that Elphin had seen its like before.

In her mind, she ran through the ideas she had about the crystal. There were four of them.

First, it wasn't a natural stone. It had been *made* – that is *manufactured* – and presumably by the giants. But whether for some particular purpose or process, or for many – that she couldn't say.

Second, sleeping inside it, like a kernel inside a nutshell, was some sort of power. This, when accessed and channelled, was formidable.

Third, it seemed in make-up to be something like a brain. Her own brain contained memories, knowledge and pictures of the world. Were these things what crystals contained? When she'd told Thorn what had happened during her last experiment, and described the three scenes, he'd fallen silent for a time. Then he told her something that made a big impression on her. It was something the Norgreen Syb had said on the day she gave him the three gifts.

"We were talking about the future. Then Minny said something like: *every possible event buds in time's deep womb. But who knows why one comes to pass and another doesn't?* So I said: *surely only one of these possibilities comes about?* And she said: *so far as we know, but what do we really know? Scarcely enough to fill a thimble.*"

"What do you think she meant?" Jewel had asked.

"Well, at the time I thought she meant something like this: that when in your life you reach a fork in the road, only chance or circumstance may cause *this* path to be taken as opposed to *that* one. But now it occurs to me that there's another possibility. What if the world we know isn't the only one there is? What if we take *both* forks: *this* path in *this* world, *that* path in another?"

"So that somewhere there's a world where my mother didn't die, where Rainy and I killed the twins before Racky Jagger appeared? And somehow the crystal has knowledge of those worlds?"

"It's a thought, isn't it? But there might also be a world where you and I never met."

"That's true. Well, all I can say is this: I'm glad I'm in *this* world and not in *that* one!"

On reflection, she thought Thorn's idea pretty far-fetched. Where would the other world – or other worlds – be? Somewhere in the sky? Next door to this one – invisible?

Her final notion about the crystal was that it wasn't self-sufficient. It required an energy source from outside to fire it up. The mind of an ordinary human being, even a Syb, was inadequate; but the mind of a Magian . . . Had there been Magians, she wondered, in the world of the giants? And if there were none, what other kind of energy had been used to work the crystals?

This brought her round to Racky Jagger. Racky wanted the crystals, but Racky wasn't a Magian, so he couldn't handle them. Perhaps he was simply mad. Still, Thorn didn't think so and neither, truthfully, did she. Both suspected Racky was working for someone else. But who *was* that someone else, and why did that someone want the stones?

Jewel passed groups of other travellers, some on foot, some on carts. She was a young girl and alone, but no one offered her any threat.

Some time in the afternoon she came to Minral How – or what was left of Minral How. The roof of its main, central portion had collapsed, its supporting timbers burnt away, leaving the gable-ends and their chimneys pointing forlornly at the sky.

On impulse, she rode down the track to the gate. It stood open. The gatehouse was untenanted. Its interior had been trashed. She went on towards the house, choosing the track that avoided the sharp descent down the giant steps.

The roof of the right wing, where Crane and Briar had lived, was still in place. But its walls were smoke-blackened, its windows blown out by the heat. The front door had gone: only a charred tatter hung askew from the uppermost hinge. Close to the doorway's right-hand corner stood a cart, partly loaded, a stretched covering over its load. The two brown rats in the traces perked up and sniffed at Retty, but ignored her rider. Jewel dismounted, to stretch her legs. As she surveyed the scene, two men emerged from the doorway, saw her and walked over. Scavengers looking for choice artefacts, she thought. One was middle-aged, the other in his early-twenties: father and son, perhaps.

"Looking for something, lass?" This was the older man, and there was suspicion in his voice.

Jewel smiled. "Just curious. I happened to be passing. How about you?"

The man weighed her question; then, concluding (she presumed) that she was harmless, he said: "We came up from Lowmoor to give the place the once-over. But the building's a total wreck, along with everything in it. A waste of time."

He might or might not be lying to her, but Jewel didn't care. She put on a sympathetic face. "Bad luck. You follow a dangerous calling, I think."

"You're right there."

"I don't suppose you can tell me what happened here."

"The story goes that the gateman was jumped by half a dozen brawny men. They overpowered him, tied him up, then went on to the house. Later he saw that the house was burning. They must have set fire to it. And they bested Rockett's men."

"What happened to Deacon Brace?"

"Mad as an armchair. Dribbles at the mouth. Talks to the trees. Some fellow turned up and took him away. Rumour has it, it was his father – though all Lowmoor's convinced his father was the devil."

"Rumour's very probably right. His father is a good man. But wasn't there a manservant? Biggs or Maggs – some such name?"

"Scraggs? He's a shifty one. Drove away on a rat-cart. Probably with a good bit of loot, if I know Scraggs."

"And Crane Rockett and Briar Spurr?"

"Burnt to death or disappeared. When the mighty fall, they go with a bang, as the saying is."

"So it seems," said Jewel. "And those six brawny men – who were they? Where were they from?"

"Now that's the strangest thing. No one knows. But Rockett and Brace made a parcel of enemies. My best guess is that those men were after revenge. Looks like they got it, too."

Jewel nodded. "Well, thank you for telling me what you know."

"You travelling alone, Miss?"

"As you see – me and my rat."

"Is that wise – a young lass like you?"

"I can look after myself. Well, goodbye now and better luck with your hunt."

And with that, she remounted Retty and rode away.

18

SIGHT AND SEEING

Next day, around mid-morning, she sighted the battered, ivy-grown walls of Harrypark. She brought Retty to a halt and sat upright in the saddle, her mind seething with bitter thoughts.

When I last passed through these walls, Rainy was walking beside me. Now here I am alone. I wanted revenge and I got it. But what's that revenge now? At what cost did I get it? Death upon death. Blood on my hands . . .

She began to cry. She cried for Rainy, Luke, herself, and for the wickedness of the world. Sliding off Retty's back, she buried her face in the rat's fur. Retty stolidly stood her ground. Rats don't cry, thought Jewel. She pulled away from the rat's flank and went and looked at the animal's face. Retty's eyes, black and gleaming, seemed devoid of emotion. She's resigned herself, thought Jewel, to her life of servitude. She scratched the doe beneath her muzzle. Then, to the girl's surprise, Retty put out her pink tongue and started to lick Jewel's wrist.

Jewel burst into fresh tears. It was some time before she was able to get herself back into the saddle.

She rode in through the old gateway and on down the avenue, then turned north towards Round Pond. She'd given some thought as to whether to call first on Elphin Loach, who lived south of the main avenue, but had decided against this. She must speak to Luke first.

But how do you break the news of his daughter's death to a man? She tried out this phrase and that, even speaking them out loud, but every one felt inadequate – a dandelion seed the slightest breeze would blow away. Facing Luke would be the hardest thing she'd ever done in her life. Going into Roydsal, alone, to rescue Thorn and Haw seemed child's play in comparison.

Reaching Round Pond, she dismounted to let Retty drink. It was then that she caught sight of a movement in the long grass on the far side of the pool. Something dark and angular had for a moment come into view. And there it was again . . . almost as if someone unseen were waving a flag at her.

She stood stunned. The scene was exactly as she'd seen it when exploring the green crystal. And she thought: I have a choice: I can turn away, mount Retty and ride on to Luke's house, or I can go and see what's there . . . It's just like Thorn said, I've come to a fork in the road of my life and I can take either path . . .

Or could she? For the fact that she was conscious of the sharpness of the choice had somehow served to tip the scales in favour of one outcome. How could she now *not* investigate? It would be spurning destiny.

Happy to leave Retty to her own devices for a time, Jewel set off around the pond's cracked, weed-pocked rim.

As she pushed into the grass: this is foolhardy, she thought. What if it's a feral rat? Nevertheless, she ploughed on. What she'd seen hadn't looked much like a rat – unless rats had taken to waving things to attract your attention . . .

She stopped dead. An owl with tufty ears and orange eyes was staring at her. So stern and unwavering was the stare that Jewel almost looked away. But that would have been a mistake. She held the creature's gaze, and after a moment the owl blinked and jinked its head to one side. One of its wings was folded, the other awkwardly extended. It was the twitching of this vane that she'd seen above the grass. The wing was broken, she was sure.

Out of its airy element, and with the indignity of its tail-feathers squashed against the ground, the bird did not seem so imposing. But, sitting on a branch, with its body fully extended, it would, she reckoned, be twice or three times her size. As for airborne . . .

"Well, Mr Owl," she said, "you've got yourself in a pickle."

She'd called him Mr Owl. He was male, she was sure.

The creature considered her, then uttered a low yelp.

Was that a form of agreement, a cry for help – or a warning? Beautiful he might be, with his yellow-brown breast streaked with black, but this, she reminded herself, is a fierce predator. He will tear the head off a shrew as soon as hoot at the moon.

Yet she was obliged to help him.

She began to talk to the bird in a quiet, easy-paced voice. What did she say? Pretty much anything that came into her head. She told him who she was, where she was going, and why. The owl listened in silence. But at some point words had to turn into action, and at last she asked him if he'd let her touch him. He yelped again. Was that yes or no?

311

She took a step towards him, then another, then a third. The great round face, with a wedge of lighter fur parting the darker-furred circles around his watchful eyes, was a mask of otherness. She was now within striking distance, but he made no move to attack her. Slowly she raised a hand and laid her fingers on his breast. There – she could feel his heart beating in its bone-cage. Be calm, she told him, be calm. And she put the owl to sleep.

First Roper's leg, now an owl's wing. Well, she couldn't complain that life was empty of challenges. She located the splintered bone amidst a mess of bloody feathers. The task was delicate . . . but at last it was done.

She moved back, and touched the sleeping bird on his breast.

The orange eyes popped open and once more considered her. There was no more humanity in them than there'd been before. Am I a square meal, perhaps?

"You can fly now, Mr Owl."

The owl uttered his low yelp, then spread his wings. They seemed enormous, bigger even than the wing of the Scarebird. He might have enfolded her in those rushes, smothered her in alien down.

Instead, with a loud clap, he leapt up from the ground. For a few wing-beats he seemed to struggle, as if fighting the earth's reluctance to let him go, then he was sweetly airborne and climbing higher into the air. He disappeared from sight over a stand of sycamores.

She remounted and rode on, directing Retty northwards up a broad avenue where the narrowest of tracks had been made in the grassland. Away on either side were high hedges of rhododendron. Harrypark was full of them. Retty plodded phlegmatically onwards. Four legs are better than two.

All at once there came a swishing of wings and a gust of turbulent air – and there was the owl, flapping away ahead of them. Well that was something. A salute? A farewell?

At length she brought Retty to a halt at the Gill house. This spot, with its four picturesque dwellings, seemed no less idyllic than when she'd visited it before. But now she was about to destroy its tranquillity.

She dismounted and tethered the rat. Then, with faltering courage, she went up to the door and knocked.

The door opened. But it wasn't Luke Gill who opened it.

"Elphin!" Jewel exclaimed.

The seer's green eyes, outlined – as always – in black, regarded Jewel from the midst of a russet tangle of hair. Elphin wore a long black dress with a purple shawl. She seemed both stern and calm.

"He knows," she said simply.

"Knows . . .?" echoed Jewel.

"Yes."

Jewel considered this unexpected response.

"So you saw something, Elphin," she said. "And you told him?"

"I saw Rainy some days ago, lying in deep water. Last night I dreamt you were riding here. So I walked up this morning. I thought it might help if I was here when you arrived. I said nothing at all to Luke. But something in my manner must have revealed what I was feeling, for he jumped to the truth. So I told him you were coming and he must wait to hear your story."

"I see . . . How is he?"

"Very quiet. He just sits in his chair. If I believed hearts could break, I'd say his is broken."

Jewel cast her eyes down. "Oh God," she murmured. "How am I going to face him? I don't know what to say."

Elphin put a hand on Jewel's shoulder. "It's brave of you to come. Luke must know that. Speak what your heart tells you – that's all anyone could do."

Jewel looked up again. "I'm glad you're here, Elphin."

Elphin smiled reassuringly, and motioned her into the house.

Luke was sitting by the hearth. There was no fire in the grate. The blind man's eyes moved restlessly in their sockets.

"She's here," said Elphin.

Luke turned to face them.

"Luke . . ." said Jewel. No other words rose to her lips.

"So you've come, Jewel," said Luke. "Elphin said you would. Elphin is never wrong." He motioned with a hand. "Bring a chair, and sit by me."

Jewel moved a chair to Luke's side and sat down. His face, which was rarely without at least a hint of a smile, was turned towards hers. His sightless eyes roved over her, and she imagined he saw right through her. This is unbearable, she thought. But I have to bear it.

She moistened her lips. "Luke, I'm sorry, so sorry . . ." Her voice tailed into silence.

The blind man turned his face to the grate. "*Sorry* won't bring her back," he said.

The chillness of his tone cut Jewel to the quick. Her heart quivered in her breast. Tears rose to her eyes.

314

Then his big hands came groping towards hers and closed around them. The backs of his fists were brown from the sun, and black-haired. His grip was strong but not unkind.

"I'm sorry, lass," he said. "That was unfair, uncalled-for. I know how much you cared for Rainy."

"Luke, I'd give anything to bring her back. I wish she'd never gone with me. She knew how dangerous it would be. I didn't want her to go."

"But she insisted on going." There was pride in the bereft father's voice. "Stubborn as a brick wall – that's Rainy all over. Even as a tot she had to have her own way. She used to drive us to distraction." Then he added, with a fractured smile and a voice strained to breaking: "And now look where it's got her."

The moments lengthened, as Luke sought to master his grief. Then, with a show of control, he said: "This lass has come a long way to be with us, Elphin. Do you think you could make some tea? Then Jewel shall tell us what happened." He squeezed the girl's hands, making her wince with pain. "And mind you leave nothing out. I want the absolute truth, no matter how grim it might be."

Elphin set about making tea. Jewel and Luke sat in silence – she with her thoughts, he with his.

Elphin served the tea. Jewel took several sips, a deep breath, and began.

Her account of events began with the departure of Rainy and herself from Harrypark, and finished with the arrival of Thorn and herself (not to mention the Great Pike) at the jetty off Nettle Island.

A silence followed her story.

Then Luke said: "So you don't know exactly what happened to Rainy in the end?"

"No," said Jewel. "She could have jumped overboard, saved herself, swum to shore – but she chose to help me so that I could help Thorn. After I left her fighting Spindle, I never saw her again. But I know she died. I *felt* it when I was in the water. I can't explain."

"You *felt* it?" said Luke. There was doubt in his voice.

"If Jewel felt it," said Elphin, "then it was so. She wouldn't be wrong. Besides, when I saw Rainy, she was also in the water. And I too knew she was dead."

"I see," said Luke. There was a pause. Then he said: "So Rainy sacrificed herself . . ."

Jewel said: "She thought of us before herself. Oh Luke, what can I say? Thorn and I both owe her our lives. And it's my fault that she's dead, for if it wasn't for me and my desire for revenge she wouldn't have been there; and if I'd foreseen the attack on the boat we would have been able to avoid it; and—"

"It's *not* your fault, girl." Luke's interruption was almost angry. "It's the fault of the men who attacked you. Never say it's your fault. No man must answer for the evil in another's heart: only for his own."

There followed a longer pause.

"I'd like to meet that pike," said Luke. "I'd shake his fin and say thank you."

"Rather you than me," said Elphin.

Luke turned to Jewel. "You'll stay tonight," he said. It was a statement, not a question.

"If you'll have me," said Jewel.

"You're welcome to stay as long as you like."

"Thank you. But I've a saddle-rat outside. I need to make provision for her."

"Elphin will take her across to Jay. He sometimes borrows a rat from Harry and puts it overnight in his shed. He won't object to housing the animal. But you stay here, Jewel. I don't want you getting caught up with Jay and Linden. You know what chatterers they are."

Jewel smiled. She understood. For tonight, at least, Luke wanted to keep her here. He knew there was more to be told, and he had the strongest right to hear it.

Jewel went out with Elphin. They stripped Retty of saddle-bag, saddle and reins, then Elphin led the rat away to Jay Sweet's house.

"You'll sleep in Rainy's bed," said Luke, when Jewel re-entered the house.

"Should I?" she asked.

"If Elphin wants to stay, she can have the couch. You're the guest, the traveller. And now I'll see about some dinner."

"Can I help?"

"Elphin will help me. You can lay the table."

So it was. After they'd eaten, they settled themselves about the hearth with pots of Jay's best ale, and Jewel continued her story. The only thing she didn't mention was finding and stealing the green crystal.

Elphin paid, Jewel thought, particular attention to those occasions when she'd made use of her powers.

As for Luke, he seemed almost to live her battle against, first, the Spetches' men, then the twins themselves. He called out

317

comments like "Well done, girl!" and "Wonderful!" And yes, she thought, he's right to take what happened personally, for I was avenging Rainy as well as my father.

When she'd finished her account of Roydsal, he said, with relish: "By gum, lass, what a trail of destruction you left behind!"

"Yes," she agreed, "but somehow I can't feel proud of it."

"But you should feel proud," he said. "And if your father was alive, he too would be proud of you. Isn't that right, Elphin?"

"That's right, Luke," the seer agreed. "Everything that Jewel has done was completely justified. I feel proud to know her. Each time she's been confronted with a problem or a test, she's taken a leap forward. Her power is remarkable, and is clearly still growing. I told her when I first met her to beware of herself, and I see no reason to change my mind."

"I remember very clearly what you told me, Elphin," said Jewel. "You said: 'Power is temptation by another name: the greater the power, the greater the temptation to misuse it.' I resented your words at the time, but I've learnt better since."

"This is rubbish," declared Luke. "Jewel would never misuse her powers."

"That remains to be seen. But this is no night for old friends to argue," said Elphin.

"Then don't provoke me," said Luke.

"I think Jewel and I understand one another," said Elphin. She smiled her crooked smile at Jewel, and Jewel smiled back.

"My pot's empty," said Luke.

"Then I'll refill it," said Elphin.

*

Next morning, when Jewel presented herself at the breakfast table, she found only Elphin there.

They exchanged good mornings. Then Jewel asked: "Have you seen Luke today?"

"I just took him some tea. I asked him how he felt, but all I got out of him was a grunt. He's grieving. Poor man, he hasn't even Rainy's body to bury. He hasn't the consolation of saying goodbye to her."

"It's cruel. I wish there were something I could do."

"Perhaps there is."

"What's that?"

"Restore his sight."

Jewel thought for a few moments. "You're thinking of Roper's broken leg. Yes, I mended that. But bringing sight to a blind man – that's a much bigger thing."

"Is it? It's healing flesh. You managed one kind of healing, why not another?"

Elphin made it sound easy, but Jewel knew it couldn't be.

"Do you think he'd let me try?"

"Now that I can't say. Luke's an unpredictable man. But ask him. If he says no, at least you'll have asked."

Jewel feigned surprise. "Am I hearing you right? Did you admit a mere man is beyond your powers to predict?"

Elphin grinned. "There's only one thing harder to predict than a man."

"What's that?"

"A woman!"

When their laughter had subsided, Jewel said: "I'd like to show you something, Elphin."

"What is it?" asked the seer.

"A sort of crystal. I'll go and get it."

Elphin watched with interest as Jewel placed the object on the table and unwrapped it. There it lay, a dull green stone.

"Seen anything like it before?"

"Nothing like it," said Elphin. "Where did you get it from?"

"I stole it from the Puckfloss sisters at Nettle Island. They had it in a junk-room inside an old jar. I don't believe they had any idea what it was for."

"Neither have I."

"Once I'd seen it," Jewel went on, "well, I just had to have it. You see, I had this odd feeling it wanted me to take it."

"As if the crystal had chosen you?"

"Yes, that's right. That's it exactly."

Elphin was looking thoughtful. Suddenly she thrust a hand out towards the stone.

"Don't touch it!" cried Jewel.

She was too late. As Elphin's finger touched the stone, it emitted a green flash. Jewel blinked. The seer recoiled with a cry.

"I'm sorry," said Jewel. "I ought to have warned you earlier."

"I'm glad you didn't," said Elphin. Her face had grown grave.

"Glad? But why?"

"Because I've just seen something. Or, rather, *felt* something. Listen, Jewel. You mustn't go to Rotten Pavillion. It will be dangerous for you."

"But I must. I've got to see Harry and explain."

"*I'll* go to see him. I can tell him as well as you."

"No. It's got to be me."

"If you go, Jewel, you'll be putting your life at risk."

"How? In what way?"

"All I can tell you is this: in the darkness lies danger. And it has to do with this crystal."

"But who else could know of this crystal?"

"I can't answer that. This thing has a life that's beyond my fathoming."

"Yes, I've felt that too. Perhaps, given time, I shall be able to fathom it. But I have to go to Rotten Pavillion, Elphin. You must see why."

"You're a stubborn girl, Jewel. If you really must go, take Parker and Jasper with you."

"No. Rainy is dead because she chose to go with me. I won't put anyone else at risk. And Elphin – you mustn't send them. *Promise* me you won't."

"Very well. I promise, though it goes against my grain."

"And Elphin – you really mustn't worry about me. Now my powers have developed, I'm not afraid of anyone."

"Then perhaps you should be. Be on your guard at all times. Trust no one – even folk you think you know."

Jewel re-wrapped the crystal and put it back in her bag. Luke still hadn't appeared, so Jewel and Elphin cleared the table. Then Jewel went to the Sweets' house to tell Linden and Jay. With them, grim-faced, were Parker Catt and Jasper Tallow. So, once again, she sat down to tell her story.

When she came back to Luke's house, Elphin looked up from some sewing she was doing, then shrugged, inclining her head in the direction of the hearth. Luke was sitting in his chair, eyes roaming unseeing over the unlit wood in the grate. He gave no indication he'd even noticed the girl come in.

Jewel went and sat beside him.

"Hello, Luke," she said gravely. "I've been to see Jay and Linden. Parker and Jasper were there too. They know what happened now."

"What's that to me?" said Luke roughly, not even turning his face to hers. "Stories won't bring Rainy back."

"I know," said Jewel gently. "Nothing can bring her back."

She glanced at Elphin, who nodded encouragingly at her, then mouthed *go on*.

"Luke," began Jewel, "do you remember me mentioning Roper Tuckett's leg – that I'd managed to mend the break?"

"What of it?"

"Well, I was wondering . . ."

"Wondering what, girl?"

"About your eyes . . ."

"What about them?"

"Perhaps – your sight . . . You could get it back . . . I mean, I could try—"

Luke laughed scornfully. "Nonsense, girl."

"I'm serious, Luke. Wouldn't you like to see again?"

"What would I want to see?"

"I don't know . . . This house, your friends, Harrypark, the fish you catch in Jugdam?"

Exactly where the fish comment had come from, she didn't know, but it seemed to spark something in the slumped, morose man. He said: "I'd swap all the fish in Jugdam for one sight of my dead daughter."

Elphin said brutally: "Well you're not going to get it. You'll have to make do with the living who care about you – and Linden's baby when it comes. You know she's asked you to be godfather."

Something softened in Luke Gill.

"Poor child," he mused, "to get itself born into such a world."

"The child's world will be what we make it," said Elphin. "And *we* includes *you*."

Luke appeared to consider. Then he said to Jewel: "And you really think you've got a chance of bringing this thing off?"

"I have a chance," she answered. "How good I don't know, but I'm willing to try if you are."

"Then try, lass, if you will."

She got him to lie on the couch, then stationed her chair behind his head. Elphin stood nearby, watching intently. Pass up the chance of seeing a miracle by a Magian? Not on your life!

"Close your eyes," Jewel told Luke. Then, resting her elbows on the bolstered end of the couch, she lowered the tip of a forefinger onto each of his eyelids – her right on his right, her left on his left. Then she too closed her eyes, and the process began.

The damage to Luke's eyes was confined to their surfaces, which had been seared by the blast that had deprived him of his sight. But the cords connecting each eyeball to his brain remained intact, and this encouraged the girl. Still, the work of repair promised to be intricate – far more so than mending Roper Tuckett's leg had been. She had to locate undamaged tissue, and from that coax out new. But the power of concentration that she had to bring to the task left no room for splinters of doubt to push themselves up in her mind.

Elphin, watching, saw nothing but minute variations of feeling flicker across the girl's face: a kind of emotional shadow play. But even at these surface echoes of inner tensions she marvelled. To have this kind of power! What must it be like? Thrilling, she thought, and fulfilling; but also burdensome. She felt both humbled and envious.

And Luke? He lay still as a stone, tolerating Jewel's ministrations in silence. He's like a man, thought Elphin, waiting to pronounce a judgement . . .

At last, Jewel lifted her fingers away from Luke's face.

"It's done," she said.

Luke opened his eyes. For a while he lay without moving, eyes fixed on the ceiling. Then he raised himself from the couch and turned to face the girl sitting in silence behind him.

"Jewel Ranson," he said. "You're just as I pictured you."

19

MOIRA BLACK

"My sight for Rainy's life. It hardly seems a fair exchange."

Luke Gill was standing in his garden, staring out over the fence at the great bank of rhododendrons that bordered the avenue.

"It's *not* an exchange," said Elphin Loach in her severest manner. "And what's more, you know it. Your sight and your daughter's death have nothing to do with one another. Take your sight as a gift. That's what it is. And *use* it."

Jewel had gone to lie down for a while: the healing had tired her. Luke's thanks had been muted, but she didn't care about that; it was enough for her that he could see. For her (if not for Elphin), what she'd done *did* amount to a recompense of sorts; she felt that she'd salved at least some small part of her guilt. It wouldn't bring Rainy back to Luke, but it might help to bring Luke back to the world.

Luke turned to Elphin, who stood beside him.

"Jewel's a pretty girl, don't you think?" said Elphin.

"Not half so pretty as Rainy was when she was fifteen. But then I'm bound to say that, aren't I? Fathers are prejudiced in favour of their own children."

"I've known a few who weren't."

"You know altogether too much."

"I know that you're a lucky man."

"Lucky and unlucky, though not in equal measure." Luke considered Elphin. "Do you know something? You're not bad-looking yourself, for your age."

"What a gracious compliment! I'm in danger of blushing. Actually, Luke Gill, I'm younger than you are."

"That doesn't surprise me. I'm forty-seven, which gives you plenty of leeway."

"You're not bad-looking yourself."

"Are you flirting with me? I thought Sybs and suchlike weren't interested in men."

"Who told you that? In my experience, it's men who aren't interested in 'Sybs and suchlike' – as you so delicately put it. We frighten them."

"You don't frighten me."

Elphin grinned. "Does that mean there's hope for me?"

"Perhaps if you persuaded Jewel to straighten up your smile . . . On second thoughts, don't. I rather like it as it is."

"Now that *is* a compliment."

"You'd be surprised how complimentary I can be, when I try."

"Don't stop trying on my account."

The afternoon was well advanced by the time Jewel had made her farewells, saddled Retty and ridden away. She'd promised Luke and Elphin – for how could she not? – that she'd come back and see them some day. But as to when that day might be . . . well, time must take care of it.

As she rode towards Harrylake, the sky began to darken and

it came on to rain: at first lightly, but soon like rats and frogs. By the time she reached the pontoon bridge linking the mainland to Lake Island, Retty was soaking and Jewel, despite her hood and thick jacket, had had her fill of the weather. She would treat herself to a night in one of Harry's luxury rooms. Despite everything that had happened, she still possessed most of the money she'd brought away from Shelf Fair.

The usual boats bobbed at the quay. The old boatman, Sam Dyker, was nowhere to be seen. Raindrops stippled the grey wavelets.

But if Retty disliked the wet, she gave no sign of it. She plodded across the bridge, paws slapping on the boards, ignoring their waterborne undulations. Then it was on down the track past the spot where Deacon Brace had waylaid Jewel and Rainy, until at last Jewel dismounted outside the rattery. The door of the carriage-house was open, and inside she could see a neat row of vehicles. She unstrapped her saddlebag, gave up Retty to the ratman (who, though she'd had no earlier dealings with him, clearly remembered her from before, for he addressed her as "Miss Jewel"), and carefully climbed the rain-slick steps to the Pavilion.

Raindrops spattered the paved pathway as she walked along to the door. Today nobody would be sitting outside, enjoying a drink in the area that overlooked the lake. She went inside and up the stairs.

The bar was busy with drinkers; as yet, it seemed, few people had gone through to the dining area. Spotting Nog, the friendly waiter she knew from her previous visit, she asked if Harry was about.

"Haven't seen him today," said Nog. "Don't think he's been out of his room."

"Depressed, is he?" asked Jewel.

"You've got it. Though as far as I can see he hasn't a worry in the world. This place is doing really well."

"Harry gets depressed because he's no reason to get depressed. But I need to see him."

Nog tilted his bony face and offered Jewel a quizzical look.

"Miss Gill not with you?" he asked.

"No, she's not."

Nog pursed his lips. "If I were you," he said, "I'd just go knock on Harry's door. And don't take no for an answer."

"I'll do that. By the way, have you a room for the night – a proper room, I mean, not the box I shared with Rainy last time I was here?"

"I'll see. And you'll be wanting dinner and breakfast?"

"Yes please, Nog."

He indicated her saddlebag. "Shall I take that up for you?"

"Er – no. I'll hold on to it for now."

She had the crystal inside the bag and, although she trusted Nog, was unwilling to part with it. Leaving him, she crossed the bar and passed through the partition into the dining area. Here no more than half a dozen people sat eating, and the small stage was empty where once she'd watched Rainy – for the last time, though neither could know it then – perform her juggling act. Inside the gaming room, a couple of tablemen were getting ready for the evening. At a side table, a single impatient punter nursed a drink. Someone who can't wait to lose his money, the girl thought.

As she threaded her way between the tables, one of the men moved to intercept her.

"Can I help you, Miss," he began. Then, like the ratman, he recognised her. "It's Miss Jewel, isn't it?"

"Yes," she said, "I'm here to see Harry."

"I'm afraid he's given orders that he isn't to be disturbed."

"Then I shall just have to go ahead and disturb him, shan't I?"

"I'm not sure—" began the man; then, apparently, thought better of objecting. "Of course, Miss Jewel," he said, and moved aside to let her pass.

Jewel knocked on Harry's door, but received no reply. Undaunted, she went in.

Harry's room wouldn't have been out of place in the junk shop of an impoverished settlement. A pair of wall-lamps, their wicks turned down low, threw only the feeblest light into the windowless space with its battered furniture.

Where was Harry? Not on his couch, where she and Rainy had found him on their previous visit. Fully clothed, he lay on his cot in the corner.

"Harry?" she said.

A muffled snore was her only reply.

Jewel went round the wall-lamps and turned them up full. Then she walked to the cot and stood looking down at it.

Harry lay on his front, his head twisted to one side. His hair was a greasy tangle, his skin shone with sweat and his mouth was ajar. Squatting down beside him, Jewel was greeted with a strangled snort and a gust of reeky breath. On the floor beside the cot were a couple of empty bottles that, by the smell of them, had held his favourite tipple – barley wine.

"Harry, it's Jewel," she announced.

He snorted again.

She put her hand on his shoulder and shook him gently. Then, when that had no effect, not so gently.

His eyes opened. Then he groaned and shut them again.

"Harry, it's Jewel," she said.

His eyes opened again. He regarded her blearily.

"Jewel? What are you . . . God, my head," he moaned, and closed his eyes again.

Jewel sighed, put a hand on his forehead, and concentrated.

After a while, his eyes opened. "My headache," he said, "it's gone. How did you do that?"

"Harry, why do you do this to yourself? You look terrible."

"Because," he said, "because . . ." He sat up on the cot and ran a hand through his hair. "Is Rainy with you?"

"No, she's not."

"Oh. I'm out of favour, am I?"

"No, it's not that. Look, there's no easy way of telling you this, Harry. Rainy won't ever be coming back again. She's dead."

Harry's face – unshaven, blotchy, creased and dark-bagged under the eyes – seemed to sag, as if setting out on a new phase of disintegration.

"Dead? But she can't be dead!"

"I wish it wasn't true, but it is. I'm sorry, Harry."

Harry regarded her stonily. "How did she die?" he asked.

Jewel told him of the murderous attack on Roydsal Dam. There was a silence when she'd finished.

Then he said: "So the light of my life is dead – and all for some money bag. Ha!" He jumped to his feet and went striding across the room, where he bumped into a table and sent it flying with a crash. "Money! I've got money! But what bloody good is it now?"

"Harry . . ." said Jewel.

"I need a drink," he declared. He went to his cupboard and took out a bottle.

"Harry," said Jewel. "Are you going to get drunk?"

"Dead right I am, girl!"

"Is that what Rainy would have wanted?"

"What does it matter what she'd want? She's not here to do any wanting. She ought to have stayed with me, instead of blundering off with you. First Tarry, now Rainy. You're the kiss of death, girl."

Jewel felt herself pale as Harry's barb speared home. She wanted to speak, but could not.

"Oh, get out and leave me alone!"

"I—"

"Out, you freak! Now!"

Utterly routed, Jewel complied.

Closing Harry's door behind her, she leant back against the wall. The guilt she'd partially assuaged by restoring Luke's eyesight came flooding in afresh. How unfair the world was. What had she done to it that it should treat her like this? Nothing, she thought, except to be born – and the unborn were given no choice in the matter. For a time, she thought of saddling Retty up and heading off: but as it was still raining that would be unfair to the rat, who was guilty of nothing except

331

powerlessness. What's more, it would be all too much like running away. Not so much from Harry, as from whatever it was she had to confront before morning.

So she went back into the bar. Nog motioned to her.

"Miss Jewel," he said. "Yes, we do have a room for you. Would you like me to take you there?"

"Yes. Please do, Nog," she said.

Had she not been feeling so low, she'd have exulted in the room. It was huge, its creamy walls hung with russet and green drapes. Rugs were scattered across the floor. The bed was big enough for three. There was a dressing table, a double wardrobe, two armchairs and a small table. Oil-lamps burned on the walls. A door led into a smaller room with a commode and a basin of cold water. But Jewel did not wash in the basin. Taking the huge towel provided, and carrying the bag with the crystal in it, she locked the room and went down the corridor to a door that Nog had pointed out to her on the way up. It bore a small sign marked with three short wavy lines.

The bath water, as Nog had promised, was pleasantly warm on her skin. And to get it, all you had to do was twist a metal tap! No inn she'd ever stayed in had run to such a luxury: heated water that ran in pipes and could be had for a turn of the hand! She reclined against the slope of the tub and poked her toes up out of the water. She began to feel a little better: Harry had been upset, he didn't know what he was saying, she oughtn't to have taken what he'd said so much to heart.

In a small bowl near her elbow lay a bar of scented soap. She decided to wash her hair. When it was dry, she'd put on clean clothes and go down and eat.

She remembered the head waiter from her previous visit – the servility that had oozed from him as he'd conducted Crane Rockett and Briar Spurr to their table. Jewel, a hanger-on of a paid entertainer, he'd barely deigned to notice. Unlike the table-man and the ratman, he didn't recognise her. She could sense the sniffiness with which he took in her slightly damp hair, her simple, well-worn clothes and the clumsy bag she carried; but she said nothing as he settled her at a table and reeled off the menu.

She ordered baked roach from the lake and a bottle of apple champagne. For one night, at least, she would live as the rich lived. Then tomorrow . . .

But thoughts of tomorrow defeated her. She couldn't imagine her future; it seemed barred off by a high wall in which no door was set.

She followed the fish with jam sponge. Few diners were left now; most had moved to the gaming room. She'd thought she might have an early night but, now that she'd eaten, didn't feel ready to do so. She rose from her chair and added herself to the general drift.

The gaming room was busy. Absorbed punters clustered around the wheel and the dice tables; others sat in circles play-ing various games of cards. Jewel lingered to see some dicing, watched the cubes bounce and settle to display their telltale spots. Groans or happy shrieks greeted bad fortune or good. Her mind threw up memories of her previous evening here.

Gilda shaking the dice in her fist and murmuring some incantation; herself fingering the plaques; Rainy, virtuously, refusing to gamble . . . Except she did gamble when she hooked up with me, thought Jewel. She gambled and she lost.

Jewel moved on to the wheel. Here, on that momentous night, she'd built up a stack of winnings only to lose them – deliberately – on a single spin. She smiled as she recalled the look of relief on Harry's face. What look, she wondered, would there be on that face now? Exhaustion? Oblivion? Rainy had loved life, but Harry seemed only to care for death. It was a waste, such a waste.

She followed several rolls of the ball, observing the way the gamblers bet. The cautious ones, the wild ones, and those who, like a snail, pushed their horns out one moment and drew them in the next.

Only one of the players seemed to be making real progress. She might be any age, thought Jewel, between thirty and forty, and had short-cropped, mousy hair and a face whose individual features seemed rather thrown-together: small ears, a large and bony nose, and an almost lipless mouth above a receding chin. This face had about it all the mobility of a mask; in it, only her eyes moved: grey, quick and intelligent. Her bodily movements were economical and decisive.

She was tall – a good inch taller than Jewel was herself – and wore a black jacket and matching trousers over a grass-green shirt. She wore rings on her fingers, but no necklaces or bracelets.

Jewel monitored her for a time. There was a definite pattern to the way the woman played. She'd bet on a colour, or odds or evens, never on any specific number. She'd hazard a number of plaques and win; then just one or two and lose. But her winnings were outpacing her losses, and she was gradually building up an impressive heap of plaques.

The wheelman announced new bets. The woman put six plaques on the red. Up it came; she doubled her stake. Then, lifting her eyes from the table, she directed them at Jewel. Their eyes met for a moment before Jewel looked away, turning as idly as she could to follow the actions of the wheelman. Still, however, she sensed the woman's eyes resting on her. Not merely resting, they seemed to be pulling, tugging at her.

Jewel looked back at the woman.

For a time, the two considered one another dispassionately. Then, without shifting her gaze, the woman lifted a blue plaque. Her lips parted and she tapped the plaque on her teeth, producing a faint clicking sound. In that moment, Jewel understood that the woman was cheating and that she – the cheating woman – was telling her as much.

The woman was a Magian. They were sisters under the skin.

Jewel watched as the woman now bet her twelve plaques on the black. The ball was spun. It came up black. This time, when their eyes met, the woman smiled mirthlessly. Deliberately, she'd fractured the set pattern of her play.

A demonstration, thought Jewel, and for my benefit.

The woman scooped her winnings into a black shoulder-bag, tossed a plaque to the wheelman, left the table and walked to the bar. Perching on a high stool, she ordered a drink.

Jewel crossed to the bar and stood beside the woman's chair.

Without looking at Jewel, "Let me buy you a drink," said the woman.

"No thank you," Jewel replied. "I don't accept drinks from cheats."

The woman turned to face Jewel. Her eyes were the colour of clouds lightly freighted with rain.

"From whom *do* you accept drinks?"

"Honest people," said Jewel.

The woman laughed. Her laughter was deep-voiced, almost masculine. "Then you won't get many," she said, and took a sip of her drink. "How about insolent people?"

"Insolent people?"

"People like yourself. You are an insolent girl. Still, I shan't condemn you for that. I was insolent at your age, among other things. But let me introduce myself. My name is Moira Black. And you are?"

"Never you mind."

The woman laughed again.

"Your name is Jewel Ranson. But you aren't what I expected. I assumed you'd be ordinary – which was short-sighted of me." She paused, then went on: "Really, the two of us ought to celebrate. Do you know, I've only once before met another of my kind. She was an old woman then, and I had to travel for two weeks in order to run her to ground. She taught me a great deal." Moira Black twisted her empty glass in her fingers. "As I, perhaps, could teach you."

"What would you teach me? How to cheat?"

"What a simple girl you are. This establishment was created

to cheat people out of their money. Anyway, I was only passing the time till you arrived."

"You knew I'd come here, then?"

"Of course. Moral people are very easy to second-guess. They generally do the right thing. Whereas *im*moral people . . ." She let the sentence hang.

"Surely they're just as predictable."

"I hardly think so. If they were, you'd know what I'm going to do next, wouldn't you?"

"Order another drink?"

Moira Black laughed and snapped her fingers. As if she'd yanked on an invisible cord around his neck, the barman hurried along to her.

"Same again," she told him. Then, to Jewel: "Sure you won't have that drink?"

"Yes."

"Please yourself."

"Are you staying here tonight?" asked Jewel.

"Naturally. Are you?"

"Naturally. I thought I'd treat myself to one of Harry's luxury rooms."

Moira's gaze wandered round the room. She said, "Then you can't be short of money."

"I have enough. How about you?"

"Oh, more than enough. Money isn't important to me."

"What is important to you then?" asked Jewel, curious.

"I think you know."

And yes, Jewel *did* know. "Speaking of leaving," she said, "I think I'll go now."

"But we've only just met. I only came here to meet you. And I have so much to say to you."

"But *I* have nothing to say to *you*." Jewel turned to go.

"Wait!"

Moira shot out a hand and grabbed the girl by her wrist. Her fingers clamped like an iron vice, but Jewel's reaction was instantaneous. Her body flared defensively and, stifling a cry, Moira snatched her hand away. Her fingers were reddened, as if seared by the lick of a flame. But as the woman examined her skin, it resumed its flesh tone.

"That wasn't friendly," she said.

"It's your own fault," said Jewel. "You shouldn't have made that grab at me."

"You're a fiery little thing. You really ought to be careful; that temper of yours could get you into real trouble."

"Is that a threat?"

The woman's stiff features abruptly seemed to slip sideways, and Jewel saw beneath them a very different face: shapely, pale-skinned, delicate-featured, altogether beautiful. Only the eyes remained unchanged: cloud-grey and cold. Then her appearance slipped again, and ugly Moira Black was back, smiling sardonically.

"Not at all. Call it advice."

"When I need advice from you, I'll ask for it – *Querne Rasp*."

"I'm afraid, Jewel Ranson, you're mixing me up with some-one else. I happen to know that Querne isn't welcome here."

"I wonder why? Or rather I don't."

"Faces are such inconvenient things, don't you think? They tie us down so. We're labelled this or that when we're any number of things. I find it useful sometimes to adjust my appearance. Even to be ugly; men avoid ugly women, and to have men buzzing about you when you're busy – that's annoying."

"I'm surprised you can sit here and talk openly of these things. What if someone should overhear?"

"Does it look as though anyone is listening to us?"

Jewel looked about her. Nobody was paying the slightest attention to them.

"Actually, no."

Moira chuckled. "That's because I've thrown a cloak of silence about us. Not only can no one hear us, they're barely aware the two of us are sitting talking here. They'd ignore us all night if I kept the cloak in place."

"A cloak of silence? I've never heard of that."

"No reason why you should have. I invented it. How old are you, Jewel – sixteen?"

"Fifteen."

"Oh, you're only a child! I barely knew which way was up when I was your age!"

"I know which way is up. And which way is down, too."

"Well, that's two directions. It only leaves a thousand more."

"Ask your friends the Spetch brothers how many directions I know."

"Zak and Lanner? What do you mean?"

"Don't you know?"

Moira Black stared at Jewel with eyes that might have frozen water. The silence lengthened. Then Jewel, whose right arm had been resting on the bar top, felt a tendril of alien sensibility touch her skin, seeking entry. She rebuffed it angrily, but this time Moira was ready, and absorbed the riposte.

"They're dead, then," she said.

"They murdered my father," said Jewel. "What would you have done in my place?"

"Probably given the killer a prize. My father beat my mother until one day, when I was fourteen, I told him to stop. So he tried to beat me – *tried* . . . He didn't beat anyone after that." She sipped her drink. "It's a pity about the Spetches. I was fond of Lanner and Zak. They amused me. But I don't blame you for what you did. People have to be prepared some time to answer for what they do. And Lanner and Zak got away with a lot for a long time."

"What about you? Do *you* get away with things?"

"Me? Naturally! Who could possibly oppose me?"

"I can't imagine."

"Let's stop beating about the bush. You have something that I want. Unless I'm very much mistaken, it's in that bag you're carrying. Now, this object isn't yours – you stole it. But, to demonstrate my good will, I'll pay you well for it. So, let's imagine a resolution of this matter. I hand over to you a bag of gold coins; you hand over to me that tatty bag with the crystal in it. Then, if that's how you want it, it's goodnight; we walk away. Game over. What do you say?"

"Racky Jagger works for you, looking for crystals, doesn't he?"

"You wouldn't expect *me* to scurry around to get them, would you?"

"Why do you want this particular crystal?" asked Jewel.

"That's my business . . . Well?"

At that moment, as the two Magians gazed at one other, Jewel experienced an opening. She was looking through the weirdly-vacant sockets of Querne's eyes into some kind of internal space. She made out a brick house, solidly built, well-kept. Next moment the building disintegrated, bricks flying everywhere. Flames leapt up where it had stood, filling the Magian's skull with fire.

Shocked, Jewel took an involuntary backward step, and eye-contact was broken. There was a pause, then she met Querne's intense gaze once more. But the woman gave no sign of noticing anything untoward.

"Your offer's fair," said Jewel, "but I can't accept it. I've taken a fancy to the crystal. I intend to keep it."

"Taken a fancy to it, have you?" Moira/Querne had gone sly. "Got its hooks into you, has it? Yes, I can see it in your eyes. You're not as simple as I thought."

Stone-faced, Jewel repulsed the Magian's smirk.

"Well," said Querne, "perhaps that changes things. *Ten* bags of gold."

"*No*," Jewel replied. "Ten, twenty, thirty – you can offer what you like, it won't make the slightest difference."

The last dregs of the Magian's fake smile drained away.

"You think you're *so* clever, don't you? I'll ask you one last time: will you sell the crystal to me?"

"You've had my answer, Querne Rasp."

"Then on your own head be it."

Moira Black slid from her stool and walked away across the room.

Jewel watched her go. Now I've really done it, she thought.

341

She stayed where she was for a time, thinking. Then she sought out Nog.

"Nog," she said, "you've a guest staying tonight called Moira Black."

"That's right."

"Has she been here before?"

"Not to my knowledge."

"Is she on her own, do you know?"

"She came in a carriage driven by a man called Spine Wrench."

"Wrench? I've heard that name before. *Gummer* Wrench it was . . ."

"The famous unlamented Gummer. Well, Spine is Gummer's younger brother. A Lowmoor man and a nasty piece of work. Has a big chip on his shoulder. Gummer never had time for him. And then, of course, the Spetch brothers took over Gummer's house."

"All right. Where will this character be sleeping tonight?"

"In a room in the carriage-house – that's where drivers normally stay."

"I see. Look, can you do something for me tonight? I'm afraid it will mean missing a fair amount of sleep. But I'll pay you well for it."

"For you, Miss Jewel, anything. Life's never boring when you're around."

I wish it was, thought the girl.

The room was dark but not pitch-black. The rain had cleared and a gap in the curtains allowed the moon to cast a livid bar of light across the bed. The sleeper slept soundlessly. Almost, it seemed, there were two heads here; for, next to the pillow occupied by the sleeping head with its dishevelled strands of hair (all of it that could be seen), was a second round object, wrapped up in a rough cloth. A hand poked up out of the bedclothes. It lay on its back, open, its fingers curling up. Sleep, one might suppose, had separated hand and object.

A faint scratching came from the door. Then it opened and a figure limped into the room. It was carrying something. Moving as quietly as a spider, it sidled up to the bed and looked down at the sleeping figure.

"That's right, girl, you sleep," murmured a hoarse male voice.

Gently he put a box with a latched lid down on the bed. Then, carefully picking up the wrapped object, the man carried it round the bed and set it on the floor in the gash of moonlight. When he'd unrolled the cloth, an object that might have been stone or glass was revealed. It was jagged and pitted, and in colour a dull green.

"You little beauty!" whispered the man.

He folded it back into its wrappings and returned to the bed. Then, unlatching the box and lifting a corner of the bedclothes, he whipped up the lid, gave the box a violent shake and pulled the bedclothes back into place.

"Bite on that, sweetie!" he murmured.

He went to the object on the floor and placed it in the box. Then, after a last satisfied glance at the bed, was out of the room and away.

As soon as he'd gone, one end of the curtain moved and Jewel stepped out from behind it. She drew the curtain back a little way and moved to the bed. In the broadened strip of moonlight she made out something crawling towards the humped shape under the sheets.

Jewel leapt up on the bed. Then brought her foot down several times, till the crawling thing was crawling no longer. Then, having gathered her bag – also behind the curtain – she opened the door of the room, went out and locked it behind her.

Two could play at illusion. If Querne Rasp could change her face, Jewel could construct a fake arm, a pretend head – not to mention a fake crystal. But the crystal wouldn't fool Querne. Jewel had to move fast.

Nog was waiting with Retty in one of the arbours in the grounds.

"Spine Wrench?" Jewel asked as he helped her into the saddle.

"Did just as you said he would. Came out of the carriage-house, slipped into the Pavilion. As soon as I saw that, I did as you asked me to."

"Where is he now?"

"Back in his room."

"You've done well. Here, take this."

She pushed some coins into his hand.

"Thank you very much, Miss."

"And tell whoever cleans my room to be careful in the morning. There's something nasty in the bed. But not to worry – it's dead. Goodbye now, Nog."

"Goodbye now, Miss Jewel. I hope we see you again."

"Who knows, perhaps you shall."

And with a flick of Retty's rein, she rode off beneath the moon.

20

THE ROOK STORM

Jewel rode out from under the trees to the edge of Lake Island. Straight ahead lay the pontoon bridge. Lake-water slop-slopped. Moonlight played on the little waves, making their crests and scarps gleam in a restless flicker of brilliance.

Retty stepped onto the planking. But, as she crossed the channel, a rat-cart pulled out from behind one of the boatmen's huts and came rattling towards the far end of the bridge. The carter, who was hooded, slewed the vehicle side-on, blocking the passage to firm ground.

Jewel reined in; something was wrong. The carter threw back his hood.

Not his – *hers*. Moira Black was gone. Querne Rasp had reclaimed her face – the face Jewel had glimpsed for a moment in the gaming room.

Querne spoke mockingly: "Did you really think I'd fall for such a trick, Jewel Ranson?"

"Your *man* did, if you didn't."

"I don't pay Spine to be clever. Let this be a lesson to you. Didn't I tell you moral people are all too easy to second-guess? Now, you know what I want from you. Give it to me and you can pass. I'm still prepared to let bygones be bygones."

"I don't think so," said Jewel.

"Then you're truly a little fool."

Quern jumped down from the cart and stepped onto the bridge. Next moment, the planking directly behind Retty was leaping with fire. The rat twisted and reared and Jewel fell sideways out of the saddle. She landed heavily on the boards, head over the edge, one arm dangling, the other clutching for a hold.

But the wetness against her hand sprang an answering idea. Moments later, a swell erupted, washed across the burning boards and doused the flames in a hiss of steam.

Querne put her hands together and slow-clapped, ironically. "Nicely done. But that's enough of that. Time I got serious with you."

The planks sprouted tentacles. They came squirming over Jewel, seeking to circle her arms and legs, to bind her body to the bridge. As fast as she repulsed them, scorching them off with energy-bursts, more swarmed to take their place. How long could she defend herself? Not as long, she feared, as Querne could maintain her onslaught. Counter-attack was impossible.

But then the impossible occurred. In a tremendous rush of wings, a shape came skimming out of the night. Taking her utterly by surprise, the bird clawed into Querne's shoulders, lifted her kicking into the air, and flew off low across the lake. There came the sound of a splash – the bird had dropped his cargo off.

The squirming tentacles withered and died. Jewel climbed to her feet. Seizing Retty's rein, she dashed to the end of the bridge. A slap on the flanks persuaded Querne's rat to pull forward out of the way. Then Jewel was in the saddle and trotting briskly away.

Off in the darkness sounded a hoot. And there, black-winged against the moon's luminous crescent, hook-beaked and rip-taloned and brute-proud in victory, sailed her tufty-eared owl. Perhaps, after all, there *was* something human in him.

Almost invisible against the curve of the forget-me-not sky, two grains of black dust were moving. For a time they'd moved in a straight line; now they went into a full turn – first the one that was ahead, then the second, copying.

It was Thorn's third solo flight. Solo but not alone, for in the leading Airbird Lucy was keeping him company, or rather chaperoning him.

Thorn had proved a quick learner, hadn't Roper told him so? Physical strength he had aplenty, but up in the air physical strength didn't count for a great deal. What *did* count were agility, quickness of mind and the ability to read air-currents and to exploit them to the full. He'd had good teachers, of course. He'd gone flying twice a day in the two-man Airbird: most often with Roper, but also with Lucy or Red. He was in love with the activity, with the freedom of the air, with the soft-sinewed winds that lived and moved in the sky, with the textures and contours of the patchwork sprawled below.

"I think you'd stay up there for ever if you didn't have to come down!" Red had joked one evening, after a long flight with him.

"What goes up must come down."

"So they say. But wouldn't you just love to be the exception to the rule!"

Haw too had flown: once in the Scarebird with Roper and Thorn, once in the two-man machine. She'd enjoyed the experience, taken it quite in her stride, but hadn't duplicated her brother's enthusiasm for learning to fly solo.

Ahead was the south-eastern corner of the great, bleak Barrens that stretched north to Lowmoor settlement and west to Harrypark. It was the second time Thorn had been this close to Lowmoor Barrens, but on the previous occasion he and Roper had turned aside some distance from its boundary. It unrolled like pallid skin, its further reaches lost where sky and earth merged in a haze.

Thorn was tired. He'd flown far the previous day, and perhaps today shouldn't have flown, should have opted to take things easy. But so eager was he to master this magnificent mode of travel that he simply couldn't say no when the opportunity was offered. He closed his eyes and day-dreamed, the breeze light on his face.

A distant voice was calling him. Opening his eyes, he saw only whiteness below. He'd crossed the edge of the Barrens! Sixteen years of urgent warnings and he'd transgressed by accident.

He scanned the sky for Lucy. Off in the distance to the east, a midge was stuck against the blue. Could she be so far away? But who else could it be?

As he moved to put the Airbird into a turn, it started to happen.

Sharp angles and edges of light flashed across his field of vision. Without thinking, he ducked away. The Airbird jolted and plunged into a fast, swinging dive. A yellow sickle came slicing through the sky towards Thorn, it must chop his body in two. He screamed as the blade passed through him. Then it was gone.

The air was a madness of lightning-jags and flashing ricochets. Yet the blade had cut through him and still he was whole. An illusion, then? He fought to bring the Airbird level.

The wind – the speed – feel your speed, he told himself. But the air-currents had died, there seemed nothing to hold him up. The Airbird was gliding downwards. He believed he'd turned east – but if he'd happened to turn too far, or not to turn far enough? How far could it be to the ground? If he hit the earth at this speed he would break everything!

He wanted to shut his eyes. Open, they were little use, but shut they'd be less still. He braced himself for the crash.

Then the light-attack had ceased, the whiteness gone. Below was green earth. He was heading downwards. But then the earth dropped away and a riser lifted his wing, pulling the Airbird into the sky. He steadied himself to play the wind. The Barrens were falling behind now, and high above he spotted Lucy, patrolling an emptiness of blue.

You damned fool, he told himself. You got away with it this time. Next time you might not.

But the Barrens . . . Now he knew why people steered clear of them. Why they warned off their children.

Time to return to Stony Close. Wing behind wing, the two Airbirds flew on. There, below them now, was the junction and the road to Minral How. The fliers tracked the road south. Far below, a train of rat-carts was moving north. Did they see us? Thorn wondered. Did they gaze up and marvel, scarcely believing their eyes?

Then Lucy, still flying a little way in advance of him, gave a shout and pointed down. Up ahead, a single rider could be seen moving south.

"Let's go down!" shouted Lucy.

As they lost height, the rider ceased to be merely a vague shape. Then they were passing overhead, and the traveller was waving at them, leaning back in the saddle.

It was Jewel. Soon she and Thorn would be united again.

Thorn and Haw listened in silence as Jewel told them of her encounter with Moira Black: of her fortunate escape, her vision of the exploding house, and the connection she'd established between Querne and Racky Jagger.

"Perhaps she's dead," suggested Haw, "killed by the fall, or drowned in the lake."

"It's possible," Jewel conceded, "but I wouldn't bet on it."

"Querne had a whistle," Thorn reminded them. "If she had it with her, she could have summoned a big fish."

"The big question," said Jewel, "is why she wants the crystals."

"Not for anything good," said Thorn. "And there's another question: why is Racky working for her? And where is he now?"

These uncertainties determined them to leave the following day. It would be a long hike home.

When Thorn that evening announced their departure, Petal and May – who'd taken quite a shine to Haw (she brought out their mothering instincts) – tried to persuade them to stay for a few more days, perhaps a week. But Thorn and Haw were adamant:

they'd been away too long, their aunt and uncle must be worrying, and a trek of more than a week stretched out ahead of them.

"It doesn't have to," said Roper.

Everyone looked at him. He wore a complacent smile, like the ratling that enjoys the best position at the feeding trough. (Except that rats don't smile.)

"What do you mean, Roper?" asked Thorn.

"I know what he means," said Red. "He's going to suggest flying you home."

"Got it in one," said his brother.

"Why wouldn't I? You're transparent as glass," said Red. "But aren't you being over-ambitious? It's a heck of a long flight – especially if you're going to skirt the fringes of the wood."

"Firstly, I've flown as far as Norgreen before – further, in fact. Secondly, we won't go around the wood, but over it."

He showed them a map he'd drawn of the area based on his aerial explorations and explained the route he'd take.

"We'll fly up the eastern end of the ridge, cross the wood where it's fairly narrow and stay to the west of Norgreen Barrens. We'll do it easily in a day."

"But there are three of us," said Jewel. "Are you suggesting Thorn flies the Scarebird, with me and Haw as passengers?"

"No," said Roper. "Fast and well though Thorn has learnt, he's not ready to fly the Scarebird. No," he repeated. "What I propose is that I take you two girls on the Scarebird, while Thorn flies solo. He's quite capable of that. But, in order to make sure that everybody's up to the task, the three of you must stay one more day. We'll take a practice flight: Jewel and Haw with me on the Scarebird, Thorn flying alongside. If all goes well, we'll embark on the flight proper the following day. Now, what do you think? Remember – you'll still be home a week earlier this way."

Haw thought that to be home in two days' time would be wonderful, and said so forcefully. She also knew Thorn would jump at the chance of a last flight.

Roper glanced at Thorn. Thorn nodded his agreement. He'd had more than enough of Judy Wood at ground level. He fancied seeing it from the air – skimming the treetops like a bird.

Jewel agreed with brother and sister. The sooner the three of them reached the safe haven of Norgreen, the better.

"Fine," declared Roper. "Flying it is, then."

Next morning, Roper took them in a loop around Roydsal Dam. Wide of its northern shore, they flew low over the burnt-out ruin of Minral How. The place appeared deserted.

The flight went without a hitch. The weather couldn't have been better, Scarebird and Airbird maintained close contact, and Thorn kept his concentration. If it had crossed Roper's mind that Haw might not cope, he was pleased to be proved wrong. Following the journey down from Roydsal, stints of work in the kitchen garden had got her fit again, and Nettle Island (seen at a distance) and Minral How, places where Thorn and Jewel had had momentous encounters, were sights she wouldn't have missed for anything.

And then the trip threw up something entirely unexpected. As, on their return loop, the flying machines moved to cross the Lowmoor-Judy Wood road, Jewel spotted a lone rider below them, moving south.

"Roper, can you go down? I'd like to take a look at that rider."

"Can do," their pilot replied.

He put the Scarebird into a glide. As they passed over the rider, he looked up and saw them. It was, as Jewel's sixth sense had told her, Racky Jagger. But though she recognised him, he wouldn't recognise any of them, for they were wearing flying helmets. Which is just as well, she thought.

In their absence, the Tuckett family had prepared a grand dinner. The four fliers were ravenous. They ate heartily. Haw was the first to excuse herself and make for her bed, but Jewel followed not long after.

"Until tomorrow, then," said Roper, as he and Thorn went to their beds.

"Until tomorrow," echoed Thorn.

He didn't get straight to sleep. His mind re-ran memories of his journey through the wood: first with Racky, then without him. He saw Manningham Sparks the Ranter, Emmy Wood and Burner May, watched the woodland cavortings of the One and the Twelve, relived his fatal encounter with Blacky – one of the yellow-feathered men.

Even when he slipped from consciousness into dream, vivid faces from that time continued to pursue him. The features of Racky Jagger dissolved into those of Mr Punch, Mr Punch into a snaggle-toothed, draggle-haired Woodman. Why was it that these images would not let go of him?

On the following morning, the sun lifted into a clear sky. The breeze was light. It promised to be hot at ground level, but would be cooler high in the air. A good day for flying.

The four would have to fly light. Each carried a small amount of food and a water bottle – though with the water, for obvious reasons, they were restricted to doing no more than wetting lips that grew dry. Jewel's crystal was in a hide bag strapped to the underframe. Thorn had refused to be parted from his fine metal bow; which, with his quiver of arrows, was similarly secured.

The whole Tuckett tribe assembled for the double take-off. There were many embraces, and still more farewells. Haw, Thorn and Jewel were implored to come back soon. There would always be a warm welcome for them at Stony Close. Haw and July, who were much of an age, had become fast friends and vowed that, one way or another, they would contrive to meet again.

Then the fliers buckled themselves into their harnesses and donned their helmets. On the Scarebird, Roper had Haw behind him and Jewel at the rear.

They were ready.

The Scarebird, with a little help from Red and Lucy, was launched.

Thorn took off when the way was clear. Next stop Norgreen, he thought, as his Airbird drifted majestically away from the hill.

Roper flew towards Rook Wood, then turned along its southeastern edge. Crossing the Wyke-Shelf road, they set themselves to climb the ridge. It took a little while, but they found the lifter they needed, and made the top of Roydsal Ridge. And there was Judy Wood, just as Thorn had seen it on his earlier flight, the billows of a treescape, green-dark and secretive, that flowed to the horizon as if to the far edge of the world . . .

Roper turned due south. A confident navigator, he often flew by the sun, allowing for its passage across the sky as the day wore on. For, like all humans, his inner sense of time was highly developed. He regretted, of course, the absence from their world of instruments that told the time with exactitude. But Jewel had described the device she'd seen in Harrypark, and he had every intention of making a copy when time allowed.

Thorn flew on the right-hand side and to the rear of the Scarebird. The sole landmark they'd see before they reached the far side of the wood would be Judy River. They were making their crossing, of course, far to the east of the Forest Road. Wherever Racky Jagger was, they'd leave him far behind . . .

As he watched the trees passing below, a memory came to Thorn from his journey up through the wood – of looking up from the forest floor at the canopy overhead and thinking how wonderful it must be to be a bird and, effortlessly, outsoar that boundary . . . Well, today he was that bird; he was fulfilling that fantasy.

He turned and looked back. The northern edge of the forest was by now well behind them. In all directions was nothing but trees, a labyrinth of wood and leaf in which a man could lose himself . . . But up here, all was sunshine, blue air, simplicity. Flying, yes, flying was the only way to travel: his Airbird was a projectile aimed at a distant target. And today he would strike that target faultlessly, dead centre . . .

A distant rook-cry came to his ear. He scanned around and saw a flock of birds moving across the treetops. It was to the east and moving at speed. Its trajectory would bring it directly across their line of flight, but the birds were lower in the air: they were certain to pass at a safe distance below the flying machines.

The flock came closer. As it moved, additional rooks emerged from the treetops and joined the rout. Their number was swelling.

And now the flock began to gain height. If this continued, its path would take it on a collision course with theirs. Soon Thorn caught its massed wing-beat – a steady drumming of feathers on air that got louder the closer it came.

Both craft were fitted with hooters to keep inquisitive birds at a distance. Roper began to sound his, and Thorn followed his lead. But the flock was undaunted. Not one bird turned aside. The hooters' screeches were nothing against the birds' raucous caws.

Roper was shouting, pointing westwards and turning the Scarebird. Thorn grasped what he was doing: he intended to run before the flock. Thorn put the Airbird into a turn. Soon he was up alongside the Scarebird, even a little in advance.

The fliers cast anxious glances back. The rooks had risen to the humans' height. But what was their intention – to attack, or merely to chase? The flock was failing to gain on them: either because it was fully stretched, or because it was content that the distance between them remain the same. Yet all the time the two flying machines were heading in the wrong direction.

A ribbon of road appeared below, angling across their flight-path. The Forest Road! thought Thorn. Then a frightening idea struck him: if this pursuit went on, they'd pass over the Woodmen's part of the wood.

He glanced back again. Still more birds had joined the flock. Was he imagining it, or were they nearer now? Their wing-beat was tremendous, a continuous battering of the sky.

Then Roper was shouting: "Down! Down!"

Thorn understood. In order to go faster, the craft must sacrifice height. The Scarebird's nose dropped, she was into a downward slide. Thorn did likewise with the Airbird.

But the birds too flew faster, gaining on the flying machines. Their wing-beat was deafening, their cawing the massed shrieking of a hell of tortured souls.

A sudden prickling between her shoulder blades made Jewel look back. The rooks were almost on them now. Three exceptionally large birds were flying a little in advance of the flock. And there was something strange about them – something about their shape. She strained to make it out. And then – scarcely believing what she was seeing – she saw that on each of their necks, legs tucked under the bird's wings, sat a man with a green face.

She turned away. None of the other fliers had seen what she'd seen, so this would be one grim secret she'd keep to herself. Perhaps, if they survived, she'd have occasion to speak of it.

The forest-canopy came closer. Roper and Thorn levelled off, their craft squeezed for airspace. It was the frying-pan and the fire: behind the birds, below the trees – a double threat and no way out.

And now the storm struck. The Airbird was engulfed in rushing, wing-flapping darkness. The craft bucked in the turbulence.

Thorn fought to keep control, to hold the Airbird level, but there was no way out of the swarm. He heard the wing-fabric rip as beaks or claws slashed at it. Again the tearing sound came; again, and then again. The flock was ripping his wing to shreds.

Then the rook storm had passed, leaving the Airbird in sunlight. Not one bird had touched his body, let alone collided with him – as if the flock had been directed by a single intelligence to concentrate on ripping apart the Airbird.

The stream of birds was sheering south – a morbid shadow sweeping the treescape. But it had done what it came to do: the Airbird was mortally wounded. Tatters of fabric flapped and rippled. The machine was losing height, drifting down towards the trees.

The Scarebird was even worse off. Wing agape with holes, strips of fabric pulling and streaming, it was spinning slowly down towards the forest canopy. As Thorn watched, appalled, it fell among swells of greenery and disappeared from sight.

The Airbird would be next.

But then, directly ahead, the lake of green parted, revealing a different terrain: stepped, stony cliff-faces.

For a moment, he wondered if what he was seeing was an illusion. Then sanity returned, and he realised what it was: a quarry – a giant excavation from the Dark Time.

Perhaps the Airbird could get there. But Thorn could do nothing to help it. The Airbird drifted downwards. The Airbird crawled westwards. He was nearing the quarry's edge.

The last tree lurched upwards, branches threatening to snag his harness. Twigs scraped the air-frame. Then he was past, and over stone, and dropping towards the quarry floor. A grove of young oaks grew there beside a pool of blue water. He was going to hit the trees. In desperation he swung sideways and the Airbird lurched away. Her left wingtip hooked a branch, then he was tilting and falling.

He smacked into water, the wrecked wing on top of him. For a long moment the Airbird floated, as water explored the holes in its fabric with liquid fingers. Then the craft began to sink.

Underwater, Thorn battled with the straps of the harness. At last he got them loose. Then made the mistake of trying to swim directly upwards. The wing-fabric clutched at him, trapping his body in one of its rents.

Whatever he did, he must not breathe. He pulled his knife from its sheath and began to hack at the fabric. It parted and his body came free and floated upwards. As his head broke surface, he gulped a lungful of air. Then he was treading water and wiping it from his eyes – wet, but alive.

Unbuckling his helmet, he let it float away from him.

"Thorn Jack," said a voice he knew. "First the earth brings you to me; now you come dropping out of the sky. Who are you fleeing this time?"

"I'll tell you just as soon as I'm out of this lovely pond," he said.

21

PURSUIT

In a screeching and groaning of metal, the Scarebird fell through the upper branches of a great beech. For a time it lurched and scraped downwards; then a twig impaled the wing-frame, and it came to a shuddering rest at a sharp angle – one wingtip higher than the other, and the three fliers dangling in a row from their harnesses.

But they were alive, and they were conscious. All had bruises and grazes, and Jewel a gashed calf. Her trews were ripped and wet with blood; but even as she examined her wound, the bleeding from it stopped: her body's enhanced defences had already set to work. The pain began to ebb.

Roper said: "Can you release yourself, Jewel, get down to that branch?"

She was the lowest of the three. The branch was directly beneath her feet, a drop of no more than a couple of inches. Some eight inches in breadth, it looked dependable enough.

"I think so," she replied.

"Good. When you're down, I'll unfasten myself and Haw, and help her down to you."

The bag containing the green crystal was still strapped to the air-frame. Jewel freed it and tied it to her belt where it bulged awkwardly. Then she disconnected her harness from its webbing and dropped lightly to the branch. Pain shot through her injured leg.

Ignoring it as best she could, she watched Roper straddle a cross-frame and disconnect his own harness. As Haw held tightly to his legs, he released her. Then, grasping her by the wrist, he let her down towards Jewel. Jewel took the girl's weight, Roper released Haw's hand, and Jewel and Haw collapsed in a heap on the branch.

Roper swung down to Jewel's cross-frame, then in turn dropped to the branch.

"So far, so good," he observed, and sat cross-legged beside them.

"Is it?" said Haw. "We've been lucky – but what about Thorn?"

"Perhaps the Airbird wasn't so damaged and he managed to put down."

"Is that likely?"

"There's every chance."

He's exaggerating, thought Jewel, doing his best to comfort the girl.

"Thorn has a knack of getting out of tight spots," she said. "He'll be all right. We've got ourselves to worry about. We need to get down to the ground."

"But how?" asked Haw. "We're really high up here."

"Well, we've got these." Roper indicated the harnesses to which they were still attached.

Haw looked doubtfully at her harness. She and Jewel could see – as could Roper himself – that even if their harness-straps were knotted in a single length, it wouldn't be long enough to span the bigger gaps between branches.

"Let's all have a think," said Roper. Pulling out his water bottle, he took a draught from it.

A slight disturbance among the leaves of a side-branch caught Jewel's eye. A bird?

No – not a bird. A black nose appeared, then a furry grey head with two bright eyes and a pair of upward-pointing ears.

Seemingly unafraid, the squirrel looked Jewel straight in the eye.

Here, as if offering itself, was their answer.

"Keep still," she whispered to the others. "Make no sound."

Haw and Roper, both sitting with their backs to the animal, responded with puzzled expressions, but did as they were bid.

Jewel sent tendrils of consciousness snaking along the branch and into a sharply-clawed paw . . .

The squirrel advanced towards the humans.

Roper and Haw watched bemusedly as Jewel, slipping past them, took some bread from her pocket and laid it on the branch.

With its long, bushy tail, the creature was twice the length of a rat. It halted and stared at them. Then, sitting back on its haunches, it picked the food up with its forepaws and began to nibble it.

"What you're looking at," said Jewel, "is our transport to the ground."

Jewel took in her friends' doubtful expressions with a grin, then outlined her plan . . .

"Right, me first," volunteered Roper. If he still harboured doubts, he was not showing them. "But," he added, "I'd prefer not to travel head-downwards."

"What, with *your* head for heights?"

"Airbirds are one thing. Squirrels are another."

The squirrel finished the bread and began to lick his paws clean. Haw went up to him and ruffled his neck fur. "Isn't he lovely?" she said.

The squirrel dropped to all fours and stretched his long body. Roper clambered onto his back, his head facing the animal's tail. Using straps from the harnesses, Jewel secured him in place.

"See you soon!" said the flier.

Off down the branch went the squirrel. Looking back at them over the animal's rippling tail, Roper flapped a laconic hand. Then the strange pairing was gone.

"He'll be all right, won't he?" asked Haw.

"Who?" said Jewel. "Roper, or Mr Squirrel?"

Haw smiled. "Both of them."

"Trust me," said Jewel, laying her hand on the girl's arm.

Time passed. One Jewel sat quietly on the branch. A second, an offshoot in and behind the squirrel's eyes, claw-toed her way to the ground. Roper released himself and retied the straps to his mount. Then squirrel/Jewel started back.

Haw was the next to make the journey.

Then it was Jewel's turn. She had the crystal to transport, and had she not been a Magian she'd have found strapping herself to the squirrel's back difficult. But she could, of course, manipulate the fastenings with her mind. Roper and Haw had travelled face-down to the animal's back. Jewel instead plumped for a back-to-back descent.

As the squirrel moved at what seemed quite a speed down the tree-trunk, its scratch-pattering paws barely seeming to clutch the bark, Jewel watched the treescape as it vertically unrolled. In a dream of sun-shaft and shadow, leaf, twig and branch slipped by – an ever-changing tapestry of brown and green shades. I might be asleep, she thought. Yet knew, in her double-natured self, that she was not: conscious always of human and animal, mount and rider.

Then her world was horizontal and Roper and Haw were welcoming her, ready fingers unbuckling her straps. As Jewel slid off the squirrel's back, Haw reached into her pocket, took out a piece of bread and offered it to him. For a moment it seemed as if he'd take it from her; then his head jerked to one side, his ears quivered and he shot back up the tree-trunk, his handsome tail snaking behind him as he ran.

"What's got into him?" asked Haw.

"Something scared him," said Jewel.

"Me?"

"I don't think so."

Dropping to her knees, she laid her palms flat on the beech mast and closed her eyes.

Haw would have spoken again, but Roper shook his head. After a time, Jewel re-opened her eyes and got to her feet.

"It wasn't my intention to tell you this, but now I must. The flock that attacked us was no ordinary bunch of birds . . ."

"It's dry," declared Thorn, and pulled his shirt down off the stone.

Emmy touched his trews with a finger. "Not dry at all," she said.

Thorn didn't care. In another place, at another time, he

might have basked as a girl cast sidelong glances at his body (even one as odd-looking as Emmy, with her pushed-in features; and her glances weren't sidelong – and were scarcely, in fact, glances). But he begrudged even the little time his clothes had lain on the stone.

Roughly oval in shape and a hundred and fifty yards across, the quarry had been gouged out of the earth by tremendous forces. Some parts of its walls were a loose tumble of scree, elsewhere ran tiers and shelves on which the quarrymen had worked. A wide road slanted down from top to bottom. Everywhere plants had colonised the bare rock, sprouting green from crevices.

Thorn had dived to the sunken Airbird and recovered his bow and quiver. His arrows were wet but serviceable. At least he was armed again. He'd told Emmy about the rook storm and the crash of the Scarebird with its three passengers: his sister and two friends. As soon as he could, he must set off to try to find them.

"I will help you," she said.

But she said other things, too.

"Rooks made you crash, Thorn Jack? That is bad."

"You can say that again."

"Rooks made you crash? That is bad?"

Had Woodmen no sense of irony? "I didn't mean 'repeat yourself'," he explained. "I meant, what else can a crash *be* but bad?"

"I see. But you do not, I think, know how bad the badness is. This is Woodmen's work."

"Woodmen's work? How?"

"We have birdmen in the tribe. They understand the speech of rooks. Sometimes they ride upon their backs. Sometimes they ask them to do things . . ."

She's pulling my leg, thought Thorn. But Emmy had spoken with her habitual seriousness. And if I can ride a rat, why can't a Woodman ride a bird?

"I see," he said. "But if it was the Woodmen who caused the Airbirds to crash . . ."

"Yes: at this moment they are hunting for you."

Thorn groaned. "This is a nightmare."

"You can say that again."

Emmy's face was expressionless. Did she understand irony now?

Thorn buckled his quiver over his still-damp jacket. Then they set off to climb the road that slanted up the quarry wall.

As they went along, he asked: "What happened that day you left me in the tree-house?"

"I led the Woodmen through the wood, but they caught up with me. They were suspicious, I had to go along with them. I could not come back to the tree-house until the next day. Then you were gone, Thorn Jack." Emmy paused. "On that day, three Woodmen died. Our trackers found their bodies – rags and bones, all that was left. Two men, they say, killed them – powerful men. One, I think, was you."

"What did you feel about that?"

"I am proud of you, Thorn. But who is this other man? Is he a greater one than you? There are tales of a strange man who lives in the woods, who comes and goes like a spirit."

"He's no spirit," said Thorn. "Spirits don't fire arrows."

366

Emmy said nothing more. Once out of the quarry, they went east – back towards the area where the Scarebird had come down.

Emmy moved quickly and it was all Thorn could do, jogging along at her heels, to keep pace with the girl. As before, she seemed to know every tree, every dell. Few shafts of sunlight found entry through the dense tree-canopy, and he thought of the Scarebird spinning down out of the sky. Surely it must be caught somewhere high up in the branches. How would Haw, Jewel and Roper get down from up there? Assuming they were unhurt, that is. He had to believe they were unhurt. Jewel will find a way, he thought, Jewel always finds a way. He had unbounded faith in her.

Abruptly, Emmy stopped and dropped to her knees. Thorn pulled up beside her and squatted. She was tracing some near-invisible marks on the leaf-mould. She got to her feet, moved forward a couple of steps and repeated the action. Then she moved through the sequence again. Thorn waited, saying nothing. At last she turned to him and whispered a single word: "Woodmen!"

"How many are there?" he asked.

"Five or six. They are tracking three people."

"Then my friends survived the crash! But they're unarmed except for knives. We've got to try to catch up."

She stared blank-faced at him.

"I'm sorry," he said. "This isn't your battle, Emmy. But if you can get me close to them . . ." He fingered the shaft of his bow.

"I will get you close," she said.

And with that, she was away through the wood like an arrow. Thorn set off in pursuit.

*

Trees and more trees, the close embrace of the wood. Just how far now had they run? Then the high foliage parted and they burst out into sunlight.

"The forest road," gasped Roper.

The broad, stony avenue sloped gently north to south.

"They're getting closer," said Jewel. She too was breathing heavily. Her leg wasn't troubling her – the tear in her flesh seemed to have knitted – but how much longer could they keep going? The crystal bobbing at her waist seemed heavier than before. Haw looked pale, but said nothing.

Well, they were armed – after a fashion. They'd paused briefly to cut three staves and sharpen them to points.

"South – to the bridge?" said Roper.

"South," said Jewel. But we're too far away, she thought. They'll catch us before we get there.

Then they were in motion again. The heavy-headed trees maintained their lofty silence as the humans scuttled beneath: what were these tiny lives to them?

The road bent away left. As they rounded a rock, they saw a wagon by the roadside. A rear wheel had come off, and the vehicle rested at an angle. Its rear doors sagged open, revealing an empty interior. The wagon was painted bright blue, but something about it snagged on Jewel. Despite the desperate nature of their predicament, she moved quickly to the side of the wagon; then, drawing her knife, she scratched at the painted surface . . . Under the blue was a different colour – a vivid emerald. She scraped away more blue and uncovered a curve of scarlet paint. Then still more, and saw:

ANSO

"This is my father's old wagon!"

"Well, whoever ambushed it took the rat as well as the goods."

"Where's the carter?" asked Haw.

Roper was already at the front of the vehicle. "He's here," said the flier.

The man who'd bought the wagon from Jewel was slumped sideways on the box. Three arrows were in his body. His eyes had been pecked out; flies were busy about his face. A stench meandered off him. The three humans backed away.

Roper said: "I think this happened yesterday."

"Woodmen," said Jewel. "Come on – we mustn't dawdle here."

They hurried off along the road, but had only gone twenty paces when, out from behind a lush spray of ferns at the road-side, stepped three men with green skin. Clad in crudely-worked hide jackets and trews and coarse shirts, they had dirty, stringy hair and beards and carried stout bows. They did not look friendly.

A sound to their rear made Jewel's little party turn. Beyond the stalled, looted wagon, three more tribesmen were approaching.

The Woodmen halted and, for a time, the three groups held their positions. The Woodmen were weighing up their prey. They muttered briefly among themselves, then laid down their bows and quivers.

Why have they done that? wondered Haw.

Drawing their knives, the Woodmen now began to move in.

"Spears at the ready," commanded Roper.

Jewel was impressed. Roper wasn't a trained fighter, but he didn't lack courage. Neither did Haw flinch. Both brought their weapons to bear as the Woodmen closed on them.

But Jewel dropped her spear and pulled her crystal out of its bag.

"Close your eyes!" she told her companions.

Thrusting the crystal in front of her, she fired a burst of energy through it. There was a blinding green flash and the Woodmen fell back, rubbing startled eyes and muttering among themselves.

But Jewel was disappointed: she'd hoped for something decisive – an explosion of virulent light that would disable their attackers, or at least cause them to flee.

It's not the crystal, she thought, it's me. The long chase, her body's rearguard action to mend her leg, these had depleted her energies. I can repeat the flash, she thought, but it will be less effective again . . . All at once, she'd shrunk to merely human dimensions.

Warily, the Woodmen were moving forward again, their knives out-thrust in their hairy hands. Jewel set the crystal down and picked up her spear.

The three backed up against a stone. They might be hemmed in, but at least they couldn't be attacked from behind. The Woodmen had fanned out, and now they moved in.

An arrow came zinging out of nowhere. It struck one of the Woodmen who'd come from beyond the wagon in the small of the back. He grunted and fell forward. The others twisted round.

A man had come out of the wood, unseen.

"Thorn!" his sister cried.

One of the Woodmen uttered a string of high-pitched sylla-bles. Two peeled away and ran off towards Thorn.

Thorn had nocked another arrow. He aimed, he fired; but the running Woodmen evaded the shaft, which thudded into the wagon. Then Thorn had thrown his bow down and unsheathed his knife and the three were squaring up.

The other three Woodmen turned their attention back to their prey. One closed in on Roper. The flier jabbed with his spear, but the Woodman evaded his lunge and stabbed at Roper's chest. Roper twisted and the knife sliced through the stuff of his jerkin, shallowly scoring his chest. Blood sprang from the wound. But Roper threw himself at the Woodman, who fell backwards with Roper on top. The two rolled along the road, each striving for an advantage.

The two remaining tribesmen grinned at Jewel and Haw, showing off their white teeth. But Haw jumped forward and thrust at one with her spear. The nearest Woodman smartly sidestepped and, as the spear narrowly missed him, grabbed it and tore it from her. In a quick, decisive movement, he snapped it over one knee and threw the pieces away from him. Then he grinned at her again.

Something erupted from the ferns. Before the Woodmen could react, it had smashed into them, sending the pair flying like skittles. Then, turning, it snarled, clamped its jaws around the nearest man's throat and, lifting him, shook him like a doll. The tribesman's scream became a gurgle.

The rat tossed him away. He dropped like a bundle of rags on the road and lay without moving. The second Woodman was crawling backwards, fear burning in his eyes. But the rat bounded towards him and there came a loud *crack!* as its teeth snapped shut on his skull.

The third Woodman had the advantage over Roper. Wresting his knife-arm from the flier's grasp, he shaped to stab him. But Jewel jumped forward and drove her spear into his back. She felt a savage excitement as the point drilled into him. The Woodman went rigid, then collapsed across Roper.

Thorn's attackers circled around him. He twisted about, trying to keep them in his eye-line. Suddenly both ran at him: one from the front, one from behind. Pivoting, he saw the front man's knife-thrust pass him, then struck up with his own weapon. It sliced into the Woodman's chest, glanced off a rib and went into his lung. The tribesman uttered a shrill cry. But the other leapt on Thorn's back and bore him heavily to the ground. His forehead smashed into a stone.

Light exploded. Then there was dark.

22

THE RETURN OF PUNCH

"You've got a nasty bump there, big brother, but you'll live!"

Haw smiled at Thorn and dabbed his forehead with a damp cloth.

He was lying on soft earth, his head comfortably supported. A dull pain was throbbing through the front of his skull. He touched it; a fine lump had indeed sprouted there.

"What happened?" he asked.

"Ask your saviour over there," said Haw with a sideways nod. "She gave that Woodman a right thump."

Emmy was standing a little way off. She stood with her legs slightly apart, both hands gripping a stick whose butt-end rested on the ground. Warily, she scanned road and trees in all directions. Perhaps she expected more tribesmen to materialise and attack.

"I thought you weren't going to get involved, Emmy," said Thorn.

"And let you die, Thorn Jack?"

"Well, I'm glad you changed your mind."

He turned his head again, winced, and saw Jewel attending to Roper, who was also lying down. His jacket was open, his shirt bloody.

"He'll be all right," said Haw. "The cut's a long one, but not deep."

Then Thorn saw the grey rat. It lay on its belly near the road. Its muzzle and fur were stained with blood. It was gnawing a purple gobbet which it held in its forepaws.

"There's a rat—" he began.

"That's Smoky," said Haw. "She was Jewel's cart-rat. What she did – well, I've never seen anything like it. Domesticated rats simply don't behave like that."

This one does, thought Thorn. Well, maybe she was hungry. She'd timed it beautifully if she fancied a square meal.

The five sat in a circle, eating the little food they had. Nearby, Smoky lay on her belly. She'd licked her fur clean, and now her black eyes moved from one human to another – but on Jewel her gaze lingered.

After the battle, Jewel hugged Smoky, kissed her fur below the ear (that, at least, was clean of blood) and talked softly to her. Smoky listened impassively. To be together with Jewel again was all the rat seemed to want.

Three of the Woodmen were dead. Their bodies had been dragged off the road into the ferns. The others had crawled into the trees to make their escape or die. This fact, Thorn saw, had serious consequences for the Woodgirl. She could never return to her tribe.

"I do not care," she told him. "I go with you now."

"Erm, right," said Thorn. What else could he say? In her Woodgirl way of thinking, did saving his life grant her some right of possession over him?

"Now what?" asked Roper. Jewel had stopped his wound from bleeding, but her energy-level was too low for her to heal the cut completely. "We've little food, no tents – nothing. What if the Woodmen attack again?"

Thorn said: "We can't be far from Judy Bridge. I suggest we make for the inn. We can take rooms for the night."

"But wasn't the landlord in deep with the Spetches' men?" Jewel objected.

"Yes," said Haw. "And I was held there for a night when they brought me through the wood."

"That's right enough," said Thorn. "And I'm not likely to forget that Racky Jagger is somewhere about. But the Spetches are finished. Jonas Legg – that's the landlord – will know that by now. And we can pay. That should be enough for him."

"I ought to make for home," said Roper.

"I see that," said Thorn. "But travelling north on your own – that's *not* a good idea, not with the Woodmen on the prowl. At the inn you could hook up with pedlars or Ranters going your way."

"And suffer the fate of our friend?"

He meant the carter, whose body they'd laid in the wood and covered with leaves.

"The carter made a fatal mistake when he chose to travel alone. But if you're travelling with a party . . . It's the best I can suggest."

"All right," said Roper. "The inn it is."

Reluctantly, Jewel abandoned the sad, pillaged wagon; it was beyond them to repair it. She fashioned a makeshift lead for Smoky. The rat would go with them. And Jewel would never sell her again.

*

The journey passed without incident. First they heard the river, then they came down out of the trees and there on the tumbled parapet was the Punch and Judy Inn, its balconies high above the water. On the uppermost of these, Racky had wrestled with Denny Sweat until the rail gave way and Denny toppled into the river. And on the other side, at the head of the stairs, Thorn had caught Blacky's heel, and Blacky had fallen and broken his neck.

This return was stranger still for Haw, for all she'd seen before were the walls of the cramped room in which she'd been confined. Now, to the remembered sound of the river, she added the sight of it – dark water, with gleams of sunlight, bubbling away eastwards through gravelled or boulder-strewn banks.

The manic head of Mr Punch leered down from the inn sign. But this wasn't a Saturday, so today the Judymen wouldn't go leaping through the wood to the *thrum-thrum* of the drums, nor put a performance on tonight.

Its rattery was located below the inn, at bridge level. Jewel arranged a stall for Smoky, then said to the ratman: "I'll settle her myself, if you don't mind. She got overexcited today. Also, she's been well fed." Jewel forbore to list the delicacies Smoky had dined upon. "Just water tonight, if you will."

When she came out, the five climbed the stairs that led to the inn.

Jonas Legg greeted them like any travellers. Yes, indeed he had rooms. How many would they like? Two, they said: one for the men, one for the women – having decided grouping together would be best for security.

"Do you remember me?" asked Thorn.

"How could I forget?" said Jonas Legg. "You were with Racky Jagger. You brought some excellent crayfish. There was a fight, and a man died."

"The man's name was Blacky. He was a hired thug. He worked for the Spetch brothers of Roydsal."

"Is that so? Well, live and learn," said the landlord easily. "I hear the Spetch brothers are dead."

"News travels fast," said Thorn.

Jonas Legg ran his eyes over the group of travellers.

"Do you remember me?" asked Haw.

"No. Should I?" said the landlord.

"I passed this way once."

"So do many people, my dear. I can't remember them all."

"Of course you can't," said Haw sweetly.

"Will you all be wanting a meal?"

"We shall," said Thorn. "Have you other guests tonight?"

"A few."

"Anyone going north tomorrow?" Roper's voice chimed in.

"Yes. A party of merchants."

"Fine. Would they welcome a fellow-traveller?"

The landlord considered the lean flier. "I don't see why not."

Jewel spoke for the first time. "Have travellers reported problems with Woodmen recently?"

Jonas frowned. "No – why?"

"Then you need to warn people. Up north on the forest road we passed a looted wagon. The carter was dead on the box with three arrows in his body." She deliberately said nothing of the battle that they'd fought.

377

"That's bad." Jonas Legg's anxiety was genuine. "I've never known the Woodmen make trouble so far east. I wonder what's got into them."

"Blood-lust," said Thorn. "Or so it seemed to us . . . By the way," he added, "have you seen Racky recently?"

"No. Not since the night you were here with him yourself."

"Are you sure?" Thorn pressed him.

"Of course I'm sure."

The landlord sounded it, too. But Thorn knew he was a practised liar.

They took their keys and went to their rooms on the uppermost balcony. Directly below ran the river, flowing out from under the arch to ripple away downstream past the little landing-stage. Haw was entranced, she hadn't seen another place to match this in the world.

In the men's room, Roper lay resting after their trek. Thorn was scouting around outside. In the women's room, Jewel fell asleep on her bed. It was a bed she'd share with Haw. Emmy had one to herself.

Later, waking, Jewel lay warm and comfortable. Across the room, Emmy lay on her back, her eyes closed. Haw was elsewhere.

Jewel began to think about Emmy. She'd seen the Woodgirl look at Thorn with an almost fierce attentiveness. Could she be in love with him? Less frequently, Emmy's gaze had come to rest on Jewel. Twice, when Jewel had noticed this, Emmy had looked away. The third time, their glances locked. With perfect coolness, Emmy was appraising her. And something more than that too: challenging her, perhaps.

Thorn had said that Emmy was no older than Haw. But Emmy seemed the maturer of the two by several years. When Jewel had asked about the time Thorn and Emmy had spent together during his journey up through the wood, the young man had been evasive. Was it possible they'd been more than just friends?

The thought made Jewel go cold and hard. Was it possible she was jealous? But Emmy was ugly, and she was pretty – several people had told her so. Well, Emmy might be ugly, but there was something about the girl that couldn't be easily dismissed. Take today – by a decisive act, she'd cut herself off from her tribe. Worse than that: declared herself its mortal enemy. That was no small thing to do, yet she hadn't hesitated. If she had, Thorn would be dead. And now her future was uncertain.

But then, so's mine, thought Jewel. After Norgreen, what then? The future was a space that remained to be filled. Above all, there was the unresolved question of Querne Rasp.

Turning sleepily onto her side, she saw that Emmy was watching her. The Woodgirl had cleaned the green stain from her skin on the way to the bridge, yet her eyes had the calculating otherness of a lizard's. Jewel let her eyelids drop, but still she felt that stony gaze. If she could be granted a single wish, it would be that Emmy would go away.

When they went down to dinner that evening, Jewel took along her crystal bag. Throughout the meal, it rested on the floor by her feet.

They ate well – trout from the river. Along with the fish came sorrel sauce and generous helpings of a vegetable called fennel.

379

Baked with herbs, it was delicious. Only Emmy had had it before. It grew here and there in the wood and was a bulbous root, she said – moon-white, with green shoots and lots of feathery foliage. You chopped out chunks with an axe.

After the meal, Roper struck up a conversation with a group of merchants. They were bound for Lowmoor. He told them of the looted wagon on the road north, and the word *Woodmen* was greeted with a chorus of concern. One of the men was for turning back, but the rest were for going on – so going on it would be. Could Roper travel with them? By all means, they said, glad of extra hands and eyes. And yes, he could share a tent – provided he shared the watches, too.

As it happened, one of the party sold tents, sleeping bags and cooking utensils. So Jewel and Thorn bought gear and equipment for the journey to Norgreen. Food they could buy from the inn.

Then they retired to their rooms and locked their doors. The day had been long, eventful, exhausting. A night of undisturbed sleep would be welcome to all of them.

Somewhere – but was it inside or outside his head? – persistent knuckles were tapping on the latched door of sleep.

Thorn came awake. Night. The room was black as a starless sky.

The tapping came again. From the window, he thought. He propped himself up on an elbow.

"Roper?" he whispered.

A sound of light breathing came from the nearby bed. His friend was asleep.

Again the tapping.

Thorn got out of bed and crossed to the window.

"Who's there?"

His voice seemed loud in the edgy quiet.

"Thorn? It's me – Burner May. Will you open the door?"

The voice was unmistakable.

"Burner? What are you doing here?"

"Get your clothes on and come outside. Then I'll tell you."

Thorn dressed quickly, buckled his knife-sheath on his belt, unlocked the door and slipped out onto the balcony. There was a tiny sliver of moon and there, lurking in a deep pool of shadow, was Burner May.

"Burner! How do *you* come to be here?"

Burner May stepped into the light. The scar Racky had given him split his cheek like a black seam.

"I've been tracking Racky Jagger through the wood. He's here, Thorn."

"Where?"

"Somewhere about."

"Alone?"

"He arrived alone – if you don't count the rat he was riding. But by now he may not be alone. He's up to something, I'm sure of it."

"I know what. Jewel has a green stone he's keen to get his hands on."

"Jewel?"

"A good friend. There are five of us here."

"Then Racky's hardly likely to try something on his own."

"Who with, then – the Woodmen?"

381

"Even Racky wouldn't dare to mess with them."

"So what do you suggest?"

"Go back in your room. Lock your door. Keep your clothes on. Try to sleep. I'll stay out here. If I need you, I'll tap again."

Thorn went back inside the room and lay down on his bed. But sleep was impossible. So, his would-be father was somewhere in the vicinity. Things tended to happen when Racky Jagger was around. Thorn imagined Burner May padding about in the moonlight. Did his scar itch when his arch-enemy was nearby? At last Thorn fell into a drowse.

When he awoke it was morning. He scouted around outside, but Burner was nowhere to be seen. Had Thorn dreamt the man's coming? But he'd woken fully dressed, so he had to have been up and about some time in the night.

As soon as he could, he told the others what had happened.

"Count on it," he declared, "as long as Racky's floating about, Burner will be near."

"Burner May," said Emmy: "is he the one you fought with against the three Woodmen?"

"He's the one," Thorn confirmed.

The Woodgirl withdrew into silence.

Feeling refreshed and strong, Jewel returned to Roper's wound. This time, when she lifted her hands from his side, the wound had closed to leave a long, reddish scar.

The five went down to breakfast together. Again Jewel carried her bag and kept it by her feet. Breakfast was uninterrupted. Roper spoke again with the merchants, who were looking nervous today.

382

Jewel, Thorn and Roper settled the bill with Jonas Legg, then went out and up the stairs to collect the travelling gear they'd bought.

They'd reached the uppermost floor and were walking around the balcony to their river-facing rooms when a couple of doors opened and the Judymen poured out: Baby, Hangman, Judge, Policeman, Judy, Devil and the two Clowns. Thorn recognised them all, their garish costumes, false heads, masks. Baby shook his rattle in Thorn's face and loudly burped.

The balcony was wide enough to allow the two parties to pass; and, to begin with, people got by one another without incident. Jewel stared in disbelief as a female figure with a huge nose, and a head topped by a floppy white cap, shouldered and rustled grandly past her. She wore a billowing flowery dress; a fat red heart and a pair of silver scissors dangled from her waist.

But then, as Policeman came level with Thorn, he whipped his truncheon out and clobbered him over the head. Thorn slumped against the railing.

Burner's shouted warning, from the river side of the inn, came too late. "Ambush!" he cried.

Death and Dog Toby leapt at him, and Burner went down amidst a thrash of arms and legs.

Around the corner, Haw and Emmy struggled with Hangman and Judge, while Jewel was hugged by a horned-and-winged figure clad in a flame-red suit. She flung him off with an energy-burst, but the woman in the white cap had contrived to snatch her bag. And there it went – tossed over the struggling heads to Baby at the end of the balcony!

Baby gave a whoop and disappeared around the corner to the

bridge side of the inn. There the Judyman threw the bag down two storeys to one of the Drummers, who sat astride a saddle-rat.

He dug his heels into his mount, which scurried along to the end of the bridge, then turned sharp right and picked his way down the track that led to the riverside landing-stage.

Abruptly, the beat of a drum sounded through the air. As if responding to a signal (for a signal was what it was), the Judymen up on the balcony left off their various wrestling matches and took to their heels. Feet slapped and clattered on the stairs. The last to make off was Death, who took some time to free himself from Burner's tenacious clutches. Evidence of the bizarre encounter could be seen on the balcony floor: a short stick with a yellow bauble, a silver button, a headless wig and a fat red heart, neatly sewn.

Then Burner's voice was calling: "Here! Come and look at this!"

Picking themselves up, they ran to the river side of the inn to find Burner at the rail. Rowing away down the river was none other than Mr Punch. Seeing the party gazing down, he pulled his oars into the boat, held up Jewel's bag and shook it triumphantly. His long-chinned, hook-nosed head sneered at them, as malevolent as ever. The bells on his cap jauntily tinkled. Then, taking up his oars, he rowed away downstream. That fluent, practised stroke – Thorn would have known it anywhere. The One and the Twelve, he thought, and the One has got what he came for.

"Racky Jagger?" asked Jewel.

"It's him all right," said Burner. "Damn and blast the man! Always he outmanoeuvres me. Well, I'm going after him."

He turned away from the rail, but Jewel caught him by the arm.

"Let him go," she said. "He's not worth chasing. Besides, he's taken the only boat."

Had anyone else said this, Burner would have shrugged it off. But something in the girl's face held him there, and he complied.

Soon the river made a bend, and Mr Punch passed out of sight.

23

THE TWO MOONS

Thorn, Haw, Jewel, Emmy, and Burner May stood on the bridge. As the string of rat-drawn wagons disappeared into the trees, Roper Tuckett, who'd lagged behind, turned and waved a last farewell. The five returned the wave. Then Roper too passed out of sight.

His last words to Thorn had been: "If ever you feel like flying, you know where to come."

Thorn had smiled and replied: "You'll see me again at Stony Close. But when, who can say?"

After Racky's dramatic departure, Thorn thought that Burner May would melt back into the wood, but Burner announced he was going with them to the edge of the wood. They'd have need of him, he said, if the Woodmen reappeared. Thorn was glad to have him along. He did wonder, however, just how Burner and Emmy would make out as companions. Was he imagining things, or was there tension between the two? To have a Woodgirl as an ally was, for a man who for a lifetime had seen Woodmen as the enemy, difficult to say the least.

Jewel went to fetch Smoky from the rattery. When she came out with the rat, Smoky was wearing a pack-girth. Jewel loaded some of their gear onto her back and the five set off.

Thorn was keen to avoid the rope-bridge at Brokenbanks, so

Burner was going to take them by an alternative route – one off the beaten track. It would add to the length of the journey, but Thorn felt he could live with that.

After they'd walked for a time, Haw asked Jewel if she could take Smoky's rein: the girl was determined to make friends with the grey rat.

"Aren't you put off by what she did yesterday?" Jewel asked.

"Any enemy of the Woodmen is a friend of mine," said Haw.

Jewel now could walk with Thorn.

He said: "I'm sorry about the crystal."

"Don't be," she answered.

She seemed strangely unaffected by her loss, and he told her so.

"Who says I've lost it?" she said.

He looked at her in puzzlement.

She laughed. "The crystal's in Smoky's left-hand pack," she told him.

"But – but Racky stole your bag . . ."

"The bag, yes, but not the crystal. The crystal was never in the bag. I hid it yesterday under the straw in Smoky's stall. I thought it would be safer there than up in our room with me. I carried the bag around so that anyone watching us would think the crystal was inside. But inside was a fake stone. And I'm sure there *was* a spy. Remember the waiter last night? He was eyeing the bag so hard I thought he'd wear a hole in it. Anyway, the Judymen knew exactly what they were after. And Racky was convinced his clever little plan had worked. If he stops to test the stone he'll be a disappointed man."

"But you never breathed a word about your ruse to any of us!"

"It seemed simpler if you all believed the crystal was in the bag. Nobody had to pretend, when it was snatched away from me."

"Jewel, you're a genius."

"Hardly," she objected. "It was obvious that Racky would try something sooner or later. If not at the inn, later on. In fact, he's bound to try again, when he finds out he's been had."

"With a bit of luck, he'll be well down Judy River by now."

"Let's hope so. I can't see him mounting another attempt inside the wood. Even so, we'd best mount a watch tonight. Agreed?"

"Agreed."

When they halted, Jewel told the others her secret. There was general applause. Burner May seemed relieved. To be outwitted by Racky went right against his grain . . .

Only Emmy Wood's response seemed a half-hearted one. Thorn's admiration for Jewel had been plain for all to see. Could the Woodgirl be jealous? Her trick with the bag had delivered an unexpected bonus for Jewel.

Later in the day Burner shot a wood pigeon. With its meat, a chunk lopped from a reddish shelf-like fungus, and some herbs from his satchel, Burner cooked a stew while the others set up camp. Haw took Smoky a number of offcuts from the bird, and these Smoky gnawed and crunched up happily.

Thorn insisted that Burner, who'd been awake for two days and a night, get an unbroken night's rest. He tried to argue, but reason prevailed. Jewel took the first watch, Thorn the second and Emmy the third. Nothing happened.

Next morning, they crossed Judy Stream by means of a fallen tree. Thorn wondered where Racky was. Would Racky have parted company with the river soon or late? It flowed out of the wood far to the west of Wyke Barrens. If Racky had followed it that far, it would take him several days to make the journey to Norgreen. Thorn would be home long before him. There he planned to speak to the Headman. The Council, he supposed, would banish Racky from the settlement. The Jack family's tormentor would never be able to return.

Meanwhile Emmy, Jewel saw, had attached herself to Burner May. And Burner didn't seem to mind. His initial wariness of the Woodgirl had dropped away; did he enjoy her company? Emmy, her former quietness shucked off like a snakeskin, could sometimes be heard chattering away at him like a sparrow.

Well, thought Jewel, it isn't as if the pair of them don't have a lot in common – far more than Emmy could ever hope to have with Thorn. On their last night in the wood, Emmy took over the cooking, spit-roasting chunks of pigeon over a crackling fire. Burner got first choice of these morsels.

Next day, around mid-morning, they reached the edge of the wood. After Jewel, Thorn and Haw had bid warm goodbyes to Burner, Emmy said: "I am sorry, Thorn Jack, but I cannot go with you."

"You can't?" Thorn smothered his relief in a masterful show of disappointment.

The Woodgirl linked arms with the scar-faced man. "I go with Burner. Burner is my tribe now."

"Er, yes," said Burner, all at once bashful, "Emmy can't go

389

back to the Woodmen, but to abandon the wood – well, that's a sacrifice no one should ask her to make."

"I see," said Thorn, to whom the thought of demanding such a sacrifice wouldn't have occurred in a month of Sundays. "Well, I'm pleased for you both. I hope all goes well for you."

"Burner will come to my tree-house," announced Emmy forcefully, as if telling Thorn straight that his own night there would be expunged from memory.

"That's – well, wonderful," he said. "But I hope," he added, "that one day we shall all meet again."

A little later, when Thorn looked back, the wood had swallowed Burner and Emmy. And that was right, for they were worshippers of leaf, branch and bole. The great trees towered up, immensely tall and densely packed, and it now struck him as sheerest folly ever to have thought he could overfly them.

How callow I was, he told himself, on that distant day when I walked into the wood. Well, I went through it to fetch Haw, and now I'm out again and here she is by my side. And not only Haw but Jewel, a very different kind of prize.

But no, that was wrong, Jewel wasn't a prize at all. She didn't belong to him, she belonged to herself. And she would always belong to herself, whatever the future had in store.

The two girls had gone ahead. Thorn hurried after them.

They reached Norgreen the following morning. Their first stop was the rattery, where Jewel saw Smoky comfortably stalled. Then it was into the settlement. What a difference there was between today's homecoming and that of Thorn and Taylor after the young man's rite-of-passage! People hailed them in the streets and warmly congratulated Thorn, while Haw's friends clustered around her, agog to hear her story.

Laughing, she fended them off: "Later!" she told them. "Later!" It was worth being kidnapped to bask in such celebrity!

When Morry opened the door and saw Haw, she burst into tears. Then her arms were around her niece, and the two were hugging one another. Next it was Thorn's turn. In her pride and relief, Morry was lost for words.

At last, Thorn detached himself. "Aunt Morry," he said, "this is Jewel Ranson — our dearest friend. If it hadn't been for her — well, we'd not be here now."

Morry clasped Jewel by the hand. "Jewel, I'm so pleased to meet you."

"And I to meet you, Mrs Flood. I've heard so much about you."

"All good, I hope."

Jewel smiled. "I've been told that you're the best aunt in the world."

"Well, come inside, come inside," said Morry, a little flustered. "Taylor's out on patrol. There's been some trouble with Wyke, and there are regular patrols."

"I see," said Thorn. He wondered if the trouble had to do with the ruby crystal. Though how Wyke could know that a Norgreener had taken it, he wasn't sure.

"Why don't you put the kettle on, Aunt?" he said.

"Good idea," Morry replied.

Job Tubbs scratched his chin and looked at the three young people. They sat in a semicircle before him and two other

Council members – Cooper Vetch and Drake Hackett. The Headman and his Councillors had listened with growing grimness to what Thorn and Haw had had to say about Racky Jagger. Questions had followed; then a silence.

Now the Headman said: "The Council must meet, and we shall do so without delay. But there can only be one outcome: Racky Jagger's banishment."

"Thank you, Headman," Thorn said, and rose from his chair.

"But I suspect," said Job Tubbs, "that we shan't see Racky again. He'll deny us the satisfaction of pronouncing sentence on him."

Thorn bowed. He knew very well how unpredictable Racky was. It was too much to hope that they'd seen the last of him.

"So, Minny Pickles," said Thorn, "I owe you a debt of gratitude. Without your gifts – well, neither of us would be sitting in this room."

He and Jewel were with the Syb. Daisy Dutton, Minny's assistant, was out making a house call.

Minny leant back in her chair and smiled a complacent smile.

"Listen, Thorn Jack. Didn't I tell you before you left that bringing your sister safely home would be thanks enough for me?"

"You did, but—"

"And what you've had to tell me of those two sisters of mine, that was well worth the hearing. An elixir of life, and made out of human blood . . ." Minny shook her head. "They've grown madder with the years. Just as well they've closeted themselves

392

away on an island." The Syb harrumphed. "Nettle Island, that's a good one! Rosy and Lily are the stingers there! And when I think what great hopes our poor mother had for them."

She shook her head again and took a fortifying sip of wine.

"Minny Pickles," Thorn said tentatively, "can I ask you something?"

"Ask away, Thorn Jack."

"It's about Racky Jagger – something he said to me on the journey."

"Didn't I tell you not to believe a word that man said?"

"You did and you were right. But this – well, I . . . You see, he claims he's my father."

Minny's wrinkled eyes glittered. There was a pause before she answered.

"Do you wish him to be your father?"

This wasn't the answer he'd expected.

"Well, of course not," he said.

"Then your father is Davis Jack. The only thing that matters is what *you* want to believe. It's our minds that make the world what it is, not the world itself."

He stared at her. What she was saying was beyond him. Surely fatherhood was a fact. Only one man could be his father – Racky Jagger or Davis Jack. So who was it? But there was no point in pressing Minny. Riddling words, that was all you ever got from Sybs.

Minny was looking at Jewel, who'd said little since she'd arrived.

"Come here, Jewel Ranson, I want to take a look at you."

Jewel didn't move from her chair. She said: "I'm grateful for your help, Minny Pickles, but I don't take kindly to being ordered about."

Minny said: "How old are you, Jewel Ranson?"

"Fifteen," she said grudgingly.

"And very much your own woman. Very well, then. Would you be so kind as to bring your chair close to mine? It would gratify the whim of an old woman who hasn't many years left on this earth, as you can see."

Jewel glanced at Thorn, but, embarrassed by her behaviour, he was looking down at the floor. Setting down her glass, she carried her chair across to the Syb's and sat down beside her.

"May I take your hand?" asked Minny.

"I'd rather you didn't," Jewel replied.

"I wonder why? Have you something to hide? If you are what I think you are, what could such a one as you possibly have to fear from me?"

"I don't fear you, Minny Pickles."

"Of course you don't. So, ought *I* to fear *you*?"

"You have nothing to fear from me."

"Then humour an old woman, and let me take your hand. *Please*."

"If you took it, what could you tell me that I don't already know?"

Minny smiled. "Probably nothing. But let me tell you this: all my life I've sought to know things that few others know. But, however much I know, I shall go to my grave believing that I still don't know enough. Can you understand that?"

Her watery old eyes seemed to plead with Jewel's own, and all at once Jewel felt herself to be stiff-necked and absurd. Why was she making a fuss about so small a matter? She offered her hand and the Syb took it.

Minny's hand was dry, the skin wrinkled, mottled and coarse. She peered into Jewel's face. For a time there was silence. Then Minny relinquished the hand and said: "Today Thorn Jack told me something of his – and your – adventures together. But it was only a small part. He said little that directly revealed *your* role in things. But that little implied much. No ordinary person could have triumphed, given the forces ranged against you. Hence my old-woman's impertinence."

The Syb sipped a little wine and moistened her lips. "Well, Jewel Ranson, in all my long life I've only before met two of your kind. Both were getting on in years and must be long dead by now. The name of one was Blanche Fuller, and she was the wisest and best person it's been my privilege to know. She taught me a great deal. When young, Blanche herself had been instructed by a Magian. One day she and I were sitting as we are sitting now, and she told me something her instructress had told her when *she* was young. Would you like to hear it?"

"Why not?" Jewel replied, humouring the old woman.

"There are two moons, Blanche said. We've all seen the full moon – how silvery-white it is, how it lights up the night sky. That, she said, is the visible moon. To become full, a moon must wax. And when it has reached full, it straightaway begins to wane. At last it vanishes. But don't be deceived, the moon is still there in the night. Only it's invisible.

"Sooner or later, she told me, Magians and Sybs must choose their moon. Which will you take as your mistress: the moon that you can see or the moon that you cannot?"

Minny's "you" was general and Jewel was not expected to answer. Yet the parable's implications were clear enough to her.

The Syb removed her shawl and unclasped a chain from around her neck. From its links hung a disc of metal. It was plain and unmarked.

"Blanche gave me this," she said. "It's made out of iron. If you hold it up to the moon, one face looks silver, the other black. Set it spinning, and it imitates the moon's wax and wane. It's an emblem of the moon, yet it's made of earthly stuff. I should like to give it to you. Will you accept it, Jewel Ranson?"

Minny regarded her earnestly. She means me to wear it, thought Jewel. Well, it can't do any harm. And it once belonged to a Magian. It was this link with another of her kind that decided her.

"Thank you, Minny Pickles. I'd very much like to have it."

"Then let me put it round your neck. It will serve to remind you of the virtues of iron. Which, something tells me, you will one day have need of."

"What virtues are those?" asked Jewel.

"Strength, obviously. But also subtlety. You know, I suppose, of the wire that, when lightning strikes a house, conducts the charge safely to the ground?"

"Yes."

The clasp fixed, Minny sat back in her chair. Jewel fingered the iron disc. Its face was smooth to the touch. She tucked it inside her shirt. The metal was still warm from contact with the plump Syb.

"You spoke of *two* Magians," she said. "It's obvious that

Blanche chose the visible moon as mistress. But what of the other woman?"

"She, I fear, made a different choice," said the Syb. "Her name was Moira Black."

All Norgreen was aware of the treachery of Racky Jagger. Patrols had been briefed to take him captive if he was seen. But when a week had gone by since Thorn and Haw's return with not so much as a glimpse of him, Thorn decided the time was ripe to retrieve the crystal stolen for Haw from its hiding place.

Haw was eager to see the stone that had caused so much trouble. Jewel was looking forward to comparing it with her own, but left the green crystal for safety's sake in the house. So, telling Morry that they were going for a walk, the three set out from the settlement. Thorn and Jewel took bows and quivers.

They'd walked for some time when Haw abruptly exclaimed: "I know where you hid it – our secret place!"

"You've guessed it," said Thorn.

"But that's where they kidnapped me!"

"Yes. But after Minny advised me to hide the crystal, I reasoned that if the men who kidnapped you were also after the stone, near the pool would be the last place they'd go looking for it. And it's very well hidden."

Emerging at last from a stand of reeds, they stood on the brink of the pool. A dragonfly was hunting over the weedy, sleepy water. As they watched, he hesitated – a bar of vivid light – then shot away, scoring a fiery track on the air.

"I see why you two love this place so much," said Jewel.

But Haw was impatient. "Where's the crystal, Thorn?" she pressed him.

He grinned. "Follow me."

He took them round the edge of the pool, then plunged once more into dense, springy grass. Soon they came to an ancient oak tree leaning over the stream. Wind, perhaps, should have felled it, but still it clutched the bank, shading the stream that dreamt beneath.

Thorn took them up to the trunk, ribbed, knotted and grey with years. He ran a hand over the wood – a dwarf daring to stroke a giant. Then, taking out his knife, he prised a piece of bark from the trunk. A sizeable hole was revealed. He put both hands into the hole, extracted a cloth-wrapped object, shook a couple of beetles off it and passed it to Haw.

"It's yours, sister. Better late than never! But careful how you handle it."

He replaced the loose bark.

"Let's go back to the pool," he said. "We can all look at it there."

The three sat in a semicircle facing the sunlit water. But they only had eyes for the stone.

Haw unfolded the cloth. Her crystal might have been brother or sister to Jewel's stone. This one too was roughly spherical, with a lumpy, jagged surface. But its colour was a deep ruby, the shade of blood from the entrails of a freshly-gutted rabbit. It seemed to brood over some mystery locked up inside itself. I don't like it, she thought. She'd have preferred something pretty that she could look at and admire. But this she couldn't even touch! It was useless, completely useless. Racky might just as well have had it, for all the trouble it had been. Yet she couldn't tell Thorn this. It would only upset him.

She said: "It's – well, it's amazing. I've never seen anything like it."

She wondered if her lack of enthusiasm was obvious. But Thorn hadn't noticed. He was staring at the stone as if his eyes were stuck to it. Jewel too was gazing at it. She lifted a hand as if to touch it, then let it fall back.

"May I hold it, Haw?" she asked.

Haw never got to answer. Without warning, out of nowhere, a net dropped over their heads. Next moment, they were struggling like fish as the mesh tightened, dragging them backwards from the stream in a confusion of arms and legs and tumbling, squashed-together bodies. The crystal had rolled away.

"Calm down, you three," said a voice they knew only too well. "Relax. It's over now."

"Racky!" Thorn spat out.

Racky Jagger threw a cloth over the crystal and picked it up. Three men stood round the net with nocked bows in their hands. They must have crept up while the young people were staring at the stone.

"These bows are aimed at Jewel," said Racky, "but there's no need for her – or anyone else – to get hurt. I have what I came for. I'm going to leave now. After a time my men will leave. Then you can cut yourselves free."

"Wait, Racky Jagger!" Jewel cried.

Despite himself, Racky paused. "Wait for what?" he asked.

"Don't take the crystal to Querne Rasp! She's too powerful already. I'm sure she's planning some great evil."

Racky hesitated, and seemed for a moment about to reply. But then he shrugged, pushed into the undergrowth and was gone.

Jewel was angry with herself. Angry at her failure to foresee the attack, angry to be reduced to powerlessness so easily. She hadn't thought it possible, yet it had happened. She thought of various ways to try to immobilise the men. But three were too many to take on together with absolute certainty of success. Something might go wrong, and Haw or Thorn might get hurt. No: better to wait.

So she waited. Imperceptibly, the sun continued its voyage across the sky. More dragonflies appeared to zip about their hunting ground, oblivious of the quiet human drama on their doorstep. The three guards said nothing. Then, as quietly as they'd come, the men departed. Though not, Thorn saw, in the same direction as Racky.

"Damn and double damn!" he cried. "Damn and blast Racky Jagger! After all we've been through – to let him get it so easily!"

He pulled out his knife and began sawing at the net. But, gripping some cords in her fists, Jewel dissolved them, making a hole that Haw was able to climb through.

Soon the three of them were free. Thorn and Jewel retrieved their bows, which had been left on the edge of the pool.

"What do we do now?" asked Haw.

"Follow Racky," said Thorn. "Did you notice that his men went in a different direction? Racky is on his own. Perhaps we can catch him. Come on."

Far from convinced that the crystal was worth chasing, Haw voiced her objections. "He'll be well away by now. And Thorn, you're hardly the world's greatest tracker."

"*You* go back to the settlement if you want," retorted Thorn. "But I'm going after Racky." He plunged into the grass.

The girls looked at one another.

"We *have* to follow Racky, Haw," said Jewel quietly, "and you know why. If Querne gets the ruby crystal . . ."

Haw nodded. "Then I'm coming too," she said.

Racky's trail was easy to follow. He'd made, it seemed, not the least effort to conceal it.

After a time, they emerged from the stretch of brushwood onto moorland. This was a country of heather and whin, twisted bushes and stunted trees. The earth was dark and soft underfoot, and Racky had left tracks all three of them could plainly see. But where the heather grew thick, they had to shield their faces from the plant's coarse sprays as they forced their way through.

A strange conviction slowly grew in Thorn's mind. At last he said: "This doesn't make sense."

"What doesn't?" said Jewel.

"Racky's heading for the Barrens."

"Norgreen Barrens? But—"

"Jewel, do you think I don't know my own country?"

"No, of course not."

"All right then."

She said nothing more, and they continued to push on. The ground continued heavy and now also began to rise. Haw was flagging. But Thorn, like a man obsessed, drove himself ahead.

Then, pushing between more wiry tufts of purple heather, they saw, directly ahead and a mere thirty paces away, a livid expanse of earth.

And there, perched on a stone on its brink, was Racky Jagger. He was wearing black gloves. In his hands was the ruby crystal.

Racky got to his feet. "You three took your time. I was waiting to say goodbye. So now I'll say it. Goodbye!"

And with that he swung round, stepped boldly onto the white land and strode away from them.

His pursuers hurried after him and halted by the stone. They didn't dare go any further.

Racky Jagger turned to face them. Behind him, the landscape unrolled its unnatural floor, its further reaches smothered in a soft, pearly haze.

Cupping the crystal in his hands, Racky held it above his head like a Ranter about to invoke the unseen spirits of the place.

The stone awoke. It glowed crimson, a rugged orb of contained fire, then shafts of light exploded in all directions like shooting stars.

"Cover your eyes!" Jewel cried.

Thorn and Haw shut their eyes tight and covered them with their hands. Even then, they were aware of the flying shafts of fire.

Till abruptly they ceased.

The three took their hands away.

Where Racky Jagger had stood, there was nothing but white ground. Like some gigantic albino pike, the Barrens had sucked him into its maw.

Thorn was first to find his tongue. "Well, that's that," he declared, "we can't follow him into there."

"Yes we can," Jewel said. "Or at least, *I* can. What's more, Thorn, I *must*. Remember my vision at Harrypark? I'm more than ever convinced that Querne is plotting some great evil. Why else does she want the crystals?"

"Well, it goes against my grain to give up the crystal without a fight. But Barrens are deadly places."

"*Not*, it seems, if you're carrying a crystal – and I have one. *Think*, Thorn: Racky went in – but he's just an ordinary man."

Thorn rubbed his cheek. "True . . . and there's something very odd about his behaviour. Why did he wait for us here? It's almost as if he *wanted* us to see what he did . . . As if he was *daring* us to go in after him . . ."

"What if it's a trap?" Haw now broke in. "You know what Racky's like."

"That's a chance," said Jewel, "that I simply have to take."

"But Querne will kill you!" cried Haw. "She's much more powerful than you! Why should *you* be the one to fight her?"

Jewel smiled ruefully. "Because I'm the only one who can?"

"*Not* the only one," said Thorn. "If *you're* going, *I'm* going."